PEN

THE O

Alexandra Campbell's first [...] a finalist for the Catherine Pakenham Award and the *Vogue* Talent Contest, and led to regular appearances on Radio 4's *Start the Week*. She subsequently worked on the staff of *She*, *Harpers & Queen* and *Good Housekeeping*, and has written for the *Daily Telegraph*, *The Times Magazine*, the *Independent Magazine*, *You* magazine, *Ideal Home* and many women's magazines, winning the Individual Journalist's Award from the National Home Improvement Council. This is her first novel. Alexandra Campbell lives in South London with her husband David and twins Frederick and Rosalind.

Alexandra Campbell

the office party

PENGUIN BOOKS

PENGUIN BOOKS

Published by the Penguin Group
Penguin Books Ltd, 27 Wrights Lane, London w8 5tz, England
Penguin Putnam Inc., 375 Hudson Street, New York, New York 10014, USA
Penguin Books Australia Ltd, Ringwood, Victoria, Australia
Penguin Books Canada Ltd, 10 Alcorn Avenue, Toronto, Ontario, Canada m4v 3b2
Penguin Books (NZ) Ltd, 182–190 Wairau Road, Auckland 10, New Zealand

Penguin Books Ltd, Registered Offices: Harmondsworth, Middlesex, England

First published 1998
10 9 8 7 6 5 4 3 2

Set in 11/13pt Monotype Bodoni Book
Typeset by Intype London Ltd
Printed in England by Clays Ltd, St Ives plc

To David, Frederick and Rosalind

I'd like to thank my agent, Sarah Molloy at A. M. Heath, for her invaluable encouragement, advice and inspiration, Louise Moore at Penguin, for her enthusiasm and brilliantly critical eye, Jennifer Munka for sympathetic copy editing, the art department at Penguin for a witty cover, Rebecca Purtell in the publicity department, and Harriet Evans, both at Penguin. Also my brother, Graham Campbell, for his legal advice, as well as my mother, Margaret Campbell, for making it all possible at home.

And in memory of my father, Stafford Campbell, who encouraged me to write stories from the very beginning.

All the characters in this book, except for Charles Worthington and Sally O'Sullivan, who appear briefly as themselves, are completely fictitious. Any resemblances to any real person are wholly coincidental and unintended. But don't let that stop you reading it.

The publishers wish to express their thanks for permission, granted by Cat Music Limited and Mr Y. Islam, to quote from 'Matthew & Son'.

chapter 1

As Clara Wheeler puffed her way through her Monday morning exercise class, she realized that she almost considered her husband's mistress as part of the family. Except that she didn't have to buy her a Christmas present. It was probably no worse than having an interfering mother-in-law or a touchy spinster aunt, or any of the other malevolent spirits so often present in the background of family life, disrupting things, and carving jagged scars through events like birthdays or weddings. Except, of course, you couldn't really talk about it. It had become an ever-growing black hole of non-communication in the middle of her marriage into which everything seemed to get sucked, good and bad alike.

Her friend Annabel asked confusing questions like, 'Do you know if he knows you know?' It was like living in a world of mirrors, hard to tell the difference between reflection and reality. You could always tell when your husband was having an affair, she thought, because he became progressively ruder to your friends, leaving social events unreasonably early while arriving impossibly late. Finding out about Edward – around ten years ago – had caused her searing, absolute agony. Now the affair merely spread a lingering feeling of unease, like some chronic, incurable illness, occasionally punctuated with flare-ups of unbearable pain when she discovered something completely new. Like Edward buying Shirley a flat. That had changed the pain into anger. She wanted her husband back.

'Breathe in on the way down, and out on the way up,' shouted the teacher, watching most of her class go blue in the face.

'Another ten.'

Clara obligingly lifted her head and shoulders off the floor, elbows out to the side and chin tucked in, as directed, to prevent neck strain. Up – puff – and hold. The only thing you could say about this position is that it gave you an uninterrupted close-up view of your body, from the chest to the bent-up knees. It was not a heartening sight, reminding Clara as it did of an unmade bed. As if someone had thrown a duvet down on top and it had landed in a huddle. And that was only her stomach. Oh well, the French always said you had to choose between your bottom and your face after thirty. Her face, she knew, was still pretty, with pink-and-white peachy skin – surprisingly unlined – blue eyes, and fluffy blonde hair that sometimes worked. On the whole, you could say that everything was in the right place – no big noses or little piggy eyes. Which was more than could be said for her bottom, where nothing was in the right place, but drooped a good few inches below the ideal. Her thoughts strayed to a copy of *Good House-keeping* lying invitingly on her glass-topped coffee table at home. It proclaimed that kaftans were back. Perhaps something long and flowing would flatter her figure. A whiff of nostalgia, as pungent as the fumes from a newly cleaned oven, caught her in the back of the throat.

She had got married in a cream cheesecloth kaftan with a circle of flowers round her hair. In Guildford Registry Office in 1974. Her parents disapproved of Edward, of registry offices and everything else about the day. Sometimes Clara wondered whether their disapproval had fuelled the whole event. She regretted getting married so young when she realized that, had she waited a few years for wedding styles to change, she could have floated up the aisle in a meringue of cream silk, flanked by a posse of little girls in frocks. Still, it had all been great fun, and she'd felt utterly secure in Edward's love.

'Up. Hold, one two three and DOWN.' She hastily looked round to see what part of the body they were torturing now, and caught Annabel's eye. Coffee-drinking signals passed between them. The post-mortem cup of coffee every Monday morning was what got Clara to class.

The Copper Kettle had recently changed its name to the Paparazzi Café, replacing its simple choice of tea or coffee, both the same muddy shade of brown, with cappuccino, espresso, herbal teas and a selection of tinted waters tasting of mild Dettol. Clara

3

supposed it was progress but felt nostalgic for the strong bite of PG Tips and thick white china. And her Puffa jacket was too bulky to hang easily over the slender chrome chairs, and jammed her uncomfortably close to the table.

'I won't be coming to these classes any more.' Annabel sounded pleased with herself. 'I'm going to train as a counsellor. Now that the older children have left home, and Freddie's at boarding school . . .' There was a questioning note about this last sentence – implying, perhaps, that Clara, too, might consider looking for a new life.

'Oh. Well done.' Clara felt a bit flat. All her girl-friends, as she called them, suddenly seemed to be launching themselves into new careers or finding absorbing interests. Her round of lunches and classes, originally planned around delivering and collecting the children, Marcus and Eliza – from school, riding, Brownies, Girl Guides, football training, extra French and specialist exam coaching – seemed to be falling apart now that Marcus had been offered a top traineeship in an accountant's office in New York, and Eliza was just about to start her 'gap' year by going to the States with him. They had grown up. She'd never really thought it would happen. Clara was easing the sense of abandonment she felt by organizing a massive, tented party, ostensibly for Eliza's eighteenth birthday and her and Edward's twenty-fifth wedding anniversary, but also for Edward to invite some 'movers and shakers' to be impressed by his conspicuous consumption.

'I simply wouldn't have the time,' she said, before

Annabel could suggest training or a career in addition to all this. She waved an arm vaguely.

'The Brambles . . . you know.' Clara had put a lot of thought into choosing the name of their neo-Georgian executive home, built in a very exclusive development in Surrey, because she hadn't wanted to sound pretentious. 'It's a lot of work. In fact . . .' this was a good point 'we're putting in a swimming pool.'

Annabel's eyes widened. 'Where on earth are you going to fit a swimming pool?' Clara wondered if tact was a requirement for counselling. Obviously not. Edward had bought The Brambles a few years earlier after a particularly profitable deal. It had a garden that estate agents would describe as 'deceptively spacious' in that the series of wedge shapes around the house added up to more than you might think. Clara had found a garden designer to make the most of it, creating an illusion of hidden depths and hinted-at vistas with a clever use of topiary and 'hard landscaping'. Edward had once said that all the statuettes, urns and pergolas reminded him of a small Victorian cemetery.

'There's quite a bit of unused space behind the double garage, and we can disguise the back of it with a summerhouse.'

'Goodness. Edward must be doing well.'

Edward was. But while Edward without money was a worry to Clara, Edward in possession of what was clearly a small fortune, apparently acquired legally, was truly terrifying. He was not the sort of man to put sensible amounts into his pension fund in good years. In fact, he probably didn't have a pension fund. And he was not, in her opinion, good at hanging on to money. Brilliant at making it, but not what her mother would have called a sensible person. The more he made one year, the more spectacularly they were likely to go broke the next. She was trying to nail down as much of it as she could – before it all disappeared again into some hopeless business venture – by filling the house with as many summerhouses, swimming pools and handmade kitchen units as was physically possible. 'It's all go here,' she was fond of saying, as the phone and the doorbell never stopped with a procession of deliveries, collections, installations and removals, refitting The Brambles from top to toe. 'Very nice,' Edward had said. 'Like Peter Jones's window displays.'

She thought wistfully of the tiny terraced house they had lived in when they first married. It had had two rooms upstairs and two down. Marcus and Eliza were both born there, and Edward, after his first near-bankruptcy, had restarted his company from the sitting room. Clara had helped him while she struggled to cope with two small children and an interminable pile of nappies. Her eyes had felt like sandpaper and her limbs ached with tiredness. All day every day. But they had been together, all four of them. A unit. She had been exhausted and worried, yet, looking back, she thought she could remember being shot through with rays of happiness that glittered like streaks of sunlight across a dirty city street. It had all gone wrong. Horribly, miserably, guiltily wrong. In just one night.

She brought herself back to the shiny tin tables and chrome seats of the Paparazzi Café. Discomfort had become so fashionable. 'Mmn. His latest deal has been quite successful.'

'Gosh.' Annabel looked envious. 'I do hope that doesn't mean you'll get divorced. You haven't been hanging on for the dosh, have you? It's such an expensive process that apparently lots of people don't do it until they feel a bit better off.'

Clara's stomach lurched sickeningly. She didn't want to think about divorce. She wanted to think about shopping. She hoped that Annabel was planning to be a little less forthright to her counselling clients.

'At least Marcus and Eliza have turned out sensible.' Clara looked at Annabel sharply. Was she accusing her children of being boring? Or just swinging the conversation round to her own problems?

'Drugs. Both Timmy and Izzy . . .' Her thoughts drifted as Annabel embarked on a familiar litany of alarm about her children's activities, all of which, Clara noted wistfully, seemed to involve taking drugs with the sons of earls or making well-connected girls pregnant. Drugs were obviously an excellent shortcut to hobnobbing with the aristocracy, she thought, far better than sitting on charity committees.

She retrieved her silk scarf, which had slipped on to the floor – it was dotted with snaffles and someone had once, gratifyingly, mistaken it for a real Hermès scarf – from the pocket of her jacket, and twisted it round her fingers, glad of the opportunity to hide her face. She should be thinking about the future, not the past. Things to look forward to. Like this evening.

'We've been invited to a publishing awards' black-tie dinner. You know, one of Edward's companies publishes magazines.'

'I thought they were technical journals.'

'Well . . . yes . . . I suppose they are, but it's all the same really.' Clara was firm. Wiggins Frean might publish *Drains and Drainage* and *The Actuarial Monthly* but they had still been invited to the Magazine Publishers' Gold Awards, the industry's most glittering event. It had been so long since Edward invited her to accompany him to anything work-related. She rationed herself firmly when it came to hope, but it bubbled up irrepressibly inside her when she thought about the evening ahead. And Clara was longing to discover the reality behind those glossy titles. Perhaps she might even meet the editor of *Ideal Home*.

'What are you wearing?' Clara had hoped Annabel would ask this.

'A Gonziaga Black.' She let the name drop casually into the cappuccinos with a satisfying swirl.

There was a short, perhaps slightly worrying, pause, which Clara decided to interpret as jealousy. There had been several articles on the design duo Gonziaga Black in the press recently. 'Why every-one's wearing Black', screamed the headlines of one article, which went on to say that, in fact, Gonziaga Black were the first designers that had really managed to winkle the fashion press *out* of their inky black uniform and into 'hot sherbets'. It had gone on to list the society women across the board who declared that their Gonziaga Black was the first thing they'd rescue in a fire.

'I don't think I'd dare even go into the shop.' Annabel broke into Clara's reverie.

Clara tried to smile confidently. Going into the shop – praised in the fashion press for deliberately satirizing the cheap boutique by installing tiny flimsy cubicles with half-doors and slits of mirrors every-where – had not been fun. The half-doors were fine for Naomi Campbell and Kate Moss, but Clara found they were just the wrong height for revealing a greyish – and rather wide – bra strap. No mirror was large enough to see herself entirely, but the bits she could see looked all right, she thought.

Yes, a Gonziaga Black would place her exactly where she wanted to be. In the thick of things. And it would cause a sensation at their own party at the weekend. She paid the bill with some satisfaction, waving away Annabel's fiver.

'No, really. My treat.'

Shirley Green carefully measured out the last glossy black drops from a bottle of nail varnish, and smoothed them to the tips of her long talons. The phone beside her rang persistently, and she looked around for someone to answer it. Smudging wet nail varnish was a dreadful waste of time. Besides, she was furious.

Harry Farquarson, passing the door on his way to

the coffee area, sighed, stepped into her office and managed to coil his six-foot frame round the edge of her crowded desk while still looking elegant in the process. With surgical precision he moved a toppling pile of papers to find a place for his mug. It was inscribed with the legend 'A Mountie Always Gets His Man'. He picked up the receiver, giving it a frown and a quick flick with his handkerchief before answering.

'Wiggins Frean Publishing.' He tossed a lock of black hair out of his eyes. It always settled back exactly where it was before. Perhaps the upper classes had access to special hair conditioners. The phone twittered for a few moments, while Harry inched it further away from his ear, topping up his mug from the executive coffee percolator with the other hand.

'No, I'm the Production Director,' he said, patiently. 'The Managing Director is Edward Wheeler.' More chirruping. 'I'm afraid he's not here. Wiggins Frean is just one of the companies he owns. Perhaps I can help you.' Shirley blew on her nail varnish. This call was obviously getting tricky. Wiggins Frean, so far, had been a satisfactory, if unexciting, sideline to Edward's main businesses, which had varied from trading in luxury cars (recently surprisingly successful) to running a travel agency for single people (which had crashed two years ago amid mounting debts and barely suppressed scandal). Edward, who collected declining companies the way some people collected china Staffordshire dogs, had originally bought it for the building, one-third of which made a very useful garage in a down-and-out part of Hammersmith. The rest had been occupied by a series of studious graduates straight from university, who were grateful for the chance to work in 'publishing', and were happy to work diligently on inscrutably technical manuscripts in return for a pittance of a wage and the chance to call themselves Assistant Editors. The manuscripts were laboriously metamorphosed into technical journals, which were mainly sold to libraries, universities and the specialists who wrote, or hoped to write, for them. He left most of the organization to Shirley, or to Harry, who had emerged from the pack of graduates as a surprising front-runner around ten years earlier, just after Edward took Shirley on as a young but stunningly efficient secretary. Harry was Production Director, as Production, to Edward, meant producing whatever had to be produced, preferably in the cheapest way possible. Wiggins Frean had survived the impecunious 1970s, the competitive 1980s and the recessionary 1990s while reminding Shirley of the pop song 'Matthew & Son' ('Nobody asks for more money, because nobody dares, even though they're pretty low and the rent's in arrears'). The point of it, as far as Edward was concerned, was that it owned the building, which his other businesses could use, but was separate enough to remain intact every time one of them went under, which was fairly often. The point of it, as far as Shirley was concerned, was that working there was like being married to Edward but without the domesticity (or, regrettably, the chance to spend all night with him, except when they went to conferences together).

Harry's eyes were beginning to roll. Shirley delicately removed the receiver from his ear.

'Hello. I work very closely with the Managing Director.' She ignored Harry smirking in the background. 'Perhaps I can help you?' There was a screech of outrage on the other end. Academics were notoriously touchy and took themselves very seriously.

'I'll get someone to ring you in the morning.' She slammed down the phone.

Harry raised his eyebrows. 'You're usually Little Miss Sunshine.'

'Am I?' She puckered up her lips and checked them in the mirror before rummaging through an untidy drawer for some more lipstick.

'Tell Uncle Harry.'

'What do *you* think?'

'Edward.'

'The office party. He's going to a publishing awards' dinner. The Gold Awards.' She whipped a tissue out of a giant box on her desk and blew her nose loudly.

'Careful. You'll crack your war paint.' Harry squeezed her arm. 'But the office party is the main event of the year. And you put so much work into it. He *can't* miss it!' He was amazed. He considered Edward a lazy two-timing sod like most other heterosexual men, and badly dressed to boot, but this bordered on actual cruelty. Shirley was Edward's very personal Personal Assistant and had organized the annual office party every November since she joined the company. It was her one opportunity to stand side by side with her lover, openly, welcoming people, and it was also the only project that was wholly her creation rather than just backing up Edward's work.

'He's been invited by John Bellman from *Heart & Soul* magazine.'

' *"Because you're more than just a pretty face"*? The glossy magazine that goes beyond fashion and beauty?' asked Harry, ironically quoting the publicity on the side of the spine. 'Isn't that for sale?' Harry, like Shirley, longed for Wiggins Frean to be a part of the real magazine world, with all its gloss and glamour. While *Zips & Fasteners* or *Tanker Trading* sat in suspiciously neat, date-ordered piles on shelves, their desks were strewn with *Vogue*, *Harpers & Queen*, and *Cosmopolitan*, so well-thumbed that the issues fell apart before they could be sent on to a dentist's waiting room.

Shirley nodded. 'I didn't think he'd go with her.'

'Clara? But John Bellman knows them both, doesn't he? He could hardly not invite her.'

'Oh, stop being so reasonable!' Shirley flung a tissue down on the desk. 'Yes, I want him to go and buy *Heart & Soul*, and *yes*, I knew he'd be invited with his wife, but . . .' her voice rose to a scream '. . . that doesn't mean I have to fucking like it.'

'Have a drink.' Harry rummaged about in the desk and came up with a miniature brandy left over from a hotel mini-bar, and poured it into her black coffee. 'Down the hatch.'

Shirley stretched out her long, bare legs, and laid her immaculately manicured toes on the desk. These were eyed and appreciated by the men in Sales – although lost on Harry – but heartily loathed by the women in the Editorial Department, where they agreed that truly intelligent people never went bare-legged. Thighs in Editorial were pale pink and wobbly, occasionally pitted with cellulite, and always kept suitably covered up with black opaque tights. Shirley's were smooth and brown, bare even in the middle of winter, and generally considered to be the result of hours spent under a sunbed. Editorial comforted themselves by pinning learned articles about malignant melanoma and ageing skin to the noticeboards.

'Like my new skirt?'

'Oh that's what it is, is it? I thought it was a belt.'

'Very clever.' Shirley filched one of Harry's cig-arettes.

'Have you ever thought, you know, of actually getting dressed in the morning? Rather than just wearing expensive vests all day?'

Shirley grinned, and didn't bother to reply. Getting dressed for work could be counterproductive if it stopped Edward from undressing her as soon as they had a minute alone together. She wondered if Harry would approve of her plans for the weekend. Prob-ably not. Harry only had one fault. He was too nice. He didn't understand what a girl had to do to get herself a fair deal. And he never wanted to hurt anyone, however dull, boring and frumpy they were. And Shirley reckoned that although she had lost the skirmish about tonight – she had made a bid to accompany Edward, but he had said 'no', and she knew better than to try to get him to change his mind once it was made up – she definitely had a good battle plan for the weekend. Several key members of Wiggins Frean, such as Harry, had been invited to the grand anniversary party at the Wheelers. Although Edward was irritatingly firm about keeping his home and office life separate, it had hardly been possible to exclude Shirley. It would be her first opportunity to fight Clara on her own home territory, and Shirley was taking no prisoners. She mentally reviewed her wardrobe. There were several items that deserved the title 'secret weapon'.

For Edward – even the frumps in Editorial agreed – was an attractive man, still retaining a shadow of his rugged army good looks in the way he always seemed too big for his suits. Shirley asked him once if he'd had to kill people when he was a soldier, and he laughed. 'The nearest I got to action was stabbing my superior officer in the back with a well-leaked memo.' She was secretly disappointed. There was something rather sexy about the idea of blood on his hands. Still, even without blood those hands sent shivers down her spine. So she made sure they stayed on her well-exercised form by sticking to leather trousers, ultra-short Lycra skirts and cropped tops, even if they were unconventional uniform for a PA.

But then, as the *The Times Business News* had written recently, Shirley was so much more than a PA. 'The new breed of Personal Assistants regard their job as a stepping stone to a board position,' explained the article. It had profiled four New Tycoons. The other three had male Personal Assistants – eager young men with MBAs and well-cut city suits. Shirley was the only woman featured, but her photograph had been printed bigger than everyone else's because of her legs, elegantly crossed on the bonnet of Edward's Mercedes coupé, and the silky curtain of rich chestnut hair that almost reached her waist. 'These young men – and women – drive their employers to meetings, but after they have parked the car, they join the high-level negotiations as more than just minute-takers,' the writer continued. 'They prepare agendas, carry out research and even negotiate on their employers' behalf. They eat, sleep and dream their job and are privy to the company's most important secrets.' Too right, thought Shirley. Clara must have enjoyed reading that. Shirley had bought six copies, and had sent one to her with a compliments slip, scribbling, 'thought you'd like to see this piece on Edward as a New Tycoon'. Of course, Edward wasn't quite as Tycoonish as the other New Tycoons, who really did own multi-million-pound companies, rather than the down-at-heel Wiggins Frean bulked out by a few profitable deals, but the reporter had admitted that his editor demanded he include a female PA, and a mutual acquaintance had suggested Edward and Shirley. Shirley smiled with satisfaction at the memory. Good legs got you quite a long way in life.

Two of the Editorial Assistants lumbered back along the corridor, twittering about the party. Shirley looked at their departing behinds – both squarish and covered in several layers of different fabrics – with distaste, as she shut the door. In her opinion, they all thought that university degrees entitled them to sport unshaven legs and loose threads dangling from the hems of their voluminous cotton skirts. But, just to be on the safe side, she always interviewed them personally before they were taken on.

Virginia Law was at her over-sized desk as Editor-in-Chief of *Viva* magazine only thirty minutes before she was due at the Magazine Publishers' Gold Awards dinner. She had hoped, at one stage, to get a quick taxi home to Islington for a bath and to kiss the children goodnight. That hope had disappeared when her lunch with David Croxley, the head of a large supermarket chain called Bettadeal, overran. David had money for advertising and, more importantly, spare cash to sponsor a supplement Virginia had provisionally titled 'Women After The Millennium – What We Want and What We Need'. The art – one Virginia was extremely good at – was to get him to write a huge cheque without *Viva* having to mention Bettadeal too sickeningly often. The lunch, in spite of the time it had taken, had been remarkably minimalist – instead of being offered bread, for example, the waiter had simply presented them with a long thin black twig laid elegantly across their plates.

'What the 'ell is this?' David Croxley sounded baffled, but prepared to do battle.

The waiter bowed deferentially. 'Burnt breadstick, sir. Our speciality.'

'Delicious,' said Virginia firmly. 'Absolutely delicious. Thank you.'

She had returned, feeling slightly woozy with the effort of drinking less than David Croxley, who had hoovered champagne for Britain without it appearing to affect him in the slightest. Then Serena, her Deputy Editor, had stumped in with an armful of pages. 'If these don't go to the printers tonight, we really will lose our date on the March issue.' She looked Virginia in the eye. 'It won't ever be printed. Four hundred and seventy thousand copies will never hit the streets. All lost.' It was a threat that Serena made quite often, but you could never be sure.

Virginia cast an experienced eye over them.

'What's this?' She pointed to the sell, a few lines of big type just below the headline. ' "Healthy eating need not be boring." Neither need articles on nutrition. Get the subs to give that feature a bit of zip.' She scribbled furiously over the other pages, frowning at captions. Eventually she came to the travel feature at the end. 'Turkey is a land of contrasts.' She crossed that out. 'I don't care if we lose the issue. I'm not having clichés in my magazine. Tell the subs that Wiltshire is a land of contrasts. And so is everywhere else in the world.' She stopped for a moment. 'Except possibly Finland, which does very much start as it goes on. All those lakes and trees. I'll be here until seven-thirty for the rewrites.' That meant a quick shower and change in the boardroom loo. A taxi over to Shaftesbury House Hotel would take less than ten minutes. She wouldn't be too late.

'Do you think you'll get the Editor's Gold Award?'

Serena hovered in anticipation. Outside Virginia's office there was barely suppressed excitement. All the senior staff members were being taken to the dinner – it was a ritual that Virginia regarded as part of good staff relations. It was the big night of the year. Some companies took husbands and wives, but Virginia thought it bolstered team spirit to take all her 'girls'. And it saved her from having to talk to their dreadful boyfriends. It also meant that Serena, who had never even been known to have a date, let alone a boyfriend, didn't have to agonize about who she was going to take as a walker. An editor, Virginia often reminded herself, had to be sensitive about these things. She looked up at Serena.

'I shouldn't think so for a moment. It'll probably go to the editor of some obscure magazine about tractors.' But she was relieved that she had managed to get her appointment at the Charles Worthington salon changed discreetly to this morning. The whisper was that she had a very good chance of getting the award this time, but nothing was worse than the thought of people saying, 'Virginia Law had her hair done specially and she wasn't even placed!' She checked the result in the mirror – yes, Charles had done very well – yet again. It was a glossy, black bob, with every hair shining and in place, framing her thin pale face perfectly. As a child she had felt angular and gawky, with great dark eyes, a nose that felt too large and thick black eyebrows, but these days, with the right lipstick and the immaculately cut clothes she could now afford, all these difficult features had rearranged themselves into something that closely approximated beauty. It was, she knew, a face that people didn't forget.

'Do you want to see the sales figures or will it spoil your evening?' Her least favourite person, Nigel Platt, the advertising director, was waving a sheaf of papers at her from the doorway.

She affected nonchalance. 'I ought to look at them, I suppose.' She hoped he didn't see her hands shaking. For an editor, checking the sales figures was like stepping on the scales. Even tiny changes could cause despair or elation. These were not tiny changes. After a lifetime of professional success, Virginia had suddenly begun to worry that she had lost her touch. The first week of the October issue had sold 60,000 copies less than last year, and she simply didn't know why. *Viva*, quite suddenly, had started haemorrhaging. She'd seen it happen to other good editors – they'd got stale, tired, diverted by something else. But that couldn't apply to her. It just couldn't. *Viva*'s last publicly recorded sales figures – almost six months ago – had shown an increase in sales of 0.1 per cent, billed as '*Viva*'s seventh consecutive rise in sales'. But Paul Long, the Managing Director of Publishing Unlimited, had made it quite clear to Virginia at the time that they had had to 'massage' the figures considerably.

'It's a short-term ploy to give you time to recover. Those losses will have to show up some time, but hopefully by then sales will have started to rise again, and they can be buried.' She had always wondered what 'massaging' entailed – someone had once told her that it meant sending a large number of copies to some British colony like Diego Garcia 'so that they count as UK sales' on a very slow boat. By the time they'd been put on the even slower boat back as unwanted, the returns would have missed the six-monthly sales figures. Well, Diego Garcia or not, she could see from the papers that Nigel handed to her that things were getting worse rather than better. She really needed that award to buy herself time to get *Viva* back on course.

She handed them back to him. 'You can never tell from the first week. If the distributors were a day late with delivery, it'd cause that kind of a drop. But we'll catch up later on in the month.' This was more than optimism. It was downright mendaciousness. You never made up later in the month. But she knew Nigel wouldn't dare challenge her. Her background in magazines was solidly gilt-edged. Over fifteen years she had moved, apparently effortlessly, from famous masthead to famous masthead, picking up a clutch of awards in the process, constantly trailing higher circulation figures, pushing circulation up here by 15 per cent, there by 20 per cent. She was sharp with money – her magazines always came in under budget – and clever with people, who mostly adored her.

Now she often lay awake in bed, aching with tiredness, wondering where all that accumulated experience had gone. Why was *Viva* suddenly slipping away from her? She wasn't doing anything different. Everyone told her it was brilliant. And then she thought about everything she had achieved – along with a beautifully balanced life – and she reassured herself that it must simply be a temporary blip. Her husband, Simon, a banker, was both successful and good-looking; Oliver, her son, had just passed his entrance exams to London's most competitive nursery school at the age of three. Her baby daughter, Agnes, was exactly where she ought to be on the weight–height graph, which was about all even Virginia could ask in the way of achievements from a baby of five months. Nothing really disagreeable had ever happened to her. Not for at least twenty years. She raised a hand to her forehead and ran it through her hair in an unconscious gesture, literally pushing that memory to the back of her mind. Nasty memories belonged out of sight, or, if they could be persuaded by a couple of mild sleeping pills, out of mind altogether. She had worked hard all her life to make sure that she had as few as possible.

In the end, she was able to get away by 7.25 p.m., as Serena offered to stay and do the last corrections on the proofs. 'Don't worry, I'm sure I'll make it by the main course,' she had said. 'And definitely there to see you win.'

'Don't be silly.' But Virginia prayed she was right.

chapter 2

Clara was used to arriving at parties alone. Edward, as usual, claimed to be tied up somewhere – probably in chains to Shirley's bedpost, she thought. Although this latest excuse, that he had to drop in to the annual office party for an hour, was probably true. He had treated them to a small, but exquisite, double room in a pretty hotel off Sloane Street for the night, and as she stepped into the Gonziaga Black and heaved at the zip, she felt her spirits rising. She clipped her necklace on, checking the effect in the big mirror in the tiny marble-lined bathroom. Her face glowed softly back at her, framed by newly set blonde hair. Pearls made English-rose skins like hers almost lustrous. Thank heavens she had one really good string of real ones. Her mother had taught her that nothing was worse than seeing a lady in fake pearls. And the little clip-on earrings were real, too. The whole thing made her feel, well, pretty. Although she knew the latest diet hadn't altered her weight by an ounce.

But there was something very unnerving about the sheer size of the ballroom entrance to the Shaftesbury House Hotel in Mayfair. And her confidence was further whittled away as slinky women dressed in black, with cries of recognition and lots of air kissing, greeted each other. Everywhere she looked, slim legs flashed beneath short skirts, tapering down to expensively shod high heels. The three biscuits she had absentmindedly nibbled at the hairdresser's churned uneasily in her stomach, cutting in at the waistband of the dress. Hardly anyone was wearing long, except for one or two in figure-hugging black sheath dresses which managed to look both understated and glamorous at the same time. They didn't seem to have heard about Gonziaga Black and the fashionable praise being heaped on them. 'Prettiness made hip,' one writer had gushed. Or perhaps nobody had managed to rescue theirs from a fire, after all. Clara caught sight of a blue shape, like a walrus in Lycra, in the mirrored glass walls. With a shock, she realized it was herself. Nobody noticed her. She edged nervously down the grand formal ballroom staircase to be confronted by a sea of black – chic black trouser suits, short, black frothy concoctions, and the occasional long black or chocolate brown velvet or beaded gown – stretched out below her. Chunky costume jewellery flashed everywhere. Hers were obviously the only real pearls in the whole of Park Lane, but somehow that didn't make her feel better. She considered spending the evening in the loo, but surely Edward would be here soon.

'Ah . . . is Edward, er . . .?' A voice at her elbow,

to Clara's relief, turned out to be their host, John Bellman, trying to marshal the *Heart & Soul* table. She wondered if all the guests were like Edward, prospective purchasers for the magazine. Once it had been quite a cult read – even down in Surrey – and it still had a reputation for clever writing and unusual articles. But even she had heard that it wasn't making very much money. The advertisers, apparently, wanted to see more beauty and fashion, and healthier sales figures too. John was genial, but harassed, and immediately looked over her shoulder for Edward. Clara began to explain about the office party, but he was already introducing her to a circle of people who were locked into conversation with each other.

'Clara Wheeler.' She extended her hand around a circle of people with decreasing confidence. 'How do you do? Hello. How do you do?' Smile, grin, shake. Shake again. Eyes flickered derisively over the Gonziaga Black and single strand of pearls. Her stiff helmet of bouffant blonde hair looked out of place amongst the smooth, shining cuts swinging casually across the shoulders, and her lipstick was, she felt, just somehow *wrong*. Too pink, perhaps? Pink had always been good with her peach-like prettiness, but she could see that other former peaches were looking a lot better with something a bit more browney, or was it wine-ey?

The last woman she was introduced to was talking about babies, a subject that Clara still enjoyed more than a decade after changing her last nappy. Sushi was seven months old, the woman told her, and she had gone back to work, full time, after eight weeks. She and Sushi had quality time together.

'Sushi? Isn't that . . .?'

The woman beamed. 'Yes, raw fish and rice cakes. Sushi was conceived after a magical evening in a Japanese restaurant.'

'Oh dear,' said Clara, before she could stop herself. It was not the right response. Sushi's mother became distinctly glacial, giving Clara time to reflect that Eliza could count herself lucky to be called Eliza, having been conceived after a Full English Breakfast in the Grand Hotel, Brighton, where Edward had concluded a rather dodgy business deal. She realized she had almost been edged out of the group. John Bellman reappeared, marching another guest by the elbow as if he was leading a winning racehorse.

Everyone else stopped talking and swivelled round. The new arrival was indubitably the most elegant woman in the group. When she was introduced to Clara, she was the only one not to glance at her dress. She looked her straight in the eye and her brief handshake was warm and confident. 'Virginia Law.' Clara was thrilled. The other names meant nothing to her, and had slipped through her mind. But Virginia Law was famous to women who read magazines.

'Are you part of this media circus?' Her voice was light, with humour bubbling gently underneath it.

'Not really. Well, my husband has a small publishing company but it's nothing to any of these . . .' Clara was not usually self-deprecating but she was always honest.

But Virginia seemed genuinely interested. 'Oh? What sort of titles does he own? Some of these niche magazines put us quite to shame with their standards.'

Clara hid a smile. Wiggins Frean was not an organization to which the word 'standards' could be applied.

'Well, they're technical journals mainly, focussing on . . .' She tried to think of a technical area that might, possibly, keep the conversation going. 'Well, some of the, er, niche' – a useful word, she must remember it again – 'areas of fashion and, er, science, um . . .'

'Virginia! Darling! You simply must come and meet . . .' It was John Bellman again, overdoing his host act, Clara thought. But she was relieved to see that his latest trophy was Edward, striding into the room with that purposeful gait, looking neither right nor left. One of the things that infuriated Clara most about Shirley was that her legs were the only ones long enough to keep up easily with Edward's loping stride, while everyone else, including Clara, either had to scuttle behind like a terrier, or take little skips every four steps to catch up. There was no reason at all, she thought, why being tall, which was, after all, only a simple accident of birth, a genetic irrelevancy, should make someone appear so much more . . . well . . . in control.

As he approached her she could see distinct signs of lipstick on his cheek. She wiped it off with a motherly gesture, but he ignored her, because John was in the process of introducing him to Virginia.

27

For one breathtaking moment Clara thought their eyes had locked in that way that she had come to think of as dangerous. But then, she knew Edward's *modus operandi* at parties by now – turn the full force of his deep brown eyes directly on someone, disarm them by pushing the slightly wayward dark hair back (still dark and thick – if she wasn't careful people would think he'd married an older woman), and talk to them, very directly and sounding fascinated, for a full thirty seconds. He was always slightly challenging, and people liked that. Then off.

Clara got very annoyed when strange women came up to her at parties and raved about how lovely he was. You try getting him out of the bath in the morning, she would think crossly, or wait at home with supper getting cold while he's heaven-knows-where conducting another deal. Or, of course, an affair. Novels, articles, and, very occasionally, other wives of successful businessmen assured her that being married to a dynamic man was like that. He got on with his life, and you scurried behind, picking up the pieces and holding it all together.

But Virginia disentangled herself first, and turned back to Clara again. 'I'm so sorry. It's been fascinating talking to you. Perhaps we can catch up with each other later?' She sounded as if she meant it, and Clara beamed back as Virginia glided off. Edward immediately turned nose-to-nose with a wolfish-looking man with a pock-marked face, and she was left with two men who were talking animatedly to each other about page rates, whatever those were, and a woman with a low cleavage and black lace sleeves who was anxiously scanning the crowd and puffing on a cigarette.

'Are you in magazines?' Clara had been brought up to make conversation to people left on their own, however unenticing they looked. The woman cast an incredulous look at her blue dress, and used the opportunity to check the room over Clara's shoulder.

'I'm the Editor-in-Chief of *No!*' she said shortly. Clara was even more terrified. *No!* was billed as 'The '90s answer to feminism. For real women who aren't afraid to get to the top'. It was an uneasy blend of semi-pornographic lingerie and aggressive articles on breaking the glass ceiling, neither of which topics interested Clara at all. She liked sensible bras with lots of support, and had never had the least desire to work.

But she persevered. 'That must be very interesting.' The Editor-in-Chief puffed again, swigged back her drink and continued to cast her eye over the crowd.

'It is.' She obviously spotted someone. 'Would you excuse me? I've just seen a very old friend.' Without waiting for an answer she was gone, leaving Clara standing nervously on the edge of the two men, who had been joined by a third – all of whom clearly found women in blue dresses invisible. She sellotaped a smile to her face, and contemplated going to the loo until everyone sat down. But the walk was just too endless and she visualized herself coming down the stairs alone when everyone was seated, with hundreds of pairs of eyes wondering whether her hairdresser had yet discovered the twentieth century.

One of the men noticed her and introduced her to a row of black-clad women, who, after establishing that her connection with magazines was both tenuous and obscure, proceeded to ignore her. Clara drank her champagne rather too quickly as she stood by a bowl of limp crisps, and ate them, one by one, until they were finished.

Finally they sat down, and she found herself between the two page-rate men.

'Hello. I'm Clara Wheeler.'

'Bill Grundy.' He looked resigned to having to talk to her. Clara could do dinner-party conversation, which, in her experience, consisted of asking men about their jobs, their interests, their families and their commuting times, and treating the answers as fascinating.

'So what are page rates?'

He failed to disguise a sigh. 'Well, you see, all the advertising in magazines is sold at a certain amount per page, and that's called the page rate. But it's a bit like a bazaar. Only the most successful magazines can expect to get their page rate, and . . .'

'Bill!' A woman with a slash of bright red lipstick was holding court on the other side of the table. 'We were just talking about you.' Bill brightened and shifted forward to hear what she was saying, and the next fifteen minutes consisted of a shouted reminiscence of some press trip that seemed to have been spent mainly in the first class lounge at Heathrow. On Clara's other side, the head was firmly bent towards a frail-looking blonde whose gossip about the supermodels and their habits commandeered the attention of that half of the table. Bursts of laughter rose regularly from the trio, and the odd sentence wafted towards Clara. ' . . . and, THEN, she ordered ANOTHER bottle . . .' the blonde was saying. Her audience rocked with laughter. Clara contemplated her plate, which had something that tasted very like pickled rhino hide on it. She had landed on an alien island, but, to her surprise, she realized she found it curiously attractive in spite of the humiliation. All the doors opened at once and an army of smartly dressed waiters advanced simultaneously on every table. It felt like an invasion of old-fashioned uniformed nannies, as they swept and cleared away plates, and replaced them with something brown and shiny, flanked by vegetables.

She had plenty of time to work out why she suddenly felt so much more alive here, looking round the table and earwigging the conversation. (She occasionally asked Bill Grundy a question out of politeness, to which he smiled blandly and offered an answer, but this scarcely constituted a conversation, and, after an initial frantic cross-examination to find something that he might want to talk about, did not tax Clara's mind.) These other women were not asking men about their commuting times. They were telling them about *theirs* (Bill Grundy clearly didn't want to hear about hers, but would obviously have listened to anyone else at the table reciting the telephone directory). It wasn't easy, but it was refreshing. Having always thought that anyone worth knowing considered publicity vulgar, she suddenly realized that this was a woman's world. Created by women for women, and it felt, suddenly, incredibly exciting.

There was a general shuffling of chairs. Last chance for the loo before the awards. Terrified of having to creep out during the speeches, Clara wandered around endless long overlit corridors before finally finding the Ladies Powder Room. It was like every other powder room she had ever been in. The compulsory gilt chairs. The regulation exhausted Portuguese or Filipino coat lady. The row of unflattering mirrors swinging back at an angle to show her double chins. She gave them a quick horrified glance and retreated into a cubicle.

There was a whoosh of water from either side of her, followed by a rush of taps filling basins as two voices began talking:

'Bill's in good form tonight. Mmm, mmm. This is a good shade of lipstick. Dior's latest. They're so good at colour.'

'Oh, I adore Bill. Who are you sitting next to?'

'Edward somebody-or-other. Seriously attractive. One of those rare men that really listen to women.'

No, he doesn't, thought Clara furiously. He was probably thinking about something else entirely.

'Mmm. Sexy in a rough sort of way. I think his wife's next to Bill. The plump one in the dreadful blue dress.' Icy horror crept over Clara.

'A Gonziaga Black. No one's wearing them any more. Except Arabs, of course. That's where the market is. And Texan millionairesses.' There was a roar of water, which didn't quite drown the next remarks.

'I sometimes think fashion features should have

Frock Warnings on them. A "Look Don't Buy" sticker across the side. Especially don't buy if you're fat and forty.' There was a giggle.

'Not a bad idea. Give each designer a Frock Warning grade. Like a Gale Warning. Gonziaga Black the equivalent of a hurricane. I feel a feature coming on. Tra la.'

They were really enjoying this, whoever they were, thought Clara, pinned in the narrow cubicle with her cheeks burning.

'A real case of the wife being outgrown and left behind I'd say. Did you hear . . .' Clara pulled the chain in order to miss the rest of the conversation. Too much champagne curdled with the crisps, along with the rest of the meal, every morsel of which Clara had scraped off her plate in a nervous effort to keep occupied. She was suddenly very, very sick.

When she had finished heaving, there was a gentle tap on the door. 'Are you all right?' This voice sounded sympathetic. Unlike the assured tones of the gossipers.

Clara unlocked the door and looked quickly around. Thank goodness they'd gone. 'Yes . . . I think I ate something that disagreed with me.' A fresh mortification struck her. Suppose this elegant woman standing in front of her – she looked vaguely familiar but Clara couldn't quite place her – thought she was drunk?

'I don't blame you. The food here is disgusting. Don't you agree? Have a drink of water.' She picked up a glass and ran a tap, then handed it to Clara.

'Thank you.'

Had the woman overheard the conversation? Would she realize that they had been talking about her? Clara's cheeks burned.

'Why don't we go back to the dinner together? Then, if you feel ill again, I can help.' Clara had planned to take a taxi straight back to the hotel, but the woman took her arm firmly and guided her through the door. The only real advantage of the blue dress, Clara reflected, was that no one could see her knees knocking together. Well, they couldn't really knock much. They felt as tightly bound by the Lycra as Chinese women's feet.

'It's such a refreshing change to see someone who isn't dressed in black.' She obviously had heard the humiliating exchange.

'I'm afraid it's not very . . . fashionable.'

'You look pretty in that colour. That's all that matters.' Clara felt reassured that she hadn't lied. So she did look pretty. That was something.

When she got back to the table, she was surprised to see both Bill and the man on her right leap to their feet.

'Now I'm relying on you to look after your neighbour properly, Bill,' said the woman. 'I look forward to hearing all about another conquest for the famous Grundy charm in the morning.' She gave Clara's arm a friendly squeeze.

'Oh, I've been looking forward to a real chat.' Bill sounded almost genuine, tucking in Clara's chair and refilling her glass. 'I'll give you a tinkle tomorrow, shall I?' This to the elegant woman.

'Fab, darling.' And with a twinkle of her fingers

in Clara's direction, and blowing a kiss to Bill, she disappeared into the crowd.

'I didn't know you were a friend of Virginia's.'

Of course. It had been Virginia Law. Bill was obviously impressed.

Clara bit back the fact that she had only met her that night. It was time to stop being quite so nice. It was a pleasure to see Bill disconcerted.

Virginia had arrived at Shaftesbury House in a black cab crammed with her 'girls'. It almost reminded her of being a bride, as they tumbled out of the back in a laughing group, vying with each other for the privilege of paying the driver. She had stepped out in a more dignified way, once the taxi had been paid, and they all hung back so that she could go in first.

It took a full half-hour to get anywhere near the coat desk – in fact, one of the girls offered to take her coat for her – because there were so many people she knew. She had to stop and talk. Nigel was there, of course, with his team – what were the advertising people doing at editorial awards? He kissed her on both cheeks, and whispered in her ear, 'I gather we're in for a triumph tonight.'

She hoped so. She didn't want to face Nigel – or Paul Long – if they weren't. This buzz had better be founded on something more than speculation.

The rest of the evening passed in a blur of kisses and asides. Virginia was beginning to feel exhausted, and took another sip of champagne. Getting up at 5.30 a.m. to catch up with work before the children were awake got to you. For a very brief moment she wondered what it would be like to be curled up in front of the television with Simon, with her feet in a pair of thick socks rather than strappy high heels, instead of standing under twenty-five glittering chandeliers and facing 100 round tables for ten, each surrounded by people dressed in black. For a moment she wondered if her colour vision had gone.

But it was the lights dimming as someone leapt on stage to announce the winners. It was some famous TV presenter, whose name flitted in and out of Virginia's tired, nervous mind and failed to leave an impression. She folded her hands neatly on her lap and assumed a composed expression. Everyone would be looking at her, whether she won or not.

Clara was thrilled. She adored all Dave Dawson's satirical chat shows, and here he was, in the flesh, presenting the awards. Behind him an exciting collection of photographs flashed up – teenage nymphets in impossible-to-wear dresses (Edward should enjoy that, thought Clara, as Dave's speech was almost obliterated by a drumming of feet and cheers from the table that recognized the pages). More images followed: brightly dressed native women scratching in the sand of some foreign desert, a girl with a briefcase taking a flying leap on to a bus.

There was a roar of applause as a slogan was stripped across them: 'Because you're a woman today'. Dave Dawson opened the envelope and read out the name. Like everyone else, Clara peered through the darkness as a spotlight searched for its target, eventually locking on to a slim woman as she stepped up on to the stage. Something slippery slid under Clara's fork. It couldn't be raw egg, surely? The woman's glossy cap of black hair swung in the spotlight as she received the award. It was Virginia Law.

Clara thought she looked beautiful. She looked across the table to see if Edward was watching but he was calculating something on the back of a visiting card. He was never predictable in his tastes. He often said that he found that buttoned-up, tailored look about as erotic as a tax return. Clara watched everything and everyone carefully, taking in every detail. She was never going to feel a frump in the wrong designer again.

As Virginia was ushered into the back of her taxi, she saw Clara get into the taxi in front. Edward stayed on the pavement, shutting the taxi door firmly behind her. Virginia couldn't help overhearing the exchange between them.

'Sorry, love, can't avoid going back to say goodbye. It is my office party, after all. You know it's a tradition not to have partners.' He dropped a chaste kiss on her forehead, adding grimly, 'And I'd better find out if anyone's been arrested or burned down the building. I'll be half an hour. No more. I promise.'

Clara looked as if she was used to this sort of thing. 'Of course, darling.' Virginia saw her give a forlorn little wave as the taxi pulled away. But Edward had already turned back and was talking to someone else. Virginia somehow felt cheated. She had placed Clara as a happily married Aga woman, with the kind of life Virginia occasionally secretly envied, revolving around a warm kitchen, filled with family, friends and dogs, and smelling of freshly baked bread. Never mind. She leant back in her seat and sighed in triumph as she reviewed the successes of the evening. But every so often Clara's face floated in front of her like a niggling reproach. Virginia told herself not to be silly. There was no reason why the thought of a woman she hardly knew should make her feel uneasy.

A mile away, in an empty warehouse that had been rented for the evening – it was difficult to find a venue that would take the Wiggins Frean office party twice – a very different party was in progress. The door stood half-open in an attempt to cool down the packed throng, but even the chill November air failed to make an impression on what looked like at least a hundred half-dressed bodies, gleaming with sweat as they gyrated to a monotonous thump. Every so often the flashing lights revealed a little more than expected – an editorial assistant lighting up a bulky joint, a lingering embrace between two people who seemed literally stuck together.

'The best L.O. drink is Pernod and blackcurrant. Tastes like Ribena, but they think it's dead sophisticated.' Derek from Sales had got a good place by the bar, and appointed himself as the evening's authority on getting laid.

'L.O.?' Kevin in Production was just as lecherous, but slower on the uptake.

'Leg Over.' Derek winked. 'I don't half fancy that Becky.'

Max from Dispatch had overheard and passed it on to the rest of the dispatch riders, one of whom had brought a water pistol. 'You get drunker quicker if you squirt it straight down the throat.' There were already quite a few stains on their shirts, and in other places, where they had missed.

Shirley didn't mind Pernod and blackcurrant, but she was keeping a sharp eye out for E or any other illegal substance. Last year Edward had sacked an editorial assistant he found smoking marijuana. On the spot. Not exactly party spirit.

She, Harry, and a pretty, plump girl from Editorial called Becky were lined up with a row of triple gin-and-tonics discussing Mike, a new recruit to Editorial.

'Footsteps on the dance floor, remind me, baby, of YOU,' crooned Harry. 'I do like the oldies.' He tapped his foot and eyed Mike, who was standing stiffly apart from the gyrations of the rest of Editorial. 'I'll bet you a fiver he's gay.'

'Just shy,' said Becky. 'You're on.' She looked at Shirley. 'Who tries first, you or me?' It was agreed that they appealed to a very different sort of man.

'Hmm . . .' Shirley looked at her nails. She had resolved that if there was any talent to find this evening, then she would find it. Pay Edward back. She remembered Mike from his final interview. Very tasty. She usually kept her flings away from Wiggins

Frean because she had this feeling that Edward wasn't one of those men who would respond well to jealousy. But perhaps Harry was right. It was time to give the impression that she had forgotten about Edward. For the time being anyway. She ached with fury. This was supposed to be her evening, but instead of being in a party mood, she just felt horribly, pointlessly, dumped with the responsibility of making sure that everything went well and no one got killed. Frankly, if it wasn't for the bother it would cause, she didn't care if the whole place burned down with everyone in it.

'Talons like those might frighten someone quiet and shy off,' advised Harry. 'Becky goes first.'

Shirley was checking over his shoulder, where a scuffle had broken out. Derek and Max were simultaneously laying siege to one of the secretaries, Judith. She had overheard them setting up a complicated series of bets because, although Judith was dumpily disapproving of men in general, her religious principles represented a major challenge to their manhood. Judith, she could see, was winning, having poured half a pint of fizzy lemonade over one of them before stomping off. Shirley had little sympathy for any of them. Judith dressed like a researcher for *Vegetarian Times* deliberately, she thought, in order to emphasize that her mind was on higher things.

'When my mother came out . . . .' Harry was hiccuping already.

'Of prison? Or as a lesbian?' Shirley inquired sweetly.

40

'As a debutante, darling, as you know perfectly well.' He topped up his gin with more tonic, and broke off at a series of shrieks from the other side of the room. Harry raised an eyebrow at Shirley, who shrugged.

'Where's Shirley?' One of the meeker Editorial Assistants appeared.

'Why?'

'There's an awful lot of sick in the Ladies. And someone's groaning.'

One of the cubicle doors was wedged shut, but the space over the tops of the cubicles was big enough to climb over if someone stood on the sanitary-towel disposal unit.

'What is this, anyway? Harry peered at the pale blue plastic bin. 'No, on second thoughts, don't tell me. You're lighter than me – over you go,' he said to Shirley.

'Hurry up, I'm dying for a pee.' He couldn't quite see who was hovering at the door of the Ladies, hopping up and down.

'Oh, for goodness' sake, go to the Men's. It won't matter.'

'God!' There was a groan as Shirley propped up the unconscious body and unlocked the cubicle door. Harry helped her manoeuvre the girl out. They laid her out in the corridor in the recovery position, as she was snoring noisily by now.

'I don't *think* she needs a doctor.' Even Harry sounded doubtful.

There were shrieks from the Men's, as Kevin disappeared inside with a bottle of red plonk and six paper cups. 'The party's in here, mate.' A waft of urine assaulted their nostrils as the door slammed shut behind him, muffling another squeal. Edward should be here, thought Shirley, beginning to panic at the thought of the party getting seriously out of hand.

They went back to find out how Becky was doing with Mike.

'I've always thought . . .' they found her in a dark corner with Derek, who was murmuring unlikely compliments into her ear ' . . . that you had the most beautiful face in Wiggins Frean.'

'Thank you, Derek. No good,' she mouthed to Shirley over his shoulder. Shirley smoothed down her tiny leopardskin skirt and set off into battle.

Mike, she was pleased to note, looked flattered at her approach. She never bothered to acknowledge new arrivals to the firm in case they started taking liberties. But the way Mike was put together entitled him to take quite a few liberties, she thought, eyeing the firm, sculpted bottom inside the well-cut jeans. It wasn't often that Wiggins Frean attracted a snappy dresser. A waft of Calvin Klein and shampoo reassured her that he was her sort of man – Derek, Max *et al* all favoured more fearsome aftershaves with names, and perfumes, that reminded her of polecats. She leaned towards him.

'In my capacity as the MD's PA, I always like to make newcomers to the company feel welcome.' She slid her hand down his arm, feeling the hard muscles beneath it with satisfaction. 'Would you like to dance?'

He politely shifted away from her. 'I'd love to.'

Shirley's instincts picked it up. Mike danced beautifully, but as Shirley undulated towards him, strips of lean brown belly flashing enticingly, he definitely manoeuvred himself away. Exquisitely, of course. But clearly. The DJ put on the Stones' classic 'Can't Get No Satisfaction'.

'The story of my life,' said Shirley, who never spent more time on a man than necessary if all she was interested in was what she thought of as the lunchbox department. 'I'm getting another drink.'

Harry was standing by the bar and Becky was nowhere to be seen.

'No go.'

Harry's eyes glittered. 'Off I go. It is a far finer thing I do . . .'

'Oh, push off. Anyway he probably won't fancy any of us.'

'We'll see. But it depends if he likes them butch. Perhaps I should have worn one of my frocks.' Harry's collection of ballgowns was legendary, and they were kept locked up in a side cupboard in the office. It was difficult to find good storage space in rented flats.

Shirley was conscious of rising irritation as she watched him go. It must be so easy to be Harry.

Usually the office party was a chance to spend the night with Edward – he could scarcely have driven back to Surrey with a skinful inside him – but tonight he would have to get back to Clara, although he would be back for what everyone called the last snog. The Claras of this world, tucked up in their chintzily luxurious bedrooms, always had to come first. She looked at her watch. It was 1.30 a.m. He had promised to be back by midnight at the very latest. There was a dispatch rider slumped over a table, and another one asleep at the edge of the dance floor. Becky and Derek appeared to be undressing each other as they swayed to the music. Out of the corner of her eye, she saw Harry leaving with Mike.

'Bodies everywhere,' said a voice at her elbow. 'It looks like the last act of *Hamlet*.'

'Edward.' She didn't know what he was talking about, but at least he was here, at last. 'How long have you got?'

'Ten minutes, I'm afraid. Clara's waiting.' Becky had her hand in Derek's trousers and was pumping away with her right hand. Edward winced.

'I don't think much of her technique. Poor Derek. Still, serves him right, I suppose.'

'Bastard.' She resolved to make it fifteen, and pulled him into a small storeroom she had spotted earlier, running her hand down inside his shirt in a way she knew excited him, then unzipping him and slipping her hand inside.

'Hang on, Shirley.' Edward seemed to be trying to look businesslike.

'I'm hanging,' she whispered, hastily peeling off a pair of wispy lace knickers and dropping them as she leaned against a radiator to hook her long legs around his waist. 'When did we last have it standing up?' Being extremely fit had its compensations. As she slid herself towards him, she reflected that Edward would never be able to do this with Clara – he'd slip a disc.

After he'd gone she finished her drink and enjoyed

a cigarette, luxuriating in feeling wicked. She'd managed to leave some lipstick on his collar, and she knew it was a particularly enduring brand. That should spoil the atmosphere at breakfast. She had been trying to force a showdown for years, slipping her laciest black knickers 'accidentally' into Edward's briefcase, buying lipsticks with maximum staying power so that any smears would linger on his clothes, and once – the only time he had ever taken her to The Brambles – leaving two smudgy black mascara marks unmistakably on the pale peach bathtowel in the *en suite* bathroom. She had never found out if the message got through – Edward was infuriatingly vague about whether Clara 'knew', and Clara herself seemed to be stubbornly refusing to take the hint. If she had any self-respect, thought Shirley, she'd boot him straight out the door of The Brambles. Into Shirley's arms.

Yes, there was a certain pleasure in sending him back to his wife looking so very well used. Put that under your chintz counterpane, thought Shirley with satisfaction. Suddenly she realized that the disco van was pulling out. There was no one else left. She hadn't thought about how she was going to get home.

There didn't seem to be anyone anywhere. The warehouse was now completely empty, with paper cups and plates full of squashed food face down on the floor, chairs and tables overturned, party streamers trailing everywhere, and piles of cigarette butts along the skirting boards. She could see several used condoms. The bare bulb dangling down in the corridor to the Ladies looked very bleak, and made

Shirley's eyes hurt. Even the girl they had pulled out of the lavatory cubicle had woken up and presumably staggered off.

'Is anybody here?' Her shouts made a hollow echoing sound. Outside there was only miles and miles of deserted railway track, punctuated with looming arches covered in obscene graffiti. There wasn't – she knew this because it had been part of the appeal of the warehouse on the noise front – an ordinary home for miles, although there were a few rundown shops, mainly boarded up, on a High Street about a mile up the road. There might be a call box there, and with any luck she'd spot a taxi on the way. Why hadn't she even thought to bring the mobile phone from the office? Because she was used to Edward looking after her at the end of the office party, that's why. No other night of the year, perhaps, but this one was special, and Clara had spoiled it by being in London. It was all Clara's fault.

She dragged the warehouse door closed behind her and set out into the dark, empty streets. Her breath froze in front of her, and the wind cut through her bare knees like a knife. She hunched up inside her fake fur coat. It just wasn't long enough, and she could feel that there was ice on the pavements. Her high heels slithered and slipped – it was like being on a skating rink. One caught in the grating of a kerb and she was flung over the road, grazing her knees and one elbow. She tugged the other shoe off. Perhaps she could go faster in stockinged feet, and it would be better than spraining an ankle. Don't think about the puddles full of dirty, stinking city water.

The sharp edge of a crumpled-up can caught the edge of her big toe, and she could see shards of broken glass glittering in heaps, catching the light like diamonds. Back on went the shoes. It was just too cold to walk. She ran five miles a day on the treadmill – of course she could run one to the High Street. It might be easier. She'd do it by counting. Sets of twenty. Like in the gym. Her arms pumped backwards and forwards as she tried to ignore the pinching of her toes. Next time she'd come to the office party in Nikes. There was a man huddled up under one of the arches.

'Got the time, love?'

'Is there a phone box anywhere?' She tried not to sound too panicky. He got up and grabbed her arm, pinching her breast painfully with the other hand.

'Get 'em off.' He had the fetid stench of someone who has slept in his clothes for weeks, and the sharp undercurrent of urine took her breath away. She could see damp running down the wall of the arches behind him.

'Let go, you stinking shit!' Somewhere, from the recesses of her memory, came the advice to yank down sharply to break the weakest part of a hand hold – where the thumb and index finger meet. He slipped and fell. She gave him a couple of good kicks to make sure he stayed down, and went on running.

There, under the flickering of a street light, was a call box. Please, please don't let it be vandalized, she prayed.

It wasn't, although she could hardly get her words out – luckily she knew the Wiggins Frean cab number by heart – but she struggled to work out where she was, begging them to hurry.

'There'll be a thirty-minute delay, love.' The receptionist clearly didn't care how cold or frightened she was. 'It's a busy time of year.' She stood there under the street lamp, hugging herself, shaking with fear and cold, while the cab took a terrifyingly endless forty-five minutes to arrive. A man looked at her curiously, and came towards her.

'Just fuck off, OK?' Fear made her snappish. She'd had enough for one night. If anyone so much as laid a finger on her, she'd kick him in the balls.

He backed away. 'Cool it, huh?'

She stamped her feet to stop her knees clattering together.

It was five o'clock in the morning before she huddled up under her own duvet, her eyes stubbornly refusing to close for what remained of the night. The grazes on her shins and elbow were beginning to throb painfully – it had been agony ripping her tights off over caked blood, and even worse trying to wash her legs and elbows clean. Two paracetamol didn't seem to be making any kind of an impact, and every time she started to drift off the stench of the tramp seemed to float under her nose, or Clara's smug face flashed across her brain, and she awoke with a start. I am sick, sick, sick of being alone, drummed through her aching head. I am not going to be the one who gets left behind. Ever again.

When she opened the curtains only two hours later, she looked down at the milkman taking bottles from the float, and the postman delivering letters. She saw a youngish man – quite sexy, too – kiss a sleepy-looking woman goodbye on the front doorstep and set off briskly down the street, while a toddler waved her fat hand after him. There was a normal life out there. And Shirley wanted it. Even if she had to kill to get it, she told herself firmly. No more Ms Nice Girl. Clara might not know it, but the days of her marriage were numbered.

It was war.

chapter 3

Clara lay alone in the pretty hotel room, aching with dread. Her throat burned with the strain of chatting politely. She simply didn't think Edward was ever going to come back, and when he did – quite amazingly early considering Shirley had to be taken into account – she couldn't be nice to him because she still felt so cross and frightened.

She wriggled up in bed, blinking in the light. 'Everything OK?'

He grunted, throwing his cufflinks across the room with such force that one rolled under the chest of drawers. Clara felt too wobbly to retrieve it. He always expected everyone to scramble after him. She leant back with a sigh.

'Are you going to buy *Heart & Soul*?' She wondered what it would be like actually to own anything so glamorous. Even with the falling sales, people still thought it was smart to appear on its pages, and there were usually top models on the cover. Or society women.

There was a short silence. He liked to play his cards very close to his chest. It was almost as if he sometimes forgot she was his wife, and thought she might be an employee. After twenty-five years, she occasionally felt she hardly knew him.

'If the price is right. If there's a market there. If I think I can turn it round and sell it on at a profit.'

A lot of ifs. She wondered why this ambition to be a glossy publisher had suddenly cropped up. Probably because, like Everest, *Heart & Soul* was there. He loved to think he'd spotted a bargain that someone else had missed. She also knew that a little leisurely 'business' on the links was not enough for him. He loved the cut-and-thrust of the marketplace, and selling off the luxury-car business, however stupendously profitably, had almost been like a bereavement for him. The remaining businesses, including Wiggins Frean, amounted to no more than a part-time job for someone as restless as Edward, and, at forty-four, he was beginning to give the impression of a big cat deprived of his hunting. When he read articles on businessmen who ran multi-billion-pound companies, Clara often heard him sigh and toss the paper away. He had done well enough to be able to stand at the bottom of the north face of the commercial and financial Eiger. From there he could see the sheer cliff that still had to be assaulted before he could call himself part of the business elite.

But, perhaps, when it came down to it, it was just

that some men were shopaholics, and instead of buying suits and trinkets they bought companies. Looking at the way his dinner jacket didn't quite seem to fit him, straining over his big shoulders, it might be worth trying to interest him in suits. It would certainly be a more peaceful life, she thought, sinking down into the bedclothes with utter, draining, exhaustion.

She woke up the following morning with a raging temperature and the feeling that someone had struck her over the head with a hammer. She was vaguely aware of Edward looking at her in a worried way, and hearing him make a phone call to the manager. She lay watching dots of dust drift upwards in the sunlight, wondering if there was any part of her that didn't hurt. Doors clicked open, and closed. A doctor unravelled a stethoscope and tapped, painfully, on her chest, murmuring to Edward. She couldn't be bothered to listen to what they were saying.

'I'm seeing a lot of this in my surgery. It's a kind of false meningitis that mimics the symptoms, but doesn't have the long-term implications. A type of flu. Short but violent in my experience. She'll be fine after a few days' rest.'

She thought about the marquee, the wedding anniversary and Eliza's farewell. 'The party.' It was even an effort to whisper. Edward sat down on the bed beside her and stroked her damp hair. His hands, usually so smooth and confident, felt like razor blades being scraped down her cheek.

'Shh. I'll look after the party.'

She tried to sit up and almost cried with the effort of it. 'It's on Saturday. Eliza . . .'

'I promise. I'll make sure everything is done. The doctor says you'll be better by then.'

'There's so much to do. You won't know what's needed.'

He took her hand. His felt cool and papery in her burning one. 'I will.' But she knew he didn't. And so did he. He was hopeless on domestic detail.

'You couldn't organize your way out of a paper bag,' she croaked crossly.

'Can't you cancel the party?' The doctor obviously did not rate parties high on the list of life events. 'She'll probably just about be able to cope by Saturday, but she can't possibly do anything much before then. And it's obviously worrying her.'

Edward squeezed her hand tightly. 'I'll send Shirley to do it. She's very efficient, and asked if she could help.'

Clara nearly screamed. 'I'm not having that – ' she was going to say 'cow in my house', but experience had taught her that confrontations always ended in tears. Hers. 'I'm not having that,' she ended weakly.

'I know. I know,' he said soothingly. Surely he didn't? This was no time for the truth game. The thought of having to challenge him with a ten-year affair when she had a raging temperature made her give in instantly.

And he was, as he surprisingly often managed to be, probably right. Shirley was a superb organizer, she was his PA and she could probably lift Clara's file up and simply pick things up where Clara had left off. There wasn't anybody else who could do it, and there was a certain grim satisfaction in making her work for her invitation. Pity she couldn't be made to eat with the staff. She nodded.

'That seems an eminently suitable arrangement.' The doctor folded his stethoscope into what looked like a black computer bag with satisfaction, his mind obviously already on his next call. 'You'll feel much better now that's been sorted out.'

If Edward hadn't been there, looking so worried, Clara would have hauled herself up on her pillows and hissed at him, 'If you think that four days of one's husband's mistress rattling around the house poking her nose into drawers and cupboards is an ideal convalescent experience, you ought not to be a doctor.'

As it was, she stayed silent. Giving in again, she thought, doing what Edward told her to do. She should have said 'no' the first time he ordered her to do something against her instincts, all those years ago. And having gone along with that, there certainly wasn't any point in standing up for herself now. That was the deal between them. She did what she was told, and he stuck by her. She knew a lot of couples who had that sort of agreement. She just wished she didn't have the feeling that there was some small print she hadn't read. Which was about to change everything.

Virginia sat in the Managing Director's office at Publishing Unlimited simultaneously wondering why

Paul Long had called her up to his eyrie on the twenty-fifth floor and whether her husband, Simon, ought to try out his tailor. He was about the same colouring and build as Paul, she thought – fair, medium height, well built, conventionally but beautifully dressed, with a signet ring and gold cufflinks. They both had that slightly windswept glow of health indicating an outdoor life, although, as each worked fifteen hours a day, she couldn't imagine why. Burnished with the flame of money and success, perhaps.

Paul studied her with the special mixture of benevolence and understanding that he used for lulling errant employees into a sense of security before terrifying them with his latest grand plan. Virginia was far too important to be terrified, and began mentally composing To Do lists as she prepared to let the words wash over her.

'Congratulations on last night's award.' He smiled but there was a briskness about it that Virginia, who was now trying to decide whether they should add the words Confidence to the cover lines for the January issue, failed to notice.

'Thank you.' So this was going to be a feelgood session.

'Now, Virginia, your results with *Viva*, overall that is, have been good. Particularly at the start of your editorship. In fact, now that you've got *Viva* so well sorted, we'd like to use your talents to turn round the Specialist Division. As the overall chief, of course.'

Virginia couldn't understand what he was talking about. The Specialist Division was a collection of under-performing titles that she completely ignored.

Clock Collecting, she thought one was called. *Your China* was definitely another. Paul had been driving all the editors mad recently talking about the potential for CD-ROMs and the Internet in this area, but they all switched off. This was not an area for glamorous, fashionable, award-winning Virginia Law to work in. You could hardly imagine Chanel inviting the editor of *Clock Collecting* to their private sales. Or top designers sending gifts – often exquisitely tissue-wrapped offerings of a suit to die for from their latest collections – to someone in charge of *Your China*.

'That's a sideways move.' She looked at him coolly, now concentrating thoroughly. It was actually a step down. Overall chief of, what, a dozen titles? Maybe twenty. Small, dull magazines. It hardly compensated for losing the job of editor-in-chief of Publishing Unlimited's most important, glossiest, highest-earning title. She couldn't believe he could be considering this kind of manoeuvre the day after she had won the magazine industry's most prestigious award.

'Only if you make it one.' He regarded her over the large leather-bound desk. He really didn't care for aggressive eyeballing. 'Come on now, Virginia, let's talk about this as friends.' He got up and walked round the desk, his feet sinking pleasurably into the thick carpet. 'Let me offer you a sherry.'

'I don't want a sherry. Or a sideways move. I've added twenty-five per cent to the sales of *Viva* in four years. And I want something bigger and better. I'd like to feel I could be in line for a seat on the board.'

'Twenty-five per cent. Up to the last ABC figure. But the sales since then – the past six months, the ones that haven't been published yet – are going flat, aren't they? Not, of course, that that's the reason behind this conversation. And, of course, a seat on the board *may* be the next step after this move. But you're tired. You need a change. A break. A fresh opportunity.' He gazed appreciatively at the way the light from the window glimmered through his sherry. 'And it's not as if you haven't proved that *Viva* can manage very well without you. Not after two maternity leaves. You weren't actually there for seven months of those two years. Of course, your skill in getting an excellent team in place is part of what makes you a great manager. That's why we'd like you to turn round some of the, er, less successful ends of the business. This is, I can assure you, a promotion.'

Virginia was filled with cold rage, pushing the thoughts of the 'flat' sales away. They had worried her more than she liked to admit, reminding her of a balloon that slowly deflates. At the moment, particularly from a distance, everyone saw the balloon as large and colourful, a perfect balloon even. Close up, you could see the wrinkles, the lack of buoyancy and brightness. Just a few more losses, a little more air out, and everyone would notice it falling slowly to the floor, bobbing along near the skirting board before it finally fizzled out. Certainly the last week's figures were more than just a puff of lost air. But that was only one week and sales always went up and down, she told herself. This was nothing more than a blip. Last night she had won the industry's hottest award. She was at the peak of her career.

'I worked through those maternity leaves and you know it. I went into the delivery room reading page proofs. I went to big advertising dinners while I was still breastfeeding.'

As she made her points, one by one, stabbing the air with an expensive pen, Paul was temporarily diverted by the thought of Virginia's breasts, which, he was sure, would be as neat and firm as the rest of her. He snapped his attention back just before the end of her tirade, which, predictably of course, threatened taking her considerable skills to the opposition, who would be only too pleased to have her. Eventually she asked him who he imagined could possibly replace her.

He deliberately misunderstood her. 'I knew you'd understand. After all, a great editor like you needs new challenges every so often. And your influence, of course, will still be very much felt at *Viva*. Your deputy, Serena. . .'

Virginia felt as if she had been punched in the stomach. Serena was so much fatter than Virginia. She was like a blobby copy of her editor and mentor, her identical bob always untidy rather than glossy, and buying the same Caroline Charles suits two sizes larger, leaving the jacket on her chair whenever she could with a sigh of relief. Virginia had promoted and trained her, guided and helped her, but had never thought of her as an editor. Admittedly, she had recognized that if she was to have her family before the age of thirty-five – and she and Simon had agreed that leaving it any later might lead to possible fertility problems – then she had to train a deputy who was both hard-working and talented. Serena, aged thirty-three and single, devoted her life to work and modelled herself on Virginia so slavishly that Virginia had never felt threatened for an instant. Even though the second maternity leave had been harder than the first, with a disrupted, anxious Oliver to reassure and a sickly, premature Agnes clinging both to her mother and her life with precarious courage. She had allowed Serena a bigger role as the public face of *Viva*, although Virginia had kept a strong hand on the reins in the background. Now Serena had clearly convinced the management that the massively successful *Viva* was safer in the hands of someone who worked fourteen hours a day than a working mother who could not be trusted to do more than ten.

'I told you Serena wasn't ready to be an editor when the editorship of *House & Home* came up three months ago,' Virginia reminded the MD, who had suggested that Serena apply for the editorship of *Viva*'s sister magazine. Virginia had pointed out that Serena rarely made a decision on her own and was too lacking in confidence to make a strong editor. 'Nothing has changed in three months.'

'Serena's been a deputy for nine years. Not yours, admittedly. I think her confidence will come from being promoted. And we do, seriously, have to get the Specialist Division right. You'd be involved in overall strategy, new acquisitions, brand extensions, selling off or closing down the most difficult titles

. . . everything. And I think you could do it better than anyone.'

He was probably right there, reflected Virginia, although that was hardly a justification for pushing her into a low-visibility job marketing *Your China* T-shirts and deciding whether the market was ready for a magazine based entirely on rose growing or collecting thimbles. She just did not want to do it. There were people out there who would jump at such a job. She was not one of them. She glared back at Paul Long. But for the time being she had said everything she wanted to say. His mind was made up. The press release announcing her move was probably already being faxed out to the media press.

And Virginia had not got to the top by losing her temper. She walked out of the room with her head held high.

'Very well,' she told Paul in clipped tones. 'But I think you'll come to regret this decision.' And without giving him time to reply, she marched out into the corridor and pressed the button for the lift.

It arrived immediately, and the doors closed on his secretary who was waving some piece of paper at her, something she had to sign apparently. Certainly not. Temporarily defeated, but by no means routed, she took deep breaths into her abdomen as she had been taught at a Women In Management Stress Conference. 'Mini-workouts' would be a good health piece for the stressed superwoman in the next copy of *Viva*, she thought, automatically, before realizing that her ideas for *Viva* would now be redundant. That's what she really minded. Being transferred away from the mainstream of women's lives. She stepped out of the lift and smiled, practising sincerity and conviction, out at the murky city that stretched out twenty floors below Publishing Unlimited. Well, Serena, darling, she murmured to herself. Let's crack open the champagne, shall we?

Serena must have known about this. That was even more humiliating. She and Paul had obviously worked out a strategy behind her back. As Virginia walked back into the vast open-plan office, divided up by luscious giant pot plants, she could see Serena's head bent over her work.

'Darling!' Serena jumped at her words. 'I'm just so thrilled for you.' Virginia swept past her, tossing the hastily prepared remarks over her shoulder. 'I've been pestering the suits upstairs to take you more seriously for months, and, now, at last, they're prepared to give you a trial.' She saw Serena flinch at the word 'trial'.

Before she could say anything, Virginia was ushering in her secretary, a gawky girl called Belinda with ambitions to be a great editor herself. 'Champagne, Belinda. And glasses. Call everyone in. I want to be the first to tell the whole office.' She wondered who Serena had confided in. She would be watching faces carefully, ready to spot signs of shock or victory, fear or triumph.

'I'm sorry . . . I . . .' Serena was looking slightly bewildered.

'My darling, you're just so brave to take on a great big job like this. And now I'm free to carry out some great plans. I've been working on this for a long time.' The words were beginning to stick in her throat, but she had a chance to pull herself together by making a great fuss of opening bottles and topping up glasses. Eventually people had been flushed out of corners, unglued from telephones and detached from computers. Everyone stood round the small square office, papered with past covers of *Viva*, and waited expectantly. Virginia carefully scrutinized the circle of faces.

'I have some exciting news for you. Serena is to be your new editor, and I shall shortly be taking up a fascinating opportunity elsewhere in the building ' She paused. Shock registered on most of the faces, dismay on several. One girl was white-faced. Virginia would remember her, and would think of her for a future job. She caught the edge of a smile from another, a plain girl that Virginia had never liked, but had inherited from a predecessor. Aha, she thought. Probably been promised the newly vacant job of deputy editor. She carried on, stressing her support for Serena while saying how much she would miss them. At the end of the meeting she saw several people leap for the phones. The news would fly round, ahead of that carefully prepared corporate press release. It was company policy to decide what quotes the editors would give to the press, but in this case, Virginia would be giving her own quotes. A small victory but it made her feel better, and stopped her shaking.

Belinda was holding two telephones up.

'The *Guardian*'s media column on one line, your husband on the other.'

'Tell Simon I'll call him back.' They had an unspoken agreement that work always came first. She gave a sugary down-the-line interview to the *Guardian*, stressing her awards, the rise in circulation and the way she had moulded Serena into a worthy successor, and how she was sure, in spite of her lack of experience, that Serena could cope with the job. The best she could do in terms of damage limitation.

Then she pressed a button. 'Get me Simon, would you, Belinda?' she said, crisply.

When his voice came on the line, warm with love and concern, she felt a lump rising in her throat and her eyes began to sting with tears. She quickly wiped them away. She knew Simon would be frantic with worry if she cried on the phone. And there was no question of the staff seeing her red-eyed.

'What's up? There's some extraordinary rumour flying around about you being sidelined.'

'How does a top merchant bank have time to hear rumours about the frivolous publishing industry?' she retorted, trying to keep the wobble out of her voice.

'We've just had a meeting with a group of solicitors who are working on a deal with us, and one of them has a client in the media.' It was the kind of convoluted explanation that made perfect sense to Virginia, as it would to anyone in the media, where communication required the bare minimum of telephone lines to propel it round a whole city. 'But anyway, I just wanted to know if you were OK.' Simon was always there for her, she knew, and would take any drop in her status as a direct personal challenge. He was not a man who was threatened by living with a high-profile woman – he even enjoyed it. Although the fact that she worked in women's magazines probably helped, because he saw it as an apparently frivolous and feminine area of business. Perhaps he might not have been quite so understanding if she worked in another merchant bank. And he had – irritatingly – started banging on about the children recently, didn't seem to realize that Virginia would always make sure they had the best of everything. Including quality time. She looked round quickly. There was no one in sight.

'It's shit. But I'm handling it.' She spoke quietly. Someone drifted up to her desk, so she put on her dynamic voice again. 'Anyway, darling, it's such a special opportunity for me. What time are you back tonight?'

'I'm due at a drinks do at Hambros – shall I skip it?' He really must care, she thought. He never missed anything to do with work, or any opportunity to exchange a few words with someone who might, one day, be important to a project. More than anything else, that made her want to cry again, so she hastily put the phone down with a cheery, 'See you then.'

The day seemed interminable. Virginia knew that she was half-expected to jump ship immediately, taking her contacts book and personal espresso machine home with her, so she was determined to keep them guessing. A large bouquet from the management arrived.

'Probably for you, Serena, darling,' she said glassily, and Serena flushed. None of the staff were doing any work, she noted, and they were all taking it in turns to keep a surreptitious eye fixedly permanently on her office. She sometimes wondered if they had long-range hearing equipment concealed inside their Psion organizers.

'To Virginia – a great editor and a wonderful person,' said the inscription. She ground her teeth inwardly. So everyone was going to play darling-darling games, were they? Well, she could darling-darling for England, and had seen too many editors blow it by losing their tempers and behaving like spoilt toddlers whose ice-cream has been taken away. Who was it who said, 'Revenge is a dish best tasted cold'? Well, Virginia could turn out a superb salad if she wanted to. She scribbled a quick thank-you note and looked at her watch. She didn't even want to leave on time because everyone was used to her never leaving before 7 p.m.

But by 6.20 p.m. the office was empty anyway and she slipped away to the tall white terraced house in Islington that she and Simon had so cleverly bought before the area really came up.

She knew she'd find Oliver in the basement, which they had turned into what *The Times Magazine* had defined as a 'contemporary country kitchen', with immaculate pale beech Smallbone units and a pot rack hung with brilliant red chillies and smart stainless steel pans. One end was the 'comfort zone', and there he was, sprawled on a kilim-covered sofa – perfect for hiding the marks from tiny feet – watching a video. She hugged his chunky body until he wriggled out of her arms in order to watch *Postman Pat* more easily, so she trailed upstairs, every step feeling more leaden than the last. Agnes was already in her cot in her pink bedroom, waving her fat little arms and legs at the nanny, a French girl called Sophie.

Virginia took a moment to look round at the little room before picking up her daughter. It gave her more pleasure than any other room in the house because it was so unashamedly little-girlie. She would have loved to own it as a child instead of the austere north-facing cell in her parents' dilapidated old rectory. Agnes's bedroom had a sherbetty-pink wallpaper dotted with tiny stars, matched with pink gingham curtains, and a smart striped pink sofa, dotted with cushions in ice-cream colours. Adorable china dolls in traditional frocks lined the top of the bookcase, which was filled with Beatrix Potter story books. In the wardrobe Agnes's tiny frocks hung up – the pretty gingham one given by a godmother, a white broderie anglaise she had worn for her christening, a cute little outfit in shocking pink and aqua that had come from New York . . . Virginia loved to finger them. Agnes let out a squeal of joy, and Virginia scooped her up, revelling in the baby-smell of soap and washing powder. The soft downy top of her daughter's head was the best thing she had felt all day, and she closed her eyes briefly to enjoy it.

'You are back zo earlee.' Sophie, the nanny, was surprised. 'Or are you back just to change ze outfit?'

Virginia looked at her vaguely, tucking Agnes into the crook of her arm. 'Change? No, no, tonight's been cancelled.' Whatever it was, she thought, in a rush of guilt. With any luck it was it was one of those interminable dos that heaved with people, not some intimate little dinner for ten people at Mosimann's.

'Don't worry, Sophie, I'll take over now.' Sophie withdrew tactfully to her bedroom. Virginia was usually out four nights a week – it came with the territory of being editor. Sophie had been shocked at first, and prepared to think of her employer as an uncaring, neglectful mother. She had been surprised to find that her relationship with her children was, if anything, more romantic than that of other mothers she had worked with. Perhaps they were just too young to know different, she thought cattily. And it wasn't fair on that lovely husband of hers. Sophie rather enjoyed seeing the occasional flash of tension between Virginia and Simon, and fancied these spats were getting slightly more frequent. She occasionally dreamed of consoling Simon. Virginia would have to get more involved with her family when they were old enough to demand something more than an employee to monitor them, she thought – when they wanted real input to their homework, for example. Or perhaps not. Sophie sighed. Virginia always seemed serene and loving, not snappy and short of sleep like most others. The perfect mother.

Downstairs in Agnes's room, the perfect mother could feel her temper bubbling up inside her like a cauldron of rage.

'I have two choices,' she told Agnes's adorably

china-blue eyes. 'I can work within the system – take the "new opportunities" and really try to set that dreary section on fire – or I can hunt out a rival magazine – someone who really wants to challenge *Viva* and take that readership away from them. Which shall I do?'

Agnes dribbled obligingly on to the Paddy Campbell suit.

Later that night, she lay awake after she and Simon had made love in a rather desultory fashion. Thank goodness he wasn't the sort of man who demanded sexual gymnastics, she thought, not for the first time. She'd always rather dreaded marrying someone who constantly craved variety, and was agreeably pleased to discover that while Simon enjoyed sex, and was perfectly happy to have as much of it as necessary (once a week, choice of two positions), it didn't seem to come top of his preoccupations. He had not, in the end, come home early, but he had not been very late either. He found Virginia sitting quietly in their all-white sitting-room – described in the same *Times Magazine* article as 'a stylish marriage of a cutting-edge interior and a beautifully restored Georgian drawing room' – with Oliver asleep on her lap, a glass of wine by her side, and her long legs curled elegantly under her. She looked tired, almost ill. He hoisted the toddler over his shoulder in a fireman's lift, put him to bed and came back to stroke her hair.

'Tell me about it.' She mapped out the humiliations of the afternoon, while he poured them both a generous glass of ten-year-old Lagavulin malt whisky. It hit the back of her throat like ice on fire.

'God, that's good. We did say we wouldn't drink spirits during the week.'

'I think that this qualifies as medicinal, don't you?' He gave her his special smile, the one that still made her heart turn over. Tonight she hardly noticed it, although she saw the worry in his brown eyes, and registered, for the first time, that his tight English curls, hacked into submission by a top City barber, had one or two grey streaks at the temples. When had that happened?

When she had finished he was silent for a while. 'You haven't really explained about the new opportunities.'

'Those.' She was contemptuous. 'Whenever the company wants to get rid of someone they can't really sack or make redundant, they offer them some grand pseudo-title in some area with zero possibilities. It's just a sop. You're not supposed to take it.'

'Yes, but what is it?' he persisted quietly.

'It's Editorial Director of Specialist Magazines and New Media. It means organizing a rag-bag of minor newsletters and anorakky special projects. You know, lots of stuff with CD-ROM applications, and things where knowing about rights really matters. You know, all that legalese and technical stuff. Nothing that needs editorial flair. Absurdly low profile, too.'

'I wonder. It's a booming area. I think you should look at it seriously.' His feet tapped on the stripped-pine floor as he crossed the room to adjust a dodgy shutter. Virginia did not believe in covering the graceful lines of the full-length windows with curtains, but Simon found that if you didn't wiggle the shutters – which were original, of course – very carefully on closing, there were some terrible draughts. He comforted himself with the thought that thick heavy swathes of drapes were bound to come back into fashion soon, and returned his mind to Virginia's predicament. 'Really, I mean it. There was a *FT* report predicting fantastic growth in that sector only last week. And you could probably negotiate to work four days a week so you could spend more time with the children.'

'For God's sake.' Why was Simon bringing the children into it? 'Look, I'm hardly a typical anorak, am I? Women's lives, hopes, dreams, fears – that's what I can tap into. My contacts are the *crème de la crème* of the cosmetic and fashion world. I don't want to disappear.' There was a silence. 'I mean, that makes me very vulnerable. This time in two years I could be a nobody in that world. What does that do to my prospects and income?' She added this in case Simon thought she was just being a prima donna. He was always extremely keen on taking the long view, and never made a move without considering what it would do to his prospects of promotion.

'If you want to take a career break, I earn enough for both of us, you know. And really, I do think it's time you spent more time at home. Agnes is easy, but Oliver's getting to the age when he does need a mother around. More often. He can't go on spending twelve hours a day with a French girl. At least, that's what I think.' He picked her hand up in his and looked at it. Virginia followed his gaze. Her hand looked small and frail in his, beautifully manicured, with shell-pink nail varnish, but suddenly much older than she felt, with the faintest trace of slack skin. When did a top banker worry about what his children were doing? she thought furiously. This was a transparent attempt to make her feel guilty because she wasn't at home every night, smiling serenely with his drink in one hand and a newspaper in the other. Middle age was obviously hitting Simon early. Children indeed. He wanted an easier life. Well, he wasn't getting it. Not at her expense.

'We'd be quite secure,' he persevered, 'if you feel like taking a few years to think about where you really want go to next.'

'You just don't understand,' hissed Virginia. 'I know exactly where I want to be. Now. That's editor of *Viva* or something just as prestigious. In spite of what you and the MD of Publishing Unlimited think, I'm not burned out yet.' She glared at her glass. 'And Oliver gets quality time with me. That's what matters. Not me screaming at him because he's dropped a chip on the floor, which is what would happen if I had to be with the children all day.' Simon was beginning to sound quite boring on this issue. And it was very insensitive of him to put her under yet more pressure when she had just lost her job.

He didn't reply for a while. He just sat there, looking at her intently. She tried to avoid his gaze, but eventually risked glancing up. He looked . . . disappointed. Well, she couldn't worry about that now. He'd known he wasn't marrying a homebody

71

when they started out. That just wasn't the arrangement they'd had in mind. And he'd always *said* he didn't want a wife who just went to coffee mornings and played tennis.

'Let's go to bed. Perhaps you'll feel better about it in the morning.'

She'd felt like asking how he'd feel if one of the companies he'd been having very satisfactory negotiations with for years suddenly decided to change its terms unilaterally. He wouldn't, she thought, like it at all.

Shirley swept several blue and purple eyeshadow compacts swiftly off the desk and into an open drawer when she heard Edward's long stride reverberating down the corridor, hastily taking her feet off the desk at the same time. She had been half-heatedly clearing out her desk drawer in preparation for clearing out her mind. Somehow Edward had settled her and Clara into a routine where Shirley got Thursday evenings and Clara got everything else, which was scarcely fair. And they both accepted it. Shirley now had to unbalance that tidy arrangement and frighten Clara into making demands and setting deadlines. Or better still, tipping him out altogether. Edward loathed demands, and if Shirley could position herself as the pliant, understanding, accommodating one, then maybe . . .

And Shirley had one big advantage. She spent all day with Edward. She knew his world. They could share things. All he shared with boring Clara was the children, who were, thank God, finally leaving home and going away, both of them, for at least a year. Probably for ever.

She remembered the first time Edward looked up from his work with a sigh and suggested they took a break. In a pub he knew that overlooked the river. 'I just need to look at some sky,' he said. She'd been rather frightened of him, he seemed so remote. That was ten years ago, and sometimes he was still just as difficult to fathom. She remembered being impressed by his smart car, his air of going places. How the lunchtime trip to the pub on the river slowly became a routine, something she couldn't bear to live without, although he'd never laid a finger on her.

The first time they talked about Clara burned even more vividly in her memory. They'd gone for a drink after work for a change. Looking back, that was when – without actually spelling it out – he'd laid down the rules. Wifey comes first. No one's allowed to criticize the sainted mother of my children.

'My wife doesn't understand me,' Edward had told her. Even at nineteen she had laughed in his face, leaning over him to stub her cigarette out and allow the curve of her breast to brush his arm.

'You'll have to do better than that.'

'No, really, she doesn't. And I don't understand her. Not any more. She's . . .' he'd gazed into his beer as if to see the word he wanted swirling in it ' . . . sad,' he concluded, sounding as if that wasn't quite what he meant. 'I find it very difficult to reach her.' He paused. 'It wasn't always like that. Only since . . . well, never mind.' He looked across the room, his eyes a million miles away from the Mason's Arms and Shirley. Not a man used to talking about himself, thought Shirley, who had got very bored of spotty teenage boys treating her to chapter and verse on the fascinating subject of themselves.

She wondered what on earth he meant, though. If she, Shirley, was married to Edward, she'd make bloody sure she wasn't unreachable. An avid magazine reader since the age of ten, Shirley had read countless articles that told women that if they let their husband think they'd lost interest, well, they had only themselves to blame if the husbands pushed off. Something like that anyway.

'P'raps it's time she tried to understand.' Even then she hadn't been able to keep the critical note out of her voice when talking about Clara. They'd only had a few drinks together, but she already felt possessive about Edward. The silly woman should watch out.

'She's a wonderful person.' He'd got up to pay the bill. 'I'm sorry. I shouldn't be sitting here talking to you like this. It's disloyal.' As he'd looked down at her, something inside her rocked violently. 'And it isn't fair on you. You're a nice kid. Thanks for listening.' He'd stroked her head as if she was a favourite cat.

Later, in the car, while she'd hugged her bag and tried to think of ways of extending the evening, he'd almost apologized.

'When you grow up, little girl, you'll find out that life isn't always a bowl of cherries. And it's never simple.'

Oh, but it is, thought Shirley. If you want something, you go out and get it. And she wanted Edward.

Clara had quickly become a no-go area between them, with Edward switching off abruptly every time Shirley brought her name up. Shirley had imagined her as glamorous and difficult with a name like that, visualizing a beauty with whom she could not possibly compete. Her first sight of Clara – when she dropped something off at the office for Edward – shattered her. She looked dumpy and tired, with a long floral skirt of an indeterminate colour and a baggy jumper that had seen better days, continually pushing stray strands of ratty blonde hair behind her ear as she loaded and unloaded innumerable Sainsbury's carrier bags from the boot of a Volvo. Clara, my foot, she thought. More likely christened plain old Clare and changed it to make herself sound interesting. Well, she needed to. Poor Edward, tied to that for life. She probably didn't even shave her legs.

And she suspected that this 'unreachable grief' of Clara's didn't make for a healthy marital sex life either. More fool her.

Back in the office, she watched him shrug his coat off and tried to read his face. Sometimes it was as if she wasn't really there. At others, she thought his face lit up at the sight of her. She went to make him a cup of thick, strong black coffee and got the diary. It was satisfyingly thick and heavy, and each page marked with scribbles. Edward was a busy man.

'Would you do me a big favour?' He was really looking at her now. Her heart leapt. Go to Paris with him? Run away together to the South Pacific? Stay late and help him out with a bid? The latter was almost as good as the others – if she was writing a book on How To Be A Successful Mistress, her number one tip would to be to ensure that your lover spent as much time away from his family, working long hours. You could devote chapters to its efficacy. It was the equivalent of dumping the wife on a desert island and sailing away into the sunset. So her friend Dawna had said when she was going out with someone who was married. Dawna, rather satisfyingly, had got him away from his wife, and was now, less satisfyingly, a mother of two herself, and rather critical of Shirley 'wasting herself' on a married man. Still. Long hours were expected these days. She smiled. The person who said that absence made the heart grow fonder had been a fool. Or, more probably, a mistress trying to get a man away from his wife.

'Was that a yes?'

She came out of her reverie. 'Whatever. I'm yours.' She was, too.

'I'd like you to work down at The Brambles for a few days.'

She goggled at him.

'Clara's got flu, and the doctor said she must rest. And there's the party to organize. I was hoping you could . . .'

She could. *Definitely*. She'd watched the video of *Rebecca* only last weekend, and it was clear that a heroine could take serious advantage of people being confined to bed. Come to think of it, there were many scenes in literature (she liked to think of videos as literature) where illness had given love a helping hand. Four days in leafy Surrey to really get to know The Brambles and its occupants.

'But what about you?' With any luck, he'd be there, too, and they could play at husband and wife. With Clara in the role of the sick old woman upstairs.

'Mmm.' He was running a finger through the diary. 'I'll have a taxi on standby for the driving. I'll need you for Thursday morning, but I'll take Judith for the meetings on Wednesday. Friday I was booked out anyway.' (He did this from time to time when he was in the early stages of a new bid. Shirley thought it was really daft not even to let your PA in on things.)

It sounded as if there would be less opportunity to spend time with Edward rather than more, but even so, four days at The Brambles would be very illuminating.

She thought about Clara, lying in bed with a cold – people never really had flu – while everyone danced attendance on her. And Edward hadn't even asked her if she got home safely. The knot of hatred for Clara simmered just under her breastbone and briefly flared into a burning pain. Yes, a few days at The Brambles would be time very well spent. She promised herself that.

'Shall I send flowers to Clara, from all of us? If she's poorly.' She held her breath. When he was concentrating on something else he often didn't think things through.

'Mmm.' He waved her away with the rather smart pen that Shirley had given him for his birthday last year. 'Good idea.'

Clara received an enormous bouquet from 'Edward and Shirley – and everyone at Wiggins Frean'. The florist had read it back to Shirley as 'Edward, Shirley and everyone at Wiggins Frean'. 'Edward and Shirley, dash,' she corrected him sharply. A woman would understand the significance of the punctuation. Edward and the florist could be trusted not to.

Edward gave Shirley his keys. In any other situation this would have counted a major victory. Shirley remembered all her friends from school, one by one, winning the keys to the boyfriend's place, or, even better, getting a joint set of keys with him. She had come to associate the rattle of these keys, brought out of handbags with an ostentatious flourish, with the end of a friendship. Girl-friends started to do things in couples. Shirley was no longer invited. Not that she'd have wanted to be included in their boring lives, but still . . .

It was easy to park outside The Brambles that afternoon because all five houses in the sweeping drive had double garages. Some even had a third car sitting in front. Shirley looked round. Each house was placed at a slightly different angle to maximize privacy, and every one had a few special features to emphasize that this was not just an average estate. It was an executive development. There were gables, beams and porches with pitched roofs on some of them, half-tiling and conservatories on others, but The Brambles had more classical lines, with a flat front, a portico, Grecian pillars and long, thin windows with rounded tops. Nice if you can afford it, thought Shirley.

The keys looked dangerous in the palm of her hand, as she gazed at the front door, painted a dark royal blue and studded with gleaming brass door furniture. The shapes of the big Chubb ones reminded her of pistols. Even Shirley's heart quailed at the thought of the damage she could inflict with them. Although, unfortunately, it didn't look as if they could be copied easily. Pity, that. But she had four days to make the most of them. She slid one tentatively into a lock, determined to ignore the shiny brass bell beside the door. No warnings, no prisoners. She stepped into the neat hallway, with its striped yellow wallpaper above a dado rail and what she recognized as a colourwash in the same shade below. It had changed since she had last been here. White painted woodwork gleamed at her and a small hall table showed off an arrangement of dried roses. She flicked through a few envelopes. Gas, electricity, postcard from abroad. She turned it over. Sam and Steven. Never heard of them. But they seemed to be having a good time in Goa. Everything smelt clean, of a sanitized pine forest. Dull. Predictable. It reminded her of a show home. She could, discreetly, mock such interiors in a few weeks' time. Make Edward laugh at himself without realizing it. Undermine his wife's dreadful dull taste in decoration. Although, secretly, she'd quite like something similar herself one day. When they were together at last.

There was a rattle of metal and the clank of brakes. A bronzed New Zealander jumped down from a truck and pressed the doorbell – although he could see that the door was wide open – and looked down at her with undisguised lust. 'Royal Marquees.' Funny to think that a few years ago, flirting with him – getting him to ask her out – would have been the pinnacle of her ambitions. Now he was just the hired help. He might do for a quick fuck, though. She looked back disdainfully, parting her legs infinitesimally as she stood outlined in the door, to give him just the tiniest hint of what he might get if he played his cards right.

'Round the back.' Not exactly the tradesman's entrance, but at least it sounded like it. She wanted to make it quite clear who was in charge.

Actually getting round the back was less easy. The expensive garden designer had not anticipated the need to shift marquee poles around. They couldn't go through the house, even if Shirley opened all the windows and tried to get them through rooms that way. Short of cutting down a rather gloomy row of cyprus firs, erected as fast-growing hedging to obscure the view of an old people's home one side, or demolishing the double garage on the other side, the only way through from the side wedge of grass to the back wedge was by opening both the door and the window in the garden shed (tucked in beside the garage) and edging the poles through, past sacks of potting compost and deliberately aged Victorian-style flower pots and fashionable long Toms. Shirley frowned. Time to move on, and find the kitchen. She was getting tired of the New Zealander looking up her skirt every time she tried to open a window. He wasn't that hunky after all.

Mrs Black – who Clara referred to as 'the daily' (as if, thought Shirley, she came every day, which of course she didn't) – was standing by the back door, waiting to leave. She regarded Shirley with folded arms. Shirley wondered how much she guessed about the 'situation'. Far too much, judging by the set of her jaw. She hoped the old bag wasn't going to be here all the time, because it would make things a lot more difficult.

'Coffee, tea, milk in fridge.' She pointed round the kitchen as if Shirley didn't speak English. 'The file. For the party. On top of the desk.' She indicated a bulging buff envelope on top of a pine bureau. 'You won't be wanting anything else in there. It's private.'

Shirley raised her eyebrows. She didn't care for Mrs Black's tone of voice.

'I've given Mrs Wheeler her medicine and a snack, and I'll be back at tea time.' She rammed a depressing woollen cloche on her head, and glared again. 'She's got my number if she needs me.'

'Good. I'm not here to look after Clara – ' she stressed the use of the first name ' – I'm organizing the party.' That should show her. There was a crash outside as a marquee pole fell. The door clattered shut behind Mrs Black's disapproving back.

'Smashed something.' The New Zealander popped his head back cheerfully. 'A light switch, and a few pots.' He obviously didn't care. Neither did Shirley. Clara was probably the only one who used the garden shed, and, honestly, it would be a blessing all round if she electrocuted herself. Shirley settled down to a methodical search of the kitchen.

New. Expensive. Painted in dark Shaker blue with a polished beech top. A dark blue Aga, far too large for the room, which was only a standard modern kitchen after all, for all its hand-painted china and 'country' wood. She pulled open the drawers. Freezer bags and crumpled tin foil. Mats with engravings of Hampstead. Knives and forks. Various corkscrews, potato peelers and things that looked vaguely gynaecological to Shirley, who wasn't interested in cooking. All useless by the look of them. The last drawer was more interesting. A hostess book, and some old letters.

A hostess book! Shirley could hardly believe her eyes. Clara was even more outdated than she'd thought. She flicked through. It was some sort of record of dinner parties, where everyone sat and what they ate. What a nightmare. Just reading it made her feel sick. While she'd been channel-surfing in her lonely bed, Edward had been eating parcels of . . . she peered a little closer . . . yes, prosciutto stuffed with ricotta cheese and pine nuts, and talking to Annabel Adams, whoever she was. Or, she struggled to decipher the handwriting, Angie somebody-or-other. And while she'd been counting the minutes till the office opened, he'd probably been gazing down this Annabel Adams's cleavage. The last dinner party had been written in two weeks ago.

Inspecting the wreckage of the garden shed after the New Zealander had finally simmered off with his mates, Shirley contemplated the light switch, which had been shattered to smithereens by a marquee pole. She was beginning to feel that this chance – no, order – to help with the party, far from being a wedge that could open the door into Edward's life, was just another episode in the saga called 'Putting Clara First'. Or its sequel, 'Taking Shirley for Granted'. Coloured wires dangled out of the switch. She didn't know much about electricity, but they looked dangerous. Still, no one was to know. She just might not mention it. There was, after all, too much else to do. She could see a van arriving to deliver collapsible tin tables and little gold chairs.

The office, which she had to drive back to at breakneck speed along the M3 at least once a day, was almost as interesting as Clara's kitchen drawers. Edward had asked her to put together costings for running a real consumer glossy, and Harry was to help her. The two of them simmered with excitement, taking piles of papers and glossy magazines into one of the airless meeting rooms and shutting the door. No one else at Wiggins Frean was allowed to know *anything*. Shirley was emphatic about that. Both Harry and Shirley suspected that he was bidding for *Heart & Soul* and using their projections and plans to help him work out how viable it was.

It would be relatively easy to find out paper and printing costs, because the technical journals shared printers with quite a few consumer magazines. And it wouldn't be hard to find out a bit about the advertising side from agencies who similarly shared clients. There were those media planners – who actually bought the space in magazines – who were quite keen on leopardskin Lycra and bare flesh, and

Shirley knew she just had to wind herself round a few of them to find out all kinds of interesting facts. But it was the hidden costs – how many staff would be needed and what kind of costs should be allocated to writers and photographers – which were a bit more baffling to someone who had simply never even crossed the threshold of a company that produced those sorts of magazines.

'Got any good holidays planned?' Harry was finding it difficult to concentrate on media planners and budgets with the thought of Shirley battling through her lonely life. He'd been very shamefaced about leaving her in the warehouse after the office party, and gratifyingly critical of Edward for not taking her home.

'He couldn't really, he had Clara to think of. It was all her fault, really,' explained Shirley, but Harry pursed his lips and clucked under his breath. Shirley needed to get out of this situation soon.

She had no intention of letting Harry into her plans. When she got Edward, once and for all, they'd go on holiday together as a real couple for the first time. Venice, she thought. Or Barbados. 'Not quite sorted,' she said, with a smile. 'How about yours?'

'Darling, you don't want to know. I'm thinking of Amsterdam.' He shuddered theatrically, and Shirley, on reflection, decided that he was probably right. Last time he went abroad he had been to a café where people paid to hang in chains above your table for half an hour. Harry was very beautiful and enjoyed being taken to places. He was also public school and very clever, and he stayed with Wiggins Frean because no one there raised an eyebrow at his life-style. Occasionally he went too far, and had to have a few days off, which even Edward tolerated, because he was unlikely to find anyone so outwardly respectable and inwardly clever at the tiny salary he was prepared to pay. And in any case, Shirley loved him, and usually managed to conceal the worst of his misdemeanors.

He looked out of the window. 'Ooh, look, there's a nice policeman. I do love uniforms.' Shirley didn't love uniforms and was always worried about policemen, having a much clearer idea of Edward's business activities than Clara did. She shot to the window.

'You bastard. It's only a traffic cop.'

Harry smirked.

'Look. I want some help from you. From your posh friends.' Shirley found Harry relaxing because she could be straight with him. There was no point in inching her skirt a little further up her thigh in order to get him to do a favour.

'For you, anything, darling.' He took another swig of coffee from a mug inscribed 'So Many Men, So Little Time'. 'But first I want to talk about your weekends. Your hols. Your free time. Your life, even.'

'There's nothing to talk about.'

'That's the problem. You're young, single, attractive . . . you ought to be packing in the parties.'

Shirley didn't quite meet his eye. 'I'm perfectly happy.' If anyone had asked her – although there was no reason why they should – she would have said that Harry was her best friend. But even with best friends, it was sensible to keep a few secrets. 'I have a good job, a flat and . . .'

'No. You *don't* have Edward. You get him on overnight rental only. Look, I love the old bugger too, but he's never going to leave Clara.'

She tried to look Harry in the eye. 'Don't worry. I've come to terms with that. Honest. In the early years, I did hope . . . but well, I'm no fool, you know.'

'I know you're no fool,' he told her gently. 'That's why I want you to realize that you've got a future beyond Edward. What do you do when you're not seeing him? In other words, most of the time?'

'Lots of things. Aerobics . . .' Shirley was proud of keeping fit, and put aside at least two evenings a week to make sure that she stayed lean and glossy, without a stray moustache hair or a stubbly leg to spoil her evenings with Edward. 'Old friends . . .' Harry's eyes narrowed. He knew she had no time for old friends. She had outgrown the crowd she went to school with completely. 'People here . . .' This, too, was not entirely true. She often had trouble hiding the fact that she despised most of the people at Wiggins Frean. She wouldn't have gone out with them if they'd asked her. Luckily they didn't, or not very often.

'People here . . . they're great, but they're young. They're not you. When did you last go to a party and meet someone new?'

She opened her eyes wide as if thinking carefully. 'Well, I was invited to one last Thursday, but Thursdays are my night with Eddie.'

Harry pinched her cheek. 'Well, next time go to

the party. Make Edward sweat a bit. He shouldn't go thinking he's got you on a plate.' Shirley wondered if she should confide in Harry, and enrol him in her plan to spring Edward from the marital home. But deep down, although he would always be her friend, she strongly suspected that he simply didn't approve of the situation. He would just try to talk her out of it all, and redouble his urges that she find a more conventional, available man. It seemed ironic, considering what he got up to. People could be so hypocritical.

'Anyway, what did you want me to help you with?'

Shirley outlined Edward's plans for ostensibly starting a new magazine, adding that she was pretty sure he was actually bidding for *Heart & Soul*.

'So that's what the old bugger was doing having John Bellman to Sunday lunch the other day.' Harry's eyes lit up. This was exciting. A seriously interesting new development. 'I wondered why he was cosying up to him.'

'Sunday lunch? At The Brambles?' Shirley deeply resented the fact that Harry was often invited to Edward's home.

'You know, networking-type event. People trying to impress each other. Clara in her best and getting rather hot.'

'What was she wearing?' She couldn't resist picking at a sore spot.

'Darling, that woman's dress sense is frozen in a 1950s' timewarp. She's so far out she's almost coming in again.' He grinned at Shirley. 'No, seriously, she's a frump. But he's sticking with her, and even Lycra isn't going to tear him away. She's his wife.'

'I know that.' Shirley was irritated. 'I don't feel guilty about her, you know. I sometimes think I'm the glue that keeps that marriage together.'

Harry blew a smoke ring. 'I wouldn't know. I just think it's time to move on.' Shirley helped herself to one of his cigarettes, and waited for him to continue.

'How are you getting on with her at The Brambles?'

Shirley shrugged. 'I've only been there for a day and a half. I haven't seen her at all. She stays upstairs and sleeps.' This was partly a relief, partly disappointing. And it meant that the revealing bits of the house – the bedrooms and bathrooms – were definitely off limits. So far, the unexpected bonus of Edward's keys had not advanced her cause much. Still, she had some good ideas for the party. A convalescent Clara, she thought, could be easily out-manoeuvred.

'I did hear some interesting gossip this morning though. A friend – ' Harry broke off to simper briefly ' – a *very* senior person in publishing, darling – rang me to say that Virginia Law, who won the editor's Gold Award on Monday, got dumped by her company yesterday. Well, not exactly dumped, but exiled to Magazine Siberia.'

Shirley got his drift immediately, thinking of the telephone number Edward had asked her to find. Publishing Unlimited's. Edward, she already suspected, was after someone there at such a high level that he did the dialling himself rather than getting Shirley to place a secretary-to-secretary call.

'Is she attractive?'

'What does that matter?'

'Oh, it doesn't. Just wondered.' But Harry wasn't fooled. She could see that. She lifted the phone to stave off another lecture. If this Virginia came on board, Shirley was going to have to keep very close tabs on her.

But for the time being she would concentrate on the party. A little under three days to go.

Clara wasn't going to make the mistake of wearing the Gonziaga Black again, and found her best old black number at the back of the wardrobe. Eliza, who'd been staying with her 'best friend' in Dorset, hurled herself through the door only half an hour before the party started, a streak of long dark hair and endless legs, scattering pieces of clothing all the way up the stairs. She threw herself down on the bed and looked at Clara. 'Oh, God, Mum, not that old thing. Won't Dad stump up for something a bit special? Hope I don't marry a meanie.' Then she rocketed off to spend an age in her bathroom, tweezing everything to within an inch of its life and pouring herself into a tiny gold number. Clara smiled fondly after her. She remembered those days herself, although her pleasure at losing a few pounds had been rather crushed by Eliza's remarks.

Marcus lumbered through the door a few minutes later and she heard him throw his suitcase on to his old bed with a thump. He came in, looking crisp and fresh, reminding her painfully of a younger Edward. He kissed her cheek.

'Hi, Mum. You look a bit washed-out. Been working too hard?'

Clara shook her head, feeling even more dowdy and crumpled. 'No, Shirley's done most of it. With your father.'

Marcus tore off a bunch of grapes from the fruit-bowl on her dressing-table and devoured them virtually instantly. 'Really?' he mumbled with his mouth full. 'She's a bit of all right, I must say.' Not Marcus, too, she prayed, deciding not to comment. He went out and slammed his bedroom door. The house shook. When did children learn to close doors gently, she wondered? When they were about thirty-five?

Clara's legs still felt wobbly as she stood up to look at herself in the mirror. 'Did you manage to do the table plan?' she asked Edward, who was contorting his face and hands around a tricky bow tie. He adjusted it finally, and stood back, satisfied.

'Don't worry. Shirley did it. We've thought of everything. Really. Just come down and enjoy yourself.' He squeezed her shoulder affectionately and strode off, shouting something about ice and chilled wine down the stairs at the catering company.

Clara was alarmed. 'Shirley doesn't know who anyone is. How can she do a table plan?'

He paused at the top of the stairs and turned to answer her. 'Don't worry. I did it, she just typed it all out. And we've got the place-cards.' She would have to be satisfied with that, she thought, as she slowly followed him down, the first time she'd ventured this far for four days. She hadn't wanted to face Shirley one second sooner than she had to.

'Feeling better, are you?' A terrifyingly glamorous Shirley fussed over her in the most surprising way. 'Everyone's getting these awful bugs these days. No one's been in for days at Wiggins Frean.' She flashed a hard, practised smile that worried Clara, but, still, she was obviously trying to be nice. In very difficult circumstances, Clara reminded herself. Poor Shirley. 'Now why don't you rest a bit in the marquee and we'll send everyone through? It's going to be a long evening, so you need to pace yourself.'

Clara felt a surprisingly strong hand under her elbow, propelling her into the marquee, and sank gratefully into a little gilt chair. She looked around. Perfect. Cascades of white flowers on every pillar. Dazzlingly pretty lilac helium-filled balloons tied to every chair. Crisp white table cloths and pots of lavender on each table. Place cards in gold writing. She ought to check them, but didn't quite think she had the energy. This table seemed fine though, all Eliza and Marcus's friends together, and Edward had even remembered to separate the boyfriend–girlfriend pair that had just split up.

Shirley ushered the first few guests through. Clara recognized the portly form of one of their neighbours, Colonel Fairbrother and his wife – nice old buffers, both of them, she thought. They were glad to sit down too. 'Looking a bit pale, m'dear,' said the Colonel. 'But just as charming as usual,' he added hastily. A few more people trickled in slowly over the next hour, and Clara suddenly realized that the real party was roaring in the drawing room. Shirley obviously hadn't had time to send anyone else through.

'If you'll excuse me . . .' she decided to try her legs again '. . . I'll just see if everything's all right next door.' She pushed into the throng, feeling as if it were someone else's party. Someone she didn't know very well. She could see Shirley, hand proprietorially on Edward's arm by the door, exclaiming a welcome to two new arrivals. Business friends of Edward's she'd never met before.

'Oh, it's Clara, isn't it?' A mousy-faced woman, married to one of Edward's oldest friends, peered at her. 'I didn't recognize you. Shirley said you were ill. It's lucky she was able to step into your shoes, isn't it?' she added, and then looked embarrassed, as if she'd said something she shouldn't.

'That's what she's doing, is she?' Clara was going to see about that. It took ten minutes to struggle through the crowd to the door, saying 'hello' to several people who looked surprised to see her there. It seemed as if no one quite met her eye, or they were falsely over-cheerful, but perhaps she was imagining things.

She could just hear Shirley welcoming people, introducing herself, saying, 'Edward and I are so glad you've made it,' or, 'Pleased to meet, you, I'm sure, Edward's talked so much about you,' at every opportunity. Above the baritone roar of a thunderingly good party – although Clara felt rather sick herself, she could see it was working beautifully – there was a hissing top-note. 'Who's that?' the whisper rippled to and fro across the room, and the breeze answered back, 'Edward's mistress.' There were too many 's's in mistress to make it an easy word to whisper, thought Clara. It carried beautifully, sibilant before the more muted rumble of responses, which varied from incredulity to envy.

She saw someone point to Shirley, overheard exchanged murmurs and exclamations, which might have been horror or scandalized pleasure. She was not so naïve as to think that Edward's affair with Shirley was a complete secret, but until that night, Shirley had been a shadowy figure that no one much thought about. Probably an occasional anecdote at dinner parties, to pad out the story of someone else's infidelities. Now she was there, in the all-too-obvious flesh, for everybody to talk about, to wonder why Edward hadn't left Clara years ago for someone so young, so slender, so luscious.

'Oh, there you are,' said Annabel. 'My God' – her eyes were popping – 'you've let *her* loose on Surrey.' She looked at Clara a bit more closely. 'You could do with some blusher. And weren't you going to wear the Gonziaga Black?'

'Something got spilt on it.' It was a weak excuse, but it would have to do.

'Well, frankly, we all feel a bit dowdy beside The Wicked Witch of the West.' Annabel obviously meant to be reassuring. 'The best thing to do is just ignore her. I mean, you've done that for ten years, much the best policy.'

Clara didn't think she had any other option, at the moment. What she wanted to do was to kill both Edward and Shirley. What she would do, yet again, was take it on the chin. But not for very much longer.

Clara looked at her watch. 9.15 p.m. And they'd agreed to sit everyone down at 8.45 p.m. No wonder people were so drunk. She could see Marcus and Eliza holed up in a corner with their friends, casting the odd incredulous glance at the wrinklies, and exchanging giggled confidences. No help there. Anyway she didn't believe in making your children share your problems. They'd have enough of their own later on. She worked her way back to the kitchens, and collared the caterers. 'Miss Green said to put dinner back,' said the top woman. 'On account of the traffic reports. An accident on the M3. Lots of people were ringing in from their cars to say they'd be late.' Clara decided to let it go. It made sense. And she could hear Shirley begin to usher people through, after all. 'Oh,' she heard her squeal, 'I've heard so much about you from Edward, we must all meet up some time.'

Clara realized she'd better check out the table plan after all. They'd agreed to do without a long top table, just keep to round tables for twelve, with Edward and herself on opposite sides of one. Shirley had placed herself on Edward's right. Clara switched the name tags, seating Shirley next to two retired bores beside the Portaloos, but was swept away by the tide of guests flowing into the marquee, bestowing kisses and nervous exclamations of 'How beautiful. You are clever,' with quick darting looks at Shirley. By the time she freed herself, Shirley had obviously managed to switch the cards back.

Clara found it hard to concentrate on what her

neighbours were saying. ' Jolly good show,' murmured one. People cast worried glances at her, then back to Shirley, eyeing the way she placed a hand so freely on Edward's sleeve in front of them. She was just discreet enough, she thought, for Edward not to notice how public the display was. At one point he lit his cigar and Shirley's hands fluttered up on both sides of the match, unbidden, to shield the flame from the breeze blowing through the marquee. It was the act of a concubine, and followed by a secretive, fleeting smile. Clara thought she saw one man look at them and say 'Lucky dog' of Edward to his neighbour.

She turned numbly to the man seated on her right. 'How fascinating,' she said, in reply to what appeared to be a dissertation on house prices.

'I'm sure you're right,' she told the one on her left, after his lengthy soliloquy on the advantages of a hothouse education. Plates disappeared, reappeared and disappeared again. Delicious, everyone told her. It all tasted of cotton wool to her.

'You'll be glad to know – ' Edward was on his feet after dinner, tapping the champagne bottle in front of him with a knife ' – that we'll be keeping the speeches short this evening. Just about an hour each.' He looked round for the laugh, and got a nervous murmur. An hour was quite possible. There was a clatter of glass and a hiss of champagne pouring, as people shored themselves up against the possibility.

'. . . my gorgeous daughter, Eliza, who's not only celebrating her eighteenth birthday today–' he walked round the marquee with his hand-held microphone ' – but also setting off on one of the biggest adventures of her life.' A rumble of applause punctuated his words, and shouts of 'speech', but Eliza, blushing and hiding behind her hair, tried to sit down, as Edward asked everyone to raise a glass. There was a roar of 'Eliza' as guests bobbed up and down with their glasses. Then Edward was by Clara's side, his arm around her. 'Of course, you all know that none of this would have happened today without some very hard work and dedication from my wife of twenty-five years, Clara.' He kissed her on the lips as a second roar of 'Clara' rang through the tent.

'But there's one more person we need to thank,' he continued, making his way back to where Shirley was dipping her finger languorously in her wine and sucking it off, watched, fascinated, by an old golf club friend of Edward's. 'As you know, Clara has been rather ill this week. In fact, she's been very brave just being here tonight – ' smiles in Clara's direction, as hands reached out to top up glasses ' – so my assistant, Shirley Green, has dropped everything' (including her knickers, thought Clara, grimly) 'and has spent the last four days rushing between here and the office, making sure that everything tonight goes smoothly. I know you'll agree that it has, and I'd like everyone to raise their glasses one more time . . .' some people were beginning to exchange glances nervously, Clara noticed ' . . . to Shirley.' He bent over to kiss Shirley's cheek, and Clara saw – quite clearly – Shirley turn her mouth aside so that their lips met. She didn't think she'd imagined the flicker of the tongue, the way Shirley held Edward for a second too long. Edward must be drunk, she thought, too drunk to realize what it looked like, how it sounded. There was a shocked silence. Clara could hear her heart pounding in her ears, and blotches creeping up her neck. Until now she'd been spared public humiliation. She'd cried over Edward and Shirley in private. Now everyone was looking from her to Edward and Shirley and back again. No one – however naïve or intoxicated – could possibly have missed such a public flaunting of Shirley's entanglement with Edward. Shirley had successfully stripped Clara of her dignity.

Suddenly Harry stood up. 'The Queen,' he shouted, raising a glass. 'I for one am dying for a fag.' He simpered. 'As it were,' he muttered to his nearest neighbour, who looked scandalized.

'The Queen.' Everyone rose from their seats, with the shuffling of feet and chairs masking the relief they felt at having been given a clear directive. 'The Queen.' It was the loudest roar this evening. When they sat down again it was like the moment after an earthquake. Complete silence for one second.

A single trumpet from the band started up. As if waiting for a signal, the hubbub resumed, with questions, answers and excited exclamations flying round the room like machine-gun fire. Shirley whisked Edward on the dance floor to begin the dancing, and Clara caught sight of Eliza's face, now white as a sheet, just staring in shocked bewilderment. She looked about to leap up, but Clara saw Marcus place a restraining hand on Eliza's arm and murmur something into her ear. This she could not forgive. Her daughter needed to go off on her first big adventure secure in the knowledge that she had a happy home to go back to. And a father she could love without any divided loyalty. Eliza should be looking confidently forward, not anxiously back. For Eliza's sake, she had to look as if nothing had happened. She smiled across the tables into her daughter's ashen face and gave a little wave.

'Come on,' said Harry. 'I bet you're a good dancer.' And he frogmarched Clara on to the floor, with an unlit cigarette hanging out of his mouth.

'Why do they stay married?' she had overheard one guest murmur to another as she twirled numbly in Harry's arms.

'Oh, you know, history, really . . .' she thought she heard the reply.

History. That summed it up. History had taken bands of steel and welded her to Edward, forged them out of their children, out of guilt, and out of the things she blamed Edward for that were really, when you thought about it, worse than having a mistress. But Eliza's departure was snapping at least one of those hoops of steel, and Clara feared that the others were rusting away and out of her control. Nothing is for ever, she thought. Not even tragedy. She turned this thought over in her mind, while fear crept up her like a cold, cold sea.

The worst of it all was that Edward had no idea what he'd done, got impatient with her at the slightest suggestion that he might have been insensitive, tactless and, well, downright disloyal, at a party that was meant to celebrate twenty-five years of their lives together.

'I really don't know what you're talking about,' he'd said angrily the following morning, gazing biliously at a glass of Alka-Seltzer. 'People have to be thanked when they go out of their way for you. That's all. I don't know why you're attaching all this significance to it.'

Clara had been too tired to see the party out till 4 a.m., and, as her knees began to give way under her, had been forced to leave Shirley reigning supreme, thanking people for coming and summarily ordering the waiters to find their coats. She didn't want to think about what else might have happened.

Edward got up heavily. 'I'd better check that they're taking the marquee down properly.'

He was, quite simply, irritated by her attitude. She couldn't seem to do anything right these days. But she was no longer merely upset. She was furious. She didn't know which emotion was lodged more firmly in her gut: grief or anger.

There was a crash as Edward came back into the house.

'What the fuck d'you mean by leaving the shed in that state? There were wires everywhere! I was bloody nearly killed. I would have been if I'd gone in at night and tried to switch on the light.' Edward was white with rage.

'What do you mean?' She jumped up, shocked out of her musings.

'I mean . . .' he spoke as if she was an idiot, or a

child ' . . . that someone has broken half the pots in the shed, and smashed the light switch. There was a live wire sticking out of it.'

'Shirley should have reported it,' replied Clara. 'She was here when they were taking marquee poles through the shed.' It was the closest she dared get to criticizing Miss Wonderful.

Edward stared at her. 'For God's sake, you're really turning this whole party business with Shirley into a major issue, aren't you?' He threw his brief-case into the car. 'I'll be back later.'

Much later, as it turned out.

Virginia Law sat in her new, bleak, office on the second day of her tenure as Editor-in-Chief, Special Projects and New Media. Belinda, who had been reluctantly transferred with her, had sulkily pasted up all her awards and covers on the wall, and insisted on the installation of a small fridge for champagne and Diet Coke. Virginia could see Belinda outside through a panel of smoked glass, continuously on the telephone. Probably trying to get herself another job in mainstream journalism, she thought, accur-ately as it turned out. In her office, the phone hardly rang. She missed the queues of people waiting outside her door to get approval for articles, ideas, pages, photographs and promotional schemes. Instead of the buzz of excitement that ran from her head to her toes when she came into the office, there was a hard lump, like a piece of coal, lodged firmly in the pit of her stomach. It settled there as she stepped through the door, and sat there, unyielding, until she could no longer find jobs to prolong the day. This office made her feel tired.

Edward's call was the most interesting thing to happen in forty-eight hours. And Virginia was used to at least two interesting events every morning. His voice boomed down the phone, sounding as loud as if he were sitting in front of her. Virginia, who was more used to the even, modulated tones of the professional publicity man, held it slightly away from her ear.

'My name's Edward Wheeler. We met at the publishing awards dinner.' A face and a shape leapt into Virginia's mind. Big, slightly shambolic, curiously attractive. Cuddly, Virginia thought suddenly. Silly thing to think about a businessman.

'I've been involved in the upper end of a number of markets – luxury cars, for example, but I've got a small publishing house, too. I want to turn it mainstream, and I'm prepared to talk money. Serious money. I've bought a magazine and want the best editor in London. You. Can we meet?'

Virginia looked hastily towards the door. Belinda had just finished a conversation.

'Just a second.' She got up and shut the door.

'Well, I'd certainly be very interested to talk . . .'

'I'm offering total editorial control, shares and a seat on the board.' (Shirley, who was listening in on the other end, hid a smile. Virginia wasn't to know that the board consisted of Harry and Edward, and one or two others who were kept strictly in the dark about everything. Board meetings rarely took place.)

Virginia tried to collect her thoughts. 'Well, as I said, I'd be very interested to talk –'

'Tomorrow?' Edward was a lazy man in his private life, but the key to his success (and, of course, his failures) was that once he had decided to do something, he never waited around.

Virginia gazed bleakly at her diary. It was virtually empty for the first time in fifteen years. 'Tomorrow's a bit tight, I'm afraid,' she said. The last time she had played these sort of games was when she brought Simon to his knees with a proposal of marriage.

'Thursday, then.' It wasn't a question, which saved Virginia from having to give an answer. 'Lunch.'

Meekly she pencilled in 'Lunch'. It looked dangerous, sitting there with so much white space around it. It told her what she already knew, which was that nothing was going to happen in this new job unless she made it happen. She sighed. She had to do something. This was living death. She was talking to other publishers, of course, but there was very little movement around in the market at the moment.

'I'll see you at The Ivy. One o'clock.' And she was left holding a buzzing telephone, wondering if this was the challenge she'd been looking for.

The Ivy, of course, was Harry's choice. 'You've got to go somewhere smart,' he told Edward. 'And wear your Armani suit.'

'The waistband's too tight,' grumbled Edward. Clara had bought it for him when Armani suits were the sign you had arrived, and he had expanded slightly since then. Privately Harry thought Edward looked best in his gardening clothes – some good white cotton shirts and a battered Panama hat that he had inherited from Clara's father. However many women Edward had in his life, he was always going to look as if he'd been yomping over the Falklands and needed his shirt-tails tucking in.

'You'd better come with me.' Sometimes Edward quite liked having someone else along to do the talking. 'And you, Shirley.' Shirley wasn't fooled. Edward wanted her along to take notes. Just like a PA.

They arrived five minutes early, and Edward ordered a bottle of champagne. 'It's the equivalent of Nescaff in these circles,' hissed Harry. 'You'll look cheap if you order anything else. And make it Krug. The best Krug.'

There was a slight but noticeable stir as Virginia entered the room. It was the equivalent of a royal progress, a kiss here, a wave there, a whispered chat and a giggle with the largest table of lunchers. The waiter hovered anxiously behind her, ushering her forward like a tentative sheepdog to where Edward, Harry and Shirley waited.

It was Harry who sprang up first.

'Harry Farquarson. You won't remember me, but we met briefly at Ellison Parson's.' Trust Harry to name-drop, thought Shirley. 'I came as a friend of Mariana Gates.' Ellison Parson and Mariana Gates were both big in the world of magazines. Virginia looked reassured, and treated Harry to a dazzling smile.

'Of course, I remember you,' she lied.

'Edward Wheeler. We met at the awards evening. My wife, Clara, sends her regards.'

Virginia rummaged through her memory for the name of Clara Wheeler and came up with a hot-looking menopausal blonde in a ghastly blue dress. The Aga woman. And that embarrassing incident in the Ladies loo. 'Of course . . .' she replied, less confidently.

Harry poured her a glass of champagne, which, after a moment's hesitation, she took.

'Well, how lovely to meet you all.' Her eyes flickered over Shirley. Far too much eye make-up, but good bone structure.

'Shirley Green. Pleased to meet you, I'm sure.'

'Shirley's my PA. I don't know where we'd be without her,' boomed Edward, surreptitiously trying to avoid her playing footsie with him under the table. Shirley deliberately dropped her napkin so that she could reach under the table and brush her hand lightly, but definitely, over his flies. She was not prepared to be part of the wallpaper on this occasion. When she sat up, the waiter offered her a menu, which she studied anxiously. It was worse than an exam paper.

Harry kicked her ankle. 'Rocket and parmesan salad's your favourite here, isn't it? And the roast cod?'

'Oh, yes.' Shirley put the menu down and smiled gratefully at Harry, hoping that there wouldn't be too many olives in anything.

Edward quickly shed his air of genial buffoon, and brought out a file of papers.

'I'm the business side of this, so I'll talk you through that first. After all, you want to know that the project's going to be well supported, and that there's plenty of security in the company.'

Virginia felt reassured watching his large, strong hands deal out costings, and projections, graphs and page rates. Advertising and promotional budgets that made her mouth water. If only *Viva* had had that kind of support when she needed it. Publishing Unlimited was cautious in its promotional approach. Edward's costings seemed sensible and well laid out. No profit expected for three years. That was about right. He finished talking and there was a short silence as she took it all in, and the first course arrived.

'I'm very impressed.' She looked directly at Edward, and what she saw gave her a shock. For the first time for a long time – probably since before Oliver was born, and certainly since Agnes – a jolt of attraction shot through her.

To Virginia, infidelity was out of the question. Quite apart from anything else, staying at the top of your job, being at least a passable mother, and getting dressed to impress took up every moment – and more – of any normal person's time. Every day was a battle to achieve it all before tiredness claimed her. She could dimly remember the days when going to a party spelt the expectation of meeting an attractive man, but those memories were so distant that they could easily have belonged to somebody else. Parties now meant deals and networking, and if a flicker of mutual attraction ever fluttered between her and one of the endless smartly be-suited men she hoped to manipulate then that was in the nature of icing on a cake. It made everything a bit easier, but would never, ever be taken seriously.

But her tiredness fell away as she held Edward's glance, to be replaced by a sudden awareness of her own self. She felt as if Edward did not see her as an editor of something, a wife of someone, a mother of someone else, but just as Virginia. This man, she thought, this man would know what to do.

Her attention was distracted by the return of Shirley from the Ladies, which gave Virginia an opportunity to take on board exactly what she was wearing. White Lycra cycling shorts and a cropped bra top, with what looked like a smoking jacket thrown on top of it. Endless brown legs tapered into white high-heeled shoes. Every heterosexual man in the room had stopped chewing, as they took in Shirley's spectacular shape. Women and gays, thought Virginia, contented themselves with a sharp, disapproving intake of breath.

Later she wondered why she had thought that about Edward. It was not as if, for example, Simon didn't know what to do. He had been initiated into the world of women by a very uninhibited and demanding Swedish au pair, and followed it up with a satisfactory chain of very articulate girlfriends at university before Virginia had put a stop to all that. Simon did indeed know exactly which buttons to press and how to press them. But that wasn't what I meant, whispered a small voice in her head. Virginia told the small voice to shut up until it knew what it was really talking about. Bed with Simon was agreeably pleasant, and few women could say that confidently of their husbands.

Edward, who was interested in women the way traffic policemen are interested in cars, was, in turn, wondering about Virginia. She was not his type – efficiently be-suited mini-men never were, but he had caught a glimpse of an impossibly thin, blue-veined wrist under the smart velvet jacket, and had suddenly wondered how anyone so fragile-looking could take on the job he was offering. But underneath it all, she's strong, he thought. Very strong. Breakable, yes, but, then, aren't we all? Virginia, he rather suspected, had probably forgotten how to laugh – if, indeed, she ever knew – but he could read intelligence and stamina in her eyes.

He put down his napkin and called for the bill.

'We've prepared a dossier for you, which, of course, is confidential. We haven't talked a great deal about editorial ideas, because that's what we'd be hiring you for.

chapter 4

Autumn deepened into winter. The trees filling the skies around The Brambles shed their burnt orange abundance and became dull grey skeletons. Victorian redbrick and twentieth-century yellow brick houses emerged from the foliage, in surprising numbers, looking sad and undressed without their window-boxes and wisteria. Treasured lawns were swamped in leaves, then swept clean, revealing patches of blackened earth. Clara felt equally bleak, but pushed it to the back of her mind.

She thought about that winter ten years ago. It had been seared into her memory with a sharp, burning pain, branding this time of year as irrevocably dark, because it reminded her of finding out about Shirley. Even though Eliza and Marcus had now left school, she still associated the last weeks of November with the autumn term, an endless stretch of time running up to Christmas, when children seemed to lose every single item of uniform in succession. She remembered the long hours spent grubbing around the lost property bin, or buying replacements, and sewing on endless name tapes in an attempt to stem the ebb and flow of games jerseys. It was looking for her nail scissors to unpick a *Marcus Wheeler* name-tape and transfer it from a hopelessly torn shirt to a new one that had driven her to rifle Edward's drawers. He was always picking up her things and absentmindedly putting them away, and she'd often found useful items like nail clippers or emery boards in amongst his boxer shorts. She pulled out two or three pairs of neatly coiled socks and rummaged around at the back where all the loose ones lay. It was probably time to have a good tidy and sort – the children wouldn't be home during the day for several weeks. Her fingers touched something flat and hard. The nail scissors? She pulled the whole drawer out and tipped it on the bed. There, at the back, was a packet of condoms. Raspberry flavoured. With one used. Her heart stopped. Admittedly she'd been depressed recently – angry even – but she knew from talking to friends that that was natural. Marriages could be difficult. Especially if one of you blamed the other. But she knew she loved Edward and that she always would. It was just a bad patch. When she felt better they'd sort things out between them. Until that moment she'd never suspected that he might feel differently. How naïve she had been.

Perhaps Edward had bought the condoms for her. But they'd been trying for a third child. For years. They'd always wanted another baby. Especially now, since . . . Like a drowning person, she struggled to grasp only the important thing. Edward had condoms. There must be some explanation. He'd won them at a Wiggins Frean raffle (she herself had won some penis-shaped ice cubes last year that had lurked embarrassingly at the back of the freezer ever since). It didn't quite explain the missing one. Frantically she raced through the other drawers, then all his pockets. Nothing. Not that she knew what she was looking for, but reading articles in magazines had prepared her for finding something like hotel receipts or love letters. She looked down at her hands, which were trembling.

He couldn't be having an affair. Because he and Clara were still responding, if not to each other, then to the monotonous temperature charts and tests that she insisted they go through. Her body simply craved another baby. No matter how often people told her how lucky she was to have two – a boy and a girl – she still ached for another. She could feel her nipples tingle and her body arch towards him, yielding and liquid, when her instincts told her the time was right. The rest of the time, she invented excuses to avoid sex, or occasionally dutifully accommodated him, mentally composing shopping lists and things to do, and keeping an ear out for the needs of Marcus and Eliza.

She went on looking at the condoms, and then piled them back into the drawer with the socks, carefully disarranging them at the back so that Edward wouldn't notice. A voice had whispered in her ear, Wait. You never know. (No, I don't know, I absolutely don't know, she screamed back at the voice.) Don't blow your cover. So she waited and watched.

She had asked Edward soon afterwards if they should stop thinking about another baby. He shrugged, looking up from the paper, shook it, re-folded it, bashed it a bit to make it flat, and grunted, 'Whatever you say. I don't suppose we could afford the school fees. By the way, Annabel called. Can you ring her back?' Her eyes stung with tears. That had been that. Of course, it had taken more than a packet of condoms to lead her to Shirley, and the way had been long and cold. That was the winter when it seemed to rain all the time.

It was time to stop this maudlin trip down memory lane, she decided, standing up and shaking her head as if to dislodge her thoughts. Just because it was raining in November she didn't have to sit in the conservatory, watching the garden turn into a muddy puddle. She should do something. Take an interest in Edward buying *Heart & Soul*.

The negotiations, along with his bid to take on Virginia as editor, had turned into the usual flurry of appointments and deadlines. Shirley seemed to be on the phone constantly – the calls started as soon as Edward walked in the door in the evening, and it wasn't as if he was getting home early. Surely all this checking of arrangements and documents could wait until morning? In her darker moments, Clara suspected Shirley of deliberately retaining information during the working day so that she could invade their evenings and weekends, particularly if she had spotted possible pitfalls. He often came off the line looking thoughtful, and made another call to his lawyer. Sometimes he mapped the problem out to Clara, who had to admit that Shirley's eagle eye was probably saving them a lot of money. That didn't stop Clara wanting to scream at her or slam down the phone. But she kept her temper. 'And my husband,' she told herself.

Shirley also seemed to have stepped up her covert messages – Clara had found a glittery earring in Edward's suit jacket pocket the other day, after he had allegedly spent the night at a car conference in Birmingham. And two long auburn hairs on the shoulder of his best suit. From what she had seen of Shirley, every hair was under control, and if any were left on Edward's jacket, it was because their owner had placed them there.

'We must have Virginia Law and her husband to dinner.' It was Saturday morning, and the winter sun was trying, unsuccessfully, to struggle through the kitchen window. Edward spoke through a mouthful of toast, smothering it in Clara's home-made marmalade. She had made 97 lb of it in January, when the Seville oranges were in season, and although he'd teased her at the time, he did prefer it to the shop-bought version.

It was an order. Clara bristled – Edward would be suspicious if she didn't – but she was secretly thrilled. Since the awards ceremony, it was the first glimmer that proved she was right in thinking that if Edward owned a proper woman's magazine, rather than those dull technical journals, then she could be more included in his life.

'Who with?'

Edward looked up from the *FT* vaguely. 'Anyone really. Well, not quite, but you know.'

'Would they actually come all this way on a weekday?'

'Probably not. Sunday lunch?'

'They've got children, haven't they?' Clara thought she could remember an article in the *Independent* recently, after the award probably, about Virginia as the woman 'who had it all'.

'We'll just have to cope with that.'

You mean I'll just have to cope with that, thought Clara. Edward would be nose-to-nose with Virginia and Simon talking business, while she played Pee-po or organized races in the garden. Still, she liked children. Pee-po might easily prove more entertaining than business.

In the end, Virginia brought her weekend nanny to keep control. 'She'll stop them from wrecking the house,' she announced cheerfully to Clara on the phone. Clara promptly made a mental note to remove her collection of china shepherdesses from the low window sill and all the snuff-boxes and porcelain ashtrays from the long glass coffee table.

The two beautifully dressed, well-mannered children who were extracted from the back of Virginia and Simon's Mercedes by a plump, pretty nanny hardly looked like wreckers. Agnes, just crawling at eight months, was adorable in pale pink gingham rompers with a Peter Pan collar, and Oliver had the same style of shirt in pale blue and Osh Kosh dungarees. Virginia later told Clara that this was a compromise between her idea of what children looked sweet in – rough tough denim and zany colours – and what Nanny had insisted on.

'She looks like a modern girl, but underneath real nannies haven't changed since the days of the night nursery and Grimm's Fairy Tales.' Virginia was propped against the Aga nursing a glass of champagne, chatting away while Clara tried simultaneously to look calm, collected and interested in what she had to say while checking up on furiously boiling pans and whisking things in and out of the Aga's three ovens. She had only installed it last summer and wasn't quite confident with it yet. She felt as if her body was a whirling dervish, while her face stayed fixedly smiling. She wished she hadn't been so ambitious about having a roast.

'I should have done something easy, like Coronation Chicken,' she admitted to Virginia.

'That reminds me of a very funny story Sally O'Sullivan told me when she was editing *Good Housekeeping*.'

Clara was delighted to hear a bit of inside gossip.

'*Good Housekeeping* ran a phone-in one day so that readers could ring and talk to an expert about sexual and sexual health problems in confidence. But the only phone line they had available was normally one of the Cookery Advice Lines, so they warned the switchboard to make sure that all the calls were diverted correctly. It worked perfectly until a woman rang in to say that she had been married for twelve years and always did the same thing, so she wanted to surprise her husband on his fiftieth birthday. The *GH* expert suggested a range of things like dressing-up, changing positions, massage with oils, mildly titillating literature and so on. There was a blank silence, and the reader finally said, in a very small voice, "I was actually thinking of a new recipe for Coronation Chicken.""

Clara thought she might grow to like Virginia very much.

'I love your sweater.'

'Thank you. It's terribly old. I bought it in a Joseph sale five years ago thinking it would be bound to go out of fashion, but oddly enough it hasn't. At least I don't think it has.' Virginia was dressed in beautifully soft cashmere. Smart but not, somehow. Clara felt stiff and hot in her Sunday lunch outfit, which was a prickly navy skirt cut to cover her knees, which she thought were too fat, and a cream silk shirt with a pussycat bow and sharply tailored shoulders which tugged over her back every time she struggled with the Aga. Noticing how the shirt gaped at the bosom, she'd added a round-necked navy sweater which sat lumpily on the buttons.

'I love the Makeover series in *Viva*. I've always longed for someone to make me over. Turn me into someone completely different.'

'Really? Who would you like to be?' Virginia had such a talent for sounding interested.

'Oh . . .' Clara decided to be honest. 'I just feel so dowdy and left behind by everything I see in the shops. I can remember when I used to read about new fashions and go out and buy them, and be really up-to-date, but somewhere along the line I found a style called Clara, and I've just got stuck in it.'

'That's just what a lot of readers say. Look, as you know, I'm talking to your husband about joining Wiggins Frean, so I can't promise you a makeover at *Viva*. But if you'd like to come up for lunch one day, I'll point you in the right direction.' Virginia produced her business card from a soft suede bag. 'This has got my direct line. Just tell my secretary, Belinda, that I told you to book yourself in.'

Clara tucked the card behind the tapes of the toile de Jouy-covered noticeboard with a deep sensation of pleasure.

A discussion about magazines was inevitable. Virginia enjoyed *House & Garden*, *Elle Deco*, *World of Interiors*, *Vogue*, *Harpers & Queen* and most of the newspaper Saturday magazines. Clara loved *Harpers & Queen* and *House & Garden*, but had always felt slightly rebuffed by the others, preferring *Woman and Home*, *Homes & Gardens*, *Ideal Home* and *Country Homes & Interiors*. Perhaps it was time to add to her reading matter. She envisaged a kitchen full of bright plastic colanders (*Elle Deco*) or old porcelain sinks found in Italian monasteries (*World of Interiors*).

Virginia wandered next door to check on the children, and there was a tap at the kitchen door. It was Harry. 'Sorry I'm late.' He produced a bunch of roses, clearly a panic buy from a station forecourt, with a flourish. 'Every time I tried to get out of bed, I was simply pulled back in again.'

'Oh, er, of course.' Clara wasn't quite used to

Harry. 'Have some champagne. They're all in the drawing room.'

Edward put his head round the door. 'D'you want some help? Stop slaving away. Come and join us.' She stopped thinking about boiling sprouts for a moment, and looked at him. He wasn't exactly what you'd call a New Man, but when it came to entertaining at weekends he worked as hard as she did – chopping vegetables, laying tables, pouring out wine – and she loved him for it. It was like the old days when she'd felt cherished and supported. At dinner he was often tired and distracted, which made him short-tempered and unhelpful, but Sunday lunches seemed to bring out the best in him.

'You've got a smudge on your forehead.'

'Oh, God.' Clara's mood was broken, and, although she knew it wasn't fair, she blamed Edward for it. Had she been talking to Virginia looking like a chimney sweep? He dampened the corner of a towel and wiped it off her face.

'There. Good as new.' Their eyes met.

Clara began to struggle away. 'What's that hissing noise? The Aga . . .'

Then, so quickly she thought she had imagined it, he dropped a brief kiss on her lips. It warmed her from inside. But the gravy was boiling dry. She broke free.

There was only one hiccup in an otherwise successful Sunday lunch. Virginia held court, telling amusing stories about famous people, while Edward, usually unnecessarily as she only took tiny sips, constantly refilled her glass. They talked about Paula

117

Yates's breasts, the new fashion for having no furniture at all in one room and several new restaurants, all of which Virginia had been to.

'What do you think of the latest mistress scandal?' Harry helped himself to another potato, and then put it back again.

'What scandal?' Everyone leant slightly forward in their seats.

'David Edwards, MP, QC, Chancellor of the Exchequer, and all that cr–' Harry caught sight of Clara's expression and retrieved the last word. 'Has been found in a brothel with two women and a hamster.' Annabel choked into her wine.

'Well, I was fibbing about the hamster. But not about the brothel and the two women. The *Sun* thinks one, or perhaps even both women, are actually men. Not that that matters, because the PM's accepted his resignation. His wife's standing by him, of course.'

' . . . should think so, too . . .'

' . . . private life nothing to do with anyone else . . .'

' . . . happened since time began, only because of the tabloids that anyone has to resign . . .'

' . . . no one in France would worry about it . . .'

' . . . security risk . . .'

The usual hubbub had broken out, while Clara tried to extract everyone's plates without stacking them one on top of each other. ('Ladies never stack,' her mother had always said.)

'Would you like Banoffi pie, croquembouche or poached pears, Virginia?' Clara almost had to shout to make herself heard. A silence fell over the table, and everyone looked at her. She felt like Boadicea, standing at the end of the table wielding a cake knife with grim determination.

'Poached pears, thank you, Clara.' Virginia scarcely drew breath. 'All I can say is that a man who lies and cheats to his wife will lie and cheat to the electorate. Marriage vows are public promises, and a man who lives a public life should suffer the consequences if he breaks those promises.' Her eyes flashed with passion. Annabel started to speak up for the right to privacy, but Clara, now seated to dole out poached pears, kicked her under the table. She did not want a political row just now. In any case this was not the house to have even so much as a brief discussion on adultery.

'I agree with Virginia,' she said firmly. It was the hostess's prerogative to steer the conversation, and this one was going to be driven very fast down a dead end.

Virginia shot her a look of surprise. 'Do you? I'm getting so used to being left unfashionably out on a limb, but it really is something I feel very strongly about . . .' For the next five minutes she bent towards Clara, talking over Anthony, explaining exactly why she thought public figures had a responsibility, and why the Press was right to reveal the facts when they discovered them. Everyone else turned back to their own conversations, and the moment passed.

Of course, Virginia wasn't going to cross a road without looking both ways very carefully. Simon, as a banker, could do what he called 'a due diligence' on Edward Wheeler. Get one of his sidekicks to look into Edward's finances, as if he were a customer the bank was intending to lend money to. She couldn't ask for a better back-up.

He came home with a slim folder of papers just two days later.

'Nice day?' Virginia always hoped the answer to this would be 'yes', or, if not, 'no'. Or even 'quite'. She dreaded the evenings when Simon came back full of news, especially as he was apt to take her through the nitty-gritty of a deal, giving her every detail except the one that would have interested her. (He could never, because of secrecy agreements, reveal the name of the client in question.) There was something about someone else's office that was never very interesting, even once one had got to know the cast of characters.

'Simpkins has threatened to resign.'

Virginia's heart sank. Simon's boss.

'Might you be . . .?'

Simon shook his head. 'I've just been promoted. So they wouldn't think I'd got the experience to go up again. And Gerry says . . .' Virginia watched him as he paced up and down, occasionally thumping one fist into the palm of his hand, as he told her what everyone else in the office thought. She had loved his passion for business when they first met. It had been appealing. Now she had to concentrate very hard on the thought of the huge telephone-number sized salary that it all brought in, and to remind herself that the pages of *Viva* were full of regrets or pleas for advice from women who had allowed their marriages to go stale. She topped up her spritzer with a little more white wine, although she would have to make up for it by missing out on a slice of toast in the morning.

Her eyes roved around the room as her husband rumbled on. If you were in Virginia's position – and she didn't think she was being too pompous about it – then you had to have the appropriate environment. The sofas, big and white, were a safe, but stylish, buy. 'The white sofa just goes on and on,' Ilse Crawford had once written in *Elle Deco*. And if ever there came a time when they didn't, well, they'd go. As well as leaving the tall, graceful windows uncurtained, she kept to as few pieces of furniture as possible and left the elegant fireplaces almost unadorned. Virginia did not like clutter. The floors looked original, although in fact, when they had ripped out the carpet, they had discovered that the boards were not in good enough condition to be sanded and varnished, so they had been replaced with recycled timbers, at some expense. And on the white walls, some quite spectacularly daring modern art was carefully displayed and beautifully lit. Off this main room was a conservatory, which had featured in *Viva* several times (Virginia had enjoyed a very good discount from the manufacturer). Simon often told her that all this decorating – or undecorating, as he occasionally called it – was a waste of money. She suppressed her irritation as the Simpkins saga finally drew to an end.

'So they'll be having an emergency meeting in the morning.'

'Did you get a chance to find out any more about Edward Wheeler?' She was conscious of an effort to make her voice sound casual.

'Well, he's certainly got the cash he says he has. A few bust businesses in the background, but anyone successful has those. He was quite honest with you about them.'

'But?' Virginia knew Simon very well. His tone had a 'but' in it.

'But there's something I'm not happy about. Call it banker's instinct if you like.' He looked at her and she saw real concern in his eyes. He was protecting her.

Suddenly Virginia felt very angry. She and Simon had been married for twelve years. In that time their careers had leap-frogged each other's very satisfactorily. They had advised each other, discussed each move, never done anything without the full agreement and support of the other. But it had been a partnership of equals. Now, because of Publishing Unlimited, she was in a position where Simon felt he had to protect her. She had become the weaker partner.

She stood up, so that she could face him directly, hoping that he couldn't spot her shaking. 'Tell me,' she said, in the clipped tones that had been so widely feared at *Viva*. 'Tell me with a simple yes or no. If this man came into your office and wanted finance for this project, with me behind it, would you and your bankers give it to him or not?'

Whatever his feelings, Simon would never lie to her. Over this or anything else. She watched his face. He wanted to say 'no'. She could see that. It was written as clearly as the electronic sign at Piccadilly Circus. He dropped his gaze, and picked up his drink. Then he looked back at her.

'We probably would lend him money. Yes, we would.'

'That's my answer, then.' She turned away from him to leave the room.

'But the bank can afford to lose money.' He got up to follow her. 'Listen, Virginia. The bank can afford to get it wrong. We can't.' He took her arm. 'I can't afford to lose you. Nor can Oliver and Agnes. Please.'

Virginia's anger melted away.

'You won't lose me. I promise. But let me take my calculated risks too. I won't be caged in with a secure dead-end job. I have to prove myself.'

Virginia enjoyed giving in her notice. Paul Long had been sorrowful rather than angry.

'Please, Virginia, I'm asking you to think again one more time. Here at Publishing Unlimited, we believe in long-term investment in people. You're talented, experienced, creative, but you've had a tough two years. You're exhausted. This new division will be big – even bigger than *Viva* – and it represents a unique opportunity for you. And, more importantly, in the short term it'll give you a bit of a break from deadlines. Although in the long run, the deadlines will be every bit as bad. That I can promise you.' He twinkled at her to show it was a joke.

'I'm sure it'll be a big opportunity for someone,' she said smoothly. 'But not for me. I know you won't take this as personal – ' she twinkled back at him to show that she knew how to take a joke – 'but I've been offered a deal I can't refuse.'

'Don't take this in the wrong way,' said Paul in civilized tones as he showed her to the door. 'But you weren't thinking of returning to your desk, were you?'

'No,' she replied, flashing a brilliant smile. 'I do know how things work. I cleared it all out yesterday. Goodbye.' And she offered her hand with courteous formality. After a moment's hesitation he took it, but she could see that it cost him some effort.

But, if the truth be known, it cost her some effort too, to sweep out of the revolving glass doors on to the street after handing her pass to Security, along with her gold company Amex card and the keys to her office. She had been determined that no one should be able to humiliate her by asking for them.

'Goodbye, Miss Law,' said the security man, who liked Virginia.

'Goodbye, Bill,' she said sadly, wishing, for the last time, she promised herself, that she was still editor-in-chief of *Viva*.

Arriving at Wiggins Frean was less fun. The first letdown was the office itself. She knew better than to expect the equivalent of Publishing Unlimited's expensively fitted tower in Mayfair, its foyer decorated with sculpture by some of Britain's most famous names and photographs taken from thirty influential years of magazine publishing on the marble walls.

But she had visited a few studios in outlying places like Hackney or Hammersmith and had found them young, vigorous and stylish, with historic industrial units and buildings stripped back to the bones and renovated with cleverly re-used furniture. One office had had Porsche car seats in its reception area. She associated it all with the kind of light and space that would cost a fortune in Mayfair.

Wiggins Frean, however, was a fifties box, occupying an entire block, with a large garage taking up around a third of it. The reception area was like a minicab office, with a few sad square chairs and dog-eared copies of technical journals. A plastic plant wilted realistically on a Formica table with screw-on legs, and the two receptionists, Chelsea and Naseem, spent more time smoking and discussing their holiday plans than actually receiving anybody. There was an overwhelming smell of cigarettes mixed with industrial detergent, and the lino floors dated from significantly before lino had become fashionable once more. Virginia had never given fire regulations a thought before in her life, but she could see that the battered filing cabinets, desks hidden under piles of paper and miscellaneous boxes stacked, apparently at random, in every office, and even in the corridors, contravened every possible official and non-official guideline.

Her own office had last been used about nine months earlier by an unprofitable division of Wiggins Frean, which Edward had managed to hive off and sell as a separate company. A dismal smell of failure still lingered in the unpromising room.

Harry happened to be walking past as Virginia was gazing at the desolation in horror.

'The chap who last worked here had a bit of a temper, and tended to throw things about a bit,' he said, omitting to mention that it had been Edward's method of making him redundant that had caused the temper in question. 'Oh dear, I think we'd better get this sorted out. Maintenance obviously haven't done what they were supposed to do. Come up and have a coffee with me, and we can make bossy calls together.'

Virginia trailed after Harry, wondering if she had made the worst mistake of her life, while he kept up an incessant chatter, showing her everything from the coffee area to the Ladies. Both were distinguished only by overflowing bins.

Harry's office was next to a big room full of what looked like teenagers toiling earnestly over piles of paper and computer screens. 'That's the Editorial Department.' He waved a hand, and a few pale faces looked up in a dazed fashion.

'Welcome to my shoe-box.' Virginia squeezed into a narrow cubicle containing two blue chairs side by side and separated by a low table in pale wood replete with a model of the Mannikin Pis, the famous statue of a cherub peeing. She looked at it rather doubtfully and Harry grinned.

'I know it's far too camp, but it was given to me by a very darling friend. Now then, darling, you just stay right there, and I'll go and sort everything out.' He shot through the door with surprising speed, and Virginia lost sight of him round a corner.

Ten minutes later she was still flicking through copies of *Disposable Industry News*, and decided to go and look for him. She found him in Edward's office, probably one of the bigger rooms in the building. On one side it looked on to an equally unpromising fifties building, grey with dirt, and on the other, over a Victorian factory that had yet to be turned into anything fashionable. This room did have a carpet, a biggish desk, and, luxury of luxuries, something that looked like a conference table. Shirley, today wearing tight leather trousers, a fringed bra top and cowboy boots, was poring over what seemed to be an address book with Harry. They jumped guiltily as she came in.

'Hi.' Shirley was the first to speak. 'I'm sorry your office isn't sorted, I think Edward thought you'd want to choose everything yourself.'

'That's fine.' Virginia did not want to appear a prima donna. She knew that once she began issuing orders, then things would happen. They usually did. She wondered where Edward was, and why he wasn't there to welcome her. She'd had several meetings with him already, including a three-day session that had also included Shirley and Harry, which had taken place in a conference room in a hotel. She'd wondered at the time why it couldn't have taken place in the boardroom of Wiggins Frean; now she knew.

She was also aware that she had suppressed her growing disquiet about the company because she enjoyed Edward's company and wanted *Heart & Soul* to succeed. She remembered the magazine in its heyday when everybody who was anybody read it. Now you could occasionally still see the ghost of greatness on its pages, but she longed to pull it round, replace the grey, dreary covers with a sparkling and beautiful woman, find an art director who could make the words look as if they were worth reading, and get rid of the sloppy, incomprehensible columns that read like some kind of an in-joke. Launching a magazine was one thing – Virginia had done that. Buying something like *Heart & Soul* and deciding who should be reading it and why they weren't was a completely different challenge. Ideally you could take all the best bits – like the fact that *Heart & Soul* had always been more than just a woman's magazine and was read by men as well – while ruthlessly discarding any areas that seemed tired, outdated or simply dull. Then, of course, you had to convince the other businesses – the advertisers and the shops where *Heart & Soul* would be sold – that what you'd created really worked. That people really wanted it. Because good support from the industry would turn an excellent magazine into a runaway success. She could transform it into a title that offered just that little bit more than the rest. And certainly more than *Viva*, which Virginia was sure would become rather formulaic under Serena. Edward was offering her this opportunity with no strings attached. She would be in charge.

As soon as she was in control. But to be in control, she had to get a secretary as Belinda had declined to join her. She'd been sure that there would be a spare secretary or junior at Wiggins Frean who would be only too thrilled to have a leg up by working for such a senior editor. Her first impressions of the company had disabused her of that idea. There certainly wasn't a spare anything at Wiggins Frean. Virginia was disconcerted. She'd never had to try very hard to find a secretary before. At Publishing Unlimited there had always been plenty of intelligent, talented, well-qualified girls queuing up to work in any capacity, and for any number of hours regardless of the pay. Virginia had never had to use an agency, or even remember the names of the dozen or so students a month who arrived on work experience. Other people did that. She sighed and set about tidying her office. It was not turning out to be a very satisfactory morning.

'It was awful,' she confided to Simon over dinner that evening. They had ordered a 'takeaway' – marinated smoked salmon with basil, and chicken grilled with coriander from a very fashionable local delicatessen which delivered to your door. Virginia could scarcely taste any of the Duchy of Cornwall non-alcoholic drink. If ever she needed a very large gin, now was the time. She smoothed down her stomach, still not quite back to washboard flatness after Agnes. The gin was definitely not on. Empty calories.

'The place is a tip. Edward Wheeler wasn't even there – he was at some car conference in Cologne.' Shirley had told Virginia this with a note of triumph in her voice, and Virginia had read another message in her eyes. Private Property. Keep Off. So that's the way the wind blows, thought Virginia. No wonder that Shirley had been the least welcoming of the three. She needn't worry, though, I'm a happily married woman. She felt a huge sense of disappointment in Edward, however. She had wanted to believe he was special, yet here he was, like some second-rate philanderer – or even cabinet minister, perhaps – having an affair with someone younger and slimmer than his wife. It was so tacky.

'The place is virtually run by his secretary,' she told Simon. 'She dresses like a tramp.'

Simon looked puzzled.

'I mean a tart, not a vagrant. Fringed leather hipsters and a bra top to match.'

'Jolly nice.' Simon pictured fringed leather hipsters brightening up the merchant bank. It was a surprisingly pleasant thought. He noticed Virginia staring at him rather hard. 'But not at all suitable for the office.' He realized he'd failed to offer the right response.

'Oh, Simon, do you think I've made the most terrible mistake?'

Simon, who *knew* she'd made the most terrible mistake, and had told her so several times, decided that it would be wiser to keep quiet at this stage.

'I don't think I could bear to face the Publishing Unlimited people if I quit after just one day,' she mused. 'I've just got to make a go of it.'

'And you'll never guess what,' she said later in bed, just as Simon was reaching towards her.

'What?' murmured Simon, who had recently been feeling slightly left out in the bed stakes. He couldn't quite put his finger on it, but Virginia, usually so compliant, was somehow becoming, well . . .

resistant was too strong a word. Perhaps he was imagining it.

'I think Edward Wheeler is having an affair with his secretary.'

'The one with the fringed bra top? It gets worse and worse. And with that nice wife. Well, I know who I want to be having an affair with. My own nice wife.' He nuzzled towards her, and gently began to tease one nipple to a point. It responded obediently. He moved across the firm, silky breast to drop his head down towards the other one, but Virginia shifted away.

He wasn't imagining it.

Virginia and Edward agreed to meet the *Heart & Soul* staff in their smart offices in the West End. They would, of course, be moving to Hammersmith – Edward had no intention of footing a massive rent bill just so that everyone could go shopping easily at lunch time, but they decided to break this news at their first meeting. Shirley and Edward – with Harry to add 'immoral support', as he put it – would arrive at the current offices of *Heart & Soul* at 9.30 a.m. with the meeting scheduled at 10 a.m. Virginia, whose role had been kept a strict secret, was to be smuggled in, to be unveiled, as it were, after Edward's introduction.

'The staff should be the first to know about important office changes and new editors,' said Virginia. 'Having rumours flying round just unsettles people.' She took staff morale very seriously.

'Might make a few of them resign,' said Edward,

who wasn't looking forward to adding massive redundancy payments to the small fortune he'd already spent. He'd costed in some payoffs, partly because he thought that *Heart & Soul* was grossly over-staffed, and partly because Virginia had insisted on being able to have her own choice of key staff. She had made it quite plain that when new editors took over, they immediately expected to fire the art editor, the fashion editor and the deputy editor – at the very least – in order to install people they had worked with previously and could trust. After a year you could reasonably anticipate the replacement of all heads of department. Edward agreed, but resolved not to pay them *all* off. In his experience, some people took fright and simply resigned when a company was taken over.

No wonder *Heart & Soul* was losing money, mused Shirley, as they stepped into its marble foyer in Covent Garden. The rates alone must be eye-watering. The rental on the plants could probably pay a junior assistant for a year, except that, by the looks of things, junior assistants here were rather nicely off. The three of them squeezed into a mirrored lift with four women dressed in designer black.

'Have you heard? Our new master's coming in to address the troops.'

The other three rolled their eyes.

'Who is he anyway?' A rabbit-faced blonde pressed the button for the third floor.

'Some jumped-up small-time businessman who thinks he can buy a glossy magazine. Not even worth bothering to impress.'

Why have you got freshly lacquered nails in that case? Shirley wondered, sure that the distinctive sweet fragrance in the air was the result of four breakfast sessions at separate hairdressing salons.

The others shrugged. 'I don't think we need worry too much about Edward Wheeler, do you?' Their eyes flickered dismissively over Edward and Shirley, and one of them trod on Shirley's expensive white Manolo Blahnik shoes as she got out of the lift. She caught Edward's eye and tried to work out if he was laughing or furious. Well, they were in for a shock.

She was impressed by the way Edward strode along the corridor as if he – well – owned the place. Not for long, she suspected. He'd already asked her to contact a number of commercial estate agents with a view to clawing back some of the murderously high purchase price he'd had to pay for the magazine. She couldn't help wondering how the harpies at *Heart & Soul* would enjoy working in the back streets of Hammersmith. Not much by the looks of things.

'If you could all gather round . . .' John Bellman clearly felt guilty about selling the magazine he had founded, and would probably have preferred to send a fax from his retirement villa in the Canaries. Hostile faces looked up from word processors, backs were turned as fashionably cut heads refused to finish telephone conversations. A plump hot-faced junior, who nobody took any notice of, was delegated to round them all up, which took fifteen minutes. John Bellman's colour rose. Edward looked unconcerned, chatting easily to John and sporadically taking calls on his mobile. Harry ostentatiously lit a cigarette and passed one to Shirley, ignoring the elaborate coughing noises and the indignant murmurs that accompanied a certain amount of frantic waving of paper in the air. It was, as Shirley had spotted in reception, a No Smoking office.

'Sell thirty thousand. Cheers.' Edward's voice was audible in the growing silence. (Later Shirley overheard someone in the Ladies say, 'He's so vulgar he answers his own phone. Just like a plumber really.')

John cleared his throat. 'I'd like to introduce *Heart & Soul*'s new owner, Edward Wheeler, and I'm sure you'll all give him a very warm welcome.' A complete, slightly menacing, stillness reigned. Shirley noticed spots of colour on the cheeks of the women who had been in the lift. 'And I'm sure you'll give him every co-operation.' John tripped over his words in his anxiety to be gone. 'You're all invited for a farewell glass of champagne in my office at midday.' As he left, a murmur followed him, hands extended to be shaken, kisses on the cheek. And Edward was left, circled by what was beginning to look like a pride of big cats moving in for the kill.

'I bought this magazine because it's good . . .' Edward began. 'It's very relevant to the twenty-first century. You – and I hope that means all of you – and I are going places. Inevitably, however, change brings more change.'

Aha, thought Shirley, he's about to start Conceptualizing. When he talked in the abstract, particularly in public, it always meant that he was going to say something his listeners didn't want to hear. She'd known cases in the past when an unsuspecting staff never fully realized what they had heard, and would still be wondering weeks later exactly when and why their division had been sold to a company in Wolverhampton.

There was a sob and an anorexic-looking girl, wearing what looked like a pair of black pyjamas, jumped up and dived into a cupboard, slamming the door. Muffled wails emerged at intervals for the rest of the session. Edward took no notice. Neither did anyone else. Most gazed out of the window, deliberately indifferent to the Conceptualizing. The words 'market forces' drifted over Shirley's head. Never a good sign. 'Forward into the future.' Another phrase he often used when he meant 'straight out the door'. Eventually he halted, having temporarily hypnotized his new staff into submission with jargon.

Round one to Edward.

'I'm here to answer any questions you may have, and then to introduce you to your new editor-in-chief.' There was a sharpening of interest. 'Perhaps you could identify yourself when you speak.'

'Maggie Dunstone-Smith, features editor.' It was the woman from the lift, her voice like gin and Capstan Full Strength. 'As you may, or may *not*' – her emphasis made it clear that it was the latter – 'realize, *Heart & Soul* is a very exclusive magazine . . .'

'You mean no one buys it at the moment.' Edward seemed quite matter of fact. 'Don't worry, I shall be addressing that problem vigorously.'

'The *Heart & Soul* reader is extremely discerning,'

Maggie Dunstone-Smith ploughed on. 'They're used to excellence. They'll never respond to cheap commercialization. What guarantees of editorial independence are you offering?'

'None.' Edward flashed her a vulpine smile. 'And if by commercialization, you mean producing a magazine that actually sells, then you can look forward to a bit of commercialization.'

His listeners edged nervously, like sheep facing a ten-ton truck on a narrow lane, Shirley thought. There was some bleating and another sob from the cupboard.

'Debbie Gordon-Brown.' A red-faced woman in a vast hat waved a hand from the back. 'I'd like to ask if there will be any staff changes or redundancies.' She spoke in a plummy tone, like a vicar's wife in a TV series. Shirley crossed her fingers. If he said yes, there'd be a riot. If no, he'd be accused of lying later.

Edward perched on the edge of the desk, folding his arms. 'That will be up to my new editor-in-chief,' he said smoothly. 'Perhaps it's time I introduced her.'

'Do you think I ought to get Camilla out of the fashion cupboard?' whispered the moon-faced junior to Shirley. This was, without doubt, the office doormat.

'No, don't bother. She can catch up later.' Out of the corner of her eye she saw Maggie Dunstone-Smith edging towards a telephone. I'm keeping my eyes on you, my girl, thought Shirley. She was Trouble with a capital T. Edward was now droning on about Virginia's awards and achievements in the build-up to announcing her name. Two or three women were viewing him with open lust. Shirley memorized their faces for later inclusion on the redundancy list. She was bound to be able to influence it. As he came to the end of his speech, finely timing a dramatic pause, the door opened, and Virginia stood silhouetted in the office doorway.

The hostility of the silence was almost visible, like a heavy fog, and Shirley could see Virginia literally pushing through it to get to the editor's desk.

'Good morning.' Her voice was beautifully modulated, with a smile just bubbling under the surface. Surely they must respond to such calm elegance, such self-control? 'I know this must be a very difficult day for many of you.' She looked round, as if taking each face in. 'You've all worked as an excellent team with my predecessor. I spoke to her on the phone this morning, and she has sent her best wishes.' This seemed extremely unlikely, considering the spitting invective that had apparently spewed forth on her departure, but Virginia was hardly likely to lie, was she? A few hunched shoulders dropped in relief.

'Janine du Blaque.' A frail, intense girl, positively vibrating anxiety, tentatively raised her hand. 'I'm interviewing one of this generation's leading dancers – now at the height of her achievements. Obviously one has to give certain guarantees of the kind of environment interviewees appear in. If I don't even know myself what this environment is, how can I, in all conscience, talk to an artiste of this calibre?'

Edward looked baffled.

'Forgive me if I don't poke my finger in that

cage,' he said finally. 'Perhaps Virginia would like to comment.'

'I have edited magazines in which many superb dancers have been only too happy to appear – ' Virginia reeled off an impressive list of names ' – so I'm sure my reputation is all the guarantee you need.' Out of the corner of her eye, she noticed Maggie Dunstone-Smith murmuring softly into her mobile with her back turned, talking to the *Evening Standard*'s gossip column, Virginia accurately surmised, about falling standards at *Heart & Soul*. 'Mass-market tactics,' Virginia heard her whispering to the mobile. Her lips tightened.

'I'd like to talk to everyone individually once we've moved into the new offices in Hammersmith at the Wiggins Frean headquarters,' she said, jettisoning Staff Morale in favour of making it clear who was in charge.

Edward gathered up his files and headed briskly through the door, with Virginia and Shirley – and a still-silent Harry, of course – bringing up the rear in a comet's tail of expensive scent.

'Is taking over a magazine always that bad?' Back in John Bellman's office, Edward looked shaken. 'Give me an office full of men with mortgages any day.'

'Compared to some, that was quite a warm welcome,' lied Virginia, who was used to being adored and deferred to, and hadn't cared for what she later christened 'an off-hand attitude'. She tried to be fair – she was, after all, famous for understanding her staff. 'We shouldn't judge them too harshly. They're obviously just terrified of losing their jobs.'

'I can't quite see what their problem is,' Harry drawled. 'Anyone would think *Heart & Soul* was an important magazine by the way they were behaving. *Vogue* crossed with *The Times*.'

'Well.' Virginia knew everything . . . 'It was very cultish when John started it. Back in the seventies.' Harry's face dropped theatrically.

'Did your predecessor *really* send her best wishes?' Shirley was fascinated.

Virginia smiled. 'Not quite, but I'm sure she would have done if I'd given her the chance. She'd want them passed on.' She met Shirley's eyes confidently. 'Maggie Dunstone-Smith. That woman is pure poison. Do we promote her or fire her?' She turned to Edward.

'Promote her?' Shirley wished she hadn't spoken up when Virginia flashed her just the tiniest look of irritation. She paused to explain, hardly sounding impatient at all. 'If we have Maggie on our side, it may be more effective than letting her loose on the industry to undermine us from outside.' She smiled warmly, but firmly, at Shirley. Conversation closed. Shirley was conscious of a creeping respect for Virginia, which, if she didn't watch out, might finish up as downright admiration. Watch out, she told herself. That sleek pussycat has just shown the tips of her claws.

'Are you scared of change?' taunted the headline in

She, above an article that promised Shirley to change her life in thirty days.

'Why should I be? thought Shirley, snapping the magazine shut. She ought to discuss her workload with Edward. Or perhaps not. It had been three weeks since the meeting at *Heart & Soul*. Spitting like wildcats, a few of the staff had been assimilated into the building in Hammersmith, although the move had been accompanied by a series of extortionate (in Shirley's view) redundancy payouts and an avalanche of bad publicity depicting Edward as a vulgar asset-stripper, Virginia as a reject of Publishing Unlimited, and making vague, confusing references to Shirley's leopardskin tops, bare legs and white shoes. Actually she'd quite enjoyed the last part although she hadn't actually been named. There appeared to be no common ground at all even between Becky and Judith and the newcomers, far less Derek, Kevin and Max. Sex pests, religious fanatics and women with visible pantie lines were not considered funny – or even really human – at *Heart & Soul*.

Maggie Dunstone-Smith had accepted a massive payoff in an attempt to stem the tide of spite – it had eventually been conceded that she'd never settle in Hammersmith, and that, fortified by a large cheque, she might turn her attentions elsewhere if set free to do so. So, Shirley reflected, it wasn't surprising that having a new magazine in the building was bound to make things difficult for a bit. They'd only been here for a few weeks. Harry wandered into her office.

'Still here? At 7.30 p.m?' Then, looking closer: 'You look awful. Tired out.'

Shirley shot up indignantly. 'I do not. I've just bought a very good new concealer from Clinique which is guaranteed to remove all evidence of late nights.'

'Well, it must have worn off,' said Harry, who thought she looked worse than he'd ever seen her.

'It's this bloody stationery cupboard,' said Shirley, not entirely truthfully. 'I just can't go on checking how many bloody pens people use, not with all the other work and *Heart & Soul*.' The dummy for the re-launched magazine was currently being market researched with 'hall groups', which meant that a group of market researchers asked around six women to give their opinion on all the aspects of the magazine they couldn't possibly know about, such as the type-face or the headlines. Shirley and Virginia sat behind a two-way mirror and eavesdropped on the proceed-ings – Virginia as the editor, and Shirley because she wanted to know what went on. On principle. She wanted to make sure that Virginia didn't have a hidden agenda. Privately, she thought it was all a waste of time and money, because you could never trust people to say what they really thought. And what did six women know anyway? But everything at Publishing Unlimited had been researched to within an inch of its life, and nothing was ever launched, tweaked or changed without everyone from the management down to the post room convin-cing themselves that every effort had been made to prevent it from failing. So Virginia had insisted on market research, and, at the moment, what Virginia said went. They were still in the honeymoon period.

'Well, don't. Pass it on to Judith,' said Harry unhelpfully. 'She was telling me only the other day that she'd like more responsibility.'

'Did she?' Shirley was irritated. She and Harry often had arguments about whether you should give juniors more responsibility. Shirley's fear was that if you gave juniors too much, where might it end? They'd all be fancying themselves PAs and there'd be no one to do the filing. Harry said that he never minded doing his own filing. 'That's not the point,' explained Shirley. 'It's more than just filing. It's the principle of the thing.'

'Pull the other one.' Harry helped himself to one of Shirley's cigarettes. 'Is Edward being a naughty boy? Or not being a naughty boy?'

'Oh, he's all right,' Shirley said wearily. As far as she could see, nothing had changed since the office party. She was no nearer being a permanent fixture in Edward's life. There had been a flurry of togetherness during the deal for *Heart & Soul*, but, like the other flurries, it had subsided. She was beginning to think that she'd have to pull something very different out of the bag.

'Oh dear, we are in a state, aren't we? I think you need a very strong drink, for a start.' Harry picked up Shirley's coat and bag, turned off her word processor and proceeded to frogmarch her out of the office. As she turned to lock the door, he suddenly realized what day it was.

'It's Thursday, isn't it? What's happened to your usual romantic tryst with the old bugger?'

'Oh, he's at some publisher's conference in Birmingham,' replied Shirley. One of the advantages of being your lover's secretary – and another very good reason for not letting Judith take over too much – was that you could be quite sure exactly where he was. She'd rung at least three times, on the pretext of urgent decision-making, so she did know he really was there. And Virginia was safely tucked up in her own office in Hammersmith. Not, of course, that Shirley suspected anything between them. But you had to keep an eye on people.

'Do you suppose Wonderwoman ever sees her children?' she said, once they were safely past the office door marked 'Virginia Law, editor-in-chief'.

Harry put his arm round her and gave her a hug.

'And why can't people just be editors any more? Why are they always editor-in-chief?'

Shirley sat in the pub, known to Wiggins Frean as The Lovers' Arms on account of the number of affairs that had started there – including Shirley's with Edward – and gazed miserably into her treble gin and tonic.

'She's OK really, Virginia, I mean. But she's just like Edward. I mean, I really want to be involved in the magazine, I can't bear to think of it going ahead without me, and she lets me do it, she's really welcoming. She just says, "Yes, great, do, I need all the help I can get."'

Harry wondered what could possibly be wrong with that. Shirley took another large slug of gin, and added, 'But I just can't manage it all. And I'm afraid that if I say that, they'll give some of my work to someone else and then I'll be back to just being a secretary again.'

Harry felt worried. Shirley never admitted fear or failure. He had never heard her be so frank, and realized that she was close to tears.

It had all come to a head that morning, and as the gin crept through her veins, she revived enough to tell Harry all about it. Edward, who could be infuriatingly vague, had slipped through her best efforts to keep him in line and had double-booked the conference in Birmingham and two consecutive meetings with major cosmetic advertisers.

Virginia had been incandescent with rage. 'What do you mean he's in Birmingham? He can't be in Birmingham, he's supposed to be in Mayfair at eight-thirty and ten forty-five respectively. Don't you keep his diary?'

'Yes, but I can't keep it if he puts things in without telling me, and then doesn't even write them in,' said Shirley incoherently. Edward was safely away from Virginia's wrath, on the 7.45 to Birmingham, probably tucking into a British Rail breakfast, she thought, knowing Edward.

'Well, you'll just have to come instead,' said Virginia, shocking Shirley out of her mental picture of Edward with bacon and eggs.

'Me?' she squawked.

'Yes, you. You know just as much about the business plan as he does. Probably more.' Then, misinterpreting Shirley's look of horror, she added, looking her up and down, 'Don't worry, I've got a spare suit in my office.'

It had never occurred to Shirley that there was anything wrong with the way she dressed. She flushed. 'You mean I look like a tart?'

'No. I mean you look like a secretary.'

Shirley gulped, but Virginia had already produced a cranberry wool suit with a calf-length hemline (not even split – Shirley had never worn a long skirt that wasn't split) and a neat, tailored waistline and collar. Shirley thought it was drab when she saw it hanging on the hanger, but it felt surprisingly luxurious and confidence-giving once she'd buttoned it up. Quite a different Shirley gazed back at her in the mirror of Wiggins Frean's deplorably maintained Ladies lavatory.

'It's not bad,' she admitted.

Virginia flashed a smile. 'I always keep it in the office in case I need a bit of extra confidence,' she confided. 'Paul Costelloe is such a brilliant cutter. I call it my bad hair-day suit. Oh, and here's a spare pair of tights.'

'I can't imagine you having a bad-hair day.' Shirley was so envious she forgot to say that she didn't wear tights and never would.

'Don't you believe it,' retorted Virginia. 'Everyone has bad-hair days.'

In the car on the way to the meetings, Virginia schooled in her in what to say and how to say it.

'Can you handle the AV?'

'Of course.' Shirley was incredulous. If there was one thing she knew backwards, it was how to get slides on to a screen. She could, if necessary, repair the bloody projector. She'd had to in the past. 'I've given lots of presentations.' This lie was, she thought, justified because it would reassure Virginia.

'Just talk directly to me, if it makes you feel more confident. Or look directly at one or two people in the audience. There won't be many – a dozen at most.'

A dozen people. Shirley's heart sank.

'The thing to remember –' Virginia was in full flood – 'is that you know this magazine backwards, forwards and inside out. They don't. You're there to tell them the facts and figures. I'm there to provide the creativity and gloss. So you'll be able to handle them easily. I promise!' Then she dusted Shirley across the shoulders and handed her a tortoiseshell clip. 'This'll stop your hair from getting in your way and obscuring your notes,' she said, tactfully.

'Executive women don't have long hair hanging loose?' asked Shirley.

'Well, not really. But don't worry.' Virginia was reassuring. 'It's your style and you stick to it. Except we all have to dress up when it comes to business. It frightens The Suits if you don't.' She gave Shirley's hand a last squeeze as the chauffeur opened the car door.

'It was awful.' Shirley shuddered as she recounted it to Harry. 'Firstly we went into this great big grey building with smoked glass windows, and sofas as big as my bed.' ('Mmm, that big?' murmured Harry.) 'And those twiggy things in big jars.'

'You mean twisted willow?' Harry was impressed. 'Very fashionable.'

'Yeah, well, looked like barbed wire to me. I like a nice bunch of flowers, not a statement of agony.'

'Never mind the flowers, what happened at the presentation?'

'First this snotty receptionist kept us waiting for hours.' It had actually only been twenty minutes, but even Virginia had been rattled by this. She had never been kept waiting when she worked for *Viva*. She ostentatiously went through work from her brief-case, scribbling answers on letters and reworking the first paragraphs of articles, while Shirley went over and over what she was going to say in her head. The tights prickled uncomfortably against her legs. Every so often Virginia raised her eyes from her work and gave her a reassuring smile.

Then a blonde with a short skirt and long hair had appeared to take them up in a circular steel-and-glass lift. That was me yesterday, thought Shirley, catching a glimpse of flesh between a tight pastel jersey top and a Lycra waistband, as the blonde raised her arm to press twenty.

The presentation room, completely featureless and decorated in industrial shades of grey, was designed to hold fifty comfortably, and looked nerve-rackingly empty with just a dozen jaded-looking young men and women, dressed in monotones of grey or black, fidgeting with coffee cups and discreetly comparing hangovers. Shirley was grateful for the long skirt because no one could see her knees knocking together as she gave the first presentation.

Business first, Virginia had explained to her. Then the ideas side. Secretly Shirley wondered if Virginia wanted to make sure that any bad impression of Shirley was wiped out by Virginia's professionalism. She'd tried to persuade Virginia to give the whole presentation, but had been refused. 'They're expecting a team, not a one-man band,' she insisted.

Shirley couldn't quite remember how she'd got through that half-hour. She knew she stammered a bit, and was completely thrown by one question, but Virginia had answered from her seat in the front row.

'You needn't worry about that side of it,' she had reassured the advertisers with a glittering smile. 'I have fifteen years of experience in magazines, and my hand will be on the helm.' Then Virginia had stepped up to the podium, and begun to talk. Shirley had watched the bored young executives shift in their seats and sit up. The women stopped examining their nails for invisible chips in their nail varnish. *Heart & Soul* was Virginia's vision of women for the twenty-first century. Shirley saw hope on the women's faces, interest on the men's.

The second presentation was quite different, and took place in a small, pretty townhouse in Mayfair, the headquarters of Dearest Cosmetics. 'Is it called Dearest as a term of affection or because they're so expensive?' whispered Shirley.

Virginia smiled briefly. 'It was started by a Russian refugee called Eugenie Derestovich, now anglicized to Dearest. Colin Dearest is her grandson.'

The receptionist greeted them as if they were famous, which, Shirley supposed, Virginia was. They were instantly ushered into a small sitting room, exquisitely decorated with Colefax & Fowler chintz and antiques, and tea and coffee, in a delicate set of porcelain, was produced. Within minutes, the door flew open and an attractive man, in his early forties with the broad cheekbones and honey blond hair of a Middle European aristocrat, walked in, followed by two unbelievably elegant women.

'Virginia! Darling! Such bliss to see you again!'

'Colin!' Three kisses ensued, on alternating cheeks, and two kisses each for the women, who turned out to be called Alison Smith and Carey Khan. Shirley concluded that either Colin was a long-lost cousin of Virginia's or he was another Harry. Probably another Harry, as Colin seized her proffered hand in both his, and gave her a long, sincere look when they were introduced.

'Shirley! I'm sure we'll be the greatest of friends. We've got a little launch party for our new product, The Best Lipstick in The World, next week – Virginia's coming. I know it's rather short notice, but we'd love to see you too.'

'Oh, er, yes, I'm sure. Pleased to meet you,' murmured Shirley, who was thrown into further disarray by Colin and Virginia embarking on a lengthy discussion about their respective children. Not a Harry then. Eventually an expectant pause fell over the company, and Virginia gave her the nod. It had felt much easier and more natural to be sitting down, although a secretary had arranged a slide projector against one wall. Shirley had forgotten she was giving a presentation and began to talk about their hopes and dreams for *Heart & Soul*. When she handed over to Virginia, she felt much more confident.

In the car going back, Virginia was generous. 'Well done. I think you did brilliantly. Does Edward know what a star he's hiding in the photocopying room?'

'Oh, it was you, you really wowed them. Especially that agency.'

'God, weren't they beastly?' replied Virginia. 'They always are. They think they know everything, and, of course, their main aim is to beat down the price, so that their clients get the cheapest possible advertising. But the cosmetics houses are often genuinely nice, I think. I know that what they're really after is for their products to be featured on my pages, but I do believe that most of them manage to do business without completely losing track of the fact they're human beings.' There was a short pause. 'Unfortunately, it doesn't necessarily mean they'll advertise. Colin is one of the most welcoming men I know, but he's extremely careful where he spends his money.'

'So is all this angst about ambition?' Back in the pub, Harry was listening carefully. 'You've decided you've gone too far to return to life as a humble PA?'

'Not so much ambition, Harry.' Shirley knew she had to be very careful how she presented all this to him. Payback time for Shirl was coming up in a big way. But she'd decided to make Edward really sit up and take notice of her, and she needed Harry's help. She gave him what she hoped was an innocent look. 'But I seem to have crossed a boundary, and gone somewhere, and I don't know quite where, but there isn't any going back. I don't think.' There was an expectant pause.

'You'll have to talk to either Virginia or Edward about it. You can't go on as you are.'

Shirley's answer surprised them both. 'Virginia, then?'

'Attagirl. Let's have the other half.'

In fact, the business trip with Shirley had sorted out quite a few issues in Virginia's mind. Firstly, she now realized that Edward had several companies, and that although he was prepared to give extra time to *Heart & Soul*, he wouldn't be spending twelve hours a day, day in and day out, making presentations to advertisers and the news trade. And that's what it took to launch or re-launch magazine. She needed him to be available for a big agency breakfast at 8.00 a.m., a few mid-morning presentations to the smaller cosmetic houses, a splashy lunch for the distributors, more afternoon presentations and then a train in the evening to Birmingham, Manchester, Liverpool or Cardiff to explain to the news trade why it was in their interest to display *Heart & Soul* right in the centre of the women's interest titles. 'Otherwise they'll put it with the medical magazines,' Virginia had muttered to an open-mouthed Shirley, when running through the business plan with her. Then back on the red-eye shuttle for another 8 a.m. meeting the following day.

Secondly, Edward was a great salesman, but he didn't quite fit into the well-polished, elegant world of the fashion and cosmetics industry. The Armani suit was beginning to look a bit rumpled, and Virginia had spotted a large safety pin on his trouser waistband only yesterday. Oddly enough, it looked rather sexy and made her want to sort him out, but she couldn't expect advertisers to feel the way she did. He went down surprisingly well with the news trade and the distributors, who seemed to enjoy talking about luxury cars and to take him at face value about women's magazines – although Virginia knew that some extremely astute calculations were going on behind the smiles and camaraderie. But the advertising agency clients – especially the fashion and cosmetics industries – were quite a different kettle of oak-smoked salmon.

When Virginia saw Shirley dressed in a good suit, with her thick chestnut hair tied up in a chignon, and her eyes shining with conviction, she'd spotted the perfect solution. Otherwise, she was going to have to give Derek Easton more responsibility, and the idea of him lumbering through the world of women's magazines didn't bear thinking about.

So when she saw Shirley standing in her doorway the following morning, looking almost supplicant, she smiled inwardly.

She let Shirley talk first. About how much she wanted to be involved with the magazine and had grown out of being a PA.

'So you see,' Shirley concluded, 'I wondered if perhaps I could be more formally involved on the advertising or sales side.'

Exactly what Virginia had worked out herself.

Being right was so satisfying. She hadn't lost her famous touch.

'I think you've earned it. But we have to have a very honest talk. Have you discussed this with Edward at all?' Shirley shook her head.

'But you two are very . . . close?' Virginia had her intent look on, a look feared and respected throughout the glossy world of magazines.

Shirley flushed. 'We're lovers.' There. She'd said it, and a little thrill ran through her. Being the mistress of a married man meant that confidences were rare – eked out very occasionally by strangers on a train, or when she was lured to the odd hen night by old schoolfriends. An admission of guilt was like a surreptitious sweet, all the more satisfying for its furtiveness. 'He and his wife have a marriage of convenience,' she added. 'They don't sleep together.'

'I'm not concerned with the morality, or the consequences,' lied Virginia, who didn't want to sound pompous. She was amazed that someone as bright as Shirley appeared to have swallowed every cliché in the book about married men. 'But I must be sure that it isn't going to affect your work. Would you accept a promotion if it meant seeing less of him? I need to know that you're prepared to devote yourself whole-heartedly to the magazine.'

Shirley looked down at her hands. 'I wouldn't be seeing that much less of him. Would I?' Admittedly, this was what Edward might call a 'high-risk, high-reward' strategy, because she'd be relinquishing her stranglehold on his diary. But working in sales or advertising should mean client lunches and suppers

– which she could persuade Edward to attend. There'd be more evenings away. She thought she could find many reasons why she needed to spend time with the Managing Director. This way they could share even more.

Virginia wondered what Shirley was really thinking. All of a sudden, she'd become very important to Virginia's plans because she knew that Shirley could manipulate Edward. A sales director brought in from outside, however experienced, would lack that vital connection. What was more, she was beginning to suspect that the top-level staff, with salaries to match, who had been promised to her at the beginning might not be forthcoming after all. She was better off working with the material she had, rather than fighting a losing battle with the elusive Edward to upgrade the sales staff.

She chose her words carefully. 'You wouldn't necessarily see any less of him.' A meaningless phrase that could scarcely be called a lie. 'But I'd want to know that you'd always put work first. If you needed to be at a Dearest Cosmetics launch instead of spending the evening with him, could you do it?'

'I think so.'

'This Thursday?'

It was a shot in the dark, but there was an answering flash of insecurity in Shirley's eyes. She took a deep breath. 'OK.' Two Thursdays gone in a row.

Virginia smiled. 'You won't regret it. The Dearest hospitality is legendary. So who's going to tell

Edward who his new magazine sales director is? You or me?'

'We both are.' Just for once, Shirley was not going to face Edward on her own. Between the two of them, he would be hopelessly outclassed. But she was going to make sure that he got a very plain secretary as her successor.

chapter 5

'I'm sorry.' Clara pressed the last traces of mint out of a peppermint and ginseng tea bag at the Paparazzi Café. It tasted of liquid toothpaste. 'I must be boring you.'

'Don't worry.' Annabel, comfortable with Anthony, her course and her still-at-home children, was aware of the need to be understanding. To allow Clara to talk about Edward and the party.

There was a silence.

'Did Eliza go off safely?' she enquired brightly.

'Yes.' What an inadequate word to describe her last sight of Eliza at Heathrow, just before she was swallowed up by Customs and the wide world beyond. Marcus put a big brotherly arm round her shoulders to guide her through, but when she turned and gave Clara a crooked, frightened smile it had gone straight to Clara's heart like an arrow. Then, with a final wave of a bulging shoulderbag, she vanished into the crowd. It reminded Clara of Eliza's pale, brave face, aged four, going to school for the first time.

'Well,' Edward had said jovially. 'That's our job over with. Two redundant parents. Can you drop me off somewhere on the Piccadilly line? I need to do a few hours in the office.'

'Is that all you can say? Twenty-something years, and just "our job over with"?' There was a choking feeling at the back of her throat. It was safer to sound angry than upset.

'God, you're touchy these days. Must be the "change" or whatever they call it.'

'No, it isn't,' she'd hissed. 'That's not due for absolutely years. Just because *you're* being insensitive, there's no need to foist all the blame on me.'

Edward had spread his hands and rolled his eyes in a gesture that spelt 'anything for a quiet life' before diving into the Underground without so much as a see-you-later.

Clara stood beside the open mouth of the tube station, shouting, 'But when will you be back?' People had looked at her curiously. One youth had laughed. 'He's left for good, love.'

Back in the Paparazzi Café, Annabel leant forward sympathetically. 'Pretty grim, eh? I was hysterical for three days when Timmy went off for the first time. They'll be back sooner than you think. Meanwhile, what about *your* new life?'

Clara had decided, very definitely, that her plans were not going to be dissected and mulled over by Annabel or anyone else keen on re-organizing her. It was impossible to make a sensible decision with people picking over it and trying to influence her all the time.

'Coming along beautifully,' she said firmly. 'I'm starting a two-week computer-and-business-skills updating course on Monday.'

Annabel, she was gratified to see, looked surprised.

Virginia was working late again, suppressing her guilt over Oliver and Agnes. She had said goodnight to them on the phone – again – but resolved that, as soon as the magazine was launched, she would make it up to them. She looked through a list of ideas sent in by one of her regular freelance contributors. Not bad. She liked the idea of taking three women and comparing the way they shopped, then getting a psychologist to analyse it and describe each woman's character by her wardrobe alone. Her eyes skimmed down the other ideas. Maybe . . .

Edward came in.

'Look. An order. Twelve bloody gorgeous months of advertising from Dearest Cosmetics.'

'No!' Virginia was elated, and almost jumped up to hug him, but that wasn't her style. 'This calls for a celebration. Once Dearest are in, the others will be so much easier to persuade. We're getting there!' She rummaged around in the small fridge for a bottle of champagne and found it.

'Not very cold, I'm afraid, but it'll have to do.' The fridge gave a petulant whine, and belched out a waft of faintly rotting vegetables as she shut the door. All the fridges at Publishing Unlimited had purred like Rolls-Royces and delivered ice-cold champagne.

'I don't think this really works properly.' She poured out two glasses. Edward raised his.

'To us.'

Virginia hesitated a second. It sounded too personal somehow. But she mustn't be stuffy.

'To us.' She permitted herself a smile. 'The first real break we've had.' This was true. She had found the advertising agencies, along with the fashion and cosmetic companies, deeply cynical about the relaunch of the floundering *Heart & Soul*, particularly by an untried company. And the blaze of publicity that had followed the purchase hadn't helped at all, focusing as it did on Edward's lack of polish, his previous dodgy businesses and his supposed intention, probably according to Maggie Dunstone-Smith, to make the magazine 'mass-market'. It had frightened away the few good advertisers that *Heart & Soul* retained from its glorious heyday. No one seemed prepared to take a chance, and more than once Virginia had wondered if she'd bitten off more than she could chew.

'Shirley's handled most of this, you know. She's done very well.' Virginia was determined to give credit where credit was due.

Edward didn't quite meet her eyes. 'I know.'

The phone rang. 'Virginia Law.' It was Oliver, begging for one more goodnight kiss on the phone. Her voice softened. 'Night, night, darling. Sleep tight, mind the fleas don't bite. If they do, get a shoe and split their silly heads in two.' Oliver giggled down the phone.

'Ni', ni', Mummy. I really really love you.'

'And I really, really love you.'

Edward was looking rather startled.

'My son, Oliver. He's only just four.'

'Oh.' Edward poured himself some more champagne. 'Do you ever get called Ginny?'

Virginia grimaced. 'Certainly not. And I'm not starting now.'

'What about when you were Oliver's age?'

'My parents were not the sort of people who would have countenanced a nickname. They were very Victorian really – they married late, and I don't think they ever expected to have children. It must have been quite a shock when I came along.' She remembered the stiff mealtimes when she had been expected to keep quiet unless she was spoken to, and could almost feel again the starch of the worn linen napkins, each rolled in its own silver napkin ring and kept in a basket on the heavy mahogany sideboard.

'And what about when you were teenager?'

Virginia had forgotten, or tried to forget, those few brief years of freedom, of sneaking out the back door when her parents thought she was safely tucked up in bed. She'd never even told Simon. What a curious man Edward was, to pick the one point in her life that no one else had ever thought to question her about.

'To be honest, I called myself Gin for a few years. I thought it sounded, you know, dangerous and different.'

'And were you dangerous and different?'

'Oh, not by today's standards. But I had a whole life my parents never knew about.' She flushed slightly. As Gin, she could remember the fumblings in the back row of the cinema and her first taste of cider, smuggled out of the off-licence by the only one of her group who'd passed for eighteen. She had been sick behind the bus-shelter after seeing *Easy Rider*, because someone had passed her a very weak joint.

'And what happened to Gin?'

An unpleasant memory floated to the top of her mind, with a stench like a blocked drain. She pushed it away again firmly.

'I grew up.' For a moment she didn't think Edward was going to leave it there, but eventually he turned away, hands in his pockets. He stared out of the window.

'It's half-past eight. Are you expected anywhere for dinner, or shall we celebrate?'

Virginia thought carefully. Oliver and Agnes would be asleep by the time she got back. Edward had shown that he knew how to choose a restaurant. There was no doubt. Dinner would be very nice.

There was something soothingly expensive about the velvety darkness of Scott's, with its soft-footed waiters and the instant champagne bucket that arrived. Virginia had only had two Diet Cokes and a Boots Shaper's sandwich for lunch, which had tasted of tarragon and cotton wool, so the alcohol went straight to her head.

'So isn't Clara expecting you back?' She decided to risk a few questions.

Edward looked amused. 'She never expects me back on Thursdays.'

'Your nights with Shirley?'

'You know about that, do you?'

'Doesn't everybody? Except, apparently, your wife.'

He ignored the 'apparently'. 'I expect you think I'm extremely selfish.' He didn't sound as if it worried him.

Virginia did, but was prepared to soften her usual hardline approach on infidelity under the influence of Edward's very welcome champagne. 'I think it's the teeniest bit wrong to tell Shirley that you have a loveless marriage and don't sleep with your wife.'

'What makes you think I don't and I do?'

She held his gaze for few moments, and he was the first to look away. She was conscious of a stab of some unfamiliar emotion. A ghostly stirring somewhere. She turned her mind back to Shirley. She was her new protégée, and deserved some protection.

'I didn't tell her that.'

'But that's what she thinks.'

He looked at her carefully. 'I believe, under British law, that I have the right to remain silent.'

Was that laughter, she wondered, somewhere in his face? She felt she might be getting into deep water, and decided to soften her criticism. 'I just hate seeing people hurt.'

'I don't want to hurt anyone, but I don't suppose you'll believe that.'

'Affairs always hurt.' Was that true? Champagne and hunger were addling her brains. 'You can't just do what you like all the time.'

'Oddly enough, my dear' – oh, dear, she'd made him angry now – 'none of this is about what *I* want.'

Oh no? It must have been once, thought Virginia, wondering what he meant, not sure whether she swallowed the concept of the noble, self-sacrificing adulterer. She could have pointed out that perhaps, in that case, it was time for him to state what he did want, and make at least one person happy rather than two miserable. But she settled for raising an eyebrow.

'Marriage isn't that simple. At least, mine isn't.' He clearly wasn't going to elaborate.

Clichés. Virginia wondered whether to challenge them. But she could feel a restlessness boiling up in him that might explode into irritation.

'Families,' she said, neutrally. Meaning nothing in particular.

'So tell me about you. Your family. Your parents. Are they proud of what you've achieved?'

'They never say anything. And they wouldn't dream of reading anything as frivolous as a woman's magazine. So I don't know.' She thought of the Stock-bridges, still miraculously clinging on in an old Shropshire rectory that smelt of mould and damp, with windows that were either shut or open but few of which could manage both.

Virginia and Simon both earned good salaries, but they spent up to the hilt, and there was rarely any money left over. Even so, Virginia had sometimes tried to help her parents out with essential repairs, but her father had angrily rejected the implication that he couldn't manage. And time and time again she had suggested they move somewhere smaller and less demanding. She had come to realize that these suggestions only upset them, and were never likely to achieve anything. She sighed.

'What's up?'

'I was just wondering why other people's lives always seem so much easier to sort out than one's own. I think my parents would be so much better off if they sold the Old Vicarage and lived in comfort somewhere smaller. But they'd rather die first. And they probably will.'

'And Shirley's life would be so much better without the complication of an affair with a married man?'

Virginia didn't answer directly. 'You see, I think that an affair is just lying to two people. If there's something wrong with your marriage, you need to address it, not run away within it. After all, the bad old days where you had to stay married for the sake of the children are gone. If your marriage with Clara is dead, then perhaps it should stop. If it isn't, don't mess Shirley and Clara around with an affair.'

'It sounds to me as if you think the honourable thing would be to leave Clara and marry Shirley.'

'I always have to remind myself of the Oscar Wilde remark, "The best thing to do with advice is pass it on." But women's magazines make you an expert at rearranging everyone's lives and re-inventing them so that they're perfect.'

He leaned back in his chair to signal to the waiter. 'I can assure you that Clara's life would not be perfect if I dumped her. Even when I was young I didn't join in when the others were pulling the wings off ladybirds.'

He has an extraordinarily high opinion of himself,

thought Virginia. His mother had probably brought him up to view himself as the centre of the universe. After all, divorced women had to pick themselves up and start again every day of the week. Clara would discover a new, liberated self. She'd be much happier in the long run. It would be more sensible. Like her own parents in their crumbling house, she thought. There was a silence between them.

'On women's magazines we always believe there is a solution to most problems. But perhaps life isn't always like that.'

'Or perhaps concentrating on other people's problems means you don't have to tackle your own?' Edward put his hand over her own and slotted his fingers through hers. They felt rough and warm, and the gesture felt much more intimate than a kiss. Virginia hadn't held hands with a man other than her husband since they had married. Twelve years. No wonder it felt different. She didn't dare look at Edward. But she had to admit she liked men with big hands. They felt . . .

She slid her hand away, ostensibly to straighten her hair.

'I'm very lucky. I have a wonderful husband, two glorious children, and a great job. I don't really seem to have any problems.' She gave a bright smile. 'Except, of course, getting *Heart & Soul* out and making it successful. No dark secrets, I'm afraid.' Her heart thumped, probably because the champagne was making her dizzy on an empty stomach. 'Oh good. Food at last.'

She was glad that Simon was already home when

she got back that evening, propped up on a mound of fine white linen pillows in their elegant cherrywood lit-bâteau bed, reading *The Economist*. She looked at him thoughtfully as she undressed. Her decorator had suggested a white muslin canopy above the head of the bed, but she was glad she had decided against it. It would have looked too fussy.

'Nice evening, darling?'

Virginia turned away to unhook her bra. 'Mmm. I went out to dinner with Edward Wheeler.'

Simon's sensitive antennae had long been tuned to a different note in Virginia's voice when she talked about Edward.

'What's he like? On closer acquaintance?'

Virginia pulled the duvet up round her, marking out her own territory with little tugs. 'Nice,' she said, thinking what an inadequate word that was to use about Edward. 'He seems to . . . care about things.'

Simon snorted. 'He's got a lot of things to care about.'

'Mmm. You know . . .' she was feeling her way through her thoughts ' . . . there's something about that marriage.'

'Infidelity,' muttered Simon.

'No, really. There's either something big keeping him and Clara together, something that Shirley can't quite break. Or perhaps it's something big keeping him and Shirley apart.' Did that sound like what her English mistress had always called a blinding glimpse of the obvious?

'His ego, I expect.'

'I don't know. I think it's more concrete. I think

he's ashamed of something. Something his wife can't easily forget. Or forgive.' Virginia knew she was into the realms of fantasy now, travelling far ahead of what she really knew.

'Shirley is something poor Mrs Wheeler can't forget. Or, presumably, forgive. And he *ought* to be ashamed of it. Anyway, all marriages have something big that holds them together. In case you'd forgotten, it's called love.'

Simon, thought Virginia, was clearly beginning to feel very defensive about Edward. She must watch out for that. Not shut him out of her life. She was mindful of many articles she had edited on 'Keeping Your Relationship Alive'. Reluctantly, she moved towards him, crossing the demarcation of territory she had mapped out with the duvet. She could feel him relax and respond as she ran her hands over his firm stomach, and murmured in return as he turned out the light. They hadn't made love for over three weeks, and any women's magazine editor knows that you have to keep marriage alive with regular sex. It was a kind of internal spring cleaning that men needed more than women. Definitely not to be neglected. Thoughts of the evening drifted through her mind, as she lay on her back while Simon pumped away.

Later she listened to his steady breathing while she watched the clock hands go round and round again. Two o'clock. Three o'clock. Four o'clock. Too much black coffee, Diet Coke and champagne, she thought. She must eat more healthily. As she finally turned over – apparently just before the alarm shrilled her into total, tired wakefulness – she thought that Simon wasn't quite right about love. There was something else that held marriages together when love didn't work any more. She wondered if she and Simon had it or not.

'How was the course?' Annabel took her duties as a friend very seriously, and phoned Clara every night to see how she was. Clara was going through the books, taking advantage of Edward's Thursday absences to catch up with chores that she'd put off because of the course. Ever since their first near-bankruptcy, she had taken over the household finances because it made her feel safer to know exactly how near broke they were. In any case, they bored Edward. 'I deal on a larger scale,' he told her. 'Conceptually speaking.'

'Boring,' she told Annabel, her mind half on the columns of figures in front of her. 'A row of grey word-processors and a chap in a ponytail called Randy.'

'No! Is he?'

'He's about nineteen.'

'In his sexual prime.'

'Ugh.' All this egging her on to a new life was exhausting Clara. Advice and support was one thing, but if Annabel and the others had their way she'd be a puppet dancing on a number of strings. All being pulled in different directions, most likely. She'd kept to her resolution of finding a course that had *not* been suggested by any of them. They were all currently behaving as if she was a derelict property ready for renovation. This one, aimed at re-introducing women to the 'workplace', was designed to upgrade and computerize the secretarial skills she'd learnt after leaving school. It had been suggested by a magazine. She'd dithered in the newsagents between three different titles whose covers promised to 'change her life' in thirty days, by Christmas and in a year respectively. She'd opted for the year on the grounds that it seemed achievable and didn't involve crash dieting. So here she was, going back to school, as the article put it. She was getting a 'marketable qualification', and was going market herself vigorously, especially to her husband.

'But I came top.' She had been secretly delighted, but hadn't really wanted to mention it. She didn't like the idea of Annabel telling everyone that they were making headway with her, after all. She changed the subject. 'I'm just going through last year's household acounts. I've only got to August. You remember that holiday we all went on.'

There was a shout of laughter from Annabel. 'Rather you than me. Must dash, the bath's overflowing.'

When Annabel had rung off, Clara struggled a bit with exchange rates from the holidays (maths had never been her strong point, although she usually got it right in the end). That meal had cost nearly £100 a head. And it had been such a disaster.

In fact, the whole holiday seemed to sum up what was wrong – and perhaps also right – with her marriage. Clara had organized two weeks in the South of France, in a villa with a pool, with Annabel and her husband, Anthony. The three of them, plus Eliza and Annabel's daughter, Isobel, arrived two days before the rest of the party – Edward was delayed by some 'business deal', which Clara interpreted as nights with Shirley. One of Edward's golf-playing chums, Fred Stewart, with his second wife, Angie, were driving down with numerous stopovers to 'make it easier for Vanilla', their eighteen-month-old daughter.

There was an instinctive line-up against Fred and Angie the minute they arrived in a Range Rover Discovery, packed to the gunnels with a vast amount of paraphernalia for Vanilla. 'Sounds like ice cream,' giggled Eliza.

'Yuk,' sneered Isobel.

Both girls then set off into 'town' to find what they called 'fit boys', Sony Walkmans chugging in their ears.

'I don't think . . .' Angie was peering anxiously into the cot that had been requested for Vanilla ' . . . that this mattress will do. It's got some very worrying stains, and Vanilla is still at the cot death stage.'

'She is not going to die of a few stains on a mattress.' Edward was unsympathetic.

'Do try to be a bit more tactful,' hissed Clara. Angie was close to tears.

'I think we'd better drive into town and buy a new one.' Finding a new cot mattress in a remote part of the South of France on a Saturday afternoon at 4 p.m. was not easy, but Angie was determined, and succeeded. On the way home she saw Isobel and Eliza chatting to some boys.

'I had no idea that lager louts came this far south,' Angie said later. 'I'm sure Isobel and Eliza wouldn't look at them in England – all they've got in common is the language. And common is the word. At least I know where Vanilla is,' she added smugly. The only trouble was that so did everyone else. Vanilla did not sleep through the night, a fact that Angie seemed almost proud of. 'I haven't had more than four hours sleep at a time since she was born.'

'I haven't had more than four hours sleep at a time since the start of the holiday,' grumbled Edward.

'Well, that's what happens when men trade their wives in for a younger version,' said Annabel, seeing the opportunity to stick up for Clara. Clara wished she hadn't bothered. Fortunately Vanilla had issued one of her trademark squeals, and Angie, hand on her heart, was thundering down the garden after her and didn't hear.

She returned, carrying a vigorously wriggling child. 'Did you see that? She practically fell in the pool!'

'She was about twenty yards away, and running in the opposite direction,' said Eliza, who wasn't being bitchy but liked to be accurate.

'I remember what it was like when you were at that stage.' Clara hoped she sounded sympathetic. 'Any sort of water was absolutely terrifying. I remember the relief when you finally swam a width of the pool. It was the day after your sixth birthday.'

'Eliza didn't swim until she was six?' Angie was clearly taken aback. 'I've been taking Vanilla to Water Babies since she was three months old.'

Clara had never known such a difficult series of menus. Fred Stewart didn't like 'messed-about foreign food'. Angie was still breast-feeding Vanilla between carefully constructed organic puréed meals – horrifying Annabel and Anthony the first time she hoiked up her T-shirt and attached the toddler – and didn't think she'd like garlic. Eliza and Isobel were both on diets, which meant that they took tiny portions, chased them around their plates and then secretly wolfed down two huge gateaux that Clara had bought for supper. Annabel was on The Hay Regime, which involved eating enormous amounts, but only of certain things. 'Honestly, the minute I deviate, I blow up like a balloon,' she explained, oiling her well-preserved size 10 figure ostentatiously in front of Edward. 'Could you just do my back, Edward?'

Clara seized the suntan oil from Edward's hand. 'Don't worry, darling, I'll do it.' The trouble with having an unfaithful husband, she reflected, was that everybody thought he was up for grabs. Edward kept going into town to make secretive phone calls, which made supper late, and Anthony tried to 'pour oil on troubled waters' by mixing a selection of lethal cocktails. Too much sun and alcohol could turn anyone into an upmarket lager lout, Clara decided.

On the last night, Edward suggested that they all go to the best restaurant in town.

'Do you think they're child-friendly?' Clara was surprised that Angie even bothered to ask. As far as she could see, she regarded Vanilla as a precious trophy that any restaurant would be delighted to be awarded. Under the impression that all Mediterranean countries adored children, she and Fred had hauled her into a number of restaurants, only to become indignant when the waiters told her off for racing around screaming. 'We don't use the word "no",' Angie reproved them. 'It has too many negative associations.' Luckily, thought Clara, the waiters hadn't a clue what she was talking about.

Isobel and Eliza were reluctant. 'We'll stay behind and babysit if you like.' This was one of the most worrying offers Clara had heard all holiday. Isobel and Eliza had not, so far, had any time for Vanilla, or indeed anyone else for the whole two weeks. A sudden desire to help seemed completely out of character. She voiced her fears to Annabel, who thought she was being paranoid. 'Izzy's a sweetie underneath that tough exterior. And she adores babies.'

Clara became increasingly suspicious as the day wore on, and Isobel and Eliza offered to do the washing-up (unheard-of), played briefly on the swings with Vanilla ('She's so good at making friends,' commented Angie adoringly. 'All the playgroup teachers say she's naturally outgoing'), and even fetched a new glass for Anthony when he broke one mixing a particularly elaborate cocktail. At one point Clara collared Eliza and demanded to know what was going on.

She turned on a bland smile. 'I don't know what you mean, Mummy. We're just trying to be helpful. After all, you have arranged a very nice holiday for us.' She then spoilt the effect by adding, 'Perhaps it's your age making you worry. Women do often go funny after forty, apparently.'

They were three-quarters of an hour late for the restaurant, with Edward and Anthony fretting that the table would have been given away, and Angie returning to the house three times 'just to check that Vanilla has settled. I've never left her before.'

'Yes, you have. Lots of times.' Fred was finally beginning to rebel.

'Not in a strange house, darling.' Angie sounded hurt.

'This house isn't strange.' Edward spoke through gritted teeth. 'We've been here for a fortnight.'

'*We've* been here for a fortnight,' corrected Angie sweetly. '*You've* only been here for ten days.'

Clara flushed in the darkness. 'Now, does anyone know the way?' It was not a good diversion because Anthony had appointed himself map-reader, and appeared to resent anyone else trying to chip in. She wished that the Discovery didn't have quite so many seats, because all six of them in a car for three-quarters of an hour seemed to be asking for trouble. At least it meant all the men could drink, as Angie had offered to drive because she hadn't drunk any alcohol since they first started trying for Vanilla. Clara, hunched up on the bucket seats at the back, facing Fred, was astonished to feel a hand creeping up her thigh. Surely not? (When she later told Edward, he had snapped, 'Don't be absurd. He was probably just feeling around trying to find the matches in the dark.' This was plausible as Angie never let him smoke either in the house or the garden as 'statistics show that children with smoking parents are more likely to be asthmatic'. Every expedition off the premises was always begun with a tremendous amount of fumbling around and lighting up.) But matches or no matches, it was a worrying sensation having a hand creeping quite so thoroughly around one's thighs. Clara, who only ever exposed herself in a regulation black swimsuit, had tried to prevent anyone from discovering the extent of her lower half by swimming either very early in the morning or late at night. Fred would be under no illusions by now.

The relief she felt on getting to the restaurant was short-lived. Everyone took ages to choose, making Clara, who had missed lunch in the hope of not getting much fatter on holiday, feel faint with desperation. She ate three pieces of French bread, liberally spread with butter and then regretted it.

'I just want to talk to the chef to make sure that he doesn't use any cream in the sauces. *Por favor,*' said Angie to an uncomprehending waiter.

'We're in France, not Spain. In case you hadn't noticed.' Edward was not taking any prisoners.

Angie looked sulky. 'Well, you translate if you know so much about it. But if I eat dairy foods they go straight to my thighs.' She smoothed her slender legs in satisfaction. 'I worked very hard to get my figure back after Vanilla. Do you know . . .' she turned to Clara ' . . . I actually left the hospital in my size 10 jeans. The nurses said they'd never seen anything like it.' Clara smiled. Annabel leant across and started explaining how Angie could eat butter without compromising her thighs just as the waiter got to her order.

'Annabel!' Anthony, who had been at least amiable, if a bit woolly, all holiday, sounded almost snappish. 'Stop droning on about your bloody diet, and tell the man what you want.' Annabel looked offended and spent the next ten minutes trying to find out what was in everything with her very basic French. Eventually Anthony took the menu away from her and ordered for her. 'You'll be able to eat all that.'

'Is that a public telephone?' Edward was away. 'Tell him I'll have the mixed hors-d'œuvres and a steak.' Everyone looked sympathetically at Clara, and Fred gave her shoulders a squeeze. She thought she felt something move around under the table, shifting her feet. Probably a cat. French restaurants seemed full of pets. As long as it wasn't that horrid dog they'd seen outside, a mangy wolf-like creature.

What with Angie jumping up to ring and check on Vanilla, and Edward's long phone call, the meal never quite got settled, and, out of the corner of her eye, Clara kept seeing the dog wander in, and be chased out of, the restaurant several times. It looked positively rabid.

Annabel started up a conversation about a new American syndrome called 'praise junkies'. She turned to Angie. 'Apparently, children who are praised too much grow to expect praise for every action, and feel that they haven't achieved anything unless they get lots of petting. Then they grow up and have to work in offices, and when no one praises them for every cup of coffee they make they lose all their sense of achievement and self-worth. Then they drop out,' she concluded with satisfaction.

'If you're insinuating that we praise Vanilla too much . . .' Angie, rather surprisingly, had taken the bait, and was treating the conversation as a direct attack – which it was – rather than a general discussion of an interesting topic, which Annabel had presented it as ' . . . then I think that's disgusting.' There was a hushed silence. Even Edward sat up and took notice. Angie backed down slightly.

'I mean, I think the whole theory is preposterous. How could you praise a child too much?'

In reply, Annabel leant forward to offer chapter and verse from this learned paper she had read, while Edward and Anthony started a conversation over her head about share prices.

'Bound to go down in the short term . . .'

'Loss of self-esteem and sense of self-worth . . .'

The nasty moment had passed, and Clara relaxed for a moment. Until she felt something warm on her lap. The dog's nose. She screamed. The whole restaurant came to a standstill. Fred removed his hand from her knee as if stung.

'Sorry, I thought it was the dog.' It was not a helpful explanation, but Clara was still shaking too much to think clearly.

'I've had enough,' Angie spoke clearly. 'First you criticize my parenting methods – ' ('I didn't,' implored Clara) ' – then you make approaches to my husband! I'm going.' She left the room, and returned two minutes later. 'And what's more, as I'm driving the only vehicle in the Western Hemisphere, you'll all have to come too.' Edward, who had been looking highly amused, found himself negotiating a flurry of credit cards and apologies to the waiter while Angie sat, stony-faced, in the Discovery, occasionally hooting on the horn. Clara made sure she kept well clear of Fred on the journey back, which took place in complete silence.

Every light was blazing at the villa when they returned. Angie spoke for the first time.

'My God. I hope there isn't an emergency with Vanilla.'

'It'll be fine.' Fred tried to put his arm around her but she shook him off.

'And you can keep your hands to yourself,' she hissed.

They all hurried out of the Discovery. Music was blaring out of the windows. 'Far too loud for two Sony Walkmans.' Edward was puzzled. They had specifically prevented the girls from bringing anything more powerful. The main hall-sitting room of the villa was deserted.

'They've been kidnapped!' Even Annabel was worried. They raced through the house to the bedrooms. There were groans coming from the girls' room. Edward put his shoulder to the door, and it flew open surprisingly easily. Isobel, naked from the waist upwards, was coiled round what Clara was later to discover was one of the 'lager louts' on the bed. The two sprang apart, doing up their jeans.

'Mummy! Daddy!' Isobel's convent education returned to her in moments of crisis. 'Have you met

Kenny? Kenny, these are my parents.' In the silence that followed a small voice, speaking from knee level, popped up from behind the other bed.

'Boobies,' said Vanilla. 'Just like Mummy.'

Two hours later, Angie and Fred had packed the Discovery and set off into the night. 'I couldn't stay another moment,' declared Angie.

'Damn fine filly of yours,' murmured Fred to Anthony, who nearly hit him.

'But what on earth was Vanilla doing in the room with them anyway?' Clara was trying to make sense of the story from Eliza, who had been discovered innocently curled up on a sofa in the back sitting-room, catching up on her geography homework, Sony Walkman blasting out all sounds of the party's return.

'She kept getting out of her cot and wandering around. And we were worried about the swimming pool.' Eliza's reply was very reasonable – responsible, even – but it didn't quite explain why Vanilla wasn't with Eliza. Unless Eliza had been doing something much worse than geography prep. In retrospect, Clara wished they'd opened a few cupboards. If Angie's initial encounter had been reported correctly, they were at least one 'lager lout' short.

The journey home was awkward. It was a relief to open the door on The Brambles, with its comforting smell of polish and pot-pourri. Eliza attached herself to the phone, and was soon out with her friends. Edward dug around in the fridge, and came out with a bottle of champagne.

'What's this?' Clara was startled.

'We're celebrating. Being home.'

Her eyes filled with tears. 'I'm sorry. I did try . . .'

'I know. And I didn't. I'm sorry.' She couldn't remember Edward apologizing before. He reached out and wiped a tear away from her cheek. 'There, there. Blow your nose.' Hardly romantic, thought Clara. She bet that when Shirley cried, she looked like a romantic heroine. Catching sight of herself in the mirror, she could see her face looking pink and puffy.

Edward sat down again, and suddenly roared with laughter. 'Thank you for the funniest holiday I've ever had.'

For one moment she felt insulted. Then she thought of Angie's face and Fred's groping and began to laugh herself. 'Were you there when . . .?' She remembered a detail of some encounter between Annabel and Angie when Edward had been phoning. It had been particularly funny. They polished off the champagne, and opened a good claret, and then had a shower together, soaping all the best bits between giggles. Her hangover the next day was terrible, and Edward had gone into work in a grump, fussing about the lack of matching socks. Back to earth with a bang. But a lingering warmth had remained.

Back at her desk in Surrey, staring at a column of figures, Clara wondered why Edward couldn't always be like that. Warm and funny and, most importantly, *there*.

She heard the slam of the car door.

'You're early.' She always tried not to ask questions on a Thursday night.

'Mmm. I took Virginia out to dinner. I thought she needed it.'

Clara suppressed the thought that she too might 'need' taking out to dinner. But no Shirley. Her heart leapt.

'You look tired.' He stroked her cheek. 'Come to bed?'

Not exactly a romantic proposition, but suddenly she wanted him very much. Her loneliness and anger melted away as he kissed her surprisingly thoroughly.

The thought that she was just a substitute because Shirley wasn't available washed over her like a bucket of cold water. She turned away.

'You go on up. I've got to finish these.'

He shrugged and left the room, shutting the door softly.

Shirley fiddled nervously with her sales sheets. Virginia had gone to a meeting alone, which always worried her, because she liked to know what people were up to. Especially Virginia. Even in the two weeks they'd been working together, they'd become very close – hardly out of each other's pockets. She liked to think that she was Virginia's 'best friend', always ready with a smile or a story, or just a sympathetic ear when things got her down. Because things did get Virginia down, and Shirley congratulated herself on spotting that. Most people saw Virginia as seamlessly perfect, almost without personal needs of her own. Shirley believed she saw a lonely woman tottering under an almost impossible burden. She made sure she shared that load whenever she could and the reward was an exclusive relationship which shut other people out. She didn't want Virginia forging dangerous links with anyone else in the company, not even darling Harry. And Shirley had so much to learn, and Virginia seemed so willing to teach. She liked to sit on the corner of her desk, or in a chair pulled up beside it, skimming through page proofs and profit forecasts, discussing strategy, and then they'd go out to lunch together, or into the West End to Virginia's favourite smart shops. And they both believed in work. Shirley and Virginia were always the first in and the last out of the building, which meant, in Shirley's view, that they could keep an eye out for people skiving or taking advantage.

She had always shopped alone before, in the market, parading the clothes before Edward later in her flat, and peeling them slowly off before sitting on his knee to kiss him. But Virginia was turning her into someone to be reckoned with, she could see that every time she looked at herself in the mirror or read approval in her mentor's eyes.

And in Edward's, as she stood in the doorway of his office before softly shutting the door behind her. It was time Edward was reminded that certain aspects of her hadn't changed. Like her hair. She tugged off the comb that held her hair back and it swung down again in that familiar curtain. His Shirley back again.

She smiled. 'How goes it?'

'Fine.'

She laced her arms around his neck and gently nibbled his. 'Tell me I look nice,' she whispered.

'You look beautiful.' His hand had its own habits after ten years and moved up from Shirley's waist, encountering several unforeseen hazards on their journey. Firstly there was the silk shirt, tucked into quite a tight waistband and which had to be discreetly rucked up after something of a struggle. Then, moving across the firm, familiar abdomen, he found his way barred by the shirt's buttons which constricted him at just the place where he wanted to splay out his hand to touch each nipple with finger and thumb. Her jumpers had always been tight, but somehow yielding, allowing his hand to move upwards until a breast dropped softly into its palm. *These* buttons had to be undone with painful slowness, and Shirley had to help him. It was time he learned not to take her for granted.

'It's like scaling a barbed wire fence.' He sounded grumpy.

'It's Jeff Banks.'

'Jeff Banks, whoever he is, obviously wasn't planning on anyone getting undressed in a hurry.'

Negotiating Shirley's skirt wasn't easy either. It was long and beautifully cut, in a soft tweed, but somehow it didn't feel right to push it up and have rolls of fabric bunched up between them at the waist. Eventually he found the hook-and-eye and tugged unsuccessfully at it. Shirley released it, and stepped neatly out of the skirt, leaving them with the problem of tights. In the past she had been bare-legged or had occasionally worn black stockings. She took them off, hanging them neatly over a chair and feeling like a schoolgirl undressing in a dormitory.

Yes, she thought, as he moved against her in a practised way, yes, we all need a little change sometimes to stop ourselves from getting stuck in a rut. She could hear from his breathing that he was more excited than he had been for years, enjoying the tantalizing blend of familiar and unexpected.

It took much longer than usual for Shirley to get dressed afterwards too, and she could see him surreptitiously watching her face and the slightly awkward movements of her body. It was a Wednesday.

'Tomorrow as usual?' She twisted the hair back into the chignon. Transformation completed.

He was back behind the desk, pulling out the top of a pile of documents with an abstracted look. 'Mmm.' Their Thursdays had been cancelled for three weeks in a row, twice because of Shirley's new responsibilities. They'd only once been able to make a Friday instead.

'The advertising agencies still aren't following Dearest into *Heart & Soul*.' Virginia ran her finger down the columns of *The Times*, frowning at the media page, which featured a tiny item suggesting that the re-launch of *Heart & Soul* was being delayed due to the lack of financial support from the advertising industry. 'Where do they get this crap from, I'd like to know? We've always said that the relaunch would be the May issue.' It was tight, though – glossy magazine deadlines were about three months, and it was now the middle of February.

Shirley was on her favourite perch, the edge of

Virginia's desk, holding a sheaf of papers. It was most unlike Virginia to swear. She must be really worried. 'And,' replied Shirley, who felt she would want to know the whole picture, 'it's taking too long to shift that posh office building we had to take on when we bought *Heart & Soul*.' Built into the calculations, she knew, had been the idea of making a bit on the turn with the property, but oddly enough, and against the predicted trend, swanky, expensive offices in Mayfair suddenly just weren't moving. No interest *at all* in six weeks. It seemed impossible. 'Prime property always moves,' Edward had told her, and so far he'd usually been right.

Derek Easton trailed in with the sales figures and held them out to Virginia, who was still engrossed in *The Times*. Shirley deftly intercepted them, and had a quick glance to make sure he hadn't changed anything since she'd OK'd them. You had to be on your guard and she didn't like surprises. He hadn't. Probably too fucking idle. He trailed out again with a dejected air, like a dog who expects to be kicked. He was clearly terrified of both women, in spite of his macho bravado. They exchanged glances as the door shut behind him, and giggled.

'What he thinks he looks like in that shirt, I can't imagine.' Since coming to Wiggins Frean, Virginia had discovered the guilty pleasures of bitchiness. Between them Shirley and Harry could stitch anyone up – it was all such fun. And looking at these figures, you needed a bit of fun.

'But *why* aren't we getting more advertising?'

'I expect they took one look at Derek and fled.'

Shirley's heart was thumping at the thought that her department wasn't up to scratch. No one could blame her, though, because virtually every good advertising deal had been one of hers. It wasn't her fault if the rest of them had about as much get up and go as an old flannel. She'd done her best to browbeat them into submission, so things must be about to change.

'He really buggered up my presentation to the Grey's ad agency,' she pointed out. 'He started leering at what he thought was a secretary, and talking about great boobs, and it turned out to be the account director.' She had no intention of taking the rap for any of Derek's shortcomings, or Short Comings, as she and Virginia called them. 'I think I might have rescued the situation though.'

'Let me see.' Virginia cast an experienced eye over the list of advertisers. 'Cosmetics – a few – no one big except Dearest. Cars – none. Washing powder – one.'

'No thanks to Derek,' interjected Shirley. 'I got that.' She glanced at herself in the mirror. Her long glossy hair was now a sleek cap, perfectly cut and shaped, and her make-up, although it still looked barely there to her, was, according to Virginia, perfect.

'Fashion. One or two, only one biggie. Homes. Well, you don't get many big spenders there anyway, but there are a few and they ought to be on board. Travel ditto. Oh dear.' She put the figures down. 'We'll have to do something fast. Or we won't have a magazine.'

'Classified is doing well, though. Mark is shaping

up really well.' It had been Shirley's idea to pull Mark Wells out of the pool to head up the small ads section, and there were now four times as many companies taking five-line boxes for iron beds, shutters, paint courses and fashion catalogues. But even so, these small black-and-white advertisements just couldn't bring in the cash the way big, colourful double-page spreads from major companies did. 'I thought he'd be good.' It was always worth reminding people. She had reminded Mark himself, yesterday.

Virginia sighed. 'What do you think is stopping them? Apart from Derek's ghastly ties, of course.'

'I think . . .' Shirley was cautious about upsetting Virginia in any way ' . . . that they still don't quite believe an untried publishing house can turn *Heart & Soul* round. It's been so bad for so long.' She looked at Virginia. Virginia would have the answer – she always did.

There was a short pause. 'I'm not untried.' She had almost snapped. 'But I think you're right about Derek. From now on, for the big bids, it's you and me, you and Edward, or me and Edward. Not Derek. But that does mean I need a deputy editor urgently.'

She had come to value Shirley's judgement when choosing staff, and Shirley had sat in on all the interviews so far. There'd been a candidate for deputy editor this afternoon, a neat dark-haired woman she'd worked with before, called Sarah, who had recently returned to work after her second baby. Sarah was clearly good, and Virginia could see that Shirley was impressed. Afterwards they compared notes.

'You worked with her before she had the children?' asked Shirley.

'Yes. She was great. Very hard-working, clever, good with headlines. And fun, too. You'd get on with her.'

No, I wouldn't, thought Shirley, who had no intention of allowing anyone in the door who might compete with her for Virginia's affection. She looked concerned. 'I thought she sounded as if she'd always put the children first.' That should put Virginia off her.

'Did you?' Virginia thought back over the interview. 'I don't think I got that impression. Anyway, her husband's a student, so she has to work.'

Shirley rolled her eyes. 'One of those. They'd all much rather be at home with Play-Doh and spinach purées. It's a real shame. I don't know how their husbands can do it to them.'

Virginia was rattled. 'Well, perhaps you're right.' It had been Shirley, after all, who had pointed out that another candidate had children of school age 'and you know what happens when you get an office full of working mothers. They all want to go on holiday at the same time.' Virginia thought of the resentment it would generate if she took time off at Easter, Christmas and during August, leaving behind a deputy who wanted to be with her children, and quailed. You had to be fair when managing staff. But Simon wouldn't wear her being at work during major holidays, because that was when he liked to take time off.

It was proving extraordinarily difficult to find

someone for the job of deputy editor who was old enough to have the experience, but didn't have children. Or didn't look as if she was just about to have them – Shirley had extracted the unwilling admission from another candidate that she and her husband might be planning a family in the next few years. 'Probably means she's pregnant already,' she had commented later. Even Virginia, who did not believe in discriminating against women because of children, and who had managed two children herself without dereliction to her duties, did not want someone going on maternity leave when the re-launched magazine was only a few months old. 'I never had these problems at Publishing Unlimited,' she grumbled.

Shirley was sympathetic. 'With a larger staff and plenty of similar magazines in the group with lots of staff turnover, I expect there was always someone to fill the gap.'

Harry tapped on the door. 'These have to go to the printer tonight, darlings, and I mean tonight. We're scarcely half-way through sending proofs to the printer for the May issue, and the schedule says we should be 98 per cent complete by now.'

'Be a love and help us with these.' Shirley jumped off Virginia's desk to make room for the proofs, and pulled a chair up for Harry. 'There's a bottle of flat champagne around somewhere.' She divided up the pages between the three of them.

'I don't know what they think they're doing with these captions.' Virginia was slashing across the proofs with a red pen. ' "Quick and easy is my motto, says the Minister for Women." Do you think she really said that?'

Becky tapped on the door. 'This fax came through our fax machine by mistake. It says urgent.'

Virginia gave her a grateful smile, although it tired her to do so. 'Thanks. That's sweet of you.'

Becky flushed with pleasure. 'Is there anything I can do to help?'

'No!' Shirley spoke sharply, and even Virginia looked surprised.

'I mean,' she said, collecting herself with a forced smile, 'that it's very kind of you to ask, but we're probably quicker doing it ourselves.'

Becky didn't take offence. 'Fine.'

'Empire building,' muttered Shirley, when the door closed behind her. 'Always trying to push herself forward.'

Virginia was lost in thought. 'You don't think she'd be a possible for the deputy editor's job? I'd be here to hold her hand and she is already a member of staff. I liked what she'd done with the psychology magazine. Which is vaguely in our area after all.'

Before Shirley could say anything, Harry fore-stalled her. 'Good idea. Of course' – he knew how to persuade Shirley, whose insecurities he understood – 'she'd never be quite as good as someone with more experience, would she, Shirley?' He could see her weighing up the relative threats to her relationship with Virginia of Becky, a known quantity, and a new person, possibly already an old chum of Virginia's.

Becky won. 'You can always transfer her back if it doesn't work out,' Shirley said.

'I'll talk to Becky in the morning. You might like to sit in, Shirley,' suggested Virginia. Shirley would, definitely. She looked down at the page proofs, frozen with anxiety. Harry scribbled a few lines. 'Better?'

'Much.' Virginia moved quickly over the gardening pages. 'A glorious blaze of late summer colour heralds the advance of autumn.' They all giggled.

'In other words, we don't know what these plants are and we've got two lines to fill.' Shirley could put her finger on a weakness with the accuracy of an Exocet missile, observed Virginia. 'Send those pages back. They've got to find out what kind of flowers are in the picture, or at least in the foreground.'

Another late night for the sub-editors, thought Harry.

Between them they cleared all the pages and opened another bottle of champagne. It was 9.30 p.m. by the time Shirley and Virginia called for taxis to take them home.

'We'll get everything sorted with Becky tomorrow. That'll free you up a bit,' promised Virginia.

Shirley felt a clutch of fear, and suppressed it.

'Well, bugger me,' said Edward.

'Ooh, darling, I didn't know you cared,' murmured Harry, as he slid through the door, scenting gossip.

Virginia, who had now got used to Harry and his badinage, and Shirley, who never noticed it, were both standing over Edward's desk in a state of consternation.

'I didn't think that kind of thing happened these days,' said Edward.

'Well, it obviously does,' replied Virginia crisply.

'Bloody idiot,' said Shirley. 'What's a diary for, after all?'

'Would someone like to tell me what's going on?' Harry affected a casual air but was dying to know what the story was.

'Well, Samantha's mother just called. She was taken to hospital last night with acute indigestion. It turned out to be a baby.' Samantha, not the brightest of girls, was Edward's new secretary, and Harry suspected Shirley of sabotage in her appointment because she hated competition. From anyone. Shirley had taken the call from a hysterical mother, still only thirty-five herself, who had called at 7.30 a.m. (Shirley had come in to prepare for an early meeting) to screech invective down the phone. It had taken all Shirley's powers to persuade her that, as Samantha had only been with Wiggins Frean for three weeks, the company could not possibly be held responsible for a baby conceived some nine months earlier.

Harry lit a cigarette. 'Do you mean she didn't know she was pregnant? But that's incredible. Just not possible. What about . . . you know . . . ?' Harry wasn't very clear about the way women operated but he had been given the basic facts of life by the biology master, at his expensive prep school many years ago.

'Apparently it's quite common for bleeding to continue throughout pregnancy. I read it in *Marie Claire*,' said Shirley.

'Will you two stop talking like an episode of *Casu-*

alty? ' Edward found this conversation very uncomfortable.

'There was an article about it in last week's copy of *Woman's Own*. If you've got a retroverted uterus . . .' Shirley was unstoppable.

'The problem,' said Virginia, steering the conversation away from gynaecological trivia, 'is that it leaves Edward without a secretary.'

'Just before the launch,' added Edward gloomily.

'She *was* a rather funny shape,' Shirley said. 'Sort of square. It *could* have been a baby I suppose. I just thought it was too many Mars Bars.'

'Well, you'll just have to get a temp.' Harry hoped she'd be one who could actually type and answer the phone. Samantha had been dismally unable to do either.

'I don't want a temp.' Edward was having a bout of worrying about money, but didn't want to say so in front of Virginia. 'They're hopeless.'

'I've got the name of a really good agency in my Rolodex – ' Virginia began, but Edward cut her off.

'Don't worry, I've just thought of the perfect solution.' He hadn't, but he was damned if he was going to get conned into paying twenty pounds an hour for someone to muddle up his diary, and then another fat fee to recruit a permanent girl. Whether you took an ad, or went to an agency, it always seemed to cost at least two thousand pounds. And he wasn't going to the Job Centre again, not after Samantha. Perhaps Clara would know someone. One of her friends was bound to have a daughter who wanted to get into magazines and could type.

*

'I'll do it,' said Clara. It was the opportunity she had been waiting for. She had recently been perfecting dishes like shepherd's pie, steak-and-kidney and treacle tart, where her habit of missing out difficult ingredients had stood her in remarkably good stead. Cookery writers, desperate to make their dishes seem different now, insisted on adding things like lemon grass, Szechwan peppercorns and crème fraîche to recipes that would be perfectly good without them. But Oriental Shepherd's Pie, in Clara's hands, had been transmogrified into the good old-fashioned variety, without the lime and coriander (often to be found in Tesco, but, fortunately for Edward's digestion and taste buds, not that day). This Tuesday evening, Edward was sitting comfortably over the homely dish, gin and tonic to one side, and the inviting prospect of *Inspector Morse*, his favourite television programme, to follow. It was their favourite sort of evening, and somehow, however bad things had got between them, they'd never stopped having them.

The spectre of Shirley hovered like an unwelcome ghost. But, thought Clara, now is the time to fight back.

'Erm, that might put other employees at an, erm, disadvantage,' muttered Edward, adding, much more firmly, 'And you've never worked in an office.' He helped himself to a fresh white roll, fluffily warm from the oven. Thank goodness that phase Clara had gone through of producing brick-like bread, packed with fibre and bits of gravel, seemed to be over.

'I've just done an office-upgrading course, and there was lots of computer work on that. And we did work together at the start.'

Edward paused. Clara knew him so well. He would want the quickest, most efficient way out of this problem, and it seemed a waste of time and money not to take the obvious option. She was beginning to pick up his sense of unease about the financial side of *Heart & Soul*. It wasn't so much that they hadn't calculated how much re-launching it was going to cost – Edward's estimates, ably assisted by Virginia's, were probably remarkably accurate. But Edward simply couldn't resist brinkmanship, in her view, and she knew he'd just go on ploughing money into this project until there wasn't a penny left – and then some. Clara had seen the spiteful pieces in the press, and knew they'd destroyed some business confidence in the re-launch. He probably hadn't budgeted for a safety net, and it was already beginning to look horribly as if they needed one. High risk, high reward, he told her whenever she questioned him. That's what business is about.

'After all,' she said, trying to make it sound casual, 'if your secretary can step in to your wife's shoes in an emergency, and organize a party, why can't your wife step into your secretary's job in the same way?' You owe me, she thought. You know you do, and I'm pressing for repayment. Something on account, anyway. Her marriage to Edward had become a series of debts, which Clara had always been very careful not to call in. Because once she did, she might suddenly find she had nothing left. But it was time to take risks, she thought. Or she might lose the game.

'Just temporarily, of course,' she added, to take the threat out of it. 'You did say that you wouldn't mind me working.'

His face was difficult to read.

'It would give me so much more confidence to start off in an environment I already know. And you know I'm very efficient at organizing your life.'

She hoped the thought of his office being organized as smoothly as his home life would sound too alluring to pass up, especially after three weeks of the dismal Samantha. It would be ironic if Shirley's possessive-ness about her job – Clara was sure that was why she'd engaged such a hopeless successor – was the factor that led to her downfall.

Edward drummed his fingers on the table. He knew she had a case, was obviously trying to work out the consequences.

'Please.' Clara tried again. 'I think I deserve a break, and I do promise to be a PA not a wife in the office.' She paused. 'I think I'm over . . . you know . . .' Finally, she finished up with the weakest line of all. 'Trust me.'

'OK.' Edward took a deep breath. 'Provided you don't undermine Shirley. She's starting a new career, and we can't afford for her to get it wrong.'

She was so delighted with the 'we' that she could overlook the considerable undermining that Shirley herself had so vigorously conducted over the years.

'You won't regret it.' Forgetting the careful lines that had been drawn between them for years, longer than she could remember, she jumped up and hugged him.

'Hey. What's all this? It's only a job, you know,' Edward protested. But he pulled her on to his lap. 'In fact . . .' he tickled her gently ' . . . the duties of my PA are very onerous, you know.'

'Tell me about the duties of your PA,' whispered Clara, forgetting to be frightened of the reply. 'Perhaps they could start now.' It was the first time in the whole of their marriage she had ever taken the initiative, and she held her breath for a second, terrified that her happiness would be punctured by rejection.

She had recently read a survey in *Ideal Home* which said that twice as many men as women thought the kitchen was an erotic place to make love. In fact, what with terracotta floors and pine tables, and creaking middle-aged joints, the kitchen was indeed less erotic for her than it appeared to be for Edward, but at least it was a change from making love under the duvet with the lights out, something that Clara had restricted herself to when she felt that her stretch marks and spare tyres could no longer compete with Shirley's smooth, long limbs.

Shirley probably had a leopardskin bed and a useful set of leather and chains instead of wooden spoons and Le Creuset dishes in her kitchen, reflected Clara. But still.

chapter 6

Clara started work two days later, setting out alone on an unpromising dark, wet and cold February morning because Edward had left the house earlier for a breakfast meeting with his bankers. Icy leaves slithered underfoot as she walked to the station, and steam rose off the packed bodies in the train. It all seemed to take a long time, and, as each mile clattered past, the knot of tension just below her heart seemed to get colder and sharper. A two-week word-processing and business-skills course was one thing, she thought, as she finally swayed uncomfortably on the tube, wedged between a man reading a newspaper and a pregnant woman who everyone seemed to be ignoring but who looked as if she desperately needed to sit down. Actually going into a real office to work, she reflected, something that she hadn't done since she was twenty, was quite another. Her suit jacket, a businesslike shade of red, chosen in haste with Annabel the day before, strained at her shoulders.

Annabel had been on a Self-Esteem course, and had urged Clara to go. 'I haven't got the self-esteem to go on a Self-Esteem course once,' she had replied, only half-joking. Several rounds with therapists over the years had rather put her off that sort of thing.

Litter dogged her steps as she walked to Wiggins Frean from Hammersmith Broadway, and her first impressions of the company did not raise her spirits. She had rarely been there, judging it to be Shirley's territory. So she was as horrified as Virginia had been when she marched into reception and was forced to stand and wait there for a full ten minutes while Chelsea tried to get a room upgrade for her forthcoming holiday in the Caribbean. Naseem was nowhere to be seen. The ashtrays hadn't been emptied that morning, and a scrumpled tin of Coke lay abandoned by the potted plant. Some of the carpet tiles were beginning to curl up at the edges.

Chelsea finally put down the phone.

'I am Mrs Wheeler, Edward Wheeler's wife, and I've come here to work.'

Chelsea looked unimpressed. 'S'not in.'

Clara waited for Chelsea to offer a suggestion as to where she should wait or who she should report to. Chelsea ignored her.

'I've got them to give me the honeymoon special as an early booker,' she called to Naseem, who was just arriving with two cappuccinos in polystyrene cups and what looked like a bun perched precariously on top. 'Complimentary fruit bowl, half a bottle of sparkling wine at the first dinner and a serenade.' After a full description of the brochure, the holiday and the island, she nodded towards Clara.

'Edward Wheeler's wife. What do we do with her?'

'Ooh, the boss's wife,' squealed Naseem. 'Ever so pleased to meet you.'

She could stay, thought Clara, but she'd need training up.

'Want to read a few mags, while you're waiting? Not that any of them are very interesting, reely.' Before Clara could reply she added, 'Fancy a bit of bun?' She tore a piece off with her fingers and held it out to Clara.

'Harry!' She knew Harry reasonably well from his lunches and dinners at The Brambles – he'd often been a useful 'spare man', but she had secretly been rather nervous of him. Now his lanky form, draped elegantly around a copy of *Private Eye*, spelt rescue.

'Clara!' Harry didn't add his usual 'darling' because he never felt it was appropriate with Clara. She was always so starched, and gabbled nonsense. And he was rather inhibited by his knowledge of the affair with Shirley, secretly feeling himself to be on Shirley's side. He couldn't see why Clara didn't do the decent thing and chuck Edward out, thereby putting an end to the pain all round. What could she possibly hope to gain by hanging on in this undignified way?

'How delightful of you to join us.' He made it sound like a garden party rather than a job. 'We're so looking forward to . . . seeing a bit of organization in the office again. Let me show you round.' Harry

200

was, in spite of his usually kind nature, really looking forward to witnessing Clara's reaction to Wiggins Frean. There was an office sweepstake on how long she would stay. Everyone had put in a tenner, written down their choice – the number of days or weeks – and put it in a sealed envelope. Derek Easton was in charge, and everyone except Virginia, who didn't approve of gambling and thought they should all be more supportive to Clara, had pitched in. The winner stood to gain the princely sum of eight hundred and fifty pounds. Harry had scribbled down four days, Shirley, with previous experience of Clara's tenacity and unwillingness to give up when she was beaten, six weeks.

In the lift, Clara tried to think of something to say to Harry. He was one of those people she knew far too much about – Edward often brought home tantalizing snippets about his lifestyle – and could therefore never think of anything that could be guaranteed a safe topic of conversation.

The fated Samantha had left both her desk and Edward's almost concealed in a mountain of paper, and Clara was relieved to set to work, piling post into 'Urgent' (so tall that it almost toppled over), 'Wait', 'Bin' and 'Clara'. She spotted at least half a dozen letters that she could probably answer herself. If she could bring herself to talk to Shirley. Well, she would have to do it some time. Ten years of hiding her feelings were about to stand her in very good stead. Or at least she hoped so. She would go and find Shirley and, mortification of mortifications, ask her what she needed to know about the filing systems and how to turn on the PC. She would smile, and defer to her. Shirley had been a very good PA, and was far more fundamental to the workings of Wiggins Frean than she, Clara, was.

In fact, Shirley was reapplying lipstick in the Ladies loo, squaring up to their meeting. Edward had cunningly announced that Clara was to take over her duties as his PA – only temporarily, of course – in front of everyone, in a meeting only yesterday. And she hadn't seen him alone since. With Virginia's cool gaze quelling her, and Harry, pushed back in his chair, watching her with half-closed eyes – probably ready to throw the contents of the fire bucket over her if she got hysterical – she'd had to sit on her instinct to scream and rush out of the room there and then. It had been like a slap in the face. Her knees had started shaking.

'Have you got last week's figures?' Virginia had tried to change the subject immediately, stretching out her hand for them. Shirley had pushed them across the table numbly, while fury burned inside her. Clara got everything that was rightfully hers. Even her job. Boy oh boy, was she going to regret it someday. For the time being, she simply raised an eyebrow.

'I hadn't realized Clara *had* any secretarial skills.'

'Samantha didn't exactly have any secretarial skills.' Edward had been curt. So that was what it was about. Revenge for the appalling Sam. Well, how was Shirley to know she'd be so useless? 'Clara's been on a course,' he'd added.

'A course.' Shirley hadn't tried to keep the scorn out of her voice. 'Oh well. That's all right then.'

'I'm sure we'll give Clara all the extra help she'll need,' Virginia had interposed smoothly, obviously with no intention of allowing this to develop into a brawl. 'Shall we move on?'

Shirley resolved that Clara was not going to last very long at Wiggins Frean. The woman was a fool to try to compete on Shirley's territory. She snapped her make-up bag shut and strode back to her office, determined to look completely cool.

'Shirley.' Even Clara could hear that she sounded like a dog trainer calling a naughty puppy to heel. But it was hard to control her voice. How does one ask advice of one's husband's mistress? She forced a deferential note into her voice, not very successfully. 'I was wondering if you could spare a moment to initiate me into the mysteries of the filing cabinet.'

For a moment, Shirley looked baffled, and Clara had the odd sensation that they weren't even speaking the same language. But she rose up from her desk and started to walk towards her, inadvertently giving Clara quite a shock.

Her brief glimpses of Shirley in the past had completely confirmed her in her preconceptions of what a mistress was like. Revealing clothes, black lace, high heels, and thick, sooty make-up plastered over her eyes. It had been a great comfort to Clara to think that Shirley came from a completely different class, and that being married to her would be less helpful to Edward than Clara had been in obtaining memberships of golf clubs.

But the Shirley who stood in front of her now looked at first glance almost dowdy, at second, beautiful or something very close to it. A figure-skimming wool suit buttoned up severely at the neck, and her hair was styled in a close-cut boyish crop that revealed her chiselled bone structure. Her shoes were almost classic, but not quite.

'I like your shoes.'

Shirley was clearly discomfited. 'Oh? These. Er, yes. I got them from Emma Hope.' Edward must be paying her well, thought Clara, who then resolved that she was never going to move forward if she kept allowing the voice of past resentment to chip in with irrelevant comments. Shirley must, from now on, be viewed as a colleague. Otherwise they would all go mad.

But it was still impossible for either to think of any small talk as they returned to Edward's office.

Shirley reflected that she could hardly ask after the children, for example, because mistresses were famously disruptive of family life. Suppose they were both on drugs, and all because of their father's infidelity?

Clara didn't feel she could ask Shirley about her holiday plans, in case they coincided oddly with one of Edward's trips abroad. If you really thought about it – and it was probably better not to – there were few absolutely safe conversational topics.

'Awful cold for this time of year,' offered Shirley, as the lift creaked painfully up to the fourth floor, pausing for a heart-stopping thirty seconds between 2 and 3.

Clara smiled with relief. 'Oh, yes, we usually still have late roses in the garden, but I've had to –' she was going to say 'force Edward out a whole month early with mulch and straw to protect the tender plants,' but she changed it to 'start thinking about frost precautions unusually early.'

Shirley had never owned as much as a window box, and wondered what frost precautions were. It sounded like some sort of drill. No wonder Edward said he found her flat relaxing.

Things scarcely improved when they started discussing the filing. Underneath the chaos left by Samantha was a system that Clara could only admire.

'It's like a well-planned garden,' she commented in approval. 'A bit neglected and overgrown, but a superb shrub structure underneath.' This was lost on Shirley, who began to seethe at the words 'neglected and overgrown'.

They exchanged another pair of desperate smiles. It was all beginning to remind Clara of the time Edward had brought home a visiting Japanese delegation, when every trivial remark had had to be repeated, explained, re-explained and then bowed over.

Then there was the question of lunch. Harry, who was protecting his investment in the sweepstake, had given Clara a stomach-churningly accurate description of the local sandwich bar. 'It's watching them lick their fingers that I can't stand. And I'm always finding a hair in my bacon, egg and lettuce bap.' The kinder side of his nature had contemplated taking her out to the local wine bar, which had come second in the *Evening Standard* Wine Bar of the Year award about five years earlier and had changed hands three times since then. But Shirley had begged him to have lunch with her: 'I'm just dreading the first morning. Please, Harry. I promise I won't ask again.'

He couldn't resist Shirley. She was his friend, after all. Edward could look after Clara, as even he could scarcely have lunch with his mistress the first day his wife came to work in his office. Harry still couldn't believe he'd gone this far, and propelled them all into this disastrous situation.

'I'm glad I'm not heterosexual, that's all I can say,' he said to Shirley in the wine bar, as he dissected a wrinkled baked potato. 'You all get yourselves into the most frightful muddles.' Shirley had sketched out the awfulness of the morning, and demanded to know whether Harry thought this meant that Edward wanted to end their affair. And what did Clara hope to achieve by barging into Wiggins Frean?

'I couldn't bear to have a marriage like that. Loveless and sexless.' Shirley ate a lettuce leaf. It was a dull, limp green, and the dressing was sharp, with a tinny aftertaste.

Harry was silent. His unconventional life meant that he quite often found himself forced to peer into other people's bathroom cabinets – only in search of basic necessities like a dab of Vaseline, which could hardly constitute stealing or prying. But he did know that in Edward and Clara's corner storage cupboard, painted prettily in shades of dragged lemon, there was a plentiful supply of the Pill, including a packet that was very much up-to-date. Or had been last August.

Shirley picked up on the pause in conversation. 'Or do you know something I don't?'

'I don't know anything about the intimate side of their marriage.' Harry knew he sounded unusually stilted. 'Shirley, you've got to move on. There's a whole world out there you could be enjoying.'

As Shirley buried her head in her hands, Harry decided she had had enough. He helped her into her new coat – a blissfully soft cashmere which simply slipped on to her shoulders – passed his Barclaycard to the waiter, and summoned a taxi.

'We're not going back to the office. You're going home and I'm coming with you.'

They spent the rest of the day, and most of the night, mixing up cocktails with the contents of Shirley's drinks cupboard, which held a wide selection of liqueurs in it, mostly brought back duty free from trips abroad with Edward.

Her home wasn't so much a flat as a single large cream-painted room which Harry would have called a bedsit and the estate agents a studio, in a vast Victorian house in Acton that had been completely gutted and turned into a dozen little flatlets. Not a single vestige of its former self remained – the developers had left only the outer walls standing before effectively building a modern block within. All the windows, consequently, were at slightly odd levels. A strip of galley kitchen led off the main room at one end, and a slice of bathroom, complete with power shower, commanded a sliver off the other. Shirley curled up on the huge white bed, and Harry on the slightly uncomfortable bench sofa inherited from an aunt.

'Now you're a homeowner, you might at least take an interest in these things,' he grumbled, feeling the moquette hot and scratchy under him. 'Make your home a pleasure zone.'

'*Elle Deco*.' Shirley's knowledge was encyclo-paedic when it came to magazines.

'Aha! So you do care!'

'I don't give a shit.' Shirley would rather wax her legs than her floorboards any day. 'The bed's all I'm interested in.' She luxuriated against two huge leopardskin cushions, a present from Harry. 'You should try it sometime.'

'For heaven's sake, darling, don't try to seduce me. It simply won't work.'

Shirley was sulky. 'Well, you never know. It might sort out both our problems.'

'I,' said Harry firmly, 'do not have those kind of problems. But it's a very nice offer, thank you for thinking of me, darling.'

'Good quality drinks cupboard, I must say,' he hiccuped a few hours later, sprawled on one end of the bed with Shirley drinking fast at the other. 'Most people have ouzo and Fundador Spanish brandy and all those bottles that taste so marvellous under the sun but like paint-stripper when you get them home.'

'Thash because I don't get taken on the villa

holiday in Spain. I'm a mishtress.' Shirley tried to focus on her glass. She supposed that they must have been drinking since lunchtime. Her alarm clock said 9.55 p.m. Too early for bed. 'I go to Luxury Car conferences in Nishe and Wieshbaden. Not Greek islands.' She seized Harry's lapels in her hands. 'I'm going to tell you shomething very important. Now what wash was it? Yes, mishtresses. They don't go on holidays. They go on what the travel indushtry call breaksh.' Then she passed out.

Harry, who was used to hard drinking, managed to rearrange her on her side in the recovery position in case she was sick. 'Love,' he told the slumped body. 'It hurts. I'm giving it up for Lent.'

Clara had finally settled for a tub of cottage cheese and a packet of Ryvita from the supermarket as the only hygienic choice for lunch, and ate them while reading through the pile of letters and memos on the desk. She was surprised, but relieved, to get a call from Harry saying that he and Shirley had forgotten to mention that they both had appointments out that afternoon, and would see her in the morning.

The phone rang again.

'Well?' Unmistakably Annabel.

'Well and good. So far.' Clara was irritated by the intrusion.

'What about, you know, Her?' Annabel clearly didn't know much about offices after all. Even if, like Clara, you had what was called 'your own office' – a shoe-box surrounded by filing cabinets and cardboard walls – rather than a tin table in the middle of a thoroughfare, which is what most people seemed to have, there was no question of privacy.

'All fine.' She tried to bring the conversation to a halt.

'Can you come to dinner on Saturday?'

'My diary's in my bag on Edward's desk. I'll just get it.' She came back in a second. 'I think that's OK.'

'Good. Oh, and Clara . . .' Annabel was determined to get in a final piece of advice before Clara cut her off ' . . . a useful tip from my psychology course. Never put your handbag on a man's desk. It represents the vagina. He'll feel invaded.'

'For God's sake. I am married to him, you know.' Clara cut her off because two other phones were ringing, and Edward, with a harassed air, had just strode past and gone into his office.

'The main bloody newsagents' chain won't give *Heart & Soul* a good position on the shelves in their shops unless we do TV advertising. It's been sitting next to the photography magazines for the past five years and no one ever notices it there. They say that *Heart & Soul* needs television advertising to convince buyers it's changed, and without that support they're not going to move it to a more prominent place. Talk about millions down the drain! Advertising on television costs a fortune! I told them to stuff their positioning.'

'Oh dear. Was that wise?' Clara knew she didn't know much about business, but telling key clients to stuff it didn't sound like normal good practice. Edward glared at her.

'Probably not. Still, it made me feel better.' Then he grinned, and put his feet up on the desk. It was, she thought, a deliberate power-ploy. He'd never have been allowed to put them on the dining table. Here, these upturned soles, in grave need of repair, now she noticed it, told her who was boss.

'I'd better send your shoes to the cobblers.'

Edward hastily dropped his feet to the floor and pretended to rifle round in a drawer. Now was her chance to tackle him about the question of Chelsea and Naseem.

'Edward. Those two girls on reception are the first contact many of your clients will have with your company.'

Edward looked amused. 'I hadn't realized I was hiring an image consultant.'

'Don't be condescending.' She had to get him to stop treating her as if she was having a fun day out before returning to her real life. 'You don't need to be an image consultant to know when a reception area looks as if the company was about to go under.' Her voice had risen slightly with indignation, and she struggled to control it. 'What do you think goes through a client's mind when he's confronted by something that looks like a down-at-heel minicab firm?'

'Most of them, my dear . . .' he was definitely enjoying himself ' . . . don't ever get to see it. When you've been here a bit longer, you'll find that generally our sales people meet clients out of the office.'

'Well, you must have *some* meetings here.'

'Real businessmen don't care about frivolities.'

Edward suddenly seemed to lose interest. 'But sort it out if you like. You can have carte blanche . . .' he obviously suddenly remembered the bills for The Brambles ' . . . within reason.' Edward was good at apparently giving in while retaining the high ground. 'But . . .' as she left the room, he called her back. 'Don't neglect the real work, will you?'

Clara seethed. He was always determined to have the last word. Well, she'd show him.

Somehow Shirley and Harry, who had made himself a bed up on Shirley's floor with cushions, couldn't quite manage to get to the office until nearly midday. Once they both stopped feeling sick, Shirley called a taxi and curled up in it, keeping as still as possible. Both she and Harry wore dark glasses.

They both stopped in horror when they got there.

'Harry,' said Shirley in a frightened voice. 'I think I'm hallucinating.'

'Don't worry, darling.' Harry tried to imbue his voice with a confidence he didn't feel. He glanced down the street, just to check they hadn't accidentally been dropped off at the wrong address by the taxi. He seized her elbow in support. 'We'll just go straight up to our offices. There must be a simple explanation. You'll see.'

Shirley nodded and tried not to look at the reception area while she was waiting for the lift. Wasn't that Naseem in the navy suit? With Clara by her side?

Clara beamed and waved at Harry. 'What do you think of our new reception area?'

'Where did it come from?' Harry felt too ill to be polite.

'Oh, it's only on rental. I couldn't wait to chuck all that old stuff out, but I wanted to give everyone time to choose something they really liked.' Clara was obviously in her element. 'And, of course, the walls will have to be repainted, so it gives us a lovely chance to start completely from scratch. Wiggins Frean, good morning, how can I help you?' This last was addressed to a telephone which had given a brief bleep. Naseem was on the other line, and another girl, not one Harry or Shirley recognized, was talking to a customer. The whole area was buzzing, rather too much so for Shirley's aching head.

As she waited for the lift to come, she took in Clara's work. Gone were the fifties chairs with black screw-on legs. 'Shame,' murmured Harry later. 'Those were genuine antiques.' In their place were restful eau-de-nil blocks of seating, curving round corners and providing about three separate seating areas, divided by low steel-and-glass tables, each one with what looked like a small potted forest on it. Copies of *Vogue*, *Harpers & Queen*, *The Economist* and *The Independent* were laid out in neat rows.

'Eau-de-nil wasn't my first choice, but not much else would go with the walls.' Clara sounded apologetic. 'And I went to New Covent Garden market at six-thirty this morning – on my way in – to get the plants. The world is so lovely at that time of the morning. There isn't a soul about on the roads.'

Harry peered over the top of his sunglasses, then hastily replaced them. 'Where's Chelsea?'

'Oh, she resigned. On a matter of principle. The reception area has become a no-smoking zone. Naseem is now Head Receptionist, and she has very kindly recruited her cousin, Zara.' Clara beamed at Naseem, who smiled back. A pay rise and a smart title had done a lot to soften the blow of having to do some work and stick to rules. And Naseem rather approved of the changes.

'Where did the art come from?' Shirley asked, appalled. Yesterday the walls had boasted a photograph of the Queen and a *Sun* calendar. Both had gone, replaced by a series of large colourful abstracts.

'Aren't those John Protheroes?' Harry once had rather a nice time at a John Protheroe private view.

'Absolutely.' Clara sounded thrilled they'd been recognized. 'John's agent's wife, Sandie, is one of my great girl-friends. We did a school run together when she was married to someone else.' These wife-types certainly got through their husbands, thought Shirley bitterly. Except bloody Clara, of course. Anyone with any gumption would be on to her third husband by now rather than clinging pathetically on to someone who didn't really want her anyway.

'These are limited edition prints, of course, not originals, but they're still rather striking, don't you think? We've promised to run a little temporary exhibition with them in the reception area. You never know, we might even sell one or two.' Finally Clara stopped talking. Shirley's head ached.

Upstairs, they both collapsed in Harry's office. Derek was already in there, looking shocked.

'There you both are. Do you know, she's even

changed the answering-machine message? I can tell you, this place is really going downhill.'

Harry had, in fact, expected Virginia to put her foot down about the answering-machine message before now, but she had probably never heard it, as she always got into the office before everyone else and left afterwards. It had been Chelsea's idea, and it started with a giggle. 'We're all tied up at Wiggins Frean at the moment . . .' (at this point you could hear Derek shout 'whay-hay!' in the background) '. . . but as soon as we're free, we'll call you-hoo.' There had then been a long pause before the tone when you could hear the distinct sound of rustling materials and the odd gasp.

Shirley was the first to break the silence.

'Well, I don't think you'll be taking eight hundred and fifty pounds home at the end of the week.'

'I do admit that my likelihood of winning looks pretty remote at the moment. But *you're* still in with a chance.'

Once he had gone, Shirley rested her throbbing head in her hands. She felt invaded. Next Clara would be wanting to organize the office party. If she couldn't be got rid of first. She counted on her fingers. The party was always held in November to be in time for Christmas. She started organizing it in July. Four months to get shot of the appalling woman. Before she encroached any further on *her* territory. Edward would have to move her tactfully back to a full-time existence at The Brambles, or preferably into some suitable place around half the size. She wouldn't need so much space when she was divorced.

*

'Hi. Well done.' Virginia put her head round the corner of Clara's office. 'Can I come in?' It was an unnecessary courtesy, because the door stood wide open and that's how Clara intended keeping it. She was sure she had read somewhere – in *Good House-keeping*, she thought – that good managers operated an 'open door policy'.

'Well, I just wanted to welcome you to Wiggins Frean. And to say you've done a great job on Reception.' Virginia was mildly irritated that she hadn't thought of doing something so obvious herself. It simply hadn't occurred to her. There had always been a facilities department at Publishing Unlimited, and every two years expensive specialist office designers were brought in to make sure that everything was kept spankingly up to date. 'Perhaps you'd like to have lunch one day this week?' She was holding her diary. 'Tuesday would suit.'

Clara was delighted.

'By the way, I just wanted to go through Edward's diary with you . . .' Virginia sounded unusually tentative, but Clara was determined that Edward's diary was not going to become a point of embarrassment. For years she had turned a blind eye, ignoring his dates with Shirley. She could go on for a bit longer.

So she picked up the diary. 'Let's see.'

Virginia explained that they needed a big push with the advertising agencies who actually bought the space in the magazines on behalf of their clients. They had to convince the top spenders that there was the money and expertise to make *Heart & Soul* a winner. Either Edward or Shirley would be needed virtually every lunchtime or evening from now until the launch. Clara was only too happy to block in large chunks of Edward's time, particularly in the evenings, with Virginia. Shirley's Thursdays were beginning to look like an endangered species.

'Are you sure that's all right? I don't want to muck up your family life.'

'Don't worry. Your family life is being messed about too. We'll all have to make sacrifices. But don't firm up those dates until I've spoken to Edward,' Clara added nervously. The last thing she wanted was for Edward to accuse her of interfering, although quite how you could be someone's PA without interfering with their life in some way was difficult to see. But she mustn't frighten him off in the first week.

On Tuesday, they lunched at Funge, a place so full of mirrors that Clara nearly lost her nerve completely. 'It's another of these huge, trendy places that everyone's talking about.' Virginia sounded almost apologetic. Clara was thrilled. She'd just read several reviews that tipped it the 'hottest spot in town'. It had once been some kind of a warehouse, and had since been restructured in black marble, glass and chrome, with several levels, each one creating a theatre-style vista of the level below. She noticed Virginia cast an experienced eye around, as she sat down, back to the mirrored wall, and asked for two glasses of champagne 'immediately'. Clara was not too keen on seeing every forkful reflected behind Virginia in the mirror.

'How clever,' mused Virginia. 'Usually it's only

the person facing the room who can see who's in. But that mirror means both of you can check it out.' Oh well, thought Clara, at least it reduced the spinach-on-teeth risk.

The menu took her around the world in forty seconds. 'Pan-fried British stoat with Polynesian salsa,' she read. 'Surely not?'

'That can't be right.' Even Virginia sounded rattled. 'It must mean "goat", although it still doesn't sound very nice.' Clara peered at the elegant, but almost illegible, writing again.

'It says it's the vegetarian alternative. Perhaps it means "oats".' It all made her efforts with Star Anise and galangal look very tame. 'The review I read did say that this place broke new ground in an increasingly overcrowded culinary arena.'

'Well, it's not breaking new ground with my digestive system.' Virginia was waspish. 'I'll start with the grilled melon, and follow with a plate of smoked salmon as a main course. They can't muck that up.'

But, because it was currently very fashionable, the service was slow, which meant that both Clara and Virginia drank a little more champagne than they had intended.

'I just wondered . . .' Clara took a deep breath. 'You see, I feel that, now I've got a new life, or at least a new role, well . . .'

Virginia's eyes sparkled with interest. Clara felt encouraged enough to go on.

'I was wondering what I should wear in my new life. You see, I read all the magazines, but somehow

I don't know how to apply it to me. And I'd like to look, well, a bit more businesslike, I suppose.'

Virginia responded immediately. 'Well, I think you – I'm speaking generally here, it's usually a good way of starting – ' she was trying to be tactful, Clara noted ' – need to begin with your hair. Get a stylish cut. Let me see . . . go to Charles Worthington. Ask for Charles, mention me. He'll sort you out.'

'I had to choose somewhere that was thoroughly stylish but not too terrifying,' explained Virginia later to Simon, who was only half-interested. 'She couldn't possibly cope with those pseudo-trendy places where they sneer at your roots and ask you who on earth cut your hair before.'

'Neither could I.' Simon was consistently amazed at what women would go through in order to be fashionable. He went to a deferential barber just off Jermyn Street and sat beside tycoons and peers. All were treated, for the twenty minutes that they sat in the chair, as if they were Royalty. Women seemed to put up with the most ghastly humiliations to achieve the latest look.

Virginia ignored him. 'Clara's quite a challenge for a make-over,' she mused.

'Why?' This was just returning the serve, conversationally speaking, but Simon was glad to see Virginia so animated. She had become rather distant lately, not just busy, but remote, and he felt, obscurely, that she was keeping all her best stories for someone else. Simon found himself making excuses to avoid going home these days. Joining his colleagues in the odd drink after work.

'Well, Shirley's so obviously perfect for a transformation. Divine body, gorgeous face, hidden under her eye make-up. And – ' Virginia's eyes were shining with conviction ' – most of her problems are to do with lack of confidence. With her great new look and a proper career, she's unstoppable, I think.'

'Mmm. I think Shirley's a bit of a minx.' She'd been round for 'weekend meetings' on a number of occasions and treated Simon as if she knew him very well. He had been, as he was expected to be, charmed by this, although also slightly worried – he wondered exactly how much Virginia had confided in her. He felt invaded by her relationship with Virginia. Women were so trusting. And he didn't think that giving someone a good job and a great haircut instantly turned them into a wonderful warm person, although he knew that Virginia believed it could.

'Be careful of Shirley,' he warned Virginia. 'There's a sharp edge there.'

'Well, you can't really blame her. She's always come second in life. To her brothers at home, to Clara with Edward. I think she's just frightened of losing what little she has. Once she's got more confidence, I think she'll relax. But that's why it's so important that she doesn't think I'm taking sides. I'll have to be very careful about giving Clara a helping hand, although she definitely needs one. It would be easier if she was thinner, but I don't think I can ask her to go on a diet. Do you?'

Simon put the paper down. 'Why not?'

'Well, I think she's one of those women who start a new diet every Monday morning, and find themselves wrapped round three Mars Bars every Tuesday afternoon.'

'Ha, ha. We don't have many of those in the bank.' Simon found women's eating habits baffling.

'Don't you believe it. Eating disorders are growing faster amongst young professional men than any other category.'

Simon grinned. He had lived with Virginia long enough to know a headline when he heard it.

'But what I can't understand is why Clara's put up with this situation for so long. Just stuck in this abusive relationship.' Virginia was back on the psychological side of the story, which, even Simon had to admit, was fascinating.

'You mean the affair with Shirley?'

'She must know about it. Unless she's completely stupid. She's just letting Edward get away with murder. I think it's a huge mistake. Absolutely the wrong thing to do. If you were ever unfaithful, I'd leave you immediately.'

They had often had this conversation, although not recently.

Usually Simon would look at Virginia intently. 'And if *you* ever had an affair, I would never forgive you either. Ever.'

But he was busy tapping through his Psion organizer. 'Mmm.'

Virginia gave her ballpoint a shake. Wiggins Frean pens never lasted, and always petered out just as she was getting to the important bits. She must tell Clara to order some decent ones. She'd been with the company for nearly a month now, and Virginia noted that she was both efficient and well liked. Unusual in the boss's wife – she knew that everyone had been determined to loathe her and make her life as difficult as possible. But she thought that Clara was very much winning through. Although she still dressed badly. With the re-launch now only two weeks away, there'd been no time for fashion advice.

Virginia could just see the March sun struggling through the clouds, barely managing to make an impression on the unwashed windows. On the way to work she had seen a few daffodils nodding their heads, probably in indignation at the sight of the diamond-like shards of broken glass scattered across the pavement. Beat Car Crime Together said the poster on the bus in front. It was a losing battle. Like getting *Heart & Soul* off the ground. She felt as if she was conducting an orchestra through a particularly complex piece of music. She had always been so good at finding and managing staff, but after the redundancies she'd found it almost impossible to get the people she wanted. Perhaps they didn't want to come to Hammersmith. If it wasn't for Shirley, helping out everywhere, she didn't think anything would ever get past the good idea stage.

And everyone wanted something from her. Simon wanted her at home by 8 p.m. Oliver wanted her attention. Edward wanted her brain power. Harry, in his role as Production Director, wanted her to get things done on time. The few remaining staff wanted pay rises (fat chance, spluttered Edward, when she mentioned it). Even Clara wanted her advice on style. Virginia had had very little help since the night of the long redundancy cheques, as some wag had put it, although Becky was being quite useful. Quite was the operative word. Shirley said that Becky was more interested in getting men, rather than magazines, to bed. Although Virginia thought that that was putting it a bit strongly, there was definitely an element of truth in the observation. The hours spent checking page proofs each night would be much longer without Shirley and Harry, neither of whom seemed to care that checking proofs wasn't part of their job descriptions. The three of them usually split a bottle and joked their way into the night.

Clara had just come into Virginia's office to confirm some diary dates. Shirley, sitting on an easy chair in front of Virginia's desk, was chewing her pencil as she thumbed through a sheaf of papers. She looked up sharply as Clara waited for Virginia to finish re-writing a piece of copy.

'He wonders if it's really necessary for him to go with you to that White Goods fair in Birmingham.'

'Tell him – ' Virginia was irritated ' – that according to *Campaign*, there's about to be a White Goods advertising war. No less than four companies are about to launch multimillion pound advertising budgets. If necessary, we camp outside their head office. This fair delivers them all on plate.'

Clara got the picture. 'Do you have any hotel preferences?'

'I do. But there's no point in even thinking about

it. Everything will be booked up. Just go for what you can get.' Virginia was kicking herself for not having focused on the exhibition earlier. She put down her pen. Shirley moved imperceptibly, as if to catch Virginia's attention. 'Better still, Shirley and I will go. We can share a hotel room.'

Shirley barely waited until the door shut behind Clara. 'What does she think she's come as in that outfit?'

'It is extraordinary.' Virginia had to admit that culottes did not flatter broad bottoms.

Virginia, Edward and Shirley sat on one side of the boardroom table. On the other side, they faced Janet, Judy, Jill and Jane of 4JPR, the public relations company that Virginia had insisted on retaining for the re-launch of *Heart & Soul*. Janet outlined their plans for promoting the re-launch of *Heart & Soul*. Clara sat at the end, taking notes.

'It'll have to be glossy and glitzy.' She opened a giant leather cuttings file to show what could be achieved by 4JPR.

'Glamorous.'

'Gorgeous.' Judy, Jill and Jane seemed keen to keep to the alliterative theme.

Virginia began to thumb through the portfolio, with Shirley watching over her shoulder.

'You got the Smith Group some tremendous coverage.' Virginia was making approving noises as she flicked over the shiny pages.

'Mmm. Great,' echoed Shirley.

Edward, Clara noted, clearly thought that public

relations was a girl's game, and not something for real men to trouble their massive brains about.

As she watched 4JPR unveil their proposals, she realized he was wrong. They knew exactly what they were up to. She could see why Virginia had recommended them. It had been a major battle persuading Edward to pay for professional advice rather than just getting Shirley to organize a party for distributors and the press. 'She does the office party brilliantly. And now there's Clara to help.'

'Shirley is the Sales Director of *Heart & Soul* magazine. Directors do not organize parties. They are far too busy getting in advertising to do trivial and time-consuming duties.'

Judy was sketching out a lavish launch at the Hempel Hotel. Or the Metropolitan. 'Luxurious but contemporary. Emphasizing that this is a new look magazine. Real champagne. Lots of canapés.'

'Real champagne at the beginning. When people are sober enough to see what the label says on the bottle,' said Edward. 'After that, the waiters can wrap *méthode champenoise* in towels.' The women all exchanged glances that conveyed the importance of making at least one concession to Edward. He had to feel in charge somehow.

'Interviews with the trade press – the magazines the industry reads – are just as important as the newspapers. If the newsagents believe in you, they place you in a good position in the shop . . .' Edward began elaborately picking his teeth. He obviously hadn't filled either Virginia or Shirley in about telling Britain's biggest chain of newsagents to get stuffed.

For a moment, Clara thought he had winked at her, and bent over her notes to hide her blush. She couldn't bear the thought of Shirley spotting a marital interchange, because she was sure that she'd cite it as unprofessional and find some way of taking it out on her at a later date.

'We'll present Virginia and Shirley as the dynamic duo responsible for revitalizing the magazine market. The established professional and the up-and-coming star, the award winner and the *ingénue*, experience and vitality, advertising and editorial, hard and soft approaches . . .'

Beauty and the Beast, added Clara mentally.

Jill mapped out back-up activity. Competitions, sponsorship, getting showcards on to the shelves of smart shops, incentives . . . Clara's head began to swim. She was having trouble keeping up with the minute-taking. Shirley, of course, was very good at shorthand. That meant that Clara's minutes had to be very accurate or Shirley would enjoy pointing out the mistakes later. And one thing she had learned about Shirley was that she was very good at spotting errors.

She had been meticulous in her handover to Clara. And it must be very hard on her, Clara told herself. She had probably hated Clara for as long and as thoroughly as Clara hated her. And here she was being positively friendly, as she completed Clara's very detailed briefing. 'You'll need to keep an eye on Judith,' she said, almost cosily.

Clara had been surprised. So far Judith had proved very welcoming. Although she did rather tend to speak in clichés, rolling each one out with amazement – as if she'd just discovered the secret of the universe. Yet Shirley was portraying Judith as disaffected and ambitious. She would have to keep her eyes and ears open.

'Oh?'

'She wants to be Edward's PA. And that would be a disaster. She's hopeless, always muddling up diaries and ordering the wrong stationery.' Clara had felt confused. Surely that wasn't Judith's job anyway?

'Do you think I ought to have a word with her? There might be something we could do to make her job more fun. And she probably needs a leg-up.'

Shirley had looked horrified. 'Better not. It just raises expectations.'

She remembered that Shirley had been doing a particularly difficult breakfast presentation that morning, and seized the opportunity to change the subject.

'Oh, how did your presentation go?' She thought she should try to be friendly. Particularly as Shirley was making so much effort.

'Fine.' Shirley clearly didn't want to talk about it. 'Now that's about all, but you've got my number if you need it.'

Virginia walked in. 'How did this morning go?'

Shirley brightened. She launched in without hesitation. 'You wouldn't believe it. An absolute triumph. We got the United Cosmetics account – 99 per cent sure anyway – but their end was chaos. First, all the audio-visual broke down – theirs, not ours luckily –

and you know their MD, the one we always call The Giant Toad? Well, he . . .'

Clara lost the rest of the story as the phone went, but Shirley was clearly being very funny and had drawn an audience of Edward and Harry as well as Virginia by the time Clara had finished the call.

'This calls for a celebration.' Virginia was looking pleased. 'Well done, Shirley.'

'Lunch?' Shirley looked round at the assembled faces. 'Harry, can you make it? And Edward?'

Well, thought Clara. She wouldn't want me at a celebration lunch anyway. And I'm only Edward's PA, even if I am the boss's wife. But it didn't stop her feeling left out, as she got out the cottage cheese and Ryvita again. It felt very quiet and lonely in the office until 3.30 p.m., when Edward returned, looking slightly flushed, and started dictating at breakneck speed. Fortunately, he never noticed that she rewrote his letters anyway – once she knew what he wanted to say, she could usually think of a quicker, clearer way to put it. It all reminded her of O-levels, which suddenly seemed very far away and to belong to a much sunnier world.

The remaining two weeks to the re-launch date flew by. Shirley continued to be outwardly helpful and pleasant while making Clara feel completely excluded from anything that really mattered. It was the first time Clara really knew what the phrase 'the smile didn't reach her eyes' meant. She had always wondered. There was nothing concrete she could put her finger on, no obvious 'undermining', but on four occasions a stationery order she knew she'd completed went missing. Even Virginia got impatient. Still, there was no reason to suppose that Shirley had sabotaged them. Once Edward got absolutely furious because one of his most important banking contacts called and left an urgent message. It didn't get through. 'Didn't you take that call, Shirley?' asked Clara, who suspected damn well she had, and that she had deliberately failed to pass the message on. Shirley opened her eyes very wide and said she had taken *a* call, but that it certainly hadn't been anyone important. 'I'd have told Edward *immediately*,' she emphasized. Edward later suggested that Clara didn't try to blame Shirley when she forgot messages – it was a very childish way to behave. 'You're doing very well,' he told her pompously, 'so don't spoil it with petty jealousies.' Clara burned, but there was nothing she could do except walk out, and she had a very good idea who that would suit.

And overseeing the launch party for *Heart & Soul* was like jumping out of a very high building with the ground rushing up to meet her. Although 4JPR were organizing it – thank goodness – there was a stream of liaison on small details that Clara didn't dare take decisions on. Unfortunately, everyone was much too busy for small details unless you collared them as they went past, or picked on them in the lift or the Ladies. Clara was beginning to feel as if she was hunting some rare wild beast.

Only two days before the launch, Shirley emerged from Edward's office with a pile of papers, and headed towards Virginia's. Ah ha. A decision-maker, although definitely not the one Clara would have preferred, given the choice. But she didn't have a choice.

'Judy wants to know if you're happy with two girls on reception for the party. Or whether you want to have three.'

Shirley thought for a moment.

'I think we should have three, don't you? But we need someone senior from here to keep an eye on things. Leaving something important like reception completely to an outside company seems very dangerous to me. I know Virginia has complete faith in 4JPR, but she's very trusting. Would you be able to take it in hand?'

Put like that Clara could scarcely say no, although she didn't particularly want to spend the whole party crossing people's names off on a list and pinning badges to their lapels. And she wasn't quite sure what kind of dangers and disasters Shirley foretold. But, she reminded herself, the world of work was very new to her.

'Should I just check with Virginia?'

'Better not. It's one of those mornings – I think she might explode if anyone else comes up to ask her something trivial. The art department are being complete idiots.' There was something almost friendly about Shirley this morning, and Clara felt so relieved that things seemed to be getting better that she let it pass. The tension was obviously getting to everyone.

A few hours later, Becky trailed up, with her normal cheerfulness punctured. 'Is Madam at home?' She pointed at the closed door. It opened and Shirley emerged. She didn't look particularly pleased to see Becky.

'I wanted Virginia to see this.'

'I'll take it.' Shirley looked round at them. 'No one seems to realize that things are critical round here. There isn't time for hanging around chatting.' She shut the door of Virginia's office again, just slightly too hard. Becky and Clara exchanged glances.

After that, Clara didn't quite dare disturb Virginia for advice on what she should wear. But, after working late to catch up with the some of the luxury-car business correspondence (*Heart & Soul* took every moment of the working day), she caught her by the lift.

'How's it going?' Virginia looked tired.

'Fine. It's fun. It beats waiting in for deliveries from Peter Jones.'

'Fun?' Virginia looked rather startled.

Perhaps work wasn't meant to be fun. 'Well, I mean, not depressing.'

'No. Oh. Well, good.' Virginia still looked baffled. The lift arrived and the doors opened. Shirley stood inside like an avenging angel. The three of them crammed into it as it creaked its way downwards. Bother. That was that chance to talk over. And, anyway, Shirley had started some funny story, directed at Virginia, about a cosmetics industry MD who had gone into a department store and found a rival trying to poach his girls.

Clothes did give you confidence, reflected Clara, who

had decided that getting past Shirley's sentry box to reach Virginia was impossible, and, on the advice of *Vogue*, had gone to several personal shoppers the day before the re-launch party. One had shoehorned her into something very like the Gonziaga Black but the other had picked out a chocolate brown silk suit, utterly plain and divinely cut. Back in the office, waiting to set off for the launch, she actually enjoyed catching sight of herself in the mirror with her glamorous new hairstyle. 'Wow,' Virginia had said. 'Turn round. That's great. Charles has done a really good job. Aren't you pleased? I'm seeing him myself again next week, so I'll tell him.'

Shirley came slinking in wearing something black that managed to combine perfect good taste with graphic revelations of every one of her delectable contours. Virginia was wearing a beautifully cut Edina Ronay suit with a few witty touches.

'What's Edward wearing?' Virginia sounded anxious. Although, thought Clara, Virginia had spent enough time with him in Savile Row last week. Clara, who'd had twenty years of tucking Edward's shirttails in, talking to dry cleaners about interesting stains and sending trousers with broken zips to the menders (did Shirley simply rip them open or something?), had been only too happy to pass the renovation of Edward over to Virginia, who had got very exercised over what everyone would wear on the big night. 'You've got more experience at this sort of thing than I have,' Clara had told her, adding under her breath, 'And I wish you luck.'

But even Edward looked superb – well polished

like a magnificent piece of furniture – in a beautiful suit. He had nearly passed out when he wrote the cheque. 'It'll last a lifetime,' Virginia had urged him. 'And just get nicer as it gets older.'

'There's only room for three in the taxi. Virginia, you and I – and Edward – ought to get to the Hempel first. Be there from the start. Make sure nothing goes wrong.' Shirley flicked a few invisible pieces of dust off her outfit, looking at herself in the mirror as she spoke. Although Clara heard them bump into Harry by the lift. 'Come with us,' Shirley urged him. 'We can easily squeeze four into the car.' Clara didn't really mind. The others – from the art and subs departments – were all tired, but much less tense than the directors, and she liked their irreverent jokiness.

Piles of *Heart & Soul* were stacked up at the reception table in the Hempel's private wing, with big blow-ups of its pages framed artistically on the walls, and asymmetric stalks of flowers, in absolutely white vases, made 'statements' on Perspex tables. Waiters stood to attention with immaculate trays of canapés, each one carefully lined up geometrically. Clara wondered if anyone would be brave enough to destroy the pattern by eating one.

After an initial quiet period, she realized Shirley had been right about needing three people to take names and check people off the list. That was the problem with her doom-mongering. Just as you began to believe she was doing it all for spite, she turned out to be right. They could have done with four people even, at one point. But the crush soon died down and the three of them were left with just a scattering of name tags and the odd latecomer. The back of the room was heaving with people, most of whom exchanged facts – or fictions – with each other while scouring the horizon over their glasses with the eagle-eyed vigilance of trained bodyguards. So many names were being dropped that Clara was surprised the immaculate white stone floor could stand the strain. Virginia was white with tension. Shirley's face looked hard under its make-up. Even Harry, usually so laid back, kept darting anxious glances towards the door.

Every so often he came out to their reception desk and fiddled with the name badges.

'You OK, Clara?'

It was kind of him to ask.

'Why don't you join the party?' The 4JPR team seemed keen to get rid of her. Or perhaps they were just being kind. But Clara wasn't sure. If any of the disasters that Shirley worried about did come to pass, and she, Clara, was enjoying herself drinking champagne, then it would be the perfect excuse for her to point out that the boss's wife wasn't up to fulfilling even the most menial duties of a PA. She shook her head. 'I'm fine here.' And, on the whole, she was, because, although receptionists seemed to be completely invisible as far as partygoers were concerned, she was putting faces to names and over-hearing some very interesting things.

'Virginia! Another triumph! Darling, it looks quite, quite brilliant. I particularly liked . . .' One woman had fallen on Virginia with a kiss on both cheeks. Yet Clara, who had been pinning a label on the same woman at the reception desk while she flicked through her copy of *Heart & Soul*, had distinctly heard her mutter something quite different to a colleague behind her: 'Not a lot new here. And the layout's pretty messy. Virginia's losing her famous touch.'

'Where's my name badge?' demanded another woman, dressed improbably in a plumed hat and a purple silk suit. 'Don't you know who I am?'

Clara fumbled furiously amongst the badges and scoured the list of acceptances in vain. 'Sorry, we didn't know you were coming.'

'It's just not good enough,' snapped the woman, turning to her companion. 'I mean, it's not as if I particularly wanted to come in the first place.'

She stood there sighing as Clara scribbled her name on a sticky label.

'I hope it doesn't mark my jacket. Or I shall send you my dry cleaning bill.' She marched off.

'What are you doing here? You ought to be at the party.' Virginia was on her way to the loo.

'Oh, Shirley thought it would be better . . .'

'Well, there's no need for three of you on duty now. You should be enjoying yourself.' Clara wasn't sure if 'enjoying' was the right concept for an evening like this. She was quite sure Virginia wasn't indulging in anything as frivolous as enjoyment.

Virginia introduced her to Colin Dearest, who kissed her hand. 'I have been looking forward to meeting you.' He seemed to mean it. 'Do tell me, how did you get such a good crowd together? It really is a superb party.'

Clara began to murmur about Judy, Jane, Janet and Jill, but Colin carried on. 'I understand Marcus went to Radley. My ex-wife and I have been thinking of it for our son, Zac. How did you find it?'

This was comfortably familiar territory. 'Oh, Marcus was very happy there. He – '

Shirley appeared from nowhere and seized Colin by the arm. 'Come and meet . . .' Her words were lost in the crowd as Clara found herself talking to their disappearing backs. Colin, to give him his due, tried to turn round and mouth 'catch up with you later' but Shirley blocked him out.

In fact, the party was nearly over, and over the next five minutes people started trailing out, and more help was needed to give them their farewell goody bags.

Edward was in a good mood as they drove down the м3. 'Great launch. Everyone came. By the way, were you OK on reception? I was going to come and get you, but Shirley thought you might feel more comfortable there instead of being dropped in the middle of a lot of strangers.'

'Oh?' It seemed very much as if Shirley had connived to keep her out of the party. 'It was for my benefit, was it?'

Edward gave her a sharp look. 'Any complaints?' He sounded irritated. Clara sat back. It probably wasn't worth discussing it with Edward. He thought Shirley was acting for the best. Shirley was clearly an expert in the kind of bullying that leaves no visible signs. Each separate incident was just a bit too trivial to complain about. Even Annabel would think she was being fussy.

'Complaints?' She tried not to sound sarcastic. 'Of course not.'

'You're not finding it all too difficult, are you?'

She could see Edward's good mood trickling away. 'No. I'm fine. In fact, I'm enjoying myself,' she added, hastily, to rescue the evening. 'It's a nice place to work.'

Edward seemed surprised. 'Is it?'

chapter 7

The May issue – the first in *Heart & Soul*'s new reincarnation – sold 50,000 more copies than the old-style April issue had done. It was, everyone agreed, a triumph.

The advertisers – the agencies and companies who placed expensive advertisements and therefore made all the difference to the profitability of a magazine – were not impressed by a total sales figure of 129,000. The rival *Viva* sold 550,00 on a regular basis. *Heart & Soul* had a terribly long way to go.

Virginia was swallowed up by the Birmingham electrical appliances exhibition barely days after the flurry of activity generated by the launch. It was a nightmare, she reported to Simon on the phone in the evening, self-consciously twisting the telephone cord round her fingers, as she balanced on the end of a boxy peach sofa in one of the Hotel Cosmo's 'executive suites'. 'Exhibition hell, darling. You're so lucky you don't have them in your business. I never want to see a White Good, or whatever they call refrigerators these days, again.'

She was conscious of sounding extra-bright. 'Shirley's got summer flu. Absolutely raging. So Edward Wheeler's up here instead.' Somehow she couldn't quite look at Edward, who was seated in an equally boxy armchair opposite, this one in some indeterminate shade of grey, flicking through a pile of papers. They were supposed to be going to the exhibition drinks party and then taking out a White Goods executive with an enormous advertising budget.

'So I thought I'd better call you now. I've no idea what time it'll all end.'

The phone went again as soon as she put it down. The White Goods executive was also struck down with summer flu.

'So it's just us, then. Unless we get invited out at the exhibition drinks party.' Edward seemed unconcerned at being stood up.

Virginia giggled. 'It reminds me of going to parties when I first lived in London. You always knew you'd be taken out to dinner after a party, but never knew who would be taking you.'

Edward looked at her with interest. 'You had that kind of a time, did you? While I was happily married.'

'Were you?' Virginia didn't wish to reveal any more about her flat-sharing days. She had got into the habit of keeping secrets about herself.

239

'Very.' Edward was terse. 'Anyway, we'd better be off.'

Virginia wondered what had happened to that happy marriage. Probably a simple case of wandering willie. Lives growing apart. They wrote about it in the magazines all the time. Men were so easily led. And wives like Clara did seem to let their husbands slip away from them. Got too tied up in PTA meetings and collecting children from Brownies and Beavers to talk properly at the end of the day. She checked her handbag for its survival kit. Business cards, notebook, impressive pen, headache tablets, small change. Good. As she left the room, she wondered if *Heart & Soul* ought to do a piece on 'quality time' in marriage. The kind of time she and Simon always made sure they had, lingering over a spritzer and chatting through the day once the nanny had put the children to bed. At least one night a week. That's what was needed. If she was out in the evening – and she tried to limit that to no more than three nights a week, although that wasn't always possible – Simon never had to trip over toys and rifle through an empty fridge. The nanny laid him a pretty table in their red lacquered dining room, a rich, warm room furnished in old, dark wood, illuminated with the flickering light of a series of massive church candles. All he had to do was pop a home-cooked – well, caterer-cooked, really – meal in the oven or microwave and pour himself a glass of wine. Simon sometimes showed signs of forgetting it, but he was very well looked after.

Edward and Virginia worked the packed throng

of the exhibition drinks party as a team, but at the end of it Virginia's feet hurt. She had smiled too often at too many men in suits, all of whom merged into one in spite of the enormous plastic lapel labels to distinguish them, and she couldn't face trying to fight her way through a restaurant queue.

'Let's just order room service,' suggested Edward. 'Then I'll take a cab back to Mrs Whatsername's.' Edward was booked into a b&b on the other side of town, because that was all a very apologetic Clara had managed to find at the last minute, Shirley and Virginia having agreed to share what appeared to be the last hotel room in Birmingham.

Virginia hesitated. It sounded so much more comfortable but it did seem a bit personal. One shoe pinched a few toes on her right foot again, reminding her of the painful alternatives. 'OK. At least there's champagne in the mini-bar.'

'It'd be cheaper to order a whole bottle from room service.'

Edward was so sensible, she thought, once installed upstairs, pulling off her shoes with a sigh of relief. All round, he was a very comfortable man. She looked at him reflectively, watching him settle himself at the other end of the sofa, tugging at his trouser legs to get comfortable and inadvertently revealing a slightly loud pair of socks. He flicked rapidly through all the free magazines, scanning them for items of interest. He could obviously read fast, and knew what sort of things he was looking for. It didn't feel at all odd being in a hotel room with him. Rather nice, really. She took the glass of champagne and sat back with a sigh. 'I hope I'm not keeping you from chatting up the exhibition lovelies.' He snapped the last magazine shut and pushed the pile away from him. 'I don't "chat up" women.'

Virginia couldn't help looking cynical. She'd seen the way the female staff at *Heart & Soul* had looked at him.

'Really? Were you faithful to Clara before Shirley?' This, she knew, was dangerous ground, but she felt she owed it to Shirley at least to find out something about how the land lay, and whether he was ever going to do the honest thing by her.

'Yes. This mess isn't about fidelity, you know. Not at the heart of it, anyway.' He didn't sound as if he was going to elaborate, but then he went on. 'Or maybe it's just that we married far too young. Perhaps we weren't really ready for commitment.'

'So why did you marry?'

'Oh, partly because her parents disapproved so much, I think.' He swirled the champagne round his glass. 'And she was very pretty.'

Virginia tried to imagine a young, pretty Clara, straight out of some sheltered, well-to-do family.

'She seemed so vulnerable. I wanted to look after her. I haven't made much of a job of it, though. Sorry, I don't know why I'm talking like this. I don't often confide in people.'

Virginia felt ridiculously flattered. And she was sure Edward knew it. God, he was a charmer when he tried to be.

'One thing I do know . . .' Edward sat down beside her and took her hand in his. It was surprisingly warm and unthreatening ' . . . is that it's not all my fault. Clara went away in her head. Lost interest. She went through a patch when she really didn't care about me at all. She actually hated me at one point. I was . . .' he paused, as if trying to decide how much to tell Virginia ' . . . very selfish,' he concluded eventually.

Show me a husband that isn't, thought Virginia.

Edward topped up their glasses. 'Still it's better than hating herself, which I think was the alternative option. At least I've done that for her.'

Virginia wondered what he was talking about. This kind of conversation was just the kind that she enjoyed. The quirks of people's relationships. And how you could sort things out for them. Clara, she thought, had got lazy. Forgotten what a responsibility marriage was. She and Simon had always promised each other not to forget.

'Have you ever really talked to her about it?'

He shook his head. 'I couldn't.' Room service came and went, along with a second bottle of champagne. Virginia felt alive again, and she could see from the sparkle in his eyes and his occasional shout of laughter that Edward did too. The evening deepened into night, and they went on talking. It was a huge relief. Virginia spent most of her days talking about how women felt, and turning it into articles and headlines, but she kept her own feelings locked up in a box marked 'private'. Edward, somehow, in the way of strangers in a strange city, had found the key. She couldn't imagine sending him off to Mrs What-sername's on the other side of Birmingham at two in the morning. Would he kiss her goodbye if she did? A peck on the cheek in front of everyone at a restaurant was hardly an intimate act. Being alone together in a hotel room would make the gesture feel quite different. She could see the faintest shadow of evening stubble, and wondered how rough it would be if she stroked it. He was much darker than Simon, and the stubble was showing stronger, and it was slightly grey. She wished he would take charge. Either go, or suggest sleeping here.

'Have another drink,' she urged him, hoping to delay the moment of truth.

'Another?' He laughed again, and took her hand. 'I must be off.'

She flushed and looked down. Of course he hadn't thought of staying. She could scarcely compete with Shirley as far as looks were concerned, and, anyway, Shirley was her friend and protégée.

Edward moved towards her, took her chin in his other hand and tipped it up towards him. 'Unless you'd like me to stay, of course.'

Virginia tried to look him in the eye, flooded suddenly with embarrassment and desire. She could scarcely ask him to stay. As if she was desperate for him.

He looked at her for a long time, and she felt herself blushing. Then he let go of both her hands and her chin, and began to unbutton her blouse gently. 'Tell me when you want me to stop.'

The words dried in her throat as she felt his fingers stroking her bare flesh, slipping the blouse off her shoulders and pushing a slender strap down. Virginia felt herself literally fall into his hands as he gently caressed one breast to a point. She sat there, turned to stone, willing his hand to move to the other breast and continue its delicious explorations.

He stopped.

She strained towards him, every nerve end tingling with anticipation. 'Don't stop,' she whispered.

He hesitated. 'Are you sure you want this?'

For a moment she was afraid that he really wasn't going to go on. The thought seemed intolerable. 'Yes,' she told him, getting up to slip her remaining clothes off. She pushed all thoughts of Simon, Oliver and Agnes away. This was like time out. A piece of life completely separated from everything else. 'I want you.' She'd never said that to anyone. Not even Simon.

But she started to feel frightened as they folded their clothes and hung them on the backs of chairs, asking each other polite questions about the loo. If they could have moved seamlessly from the sofa to the bed, if clothes and toothbrushes didn't even exist, she could have held on to the feeling of abandonment, but this was a sudden burst of practicality and domesticity that quenched her passion as effectively as a cold shower. She worried about stretch marks and imperfections, about seeing his, about what madness it was to sleep with someone you worked for. And how betrayed Simon would feel. Most of all, she knew she didn't like sex, that she was awful at it. But Virginia Law was never bad at anything.

She lay between the cold sheets, clenching up inside, and trying to reclaim the warm liquid feeling

245

of a few moments ago. She knew she had gone too
far to turn round and refuse him now. It wouldn't be
polite. There was only one way forward. She gritted
her teeth. It was only sex. She didn't have to let it
change her life. She could put on an act. She often
did with Simon, and he'd never complained.

Edward slipped in beside her and pulled her to
him. She felt wooden in his arms.

He drew back. 'Come on, this isn't an operation,
you know.'

She was mortified that he had noticed.

'What do you mean?'

'I mean that blood sports aren't my line. We don't
have to go any further unless you really want
to.'

She tested her feelings like a dentist checking a
filling. Relief? Disappointment?

'Don't you want me?' Disappointment, then,
perhaps.

'Of course I bloody want you. But I'm not a rapist,
or a philanderer, whatever you might think.'

She didn't think he'd probably got the definition
of philanderer quite right but decided not to tackle
him about it now.

'I do want you. Really.' She didn't even sound
convincing to herself.

He sighed. 'Look, I don't sleep with anyone unless
I know it's something very special. You could call it
love.'

'Could you?' Virginia thought this was rich,
coming from a man who had a wife, a mistress and
now . . . well, what would she be? An encounter

246

perhaps? 'Anyway, what's love got to do with it? We were supposed to be having a good time.'

'You could have fooled me. And what does love have to do with it? Tell me what the word means to you.' Edward sounded genuinely curious.

Virginia thought for a moment. 'Well, it starts with your parents, doesn't it? Although heaven knows mine had a strange way of showing it. They always used to say, we only want the best for you.'

'The best schools, careers, husbands?' Edward made himself comfortable, drawing her into his arms.

Virginia nodded. 'Husband in the singular. They would be terribly shocked if I divorced. And so would I. But they were very keen on what was proper for a Stockbridge – that was my maiden name – and how we were better than everyone else.'

'Tell me what happened to Gin. Something frightened her, didn't it?

For a moment, Virginia wondered how he could possibly know. Then she hid her head in his bare chest. 'Please don't ask. I've never told anyone.'

'Look at me. I know I'm probably not the best person to lend money to, but I'm completely trustworthy otherwise. And I get the feeling that this is something you need to talk about with someone who's outside your life.'

Virginia's eyes filled with tears. 'You're not outside my life,' she managed to croak.

'No.' Edward stroked her gently, as if she were a favourite cat. 'But you can still trust me.'

Virginia didn't believe you could really trust anyone about certain things, but she had carried this particular secret too long. God, Clara was lucky to be married to a man you could really talk to. She sat up and wrapped the bedclothes around herself protectively.

'We had a gang. You know the way you do when you're fourteen. I went out with Dave, the butcher's son, who went to the local grammar. I met him through my friend, Sally, whose parents couldn't afford to send her away to a posh boarding school like mine. Not, I might add, that mine could afford it. My father was a JP and my mother a school governor, and they sat on church committees, and we lived in a big, freezing house, so we were gentry. But I was never allowed anything new. My parents told me that materialism was common, and it was more genteel to have an old tennis racket and turn your sheets.'

'Turn your sheets?'

'You know, cutting worn sheets in half and sewing them back together again, so the outside becomes the middle. Your mother must have done it.'

'We were too poor to have sheets.' Edward was teasing.

'Don't be absurd,' snapped Virginia. 'We're not having a competition on who had the most deprived childhood.'

'Go on.' Edward kissed the palm of her hand.

'Anyway, I knew they'd disapprove of Dave without even asking them. They'd want to know who his "people" were and what they did, and they'd have been shocked to find out. It made him even more . . . well, exciting, I suppose. And he was the one everyone wanted. Leader of the pack and all that.' He had been Heathcliffe, Romeo and the boy next door all rolled into one, with dark, chiselled good looks and a muscular body that had Sally and her friends tittering every time his name was mentioned. Virginia had been thrilled to be chosen as his girl, although she knew she could never take him home.

Dave had discovered a derelict house nearby, a Victorian monstrosity which reminded Virginia of Brixton Prison. Made of red brick, it sat squatly at the end of a short, but pretentious drive, now overgrown with rhododendrons and brambles.

'Dave broke a back window, and we used to climb in, with Sally and Pete, Dave's mate. For a few weeks it was like our own home – we used to take candles and torches, bottles of cider and sandwiches, and talk and talk.' She remembered the strips of wallpaper hanging off the walls, great faded cabbage roses wilting in the damp. They had trodden carefully to avoid the missing boards, and once, when Dave leant on what looked like a marble mantelpiece, it turned out to be made of rotting plaster and a chunk had dropped off. They scratched their names in the wooden window sill, linked by a heart.

'And, of course . . .' She was coming to the difficult bit.

'Sounds like a great place for snogging.'

Virginia laughed. 'I haven't heard that word for ages. Not since then.' She was serious again.

'Because, of course, when you're both fifteen, it's all about snogging.'

'And How Far Can You Go. That was what we boys always wanted to know.'

Virginia wondered if Edward was deliberately making things easier for her. He had a great talent for listening. She remembered talking about it with Shirley once, who had said that Edward was one of those people who always made you feel as if you were being very witty, 'as opposed to those people who make you feel much stupider than you really are'. They had both giggled.

'We did go a bit further each time. You know.' She was sure Edward did know the progress of adolescent fumblings all too well. Hand on the breast. Hand under the bra. Bra off. That could take weeks. Then below the waist.

'You get to the stage when things come off. Sally and Pete were doing the same in another room.'

'Knickers and knockers, we called it.'

Virginia nodded, remembering the unbearable excitement. And the discomfort. Using their folded coats as pillows. The hard boards against their elbows and hips. The muffled giggles from Sally and Pete next door. 'Here – ' Dave had guided her hand ' – pull it gently.' That had made her arm ache, but was part of a whole payback of sensation. She had always believed that they could never, never, go All The Way. She wasn't That Kind Of Girl, so there had been a leisurely enjoyment about this exploration that had never been repeated since.

'We'd gone further than we'd ever done one night.

We, well, we, you know what I mean.' She twisted the stiff hotel bedspread round in her fingers, working it so hard that her knuckles went white. 'Then suddenly an incredibly powerful torch was shining down on us. They could see everything. Two policemen. I think they might have been watching for some time.' She remembered the panic-stricken scrabble for her knickers and tights. The awful fumbling to get dressed as they watched. One in disgust, the other, even worse, clearly excited.

'I never spoke to Dave again. I wouldn't. He used to hang around waiting for me. Because you see, it was a bit more than necking.' She swallowed nervously. 'It was enough to get me pregnant. That was how I lost my virginity.' She remembered the combination of terror and shame, wiping out the sweeter sensations, the sharp, stabbing pain washed over with pleasure. And guilt. She had tried to wash it all away from between her legs, but had felt the slippery wetness for days afterwards, marking her out as different, tarnished. She shivered and pulled the sheet around her to protect her.

'The nightmare went on and on. When I started to feel sick and heavy, I didn't know where to turn. Dave was going out with Sally by then and I'd dropped them both. They thought I was a stuck-up bitch. Which I was, I suppose.'

She had gone to a clinic in London that advertised on the tube, and had been met by professional, uninterested eyes. A feeling that she was distasteful to the people who were prodding her so intimately. It was officialdom, dealing with her efficiently, but without mercy, leaving her suddenly empty and alone.

She leant back on the bed, her body uncoiling as the tension unfolded. 'After that I concentrated on work. Got into Cambridge. Stayed away from boys. Was terrified of seeing my name every time my father opened the local paper.'

Edward traced a hand around her collarbone and down the fragile breastbone. 'And Cambridge?'

'I had boyfriends there. You sort of had to.' There. An admission of guilt. Now he'd know that she didn't really like sex.

Edward was sympathetic but scarcely horrified.

'The fuzz give you a hard time when they catch you young to frighten you into staying straight.' He thought for a moment. 'Not that it always works.' He leant back and stared up at the ceiling.

'I got caught shoplifting when I was fourteen. First the shop. Then the police. They took me to my headmaster. Then my Dad, who walloped me. I remember thinking it was a mug's game.'

'Shoplifting?'

'No, getting caught. Well, perhaps shoplifting too. You only do it for the kicks. I was trying to filch an LP I already had.'

'Aren't you afraid of people finding out?'

'Not really. Everyone's got something to hide on their tax return.'

'I haven't.' Virginia was indignant. 'And I hope you're not doing anything illegal while I'm working for *Heart & Soul*.' Even as she said it, she realized that she too was thinking more about being caught than doing wrong. And she had always thought herself to be so honest.

'What about Clara?' This was a bid to change the subject, but it came out like another accusation.

Edward leant back against the wrought-iron head-board. 'What about Simon?'

'He's my best friend. Definitely. I knew he was the one for me the first time I saw him.' Then she added, pushing disloyal thoughts away, 'It's been a very good marriage. A real partnership.'

She had seen him at a party, in the kitchen, where the action always was, leaning against some cheap Formica surface, laughing down at a girl. He shone with health and good living, with faint sun-induced crinkles around his grey-blue eyes, although he only appeared to be in his early twenties. He was wearing a short-sleeved sports shirt and a pair of jeans – it was a bring-a-bottle barbecue in high summer – and she could see the blond hairs on his sturdy forearms. She had set about the business of making Simon Law notice her, invite her out, fall in love with her and marry her, with the same drive and efficiency that she had done everything else. It had been one of the most enjoyable and satisfying things she had ever done, and she had never regretted a moment of it.

She looked back at Edward, noting idly that the clock already said 2.30 a.m. She would feel terrible in the morning.

'I think, perhaps, we shouldn't be doing this. I've never cheated on Simon before.'

'No, we shouldn't.' She was surprised he had agreed so easily.

'But we're going to.'

It was a statement of fact. Virginia relaxed. It was inevitable. The warmth flared up in her again as he rested on one elbow and moved his hands smoothly down her body. She explored him with her fingers, feeling her way around the unfamiliar bones and muscles, marvelling at each sensitive spot. When they finally stopped tantalizing and teasing each other, and he moved his weight on to hers, it felt both terribly right and utterly wanton. Virginia sighed in satisfaction. She didn't have to act any more. It was a revelation.

'Do you think we could manage that again tonight?' she asked him, laughing.

'I am a middle-aged man,' he replied, quite seriously, kissing her on the nose. 'We'll have to wait at least half-an-hour.'

In the morning, she got dressed very slowly, feeling Edward grow further and further away from her with each layer that went on. As soon as she buttoned up her shirt, she felt like Virginia Law again. Then the well-cut wool jacket doused her passion like a fire-blanket, until she stood there, fully dressed, looking at Edward, who was still in bed.

'I'm sorry.'

'What for?'

'This mustn't happen again.' She wished she didn't sound quite so like a Sunday school teacher discovering a broken window. She tried to soften it. 'I hope this won't, you know, change our friendship.'

Edward laughed. 'I've stayed friends with every woman I've ever slept with.'

Virginia was stung. 'You must have a lot of friends.'

'Very few. I keep telling you.'

She suddenly felt extremely fond of him. 'Let's be proper friends. You and Clara. Me and Simon.'

Edward laughed again. 'If you like. But I may not be Simon's type.' He swung out of bed and headed towards the shower.

'Oh, everyone's Simon's type,' she shouted over the rushing water. 'He's incredibly easygoing.'

'Thank you for that vote of confidence in me.' Edward emerged, towelling vigorously. She went over to him to give him one last hug.

'No, really. Thank you for last night. Come to supper soon. With Clara.'

He smiled at her. 'Better leave separately. In case some White Goods men spot us.'

'It's really time we did some entertaining. And we must introduce Shirley to someone eligible. Someone who'll make her forget Edward.' Virginia longed to see Edward again out of the working environment, and she needed an excuse for a dinner party. It had been three weeks since Birmingham and although there seemed to be a warmth and gentleness between them that hadn't existed before, Edward had made disappointingly little effort to be alone with her. But she had laid down the rules, she reminded herself.

Virginia and Simon were working their way through the Sunday papers – all the broadsheets, plus the *Mail on Sunday* and the *Sunday Express*, snipping items that were of interest, and filing them away methodically.

Simon looked up. 'Shirley's quite capable of looking after herself. I'm sure people have been trying to prise her away from Edward for years.'

Virginia thought for a while. Shirley, in her opinion, was just about ready to try her new personality on a romantic challenge.

'Well, she's very capable in most ways, but hopeless about men. She's been freeze-dried by her affair with Edward. It's completely fossilized her dating skills.'

'Hmm.' Simon was only mildly interested in people's dating skills.

'And Colin Dearest is free again. He's a nice man.'

'Quite a nice man. But being his fourth wife might not have much more of a long-term future than being Edward's mistress.'

'Oh, I don't know. Better payoff, I suspect. And she might get a few kids out of it. What about a week on Friday?'

'God, women are cynical.' Simon consulted his Psion organizer. 'You'll never get Colin Dearest at that short notice. But it's OK by me.'

'We could have Edward and Clara Wheeler, too.'

Simon closed the Psion with a detectable click. 'I thought you were trying to get Shirley *away* from Edward. Why have you suddenly decided to have the dinner party from hell?'

Virginia sighed. 'We ought to have the Wheelers at some point anyway – we owe them. And this will give him a chance to cosy up to Dearest Cosmetics.

Shirley is far too sensitive and insecure for us to have the Wheelers *without* her. She'd think I was taking sides. So we might as well have them all together.' This was true, and she'd often talked about Shirley's lack of confidence with Simon. 'Clara will be there,' she added, 'which should keep him in line. And Clara and Shirley work together perfectly well.' Virginia had been determined to ignore any tensions and had largely succeeded. She hoped that Simon didn't realize that showing off to Edward, demonstrating her perfect lifestyle to him, was the main point of this dinner. She thought she'd done a good job of disguising her motives, even if it was likely to lead to a slightly tricky evening.

'Well, if you're going to go ahead – and my advice to you is don't – then for goodness sake, have some other people too. Let's go for a full table, and I'll have Clara Wheeler down my end where she can't see what's going on.'

'You are kind.' Virginia meant it. Of all the men she knew, only Simon would be worrying about the feelings of a woman he had hardly met.

Simon was flicking through his Psion again. 'Mmm, we owe the Curtises. And the Elliotts can be trusted to behave.' Virginia knew this was a dig at her media friends, who Simon had often said treated anyone who was not in the same line of work appallingly. The men were quite capable of sitting at a table like regal cuckoos, waiting to be fed conversational titbits by lesser folk, and the woman shrieked insider gossip over everyone's heads. Or so Simon alleged. Virginia retorted that banking, too, had its share of self-important men, to which he had replied that at least their wives had the grace to grit their teeth and look pleasantly interested in whoever was talking. In the past, the combination of bankers and journalists had frequently proved a sticky one, but Virginia decided not to argue with Simon. She wanted to have Edward to dinner and see what he was like out of his own territory. Whenever she had a quiet moment, she lingered on the feel and smell of his body, and the delicious things he could do with it. She replayed the moment he had unbuttoned her shirt over and over in her mind.

'What's she really like anyway?' Simon had scribbled a few more names on a sheet of paper.

'Who?' Virginia snapped out of her dream.

'Clara. There you are, my suggestions for this daft dinner party.'

'Oh, you know, menopausal empty nester, doesn't know what to do with herself now the kids have left home, thinks any husband is better than none at all.'

'That's not very sisterly.'

Virginia felt ashamed when she saw the surprise on Simon's face. After all, hadn't she commissioned hundreds of articles about the energizing liberation of the time children left home, or features promising to show empty nesters how they could change their lives by September and become company directors or aromatherapists? Positively managing change was the phrase, she remembered. And she'd felt positive about it all herself, really looked forward to it, when she'd commissioned the articles. She wondered why she'd changed.

'You're right. She's OK really. Just very difficult to get through to. There's a wall up somewhere. She's the sort of woman who's completely confident at bossing builders and waiters around, but freezes up and gabbles when there's someone intelligent about.'

'Well, I'm not surprised. It can't be much fun having to share your husband.'

'Oh, she doesn't know about that,' said Virginia airily, not quite believing it herself.

Virginia had been half-hoping that Colin Dearest would scotch the whole scheme by not being able to come, but he was at a loose end. The third Mrs Dearest had managed to retain their country 'cottage' – a six-bedroom mansion swathed in Colefax & Fowler chintz – as part of the divorce deal, temporarily leaving him with nowhere to retreat to on a Friday night. Then Clara accepted the invitation with such genuine enthusiasm that Virginia's heart turned over with guilt.

Shirley originally refused to come on the grounds that she wouldn't know how to behave. 'I've never been to a posh dinner party. Not like in the advertise-ments, with liqueurs and After Eights.'

'Never?' Virginia found it difficult to imagine what people did with themselves in the evening if they didn't go to dinner parties. 'What do you usually do then?'

'Well, Edward and I eat in, or out.' Shirley paused. 'And there's my aerobics class twice a week.' No wonder Shirley had such a wonderful body, reflected

Virginia. 'Sometimes I see a girl-friend. Or Harry.' She didn't think Virginia would approve of her going down the clubs on a Friday night. She sensed a distaste for easy sex that might change Virginia's opinion of her were she to know what Shirley really got up to sometimes. And, in fact, with the new job, she'd had very little time for solitary clubbing. Recently Shirley either went out to press functions or worked in the office until 10 p.m. She simply didn't seem to have a private life.

All the other invitees had, surprisingly, been able to come too, so they would be seating twelve, around the pale English elm table that Virginia had commissioned from a fashionable cabinetmaker, with three leaves in it so that it could expand from a family table for six to a grand dining table. The seating plan caused her several uneasy moments – Colin Dearest would have to sit next to Shirley, but Shirley couldn't be near Edward or Clara, who, of course, had to be kept away from each other. Eventually, using the Curtises, the Elliotts and a husband-and-wife solicitor team, the Ponsonbys – who were reputed to earn around £10,000 a morning for just going into court and saying 'no' – as discreet padding, the whole thing was arranged to her satisfaction. She looked forward to showing off her superb organizational abilities, glamorous lifestyle and, perhaps, even a tantalizing glimpse of bare skin to Edward.

For she had been shopping earlier that week with Shirley, who had begged for her advice on dinner party dressing. For the first time, Virginia found herself analysing what one wore for a dinner party and why. It was a bit like trying to explain some obscure English custom to a foreigner.

'Sexy?' asked Shirley.

'Well, sexier than for lunch. But you don't want to go too far.'

'Smart?'

'Mmm. Quite smart. But not Ascot hats and tailored suits.'

Shirley pulled a clinging velvet black dress with tiny straps off a rail. 'This?'

Virginia quailed. The velvet caressed Shirley's magnificent body like a wave. Colin Dearest would be transfixed. So, unfortunately, would Edward, Simon, David Curtis and Hugh Elliott. Charles Ponsonby might even switch off his mobile phone. The thought was too tempting to resist. 'Go for it. But keep everything else understated. Just tiny diamonds in your ears, and a diamond at your throat.'

'Diamonds?'

'Oh, get them in paste from Butler & Wilson.' Virginia urgently needed to find something equally sensational for herself. Her wardrobe was full of suits and little black dresses, divinely cut, of course, but nothing remotely surprising and daring. She could do with a touch of Shirley's tartiness to liven things up.

They'd trailed fruitlessly up and down Sloane Street and finished up at Harrods, where, to her surprise, Shirley had found a tiny, shimmery silver dress, hardly more than a wisp on the hanger. It slipped over Virginia like a second skin. She had never worn anything quite so revealing, but when she looked at herself in the mirror, the years fell away and she saw Gin again. Dangerous, difficult Gin. Quickly she pushed the bad memories away. She couldn't stay buttoned up inside beautifully correct suits for ever.

But she felt uneasy about what lay ahead, as she tried out several different pairs of earrings. Too chunky? Yes. Too obvious? Probably. She settled on a discreet platinum design, hardly more than a pair of silver raindrops.

Simon was amazed. 'Darling!'

She moved away, embarrassed. The dress might as well have 'I am planning to commit adultery (again)' written all over it. She hated wearing sexy clothes. It made her feel . . . at the very least it was awkward appearing as someone different to her own husband.

'I just thought it might be nice to have a change.' She made a great effort to work on her lipstick, applying it with a brush, powdering, then blotting. It gave her the chance to watch Simon in the mirror.

'Wow!' He was obviously going to leave it at that. She saw him walk across the room, his body as lean and chiselled as it had been eighteen years ago. Just a little more spare and defined, perhaps, the way fit men age, bone and muscle worked together almost architecturally, with no softness to spare. If you merely compared photographs, Virginia could see that Simon was far, far more attractive than Edward. But, in the flesh, he didn't have the same kind of dynamic energy and raw, sexual vitality. Simon was very able. And intelligent, she reminded herself.

His wardrobe was open, with neat piles of folded shirts and jumpers, all in subtle powdery male colours on display. When she first met Simon she had thought he was very rich because his clothes were so beautifully soft and worn, faded preppy polo shirts and sleek suits with the unmistakable stamp of good tailoring about them. He was polished, like a piece of fine antique furniture, glowing with privilege and the patina of wealth. She had later discovered that his family were no wealthier than her own, impoverished army with pretentions to grandeur, just a very distant duke dredged up by his pushy mother on every possible occasion. But Simon had always chosen his clothes with care, like a connoisseur, and looked after them as if they were precious.

The doorbell rang.

'Don't worry. Cindy will answer it.' Cooking was not Virginia's strong point, and she wouldn't have dared expose her weakness by cooking her own food at dinner parties. A culinary disaster would not fit the image. One reason why Simon had to check all their bank statements very carefully, with a furrow of concern on his face, was that they spent every penny of their two substantial salaries. Nannies, cars, holidays, school fees, restaurants, and entertaining swallowed up hundreds, or even thousands, of pounds at the stroke of a pen. They both agreed that the point of parties was to get to know other people better, especially useful people, whereas there was no point in getting to know any more about the limits of one's exhaustion. So having a dinner party meant ringing Lorna Wing or The Admirable Crichton and choosing a menu. It would then appear in all its deliciousness and be magicked round the room by almost invisible hands. And a fairy godmother cleared up the kitchen afterwards.

Clara was the first to arrive. Without Edward. Virginia was hardly surprised. She looked hot and trussed up in an emerald green suit with a fussy blouse underneath. Her efforts at dressing the part of a career woman were still a disaster, in spite of Virginia's occasional hints: she still favoured boxy, bulky suits in traffic-light colours and blouses with pussycat bows at the neck. Virginia itched to sort her out properly, but somehow there had never been quite the time.

'What a lovely house.' She sounded genuine, looking round at the white walls, white sofas and bare varnished boards, punctuated with the odd piece of colourful modern art that Simon bought so cleverly at auction. 'But don't you find all this white hard to keep clean?'

Virginia was perplexed. The cleaning lady, Sonia, did all that. 'I think it's all washable,' she said vaguely.

Clara placed her glass of champagne gingerly on the Indian thakat coffee table, its rich weathered wood covered in intricate carvings. 'This is nice. Do you have a coaster?'

'A what? Oh, I see . . . no, don't worry about rings. Cindy or Sonia will sort them out in the morning.' Virginia wished someone else would arrive. She felt like a stranger to herself – a glittering being who bore no relationship to the friendly, professional Virginia she, and everyone else, knew so well.

'I love your dress.'

'Oh, thank you.'

Clara fiddled with some terracotta bowls laid out on the table, filled with olives. 'How pretty.'

'They're raku-fired. Quite a find.'

Clara nodded, knowledgeably, she hoped. The vocabulary of interior design required almost daily study if you wanted to stay ahead, she had discovered. No sooner had one learnt to chat knowledgeably about goblet pleats versus tab headings in the world of curtains than the whole lot got swept away and replaced with a simple roller blind, and you were suddenly required to know all about raku-firing.

'Um, where's your . . .?' Clara thought that going to the loo would fill in the time. And she had been sent with strict instructions from Harry to check out Virginia's downstairs WC. She'd better do it before she got too drunk. Harry had explained the principles of loo style to her. 'In Virginia's circle you're nobody until there's been a cartoon about you in a newspaper. And the downstairs loo is where you hang it. Same for awards, photographs with really top film stars, prime ministers and pictures of dogs from The Rescue Home. You can tell a lot about who people think they are, or want to be, from their downstairs loos.' Clara had gazed at him open-mouthed, thinking of her framed Kipling's 'If' and a small tapestry that Eliza had done 'for Mummy'. And two really revolting china plates that had been sent by aged great-aunts, which she hadn't the heart to hide in the attic.

'Lots of people dress up in uniforms they're not entitled to and have black and white pictures done for the downstairs loo,' continued Harry. 'I'm fairly sure I've even seen an old school line-up which had been doctored to include someone who certainly didn't go to Eton. But it's the perfect place for discreet showing off – because no one can say you're being pretentious, but everybody's got to go in there at some point. And there's plenty of time when they're there to read the walls. It's today's equivalent of the family cuttings book. And anything that seems out of place with the rest of the house belonged to the husband before they got married – that's where wives always relegate boating trophies and paintings they hate. You'll get the hang of it all once you've worked out the principle,' he added, with a grand sweep of his hand.

Virginia's loo had *two* framed cartoons of her from national newspapers, a photograph of herself and Simon with the Prime Minister (and several more of them with vaguely familiar-looking people), one of Oliver's nursery school paintings, framed under glass ('Very caring, I'm sure,' Harry muttered later) and a whole wall of awards. Definitely a power lavatory. Clara spent as long in there as she could, wishing she hadn't chosen that particular shade of green for her suit, and thumbing through books that had been signed 'To dearest Virginia, always such an inspiration', and other variations on the theme, from several authors. There was a burst of conversation from the hall, and she emerged again, plumping down on the massive white sofa just as two couples arrived, with coo-ing cries of ecstasy at the flowers, the room and Virgina's outfit. Two giant creamy candles, the size and shape of beer barrels and each fluttering half-a-dozen wicks, were pronounced particularly clever. Not so much clever as expensive, commented Clara inwardly. She had seen the candles last month in *House & Garden* and knew they cost £700 each.

The Elliotts and the Curtises had arrived together, having shared a taxi from Wandsworth.

' ... now worth over six hundred thousand pounds,' she heard David Curtis say to Hugh Elliott.

' ... exams for Colet Court.' Gail Elliott to Susan Curtis.

On to property prices and schools already. Clara abandoned any hope of inserting a wedge in this conversation. The dark green olives in the raku-fired bowls gleamed fatly on the table in front of her. She tried a nibble. Very good. Stuffed with anchovies and chillis, and, even, possibly, an almond. She had no idea you could get so much into a single olive. She found herself reaching out for another, and then one more. They heaved and bubbled in her empty stomach. A mistake. She swigged back another mouthful of champagne in the hope that it would settle them. It didn't.

Virginia was wondering whether Edward would be hopelessly outclassed in this atmosphere. He was such a rough diamond. Clara looked terribly out of place and wasn't talking to anyone. Perhaps this had all been a bad idea after all.

The doorbell rang again, and Shirley appeared, looking like a goddess with her swanlike neck and sculpturally close boyish crop setting off the soft black velvet curves. The hall rang with her bubbling laugh, and that slight twang that sounded almost mid-Atlantic when you heard it first time, but probably owed more to her attempts to cover up her East London origins. There was a touch of sparkle at her throat. Virginia wondered if Edward had bought something for her at Tiffany's. David Curtis and Hugh Elliott stopped talking, and looked as if they wanted to touch her. Susan Curtis and Gail Elliott, both wearing silk blouses with pie-crust frill necks and pearls, their neat bottoms tightly encased in short taffeta silk skirts (one red tartan, one royal blue), looked momentarily affronted, but quickly sellotaped pleasant smiles to their faces.

Too soon afterwards, the bell rang again and Edward was there. Clara could hear him joking in the hall with Cindy as she took his coat. The colour crept up her neck in blotches. Virginia dared not look at Simon. The expression on his face would be 'I told you so'.

Edward entered the room like a lion at a vicarage tea party. He was wearing one of the expensively tailored suits that Clara, Shirley and Virginia had all separately insisted he have made, but he already almost seemed to be too big for it in some indefinable way. Everyone was instantly aware of him, watchful, cautious; women glancing at themselves furtively in the mirror, men flicking invisible dust off the arms of their jackets, and straightening their ties.

Yes, thought Virginia. He is someone. She had wanted to subject him to the greatest test of personality she knew – to take it out of context, and see if it withered. But Edward, in her own home environment, exposed to all the ridicule her smart friends could muster, was still Edward. He could so easily have come across as brash and cheap in these expensive, sophisticated surroundings. Instead he dominated the room, changed it, made others assess themselves more carefully.

'Darling.' Virginia saw Clara stumble over the thakat table in her eagerness to stake her claim to him. 'You're late.' He gave a her a cursory peck, his eyes on Virginia.

'Traffic was terrible.' Shirley turned ostentatiously away. Virginia felt a spurt of anger.

There was something feral about the way Edward moved round the room, as she introduced him. But when she left him with Gail and Susan, she could see them begin to sparkle in response, finding themselves unexpectedly witty. She sighed in relief. Edward would, after all, make the evening all right, and, as the hostess, she had the right to claim him for herself during dinner.

The Ponsonbys, of course, were even later, because Charles was wrapped up in some takeover deal, and Sarah Ponsonby was acting for the other side (apparently she earned twice as much as he did, which caused a great deal of friction).

'Darling.' Sarah touched Virginia's cheek with

hers. It felt soft and powdery, and there was a waft of expensively air-conditioned office around her, reminding Virginia of soap in British Airways' First Class.

'Virginia, my dear. How splendid you look.' Charles's stilted courtesy probably meant they had been arguing in the car.

Colin Dearest was the last to arrive, carrying a vast bouquet of flowers, which was borne away by Cindy, to reappear again five minutes later in a metal vase.

'Darling!' They exchanged a kiss on each cheek, three times.

'Let me look at you! Divine!'

'How heavenly to see you!' Virginia always found Colin very cosy, and was surprised he had managed to work his way through so many wives. She introduced him to Gail and Susan.

'Virginia has been so kind to me, inviting me here tonight. I'm between wives, you see,' he said in confiding tones. 'Or perhaps not,' he added, catching sight of Shirley.

Susan and Gail scuttled back to the relative safety of their husbands, partly, Virginia suspected, to block their view of the curve of Shirley's bare back.

Clara looked as if she was stranded with Sarah Ponsonby, who was being distantly condescending.

'A secretary. How interesting,' Virginia heard her say. Clara ploughed bravely on with an amusing story about Wiggins Frean.

'How frightfully funny,' said Sarah, looking over her glass for rescue.

'*The Times* is far too much of a tabloid these days, and as for the *FT*, well, its views are probably right half the time, but the trouble is you don't know which half.' Charles was treating Simon to a rundown on the British press. 'And does anyone read any of the others any longer?' He obviously didn't count several million people, thought Virginia. Thank goodness she hadn't had any of her mainstream media friends here, or he would have spent the evening telling them where they were going wrong.

Virginia enjoyed the conversation her end of the table so much, flanked by Edward, who was being dangerously funny, and Colin, who was alternately camping it up and flattering both Shirley and Virginia simultaneously, that she felt rather guilty about the carnage that might be taking place at Simon's end. On her way back from the loo, she overheard snatches that did not bode well. They were about the Royal Family, always a sign of desperation. She overheard Simon moving on to the more select rumour that Queen Victoria was illegitimate.

'Porphyria disappeared completely, and haemophilia popped up from nowhere. They're both genetic diseases,' Simon was saying.

The Ponsonbys had clearly accepted the invitation with the express intention of finding a safe environment for a row – Virginia, as an experienced hostess, was well used to the syndrome of the couple whose marriage is so rocky that they dare not argue at home and have to do it with the protective presence of other people, but it never made it any pleasanter for the onlookers.

'I told you several times,' Sarah was shouting across the table. 'You just never bother to listen.' And David Curtis, whose insecurities had been stirred up, either by Edward's leonine presence or Charles Ponsonby's scorn, was name-dropping frantically, and bringing his stories of his childhood – which had been quite grand, but not quite as grand as he made out – into the conversation whenever possible.

'These days, the role of under-nanny has completely disappeared,' he was telling Clara. 'We always had one at Clusters, of course. The last one married a Texan millionaire in the end.' Gail Elliott could scarcely contain her yawns.

At the middle of the table, in a pocket which contained neither Edward, Clara, nor Shirley, they were talking about unusual marital relationships: 'My uncle's mistress lived in the top-floor flat of the house he shared with my aunt. They were all frightfully good friends.' Virginia frowned discreetly at the speaker. She knew what had brought that conversation on, having dined out several times herself on the unusual threesome at Wiggins Frean. People always came up with other examples of three-way relationships, and it made her feel rather giddy. And she certainly didn't want either Clara or Shirley to overhear this one. If there was going to be a showdown, it wasn't going to be at one of her dinner parties.

She settled back down as Colin leapt up to tuck her seat in and Edward refilled her glass. A gust of laughter blew up the table, and she saw Shirley look up sharply to see what she was missing. Clara's last words were lost in a roar of laughter from Simon. Perhaps things weren't quite so sticky down there after all.

Simon was still smiling as he sank back into the sofa after the front door had closed for the last time at 1.30 a.m. He put an arm out and drew Virginia to him.

'Well done, darling. Another beautifully executed dinner party. I don't know why I ever doubted you. Have a last snifter.'

Virginia was shocked. He hardly ever drank port.

'Nice woman.'

'Who?' (Surely not Sarah Ponsonby?)

'Clara Wheeler. She really rescued our end of the table. I'd forgotten how bloody pompous both the Ponsonbys are, but she even managed to get a joke out of him. And did you know about his charity work? I'd no idea that he not only funds a major enterprise for rehabilitating disturbed youngsters, but actually works with them himself for two weeks a year. Clara wheedled it all out of him.'

Virginia's better nature tried to suppress a spurt of irritation and failed. 'She dresses so badly though.'

'Does she?' Simon was humming happily. 'I hadn't noticed. Oh well, clothes aren't everything.'

Perhaps not quite everything, thought Virginia crossly, but they counted for quite a lot.

'You looked wonderful, darling.' He drained the last of the drink. 'And so did Shirley. Your plan to throw her into the arms of Colin Dearest is well on its way.'

Isn't that curious? thought Virginia. If sides are to be taken (and they are not, her better nature interjected firmly before being swamped again), then Simon is on Clara's. And I – well, I am on Shirley's.

It was a tiny crack in their marriage. Hardly even a disagreement, let alone a row. But it worried her. She went upstairs quickly and was already in bed, pretending to be asleep when he opened the door.

Shirley knew that tonight had been a triumph. Colin, now one of London's most eligible single men, had taken her home from a dinner party and solemnly written her telephone number in a small leather note-pad he kept in his breast pocket. She liked the look of him – neat, tanned, and suave, dressed in a navy blue blazer and expensive Jermyn Street loafers, with the subtle fragrance of Dearest for Men wafting its citrus and sandalwood aroma at her. Squeaky clean and tall enough for her. Just. She had passed the social test that Virginia had set her – she knew that was what it was – with flying colours. And she had looked, she knew, better than she had ever looked in her life. Clara had been a boring old frump as usual.

She had begged Edward to give her a lift to the party. 'We won't go in together of course,' she reassured him. 'But I've never really been to a dinner party like that. I'd be dead nervous on my own.' She crossed her fingers under the desk, hoping that Edward wouldn't remember that she had nerves of steel. But it was true, well, a bit. Just because she could tackle terrifying managing directors with an insouciance that had them almost slavering over her, that didn't mean she could face them over dinner when policed by their hatchet-faced wives.

Edward had sighed. 'I ought not to.' This was as good as a yes.

He'd arrived ten minutes early. Expecting sex, thought Shirley. She was going to surprise him.

'Like it?' She twirled in front of him, slipping one of the tiny straps down to tantalize him, before shrugging herself into her coat. 'Let's go, then.'

'We shouldn't arrive too early.' He moved towards her, but she dodged away.

'We're not too early. Virginia said eight for eight-thirty. And the traffic's always bad at this time of night.'

It wasn't, and they sped up to the elegant Islington square, finding a parking space just round the corner from the house, almost totally overhung with a dusty plane tree. Perfect. As Edward turned off the ignition, she ran a finger down his sleeve.

'Fancy a bit?' He had not been pleased to be rejected in the flat, she could tell.

She had really shocked him now. But he wouldn't have looked round like that if he hadn't been intrigued.

'We couldn't possibly. This is a public street.'

'It's quite a private public street.' She dropped her head down on to his lap, and he tried to tug her back up again. Not for long, though.

'Pretend you're reading the paper.' It came out as

a mumble. The *FT* rustled above her. It was all very uncomfortable, but Edward wasn't to know that. He was, she could tell, hopelessly excited. She felt, well, a sense of victory. Clara could be walking past them down the street at this very moment. She had gone to Charles Worthington's to have her hair done, so she'd be coming by tube. She could easily walk straight past the car. Or a policeman might come by and do them for indecent behaviour. That would really blow the whole thing wide open.

Neither Clara nor the police obliged.

'God, that was good.' Edward looked at her reflectively. 'You're still full of surprises, aren't you? After ten years.'

'I'll be full of surprises in another ten.' It was the first time she had ever dared refer to the future.

She couldn't read his face. She opened the glove compartment to give herself somewhere to rest her bag and busied herself emptying it. 'I must fix my lipstick.' She risked a glance. 'Don't look.'

'Why not?'

'Because it's private.' Edward snorted, but got out of the car to zip up his flies.

Shirley allowed the lipstick to roll into the glove compartment and quickly hid it behind the *A–Z*. Pity it couldn't have been a tiny pair of black lacy knickers, but less was more, she told herself, and, in any case, Edward would suspect deliberate sabotage. She suspected that Clara *had* discovered a pair of her knickers once, in the early days – a genuine accident – and Shirley had been furious, because it had been a very ordinary stretchy pair of white cotton ones from Marks & Sparks, slightly grey from a disastrous wash.

She shut the glove compartment with a satisfied click. The lipstick would lie there like a landmine until Clara discovered it.

Clara sank gratefully into the passenger seat of Edward's Jag, as they bowled through the empty early morning streets towards Surrey. She was about to suggest that they buy a little flat in London for these occasions, when she remembered, with a stab of bitterness, that he had, in fact, recently bought such a flat. For Shirley.

'That was fun.' Surprisingly, it had been. Like quite a lot of things these days. The beginning had been simply awful, up until the point when Edward and Shirley virtually arrived together. Catching sight of herself in the giant mirror above one of the sofas, she had flinched. And she had seen the evening stiffening like a setting jelly as the Curtises and the Elliotts arrived – they obviously knew each other far too well. But she had complete faith in Edward to liven up dinner parties, however much he embarrassed her in the process. One big plus about being married to him, and possibly, now she thought about it, almost the only plus, was that he did make things fun. Seeing Colin Dearest flirt quite so openly with Shirley had been reviving, and so too had noticing that Edward really didn't seem to care. And when Colin had wrapped Shirley in her expensive coat and whisked her home, there hadn't been a moment's unease on either side.

'Virginia looked wonderful.'

'Mmm.' The fact that Shirley, too, had looked wonderful hovered in the air between them.

'She's married to an awfully nice man.' Simon had been utterly charming. She really felt she'd found a friend.

'I think we've taken the wrong turning. This drive is a real pain, isn't it? Perhaps we should buy a place in town.' Clara's heart leapt, as she unlocked the glove compartment to find the *A–Z. We.*

'Can we afford it?'

'Probably not at the moment. Things are a bit tricky. Don't worry, I don't need the map after all.'

She shut the glove compartment again with a snap. 'Oh?'

'*Heart & Soul.* The advertising. It's just not coming in.' Clara knew that advertising was the key to the magazine making money. Of course, it was important that women bought the magazine, and as far as she could tell from the newsagents' weekly reports they were. But without chunky, regular bookings from Britain's biggest advertising agencies, they were looking at a drain down which money would pour every month.

'Do you think . . .' Clara knew she had to tread cautiously, but she was getting increasingly worried about the atmosphere at Wiggins Frean ' . . . that perhaps Shirley still needs too much guidance to be a really effective sales director? Everyone thinks she's a bit too dependent on Virginia.' There, she'd said it.

Edward was silent for a bit. If he was honest, the same idea had crossed his mind a few times, but he'd eventually rejected it as mere jealousy. He did feel slightly shut out by those two, but he had no right to ruin a good friendship for Shirley. She'd had few enough breaks. It had always been his intention to set up *Heart & Soul*, and slowly get less involved as time went on. That was how he worked, moving from project to project. The fact that Virginia and Shirley worked as a good tight team – and Virginia couldn't be a better mentor – meant that that time would come sooner rather than later.

'When you took this job . . .' he kept his voice even, determined not to trigger off a row ' . . . it was on two conditions. One, that you didn't try to undermine Shirley. If you're in a position to know what "everyone" thinks about her relationship with Virginia, you must have been talking about her behind her back. Which isn't fair.' Clara tried to interrupt, but he cut her off. 'Two, that you behave like a PA. One of the classic ways a company can go wrong is when the chairman's wife gets too much say in what goes on.' He looked at her, not unkindly. 'Do I make myself clear?'

She was only trying to help, she thought indignantly. He'd condemned her motives without even listening properly to what she'd said. 'Just because I *am* your wife, there's no reason simply to ignore everything I say. If someone else said it, you'd take more notice.' Edward tightened his grip on the steering wheel and pressed his foot slightly harder on the accelerator. If they hadn't been travelling at

80 mph, she'd have jumped straight out of the car and stormed off into the night.

Perhaps the friends who occasionally urged her to pitch Edward out were right. There wasn't much point in being married to someone who thought her only talent was shopping.

chapter 8

Defying the predictions of disaster that still emerged in the press from time to time – probably from disaffected former staff members of *Heart & Soul* – the June, July, August and September issues of the magazine came out, each selling 5–10,000 more copies than its predecessor. They were reaching the 200,000 mark, the minimum point at which most women's monthly magazines were likely to prove profitable. Of course, *Heart & Soul* wouldn't be expected to reach the dizzy heights of half a million copies immediately, but Virginia wished things could move a little faster. She knew she would probably be meeting Paul Long at a prestigious press lunch that day, and she'd like to see him just a little bit more concerned about the competition.

But the day started badly. Shirley – who had been going with her – discovered that she was double-booked and that the other lunch was a key meeting with the Dearest Cosmetics team. Virginia called

Clara and invited her instead, against Shirley's advice: 'She's going to feel like a fish out of water. It really isn't fair on her.'

For once Virginia was brisk. 'She'll just have to learn to swim. She's a grown-up now. I don't want a no-show against our name and it's too late to cancel.'

Their taxi fought its way through the solid, bakingly hot, fume-ridden September traffic to the Savoy Hotel. Virginia usually loved it when the sun continued to shine after August, but this particular Indian summer had triggered off a reminder from Simon that these precious years before the children went to full-time school could never be reclaimed, and that Oliver and Agnes should be spending more time with their mother outside.

She fidgeted impatiently as she and Clara waited on the stairs to be ticked off the guest list and fitted with a name badge. Then it turned out to be one of those pointless affairs where, even if you arrived half-an-hour late, you spent an hour in a barking, braying throng before the toastmaster banged on the gong to announce lunch. She got stuck with Elaine Cartwright, a rival editor, who insisted on talking about how many promotional dinners and lunches there were around at the moment, several of which Virginia was mortified to realize she hadn't been invited to. *Heart & Soul* obviously still wasn't on the A list. 'Don't you find it's absurdly hectic?'

Virginia agreed. 'Will I see you at Dearest's little dinner at The Bluebird on Tuesday?' This was a mischievous question, because the dinner was a private one given by Colin, to which Virginia and

Shirley had been invited as friends. But Elaine wasn't to know that, and would assume she'd been downgraded.

'I can't.' Elaine was unruffled. 'I'm on *Question Time*.' Virginia mentally kicked herself for falling into that one. The whole conversation had clearly been engineered so that Elaine could swank. Elaine chuntered on.

'It's going to be a terrible squeeze that evening, because we're invited to Number Ten beforehand for drinks.'

'Oh, you wouldn't want to miss that.' Virginia was gracious. 'The first few times one goes, one does find it such a special experience.'

Elaine bared her teeth in a brief smile. 'I do find it so very difficult to think of him as the Prime Minister. After all, we were at university together. I remember getting drunk with him in the Junior Common Room.'

Bet she didn't. She'd probably passed him once in the corridor. If, indeed, their time together had even coincided. Which Virginia doubted, knowing what a bullshitter Elaine was. But it was impressing the circle of people who had gathered round at the words '*Question Time*', and Virginia slipped away so she didn't have to hear Elaine playing any more games of one-upmanship. Why on earth should *she* be on *Question Time*? When Virginia had still been at *Viva*, it was Virginia the big programmes had approached. Her throat caught at the thought that she was slipping into the second league.

Everyone shuffled through a highly ornate double

door to a series of big round tables, liberally decorated with flowers in the colours of the company's logo. She was horrified to discover that she'd been seated next to Paul Long. Someone with a vicious sense of humour had obviously done the table plan. Or perhaps it was an industry ploy to discover if her departure from Publishing Unlimited had really been as amiable as both Wiggins Frean and Publishing Unlimited had made out.

He greeted her with an urbane smile, straightening his Guards tie, and shooting his elegant grey cuffs. He almost immediately locked into conversation with the person on his other side. She didn't have to worry about him until almost the end of the meal.

'Congratulations on your first half-year.' Paul was always courteous, but Virginia didn't like the glint in his blue eyes. He wasn't going to give her an easy ride. She didn't have to wait long. 'When do you think the advertising revenue will start to reflect your success at the news-stands?' She wondered if *Heart & Soul*'s dire financial position was common knowledge. There'd been a serious disappointment that morning. A big flooring company had booked a series of six double-page spreads, one in every issue from July to December. They had just cancelled it with immediate effect, pleading a sudden need to switch budgetary priorities. But Harry had heard that it had gone to *Viva* instead.

'We're already seeing some fantastic gains on the advertising side. A bumper month.' Professional exaggerations weren't exactly lies in Virgina's book. She decided to try a dig herself. 'It's clear that advertisers and readers are really looking for something . . . shall we say . . . a little bit different. That old formula of fashion, beauty and knitting patterns punctuated with royal stories is beginning to lose its popularity. Although, of course, *Viva* does it very well.' This was unfair, because *Viva*, of course, was better than that. But she did think that *Heart & Soul* was more original than *Viva*, and that it gave a slightly different slant to the same old subjects. Their first batch of reader research showed that people enjoyed the extra gossip the magazine offered them, along with the behind-the-scenes features on everything from how a suntan lotion was developed to who taught top actors to act. *The inside story – you can't afford to miss it* was now printed along the spine of the magazine, and it functioned as a motto for staff and readers alike.

'How interesting.' Paul seemed unconcerned. 'You've seen that *Viva*'s made some spectacular leaps. All helped by your excellent groundwork, I'm sure.'

I'm sure too, thought Virginia crossly. Publishing Unlimited had obviously been buying market share. Giveaways, publicity campaigns, all the money Paul had refused to spend when she was editor.

'And without any below-the-line spend. No special promotions or giveaways.' Paul wasn't taking any prisoners.

'None at all? That is an achievement.' Virginia's tone made it clear that she didn't believe him.

He did look faintly uneasy and switched his line of attack.

'I gather there's rather a, well, shall we say, interesting, situation at Wiggins Frean.'

'Is there?'

'So my spies tell me. It must be much more fun than Publishing Unlimited.'

Virginia went cold. Paul Long was well known for having eyes in the back of his head, but surely they couldn't see as far as Birmingham.

'Really?' She was playing for time.

'A very glamorous sales director, I understand.'

Shirley. 'Shirley's a very able salesperson.'

Paul grinned. 'Indeed. And there's a new twist. The boss's wife is now his secretary. Must be a bit close for comfort.'

'She's extremely good at her job. One of life's natural organizers.' Virginia was not going to let him make jokes about Wiggins Frean. 'Perhaps you'd like to meet her? I can assure you there's no one at Publishing Unlimited quite like her.'

As if summoned by a genie, Clara materialized at her elbow, laden down with carrier bags. 'Our taxi's outside apparently. Look, how kind – a full set of everything in my favourite scent. And I got you your goodie bag too.' She was pleased as a child at Christmas. Virginia winced.

'Clara, this is Paul Long, who's been dying to meet you.'

Paul stood up to shake her hand. Clara dropped one carrier bag and got tangled up in the other trying to respond, while Paul watched in amusement and Virginia in horror. Eventually the whole lot tumbled

286

to the floor, and Paul surprised Virginia by dropping to his knees to pick it up. So did Clara.

'Virginia! Darling!' It was Bill Grundy.

'Bill, how are you?' Eventually Bill had finished
mapping out how busy, busy, busy he was, and Clara
and Paul had finally extricated themselves, rather
surprisingly exchanging kisses and laughter.

Clara leant back in the taxi. 'That was fun.'

Fun? The woman was a sucker for punishment. It
had been a combination of the rush hour in Piccadilly
Underground Station and the most boring wedding
Virginia'd ever been to. 'I think I've been to rather
too many similar events,' she said. The taxi seemed
not to have moved an inch. The evening sun – it was
nearly four o'clock and more than half the day had
been wasted – glittered on hundreds of car wind-
screens. It was going to be a long journey back to
Hammersmith. She looked out of the windows at
endless glass-fronted offices, punctuated with red-
brick mansion blocks and the occasional row of
shops. Edward should be here, not Clara, she
thought, and something melted deep inside
her.

'How's Edward enjoying *Heart & Soul*?' She knew,
but she wanted a chance to talk about him. It wasn't
as if one could feel guilty about Clara, because she
didn't really have him anyway, except in name. It
had been nearly five months since Birmingham and
she and Edward were rarely alone together for long,
but when Virginia lay awake at night she thought
about his hands and his mouth and the warm weight
of his body. When she dressed in the morning, she

now chose her clothes for Edward's casual glance of approval. It was like a fever. He usually came into her office on his way in, to enjoy her coffee and a ten-minute chat about the day, and she'd come to look forward to this contact more than anything else she did. But she felt guilty because she knew she was keeping the best of herself for those ten minutes with Edward, and that Simon, whether he knew it or not, was getting left out. Still, he didn't seem to notice. Not really. With an effort she snapped her attention back to Clara, who was talking.

'Oh, he enjoys it. In fact, it's really given him a new lease of life.' There was a pause, and Clara added brightly, hoping it sounded like a non-sequitor, 'Shirley seems quite keen on Colin Dearest. Don't you think?' Virginia's heart sank. She didn't think she was quite up to confidences from Edward's wife. She opened her briefcase and began to flick through a pile of prospective features. She wished reading in cars didn't make her feel sick.

Shirley had enjoyed her lunch slightly more, but was deeply uneasy about several aspects of it. On the plus side, there had been a fresh opportunity to tweak Colin Dearest's strings, and get him dancing to her tune. Colin was becoming a very important part of the whole plan. On the minus, she didn't think that having Virginia and Clara going off together in a taxi was a good thing at all. Clara was sure to try and undermine her, Shirley, and look for a way of getting Virginia on her side in some kind of wifely conspiracy. And Shirley didn't quite trust Virginia not to fall for it. Virginia was just too nice. She never saw what people were really up to.

They found Shirley in Virginia's office going through Virginia's diary.

'Oh, hi,' she said, easily, 'I'm just trying to find a window for us to see Global Cosmetics together.' Her eyes narrowed as she caught sight of Clara behind Virginia.

Virginia sat down with a sigh. 'Go ahead, do. Preferably in the evening. Simon's being rather trying at the moment.' She smiled her twinkly smile to show she was joking but Clara saw a look of surprise shoot across Shirley's face.

'Where's Becky? We need to have a features meeting.'

'A crisis with her cat, apparently.' Shirley's voice was heavy with disbelief. 'The second this week, would you believe?' Clara felt like pointing out that if you had a sick cat – or a child, a husband, or even a potted plant – then the chances were that it would cause some disruption over a period of days.

'Did she say what was wrong?' Virginia obviously wasn't quite certain whether to be supportive or disciplinary. Of course, if a loved pet was seriously ill, staff should be offered the maximum sympathy and support.

Shirley shrugged. 'Toenail clipping, I expect. Or I thought I heard her say something about vaccinations. Some sort of injection, anyway.'

Virginia clearly repressed her irritation. 'Oh, well,

we'd better manage without her.' She suddenly remembered Clara. 'Have you ever sat in on a features meeting? No? Well, now's the time to start. Don't worry about whether you're in the right or the wrong. Just say what you think. After all, this is a magazine for ordinary women like you.'

Thanks, thought Clara, with amusement. Ordinary. But she pulled up a chair, trying not to notice Shirley's look of resentment.

'Hmm.' Virginia flicked through some market research on the readership of the three first issues. 'Interesting. A lot of divorcees and people who define themselves as "second time round-ers" amongst our readers. Now what buttons should we be pressing there?' She tapped her pen thoughtfully against the research.

'Depression. They often commit suicide, these divorcees,' said Shirley, her green eyes fixed on Clara. 'They know no one wants them and can't face a life alone in a dreary little flat, with their children miles away and not enough money to visit them. Men – ' there was a certain amount of scorn in this ' – always know how to hang on to the dosh, and really, old age without money, and without love, isn't worth living. Is it? You're better off dead.' She rarely spoke to Clara, except when absolutely necessary, but this was undoubtedly aimed directly at her. It was a threat, Clara thought. And so much a reflection of Clara's own fears about her future that she caught her breath, conscious of a cold pit deep down beyond her heart and her stomach. Shirley was telling her that if she went on holding out, there'd never be a fair settlement or a civilized divorce. Not if Shirley had anything to do with it.

'Good idea, Shirley,' Virginia said approvingly. 'Perhaps we could take it one stage further. All the euthanasia arguments have focused on ending a life full of physical pain. No one talks about mental pain.' She looked reflective. 'It'd be very contentious, but we ought to get someone really clever to put forward an argument for allowing euthanasia for serious depression. We'd get a lot of publicity.' She stopped for a moment. 'Of course, we'd have to make it clear that we were just illustrating how seriously painful mental illness can be. How it still doesn't get the resources and attention allocated to physical illness. And we'd have to avoid talking about old people. The advertisers wouldn't like it. No, young – well, young-ish – still quite attractive divorcees' – her eyes drifted over Clara without realizing it – 'in the depths of despair. "Would you help this woman die?" What a headline.'

Clara felt as if they had both got her divorced, into the depths of depression and on the verge of suicide in a few short moments. Were all features meetings like this? Virginia's mind drifted back to the magazine again. 'I wonder if we're getting a bit negative here. I must admit . . .' she was off on one of her digressions ' . . . I've always been with Dorothy Parker on suicide. So difficult to do it tidily that one might as well live.'

'Oh, I don't know,' said Shirley, still looking at Clara, 'throwing oneself off the top of a building like this would be quick and easy. It would solve everything.' Clara saw the car park at Wiggins Frean beckoning to her from the roof in her imagination. It was so vivid that she almost began to sway.

'Anyone for a cup of tea?' Harry was leaning against the door with a cigarette hanging out of his mouth. His voice cut refreshingly through the fog of outrage that had misted up Clara's vision. 'I'm thinking of making a proper pot. Of China Hunan. But it never seems worth it just for one.'

'Wonderful, darling.' Virginia looked up. 'Honestly, Harry, you must be the only person in an office who uses a proper teapot.'

'You should get Judith to do it,' said Shirley, 'she's got nothing else to do.'

'On the other hand,' said Virginia, once the door had closed on Harry, 'one should always try to portray a positive view of women's lives in a magazine. Perhaps something a bit more upbeat like "Dating second time round"?'

Thank goodness, thought Clara, feeling as if her head had been metaphorically removed from the gas oven, given a treatment at the hairdresser's and settled in front of an attractive man over a romantic dinner table. She could see Shirley frowning at the thought.

Harry came back with tea on a tray, with, amazingly, a plate of biscuits, beautifully arranged. 'By the way, I've sent Becky home. She came all the way back from Clapham after having her cat put down because she was worried about work. But I told her you'd understand.'

'Oh, of course.' Virginia looked startled. 'Poor

Becky.' She looked sympathetic, but Clara could see that her mind was already back on headlines and readership profiles.

'It's Paul Long.'

There was a silence while Clara tried to work out what he could possibly be calling Edward about. It had been a month since she had met Paul at the Perfumery Partners press lunch she attended with Virginia, and she had bumped into him once at another press event since. She found him a charming man who had been extremely helpful. She couldn't see why Virginia disliked him so much. But he'd never called Wiggins Frean before.

She tried to eradicate the surprise from her voice. 'How are you?'

Paul did not bother with the preliminaries and ignored her question.

'I'd like you to come and see me. In confidence. Do you think you could manage that?'

Clara was used to saying 'yes' to anything, however unusual or surprising. She occasionally read articles about how to say 'no', wondering who they were aimed at. 'Well. Yes. Of course. When?'

'Tomorrow. 8.30 a.m.?'

'Er . . . yes.'

'Good. You know where we are.' It was not a question, and Clara was left looking bemusedly at a buzzing telephone. What on earth could Paul Long want with her? Did he expect her to lure Virginia back? Should she tell Edward? (This last was not really an option, as both he and Shirley, painfully, were away at a conference together. Bloody, bloody Shirley. Just because he was with Her, Clara didn't feel she could call him on what he might see as a flimsy excuse. And it would just be too embarrassing if Shirley answered the phone, which, in Clara's experience, she would if she possibly could.) Paul Long probably wanted to know about some charity committee or something – in their brief chat after he had helped her pick up her packages, they had both talked about their charity work. He had asked some very flattering questions. He'd mentioned that he supported a very worthwhile concern with a name like Drug-Crazed Prisoners.

It was not about a charity committee.

'This is highly confidential.'

'Of course.'

'And this isn't exactly a conventional approach . . .'

Clara found herself agreeing that it wasn't.

'This is an informal offer – which I'd like you to take to your husband, and no one else.'

'Yes?'

'From Publishing Unlimited. To buy *Heart & Soul*.'

Clara thought of the debts that were stacking up. The final reminders that the accounts department seemed to ring her about almost daily. The increasing panic in Shirley's eyes – and concern in Virginia's – as the advertising revenue stayed stubbornly below what was needed. The monthly sales figures, which were satisfactory – quite good, really, considering what they had been – but which still weren't enough.

The thought that there could be a way out, just like that, was incredible.

Then she thought of the passion that Virginia put into the magazine, of the feeling of a job half-done that would linger in the offices of Wiggins Frean. And just a small bit of her that said she was having the most interesting time of her life – if you discounted that menace, Shirley – and how terribly dull it would be without the magazine. She also knew Edward, and that he wouldn't even contemplate selling unless he thought he could make a killing. His pride would never allow it.

She sighed. 'I really don't know what he'd say.'

'It wouldn't have to mean losing your job. We couldn't keep him on – he'd understand that – but everyone else's roles would be guaranteed. As for you, there's a shortage of organized people with both feet planted firmly on the ground in this world. You'd be surprised at how far you could go.'

Clara shook her head. 'I work for my husband.' The offer came as such a shock that she couldn't think of anything coherent to say.

'You're loyal. I like that. But don't you think it's time you took stock of your life? Things aren't exactly, well, conventional at home, are they?'

Clara felt her heart thump unpleasantly. 'What do you mean by that?'

'I'm very much afraid that it is hardly a secret. Is it?'

Clara looked down at her hands. 'Well, of course, there are always a few rumours flying round in any industry. They're not usually absolutely accurate.' That should show him. 'As for the business, I believe everything is going to plan. I'm very proud of what Edward and Virginia have achieved in such a short time. But, of course, I'll talk to my husband.' Clara could feel a flush spreading down her neck. 'And thank you for the tea.' She indicated a bone-china cup of untouched tea in front of her, then got up.

Paul waved a disbelieving hand at the ceiling. 'Whatever. And the job offer stands, whether you sell or not.' It did? As she left, she almost bumped into a tall, lean man with a moustache. In his late fifties, she thought, and exquisitely dressed.

'I'm so sorry.' He had an old-world, courtly voice.

'Clara, do you know Sir Ralph Headcorn, Chairman of Publishing Unlimited?'

Clara shook hands briefly, and extracted herself as quickly as she could. She felt disloyal – to both Edward and Virginia – just by being in the building.

'Where the fuck is the sellotape?' Edward was raging up and down the stairs. He had returned from the conference the day before in a toweringly bad mood, and Clara had tried to discuss the offer from Publishing Unlimited on several occasions. He'd cut her short each time.

Now he stormed through the bathroom. 'Ever since you started work, the house has been a complete shambles.'

Clara felt that this was unfair. 'No, it hasn't.' She scrambled down the stairs and whipped open the desk. 'Look. The sellotape is exactly where it ought to be. And where you left it last time.'

He snorted and whisked upstairs again, slamming the study door behind him. Not the right atmosphere for discussing offers.

He emerged again, grim-faced. 'I've called an emergency meeting. At Virginia's house in London.'

'But it's a Saturday.'

'I don't care if it's Christmas, Easter and All Saints' Day rolled into one.' He threw her the car keys. 'Can you drive? I need to concentrate on what I'm going to say.'

Clara's hands trembled slightly on the steering wheel.

'We're bleeding to death.' Edward was blunt. They'd all hardly sat down. 'We've been on the shelves for seven months – '

'And our sales are steadily climbing,' Virginia interrupted sharply. Clara was surprised. Virginia always spoke softly to Edward, eyes sparkling and almost deferring to him. She'd sometimes wondered if this was Virginia's way of flirting with him.

Shirley filed her nails.

'Revenue from advertising does not even cover our costs. And that revenue is *not* climbing. The advertisers won't switch their budgets until they see us taking market share from the other magazines. And although *Heart & Soul* increases its sales month by month, no one else is losing out. *Viva* is stronger than ever, for example.' He banged his hand down on Virginia's well-oiled English elm dining table and the white lilies shook tastefully in their Conran Shop vase. Virginia looked taken aback. Personally hurt, even. She'd obviously never seen Edward in a rage. Harry and Shirley exchanged glances. They had seen it all before, thought Clara.

'There is one way we can wipe out *Viva* for two months running.' Virginia took control of the meeting. There was a silence, while Clara wondered why Harry looked so tense these days. He was usually such a rock in his funny way. She'd come to be quite fond of him, now that she'd got used to him.

Virginia addressed herself to Edward as if there was no one else in the room. That warning note sounded in Clara's heart. Virginia and Edward? 'If we can just show that we're gaining readers while others are losing ground in one set of six-monthly figures, it'll probably help bring in the waverers. Take *Marie Claire*. Or *Hello*. No one thought they'd work when they first came out, but in their time they changed the face of the market for magazines. Now everyone's looking for the next *Marie Claire*, and we've got to make them believe it can be *Heart & Soul*. The title's right for the millennium, and we know we've got the expertise to provide what women want to read. So we need to strike a death blow.' Edward's gaze locked with Virginia's, and Shirley leant forward in her seat, eyes flicking from one to the other, obviously determined not to miss a single nuance. Clara pretended to scribble notes. She had to believe there was nothing between Virginia and Edward, but this no longer felt like a meeting. It was a showdown between two powerful personalities, and there was an electricity between them that no one could miss. Except, unusually, Harry, who was looking unhappily out of the window.

'We do a big TV campaign – just for two issues – and we drop the price of the magazine. Drastically. To ninety-nine pence. Remember *The Times*? It wiped thousands from rival circulations when it dropped to ten pence. Magazines are just as vulnerable. No browsing punter will buy *Viva* for two pounds fifty if they can get an equally glossy *Heart & Soul* for just ninety-nine pence. Even if they're committed *Viva* readers they'll probably buy *Heart & Soul* as well.'

'Except that we don't have the money to do that.' She could see Edward trying to control some strong emotion. Anger, perhaps. Desire? Almost certainly, she thought now, watching the way they looked at each other.

'Then we'll have to find some from somewhere. Otherwise we lose everything.' Clara wasn't sure about the 'we'. As far as she knew, all Virginia stood to lose was her job – with a nice high-earning husband behind her. It was Edward and Clara who did stand to lose literally everything. And Shirley, she supposed, because her job was everything to her.

'Er . . .' Clara tried to get Edward's attention. 'I think there's something you ought to know . . .'

'Not now, Clara.' Edward waved her away. She felt like throwing the Publishing Unlimited offer in his face, but Paul Long had stressed that it was confidential, and she certainly didn't want to discuss it in front of Shirley.

Suddenly the spell between Edward and Virginia was broken, and Edward obviously began to consider her suggestion seriously as a businessman. 'What if *Viva* choose the same month to promote? Or *Good Housekeeping*, or any of the others?'

'*Viva*'s our main problem. And they simply don't do those sort of promotions. I've never known Publishing Unlimited discount or do TV. It's too commercial a route for them to take.'

How interesting, thought Clara, picking up an almost undetectable note in Virginia's voice. She is still so bitter about everything. Clara wondered if Virginia had a much more personal agenda at Wiggins Frean than her cool manner suggested.

Simon put his head round the door. 'Harry? There's a call for you.' Harry sprang up nervously, and was absent for the rest of the meeting. He strolled back looking much more cheerful.

'I didn't think you really needed me, darlings. Such an important call from my tailor. Did you know . . .' he turned to Virginia, who was always interested in clothes ' . . . that he says I should be widening my lapels again?'

'Oh, Simon doesn't think so . . . he . . .'

Clara let the conversation drift over her. Tailor my foot. The final destination on the mental board in front of her slotted into place with a definitive click. Harry had been waiting for that call. Twitching with desire. He was in love. And lying about it. Oh well, things were bound to be difficult for him. They were for everyone else.

'Assuming we get the funding . . .' Clara noticed

that Edward didn't look at her. That meant he was thinking of taking out a loan against everything they owned and more ' . . . which issue shall we go for?' So he'd decided.

'We don't have a choice. The next two issues. January and February.'

Later, in the car going home, while Edward scribbled furiously on the backs of envelopes and left terse messages to people from his mobile, Clara told him about Publishing Unlimited's offer.

He exploded with irritation. 'Of course they bloody well want it. It's a going concern now – which it wasn't when I bought it. *Heart & Soul*'s potentially a real threat to their other titles. Look, Paul Long suspects we can't afford to wait. If we could, *Heart & Soul* could be big. In two years. We've invested in it. We're on the up-and-up. They need to get rid of us while we're still small.'

'He did say that everybody's jobs would be safe.'

Edward made a noise that sounded like 'hrmph'. 'Very possibly. Publishing Unlimited has over fifty titles. They could re-deploy people. But they'd close *Heart & Soul* down like a shot, or incorporate it into one of the other titles. In the long run, buying us would be cheaper than fighting us. A company like that can afford to take the long view.'

'And we can't?' She hoped that he wasn't being too influenced by Virginia, and her obvious desire to humiliate Publishing Unlimited.

'No. But we can't afford to sell it for anything less

than what I've put in. And that's way over the current market value.'

Clara looked puzzled so he went on. 'Look, if you buy a derelict house and do it up, you don't sell it halfway through. You don't get your money back then. But provided you can complete the job, then you'll get it all back plus a profit. This is just the same.' She still looked doubtful.

'Tell you what,' he added. 'They'll be a sight more worried – and pay an awful lot more – if we sell *after* this promotion wipes out two months of their sales.'

Clara was not convinced.

chapter 9

'But who shall I take?' wailed Judith. 'All the nice men are married or gay.' Wiggins Frean, apparently unaware that its future hung in the balance, was in a furore about this year's office party. From October onwards it was almost the sole topic of conversation, and now, the day before the party, excitement had reached fever pitch, except amongst Edward, Shirley and Virginia, all of whom seemed to be above such things.

Max went down on one knee, a reasonable position, Clara noticed, from which to peer up Judith's skirt, which spanned her legs like an elastic band round a pair of skittles. 'Judith, please be my fairy godmother and take me to the ball. I promise to be a very good boy.'

'I wouldn't go with you if you were the last man on earth.'

'Max!' Clara quelled him with a look before he could make an obscene reply. He obediently slunk away. There were two spots of colour on Judith's cheeks, but she seemed otherwise unworried by his attentions. Clara hoped she wasn't going to take any of the sex pests to court for sexual harassment, and went back to worrying about whether she'd done all the right things when she organized the party.

It had been Shirley's suggestion that they break with tradition and take partners, and Clara, wary of causing waves, had agreed with misgivings. Perhaps Shirley was longing to show off Colin Dearest. Or not.

'But you've never had partners before.' She'd been worried about Judith and several others who appeared to have no one in their lives.

'They don't have to be husbands or wives. Or even girl-friends. Everyone's got a friend of some kind. And it would interesting to meet them. Create the feeling of one big family.' Create the feeling of one big row, Clara had fretted. But Shirley had been persuasive, and Clara, who hadn't been looking forward to hanging on to Edward for a whole evening in the face of an onslaught from Shirley, had to admit it would solve a lot of problems.

No one seemed wild about the idea.

'Are you sure it's not a recipe for disaster?' Harry popped his head round the door of Edward's office to check that this was still the policy. 'I'm not bringing anyone.'

If it wasn't the recipe for disaster, it certainly had all the ingredients, thought Clara. 'I just think Shirley would like to come with Colin Dearest. I couldn't be certain, but I felt it really quite mattered to her.'

'Well . . .'

Clara was still worrying about the drink too. Each year had its special cocktail, Shirley had informed her. The stronger, the better. 'Or they'll think you're being stingy.' She had decided not to take Shirley's word for it (she had also suggested an Irish fiddle quartet instead of a disco), but discovered she'd been right. 'Pernod and blackcurrant last year, Three Kisses the year before,' Harry told her. 'Something sweet and sticky, I should think. And, no, you're right, not an Irish fiddle quartet.' But then, just as she thought she could go through arrangements with him, there was a distant trilling of a telephone from his immaculately ordered desk, and he scuttled back to his cubicle. He was like a cat on a hot tin roof these days.

Edward was no better. 'Yes, do,' he murmured vaguely when, just to test him, she suggested hiring a troupe of strippers from Soho to brighten things up at the last moment. Then, realizing what she'd said, he flung down a sheaf of papers he'd been going through, and pushed them away from him, knocking several plastic pens off the other side of the desk. 'Oh, really, I can't be expected to think about things like that at a time like this. Just do what you think best.'

There was no point in even trying to discuss office parties with Virginia, thought Clara, as she scrabbled around under Edward's desk to get the pens. She expected other people to organize such things. Was that a used condom? She prodded it gingerly with one of the pens. It rustled rather than slithered. Good, just a toffee paper. She sat back on her heels in time to hear Edward bark 'Hello' into the telephone. Still, at least taking partners meant it was easier to hire a venue – she'd managed to find a relatively respectable hotel which had agreed to take them. 'We don't accept office parties without partners,' the receptionist had said. 'We find they get a little out of hand.'

'Did you know Mrs Derek was a social worker?' Shirley followed Virginia into Edward's office with the latest gleeful fact about the ghastly Derek. The new policy was certainly flushing out some interesting, if incredible, facts about people.

'No! You must have got it wrong, Shirley. How on earth does she put up with him?' But Virginia looked quite amused. Clara could see Edward signalling for silence.

'Well, it takes all sorts to make a world,' whispered Judith, who'd come in after them with a pile of documents. She stumped out, leaving Virginia and Shirley to exchange glances and roll their eyes at each other. Clara suspected that they giggled about her when she left the room, but you could hardly stay in a room indefinitely just to stop people talking about you.

'We're off. That was the last hurdle cleared. Nick's board agrees.' Edward crashed down the phone and looked exultant.

'No! I can't believe it!' Virginia actually hugged him, and, for one moment Clara saw his hand tighten on her shoulder. 'This deserves a kiss,' Virginia added, and then blushed, moving quickly away. 'I'll get the January dummy cover in.' Clara could never get used to the time frame of monthly magazines. You were always at least two months ahead of yourself. To her, it was early November. To Virginia, it was January, because that was the issue she was working on.

Clara thought about what the telephone call meant. Edward loved living dangerously. She hated it. He'd raised another two million, using Wiggins Frean and The Brambles as collateral, and was convinced that *Viva* – and all *Heart & Soul*'s other rivals – were living on borrowed time.

Virginia brought in the proof of the dummy cover, already designed in the hope that the bankers would agree. This was a rare concession – she was usually too protective about it to allow anyone except Harry and Shirley anywhere near. 'Wives who get paid for sex' read the top coverline.

That had been Shirley's idea, and she explained it again to Harry, who was now pacing in and out of the room restlessly. 'I met a divorce lawyer, who told me that it was amazing how many men paid their wives for sex. You know, little presents. A car, a painting, a new handbag. Even a little job, sometimes. If they own their own company. Then they can write it off against tax.' The green eyes swivelled round to Clara. 'But if they try it while the marriage is breaking up, the wives feel cheap and cite it as unreasonable behaviour.'

Clara flushed, remembering the evening Edward had made her his PA. She almost said that it hadn't been like that, not at all. It hadn't.

'They must value these wives very highly then,' she replied, but Shirley affected not to hear.

Virginia propped the cover up on the windowsill, walking away to see it at a distance, then going up close. 'Lose 10 lb in ten days. For ever', screamed the next, and then a big splash, 'Confidence, Control, Cash – how to achieve the three magic Cs and find a New You'. 'Do you think the last one strikes a wrong note?' she fretted. 'Cash sounds a bit . . . well, avaricious.'

'What about Charisma? Or Charm?' suggested Shirley.

'Brilliant, darling. Do you think *Just 99p!* is bright enough? For the strapline?' The words splashed across the top left hand corner of the cover were a lurid citric orange. Then there was the advertising campaign. They'd got an advertising agency who had proposed the slogan 'A woman for all seasons, a magazine for all reasons'. Nobody was very convinced about it.

'What's a free Lip Slave?' asked Edward, studying the bottom left hand corner carefully. '"For every reader". That would definitely change my life by Christmas.' Virginia frowned.

'Er . . .' Clara tried to catch someone's attention to see if they thought she needed a special cocktail as well as the theme of Pink Drinks (which she had chosen because it meant that Virginia could have pink champagne and the few non-drinkers blackcurrant juice without anyone feeling left out). It was no good. Annabel would have told her to be more assertive.

'Lip Slave?' Harry looked fascinated. Clara sighed. She had tried asking 'the troops', as Harry called everyone else at Wiggins Frean, about the office party, but they seemed so startled to be consulted that most had mumbled 'Shirley usually . . .' But she knew that if she got it wrong, the complaints in the Ladies loos would be vociferous. A good office party, Edward had once said, could cut the need for a pay rise by about 2 per cent. Not that he seemed to have remembered this important fact. Oh well, if everything went belly up, the only comfort was that next Christmas there wouldn't be an office party.

Virginia was thoroughly cross by now. A typographical error on the cover was not up to her usual demanding standards. 'Lip Salve,' she corrected Edward, as if it was his fault. 'With aromatherapy oils. Free for every reader,' she muttered, whisking the offending cover, citric orange strapline and all, out of the room.

'What a shame,' murmured Edward. 'I bet a Lip Slave would boost the circulation no end.' Clara didn't look at him. She didn't, these days. This was the first time for years that he'd actually endangered their home. She hoped she could keep her temper until after the office party.

She couldn't. When they got home, Edward flicked idly through the post and threw half of the letters away without opening them.

'Edward!' He often did this, but tonight her nerves were jangling. 'There could be something important – or a cheque – in there.'

'There isn't.' He wandered through to the kitchen, whistling, while Clara retrieved and opened the crushed envelopes. Two were charitable requests, one was a suggestion that they upgrade their software – something they'd bought ages ago for Marcus – and the fourth a round robin from the local PCC about Harvest Fayre. It wasn't a church they ever went to, not even at Christmas, but Clara decided to keep it to prove her point, and tried to throw the others away without Edward spotting her.

She failed. 'See?' he said. 'All you've done is wasted ten minutes.'

'Five,' she replied, hotly. 'And it's the principle. You've no idea what you've missed by doing that sort of thing.'

'Ah, but I do, my dear. That's the trouble.' He tried to caress her, but she twitched away from him. 'Life can be very predictable, sometimes.' He reached out for the phone, and, before she could stop him, started dialling again, settling himself into the sofa cushions with a satisfied sigh. When he finished she calmly unplugged the phone and took it outside before coming back and locking the door behind her.

'Right,' she said, tucking the key into a pocket. 'We're going to talk.'

He raised an eyebrow. 'We've been talking all day.' He sounded genuinely bewildered.

'No, we haven't. Either you've been giving me orders and I've been following them, or I've been talking and your mind has been a million miles away. I don't call either of those a conversation.'

'It's a critical time for the company – you must

know that. I can't be bothered with domestic trivia – and,' his voice gathered conviction, 'I'm waiting for several important calls. If they can't get through, it could blow everything.'

'The answering machine's on in the kitchen. And I don't call mortgaging our home domestic trivia. It's my home, too, and I don't want you to do this.' She hadn't meant to start with a demand. It was all coming out wrong.

He sighed. 'Listen. This is the big one.'

'I've heard that before.'

'And it's been right before.'

'Not always. What about Brown's Boots?' That had been a company he'd bought to turn round, which had sunk so fast it had nearly taken them with it. 'Or the flower shops?'

'The market turned against flowers. No one could have predicted that. What about the luxury car deal?'

'But you promised that was the last big one. That we'd never have to worry again.'

'You don't have to worry. Leave that to me.'

'Don't be so condescending.'

'I'm not,' he said sharply. 'I earn the money, you spend it. It seems to me that you'll take the rewards without taking the risks.'

'That's not fair.' It sounded childish, even to her own ears. 'You never talk to me about the risks. You don't give me a chance. Until it's all too late.'

'I don't want you to worry.'

'Or you don't want me to point out where it could all go terribly wrong. Because you've got Miss Negative Shirley for that.'

'Leave Shirley out of this.' Edward looked wary.

'Shirley hasn't exactly tried to leave herself out of it, has she?' Clara couldn't help herself.

He chose not to take up her challenge. 'Shirley does have a very good critical brain. And yes, I've listened to it. As I've listened to Virginia. And my bankers. I don't take these decisions without weighing everything up very carefully.'

'You don't listen to me.'

He sighed. 'I do. But not on business matters. You don't have any commercial experience.'

'At least I don't lie. Or bully. Or twist facts to suit whatever purpose I happen to have at the time.'

'And what's that supposed to mean?' The indulgence had gone from his face now, and she could see he was getting angry.

'You know exactly what I mean.'

'I'm afraid I don't,' he said. 'You'll have to explain yourself a bit better.'

'Your precious Shirley. Miss Wonderwoman is a liar, a cheat and a bully. She terrorizes staff. She's completely bamboozled Virginia. And you're relying on her judgement?'

'Firstly,' he said, almost shaking with anger, 'I do not "rely on her judgement" as you put it. I rely on my own. Secondly, you can scarcely be surprised that I don't rely on yours when you turn what was purportedly a discussion on whether we should mortgage the house into an unwarranted attack on someone who works extremely hard – and extremely well – for the company, and has done for years.'

'She works extremely hard and extremely well for

herself. And don't you forget it for a minute. If you can't see how deeply unhappy your staff are under her despotic rule, then you're a pretty poor manager. There isn't an original idea that comes out of that company that isn't hers or Virginia's, and that's because the staff are too frightened to speak, let alone think. Do you really believe that's a healthy way to keep a company strong?'

'There isn't an original idea that comes from anyone else because they don't have any original ideas. If they did, Virginia would listen. In a home, you can be all soft and understanding, but when it comes to business, you need some discipline. Shirley runs a tight ship, and people know they can't take advantage of her. That's good management. I'd have expected even you to understand that by now.'

'Shirley treats them as scarcely human.'

'My God,' he said. 'I really blew it making you my secretary, didn't I? I only asked you one thing – that you didn't undermine Shirley. Who's given far more of her time to the company over the years than anyone had any right to expect, and, underneath it all, has surprisingly little confidence. Who deserves a bit of support. Now I find you've been turning the staff against her.'

'I have not. I didn't need to. They already hated her. And anyway, why should I?'

'Because,' he said, looking at her levelly, and, with a shock, she realized that she had pushed him to the point of no return, 'as you are doubtless aware, I've been having an affair with her for quite some time.'

Clara's heart turned to ice. 'And what – ' she tried

to keep her voice steady – 'are you planning to do about it?'

He looked at her, and she briefly imagined that he looked as sad as she felt. 'I don't think that I have much choice now, do I?' He looked pale but determined. She hadn't seen him look like this since . . . oh, for years. She pushed the memory of that morning away, but it surfaced again. But this time she wasn't going to sit and listen to explanations and justifications. She had had enough.

Don't leave me, she thought. But her anger took over.

'I'd suggest you go. Now.' She was swept along by rage, determined to hurt him, and to be the first out of the door. 'I'll leave you to pack.' She got up and headed for the door. 'Don't expect to find me here when you come back.' She turned back. 'Of course, silly me, you weren't coming back, were you?'

'Clara.' His voice was thunderous. 'Will you listen to me?'

'No.' She didn't stop. She had spent a lifetime listening to him. 'I should never have listened to you. Ever.'

'I hope you're not bringing that up again.' His voice was menacing. 'My God, you really are as cold as charity, aren't you? No wonder I've had to find some comfort elsewhere.'

'You went elsewhere because you couldn't face yourself. You know that.'

'I refuse to put up with this childish behaviour.' He was really angry now. Good.

'You don't have to refuse . . .' she knew she had to

get out before she cried ' . . . because I won't be here to talk to you about *childish* things. I'm leaving.' It felt better to have beaten him to it, even if only by about thirty seconds.

She was out of the door before he could physically stop her.

'Clara!' he roared, as if he was calling a dog to heel, she thought. Ordered to 'sit' and listen to things about solicitors, division of property and payments. The door of the car was unlocked, with the key dangling in the ignition. She slipped in, and locked it. His furious face was pressed to the driver's window, and he had to jump back as she pressed her foot hard on the accelerator. She almost laughed. It always took him ages to find the keys for his car. By the time he'd searched all the pockets of all his coats, she would be on the motorway. Where to, exactly, she hadn't decided. But she'd think of somewhere. And she drove blindly down the road, not knowing where she was headed but unable to watch him throwing his possessions in a suitcase or see his car departing.

After five minutes, she parked and got out. She walked, and walked, along the neatly manicured lanes, restlessly in and out of various triangles of newly created roads, past dark, looming, clipped hedges, oversized metal gates that dwarfed the sub-urban houses behind them, crossing the roads to avoid teenage boys hanging around on street corners with cans of lager and talking in frighteningly loud voices, stepping around endlessly parked cars and lamp-posts. One foot in front of the other, for hour after hour. Someone clearing out his garage looked at her curiously. She must have passed him twice already, stamping along the same familiar route over and over again, trying to make her feet hurt so much that they drowned the ache in her heart. Past the nursery school where Marcus, then Eliza, had started to find their own way in the big wide world. It was closed now, boarded up with thick metal mesh panels screwed to the fronts of the windows and yellow spray paint proclaiming 'fuck the council' across the doors, waiting for the demolishers. It was going to be a big new supermarket. As she brushed past the suburban hedges she caught the cloying scent of the last of the year's roses, a sudden sweet fragrance from a few lonely late-bloomers, and the sharp smell of privet, yew and cypress. Even the gardens, boxy, small and packed with plants, told her she'd made mistakes all along, from the nodding disapproval of the autumn crocuses, and the prickly criticisms of the glossy red pyracantha berries, all gossiping away. Shirley's so much thinner, you can't blame him, she imagined them saying. She never criticizes him, men don't like it, murmured a few late Japanese anemones. Just be sweet and fragile like us. It's time for a new start, trilled the birds, settling down to search the suburban gardens for the most liberally supplied bird table to take them through the winter. Shut up, the lot of you, she told them. This is my life, and I'm entitled to make my own mistakes. People who don't make mistakes, she told the glossy dark-green leaves of one particularly gloomy rhododendron, don't make anything at all. Someone walking a dog on the other side of the road looked up. She smiled back firmly to show that she was quite sane, and the dogwalker jerked nervously on the lead and quickened her step.

The lights were on when she got home, and her heart lifted, just for one second. But Edward wasn't there. He'd noticed that she'd walked out without her keys, and had slipped the spare set into their hiding place. There was a note wrapped round it. 'Sorry,' was all it said, although he had started to say something else, and scribbled it out. She tried to see what it was. 'I something.'

She lay awake all night, too frightened to cry, her eyes staring into the darkness trying to make sense of the shapes the streetlights made. At ten to five she allowed herself to get up and have a bath. Her legs were trembling too much for a shower. One day at a time, she whispered to the mirror, looking wistfully at an old bottle of prescription tranquillizers in the bathroom cupboard. But she knew they wouldn't even take the edge off her pain, and she needed to get through this one day with dignity. She couldn't risk feeling muzzy.

Because it was the office party, and, as the organizer, she had to be there. She couldn't let them down, and she had no intention of giving Shirley the satisfaction of queening it over everyone so soon. After tonight – well, then she could fall to pieces, or run away, or whatever.

'Pink Drinks.' Shirley fingered the invitation yet again, which had been designed by the Art Department on an Apple Mac, in irritation. 'What does that woman think she's up to?'

Oh, I think it's quite clever.' Virginia was dreading the Office Cocktail, and Clara had reassured her that Pink Drinks included pink champagne as well as campari, rosé wine and a selection of suitably fiendish cocktails.

'I thought all those themed things had been done to death.' Shirley didn't want Virginia praising Clara. What she did want, on the other hand, was to discuss why Clara was in the office at all. Seeing her sitting at her desk, working away quietly, as if her husband hadn't left her the night before and come to Shirley, had taken her breath away. The barefaced cheek of it. Either the woman was a battleaxe beyond even Shirley's wildest suspicions, or she was playing some game which Shirley could only guess at. Instead of the victorious, happy day, full of congratulations, kisses and flowers that Shirley had envisaged when Edward had finally appeared at her door with 'it's all over' written on his face, she was reduced to skulking around wondering what Clara's real agenda was. What could she hope to gain from such insensitive behaviour? Wasn't she humiliated to see her husband walk in with another woman? Had she no pride? After careful consideration, Shirley decided not to discuss it with Virginia, because Virginia was simply far too kind, was bound to urge everyone to look after Clara in her defeat, might even praise Clara as 'courageous'. As if anyone as bone-headedly stubborn as Clara needed looking after. And, although nothing had ever been said, she instinctively felt that Harry, at some point, for some reason, seemed to have changed sides, which showed you how devious Clara could be. As for Edward, Shirley had tried expressing mild astonishment at Clara's behaviour and had been sharply cut off. 'She's very conscientious. That's all.' No, it was not all, but Edward was so blinded by the Saint Clara image that he couldn't see that she was up to something. There literally was no one she could discuss this with. Shirley was beginning to think that she was going to have to take extreme measures to get Clara out of her life. The woman simply hadn't the nous to see when the party was over. She'd have to keep an eye out, and meanwhile behave as if everything was normal.

'What are you wearing?' She flicked through the dummy of the March issue, picking out badly placed advertising, tutting over Derek's insensitivity in placing an advertisement for Hermesetas next to an article on anorexia, and another for diarrhoea remedies next to a page of recipes for curries. 'God, you have to do everything here yourself.' Edward had insisted that they all act as normal this evening. Everything a deadly secret. And besides, she wanted to go on stringing Colin along a bit longer. Just to show Edward. Make sure that he did what she wanted in the matter of getting divorced and giving Clara as little money as possible. Having lived for ten years at Clara's beck and call – which was what it had felt like – she was not going to let the woman ruin their lives together by leaving them completely skint. Now that the children were grown up, Clara really didn't need much. And Edward would have to be shown that. Shirley was not fooling herself that the battle was quite over. Nearly though. She smiled.

'Little black dress from Harvey Nicks.'

'Mmm. The one with the lace back?'

Virginia nodded. 'What about you?'

Shirley's eyes lit up. She was wearing a very small scrap of fabric, immaculately cut to conceal and reveal in tantalizing turns. Hardly what Harry would even call a belt. It had been extremely expensive and was very sexy. So the mirror had told her.

Virginia's phone trilled and she looked around for Judith to answer it, but Judith was in the Ladies struggling into a worryingly hot-looking red velvet number. With a cleavage, Shirley had reported with a wicked glint in her eye.

'Yes.'

'It's Simon.'

'Darling, what time are you going to . . .?'

His voice cut across her. 'Look, I can't make it tonight. Something's come up. But we've got to talk.'

Virginia went icy cold. She had been trying not to talk for months. Six and a half months, to be precise. Since Birmingham. In case she said something that gave the game away. She couldn't really look him in the eye, and she felt angry with him. In bed, she pretended he was Edward, by keeping her eyes shut and moving her hips urgently against Simon to satisfy the glorious desires that Edward had uncovered in her in Birmingham. Oddly enough, it worked quite well. She could now see why people claimed that having an affair spiced up their marital sex life.

She kept her voice light and even. Virginia Law did not have marriage problems. 'What about?'

He sighed. 'Something very important, I'm afraid. I've been meaning to say this for months. Now things have rather come to a head.'

They had? What sort of head? Virginia was surprised to feel her knees shaking. Could this be another instalment in the book he seemed to be writing about Virginia's imperfections as a wife? Perhaps he was going to lay down the law about her attending more evening functions with him. Or demand that they eat together twice – or even three times a week – instead of just once. Well, perhaps she ought. Just for a time until he got rid of this obsession that her career was getting in the way of their family life. She could find some way of keeping him happy without having to give anything up. Of course, she could. Simon suddenly seemed terribly important. Very dear and very far away.

'Look,' he continued. 'It's pointless trying to talk on the phone, because what I want to discuss really matters to me. I'm afraid we'll both say things we don't mean. And you have to go to the office party, and I have to go to this . . . well, never mind. We'll talk later. I'm sorry to make an appointment, as it were. But otherwise I don't think we'll ever see each other.' And he was gone. What did he have to go to? And what did he mean by 'months'? Virginia calmed herself by getting up and smoothing down her little black dress, holding it against her face and looking in the mirror. She looked just the same on the outside. She tried to think how he could possibly have found her out.

'Bad news?' Shirley didn't miss much.

'Not really.' Her voice sounded almost normal too. 'Simon can't come. But I'll catch up with him later.'

'Just don't get too drunk on Pink Drinks and ask him for a divorce.' Shirley was rummaging around for a deeper red shade of lipstick in her make-up bag. Perhaps it had been waste to leave the Chanel in Edward's car, after all.

Virginia failed to keep control. 'What do you mean?'

Shirley put her make-up down. 'Keep your hair on. I was only joking.'

'It didn't exactly sound like a joke.'

Shirley sighed. 'Look, remember that divorce lawyer I met? Well, she also told me that office parties are peak time for triggering off divorce because everyone gets very drunk and decides they've had enough, so they stagger back to their husbands and wives and either confess all or demand an out.' She wondered if Virginia had been screwing around and, if so, who with, but didn't care for the obvious answer. But perhaps it was Simon doing the screwing.

'Thanks for the tip.' Virginia's first instinct had been to calm herself with a drink, but Shirley had a point.

'Party glamour – how to look your best this Christmas.' The December issue of *Heart & Soul*, out in early November in the way that magazines have, was full of advice for twenty-first-century Cinderellas, slaving over hot turkeys and cold white wine. Time, rather than expensive products, was the key, the article informed Clara, who had read it minutely, noticing that a number of expensive products had nevertheless been featured. She had marked the countdown in her diary – there were two, one for those at home, and the other, tactfully worded, for 'those who work in paid employment outside the home' (Virginia was particularly sensitive to such nuances). Clara's eyes felt like sandpaper, all swollen and sore, and her skin was papery with tiredness. But she owed it to herself to look as good as possible. As if nothing had happened.

Edward had come into the office that morning at the normal time – alone, thank God. He had stopped suddenly at the sight of Clara at her desk as usual. 'Are you . . .' he obviously didn't quite know what to say ' . . . all right?'

For a brief moment, her heart had contracted painfully at the sight of his familiar face. 'Perfectly,' she had replied, coolly, making it clear that she had no intention of continuing the conversation by picking up the phone and pressing the numbers.

He had drawn a breath, as if to say something, but stopped and turned towards his office, shutting the door with a precise click. Disconcerting him was a small victory, but it made her feel more in control. She was going to leave Wiggins Frean in her own time, not get pushed out by her husband and his mistress. And she was determined not to let him – or anyone else for that matter – see how much she hurt. She wasn't going to have them – Shirley, Virginia and Edward – picking over her pain or her anger, talking in hushed tones and being 'understanding'. She hadn't allowed herself any pride – or rage – for the past ten years, but now her emotions were her own business. She didn't have to think about anyone else any more.

It wasn't easy, though, and she tried to concentrate on the 'pampering schedule' to take her mind off everything. It should have started with a lunch-time trip to Charles Worthington's for a wash and blow-dry. This was cancelled when Virginia and Shirley both said they were going to the hairdresser's and that Shirley had given Judith permission to go to the chiropodist. 'Someone responsible needs to answer the phone. It looks so unprofessional when switch-boards take messages. And the phones go mad at lunch-time. Don't you think, Virginia?' commented Shirley, before Clara could suggest Naseem. Her brief, feverish glare made Clara decide not to challenge her. Anyway Clara's head ached so much that she thought she'd probably fall asleep in a warm salon.

Shirley had looked astonished – even frightened – to see Clara at her desk. She'd obviously thought that Clara would run away. Clara revelled in remembering the expression on Shirley's face. Thoroughly trumped, for a change.

Today already seemed endless, but she was damned if she was going to look frumpish at the office party. She would go down with all her guns blazing. Or flags flying. Or whatever, she thought tiredly.

'Mmm.' Virginia didn't really contradict Shirley and her mind was clearly on other things. Clara felt like pointing out that, in fact, very few phones ever rang at lunch-time, probably because most people were eating lunch. But it would sound like whinging, and would involve talking to Shirley directly. She turned away to open a cupboard to hide her face. Bloody woman. Never mind, her cut from last time still looked good.

The article suggested a five-minute facial massage in the Ladies loo, but she had to break off halfway when someone shouted through the door that the hotel was on the line with an urgent inquiry. She dashed out, face gleaming like a well-basted turkey. The lift door was just closing on Virginia and Shirley, who looked respectively horrified and amused. It was not urgent – of course – but the next six calls were, and by then the cream had sunk in, and couldn't be tissued off, so all the dead cells the article had promised could be sloughed off would just have to stay there. Plumping out the wrinkles with any luck, thought Clara. 'No matter how busy you are, take the phone off the hook for 15 minutes, put your feet up and treat yourself to a manicure,' advised the countdown.

'I'm waiting for an urgent call – make sure the lines aren't tied up,' said Edward, disappearing into a meeting. He wasn't speaking to her, except to bark a command. She hadn't spoken to him at all, and was putting his calls through without telling him who was on the line. Somehow, incredibly, no one seemed to have noticed that anything was wrong.

'Did you know you had something shiny on your face?' asked Judith, returning from the chiropodist's too late to let Clara get away after all. Oh, well. The phone had a hands-off button, so perhaps she could do the manicure anyway. She had just got the fingers of her right hand wedged into a small bowl of warm water when a man with an earring in his nose appeared. He staggered under the weight of a massive box. 'Stationery delivery. Sign here, please. Where do you want it?' It took half an hour for him to troop up and down with boxes, each of which had to be directed to a different department. Everyone had something to ask about the party, and Clara struggled to remember the answers. All she really wanted to do was find a quiet corner and cry. But back to the manicure. The water was cold and the office was full of people wanting to see Edward by the time it was over.

The final stage of 'looking your best ever' was make-up. 'Find a big mirror in a good light, preferably natural daylight.' At six o'clock in the evening in early November? Could the writer be serious? The Ladies loo reminded her of news footage of the Tokyo subway. Virginia had a mirror in her office, but Shirley was bound to be in there, and it would be impossible to put lipstick on under her scornful gaze, much less 'blend, blend, blend' in the way the article insisted was necessary for a truly professional finish. That left the mirror on her eye-shadow compact, dusty with the residue of a shade called Moonlight

Beige. She could only see small squares of her face at a time, leaving her with the suspicion that she might be adding quite a different amount of eyeshadow to one eye than the other.

'We need to get that heads of agreement letter out before the last post.' Edward appeared in the door, scuppering any chance of using a lipliner, a lipbrush, then blotting, powdering and repeating the process in the approved manner. A quick swipe of lipstick would have to do. She could re-do it later.

At least her silk trouser suit, in a blissful shade of moleskin brown, made her feel thinner and altogether more elegant, and she had the perfect earrings.

'Has Judith ordered any taxis?' Virginia put her head round the door. 'You look terrific, Clara. Have you lost weight?' This was praise indeed from Virginia, who worshipped slenderness. Some of her sparkle seemed to transfer itself to Clara.

'Of course. For seven-fifteen,' Judith returned, a vision in scarlet, already looking rather blotchy.

'You look great, too, Judith.' Virginia believed in encouraging people. She left to get changed, and, shortly after, Shirley followed. Tweedledum and Tweedledee, muttered Clara, who never usually criticized Virginia.

She resolved to get away earlier than Edward – sharing a taxi with him or Shirley would be altogether too much. As soon as the call for the taxi came she slipped off to get Harry to go with her.

'Just a sec.' He neatly ranged his pens along the

desk, filed his paperwork and, finally, put on his jacket and straightened it. 'Right, off we go.'

Shirley, Edward and Virginia were standing at the lift, which arrived before Clara could suggest the stairs. They squeezed in, and Clara fixed her eyes on the illuminated numbers denoting the position of the lift. They were terribly squashed – she froze every time Edward's arm accidentally brushed hers, but tried to conceal it from Shirley, who, she could feel, was watching everyone like a cat.

'I hope you'll be warm enough, darling.' Harry, usually Shirley's champion, seemed irritated by the endless expanse of long leg and bare back. Clara's silk trouser suit, so deliciously soft and luxurious when she put it on, suddenly felt as stiff and dull as an army blanket.

Virginia's Arpège fought with Shirley's Knowing, competing gusts of what Clara had now learned to call 'fragrance', completely drowning Harry's Dune For Men. She realized that she'd completely forgotten about scent herself. Still, no one would notice. Edward was silent, probably thinking about advertising campaigns and bank loans, she thought.

'I'm a bit worried about the food.' Clara was – a bit – but really thought that any conversation would be better than none.

'Oh, Shirley never did. We just had lumps of soapy cheese, doorsteps and coleslaw. So there isn't anything to live up to.' Had Harry and Shirley had a row? It was unlike him to be so waspish at her expense.

Shirley, who wasn't interested in food, but didn't

like to appear anything less than perfect in front of Edward, looked up at the floor signs in irritation. 'I think the lift's stuck.' But the doors creaked open at the first floor, and a few faces, seeing how crowded it was, didn't even try to get in. The doors squeaked shut again and the lift set off ponderously.

Virginia stared at her hands. What did Simon want to talk about? They had been ships passing in the night for so long that she could hardly even remember what he was doing at the moment. Was there something about a new job? His secretary sounded very attractive on the phone. It was well known that men really didn't want to be married to strong, successful women. Still, she had to get through the evening somehow.

'Lovely suit, Clara,' she said dutifully, like a polite girl at a party. She'd obviously forgotten that she'd already praised it.

'You've lost an earring,' commented Shirley, addressing Clara directly for the first time that day, with a glimmer of triumph in her eyes. Clara realized she'd left it on the desk answering a last call.

Clara and Harry seized the first taxi, and Clara ushered two sub-editors inside as well to stop Edward or Shirley joining them. Then she regretted it. What would Shirley and Edward get up to left on their own in a taxi? None of your business any more, she told herself firmly. And Virginia would be with them.

The Lancashire Hotel was surprisingly pretty and warm, with chintzy wallpaper, huge bowls of flowers and, very unusually, book-lined corridors. It reminded Clara – which was why she had chosen it

– of a shabby country vicarage, a real one, upholstered in faded Colefax & Fowler English roses. Wiggins Frean staff like Derek and Kevin, ushering unfamiliar-looking women, were tip-toeing down the corridor, peering around nervously as if they had just landed on the Planet Zog.

'Well, all this is a bit different.' Derek was standing in 'The Ballroom', which was a bit cold and rather too brightly lit, with a forced, jovial note in his voice.

'Is it?' Clara was alarmed. 'I haven't been to any office parties so I don't know. Shall I get them to turn the lights down a bit?'

'I'll do it.' Derek seemed keen to get away, possibly from Mrs Derek, who had been introduced as Shauna, and was looking round with disapproval. 'This hotel doesn't seem to have any disabled access.'

'Oh, dear, are you . . .?' Clara had a quick look round for a pair of crutches or a wheelchair.

'It's the principle of it all.' Shauna spoke severely. 'What is your minorities employment policy?'

'Well . . .' Like a mission statement, this had been suggested by Virginia, but never carried out. As far as Clara knew, the nearest thing they'd ever got to a policy was Derek, who maintained that 'women work much harder for less money. And they don't smell.' She shuddered to think what he might say about the disabled, or ethnic minorities. 'Hasn't Derek discussed it with you?'

Shirley pressed a Pink Drink into everyone's hands. Kir Royale. Clara took it absentmindedly. It set fire to the back of her throat as it slipped down,

330

and even Shauna looked a little more welcoming through its golden haze. Only briefly.

Around her conversations were being started up, only to peter out. Edward, whose mind was still clearly on the two million pounds, had that shut-off expression that she privately called his 'going-into-battle look'. Shirley was incandescently sparkling at everyone and anyone, swooping terrifyingly into clusters of people who seemed to be struck dumb by her, and leaving them just as unexpectedly. Virginia stood staring sightlessly over her glass, smiling faintly at anyone who addressed her. Harry had disappeared. Clara sipped her drink nervously and too fast. It was quite strong for a Kir Royale. Must remember to have a non-alcoholic drink next.

People swirled and eddied around her, looking nervous and formal. She overheard two men, both obviously other halves of Wiggins Frean women, exchanging nuggets of information without any apparent need for them to intersect at any point.

'I've always found that the 5.35 is too early and the 6.15 too late, but if you get the 5.50 and change at Wortley, you always get a seat.'

'We bought the DX486 when it first came out, but it outdated far too quickly.' Their wives looked earnestly into their drinks, perhaps exhausted of conversation by the presence of their other halves.

'And what do you do?' she asked a worried-looking woman, who had come with one of the editorial staff. The woman looked offended.

'I look after my children. It may not sound very interesting to you . . .'

The more Clara protested that she, too, had stayed at home to look after her children, the worse it sounded. Derek, deprived of his main topic of conversation by Shauna's rigidly disapproving presence, hovered silently, topping up people's drinks, but Max, who had not brought anyone, had no such inhibitions.

'Didn't we sleep together once?' she overheard Max asking Shauna.

'Luckily I didn't notice, or I would have been very cross,' retorted Shauna, who could clearly look after herself.

Someone from the post-room had already started snogging a blonde, which looked obscene under the over-bright chandeliers of The Ballroom, but at least kept him occupied. They were doing things with their tongues that made Clara feel quite queasy. And she seemed to be going for his trouser zip. 'I think I'll just have the lights turned down a bit more. And the music up,' said Clara hastily. 'You couldn't be an angel and divert Max for me, could you, before he makes anyone cry?' Judith's eyes lit up. She knew a mission when she saw one. 'Well, I'll try anything once. As I always say, you're a long time dead.' She adjusted her cleavage, heaving the velvet up with a practised twitch, and trooped off. Poor Max, thought Clara. He was, she suspected, no match for Judith on the offensive, armed with the twin certainties of religion and psychology, and determined to save him.

As Clara came back into the room, Shirley was handing out drinks again. 'Here. Your glass looks empty.' It seemed quite strong, but Clara felt she needed it, although it seemed odd that Shirley was acting so . . . normally. Still, she always did, in front of people. A waiter appeared with a tray of indeterminate beige blobs. They were hot, crispy and perfectly pleasant, although she couldn't tell whether they were deep-fried mushrooms, onion bhajis or Thai fishcakes, all of which had been ordered. They left a film of grease over her fingers.

'Here's Colin.' Shirley fluttered off like an exotic butterfly, dragging him on to the dance floor, and wrapping herself round him. Clara overheard Virginia invite Edward to dance: 'I think we ought to set an example. It'll get things going.'

'That leaves you and me.' Harry had appeared from nowhere, looking slightly happier again. Clara knew he was just being kind, but it would be heaven to be dancing, rather than standing on the sidelines feeling like a traffic warden. He pulled her elegantly to him in what could almost be called an old-fashioned waltz.

'How's things?'

'Grim. He's gone. Left last night.' She could be honest with Harry.

He whistled. 'Brave of you to be here.'

'Not really. I organized this, and I'm not going to run away. I can't promise what'll happen next though.'

Harry looked worried. 'Be careful, won't you?'

A flutter of fear caught at her throat. 'What do you mean?'

'Nothing.' His eyes raked the room, searching

for Shirley. 'Nothing, really.' He squeezed her arm. 'Forget I said anything.'

Clara tried to, but the words rattled in her mind like a war dance. Harry gazed over her head, looking remote. 'No, please tell me what you mean.'

He came down to earth. 'Don't be silly. I promise I didn't mean anything. Except, you know, look after yourself. Just that.' He obviously didn't think Clara looked convinced, and added, 'I'm sorry, I'm just a bit bound up in my own complications.'

'You're in love, aren't you?' Harry just nodded, with what Clara could only think of as bleak resignation. He was so clearly unhappy that Clara forgot about Shirley.

'Doesn't he love you back?'

Harry surprised her. 'He adores me. And I adore him. He's everything to me. I never knew it could be like this.'

'So what's stopping . . . ?'

'He's too important, and I'm too . . . well, conspicuous.' Harry sounded bitter. 'It makes me wish I'd been a bit more cautious. Then I could move in with him and pretend to be a friend or a flatmate, or even a "business partner". But no one would be fooled for a minute the way I am.'

'I really don't think they'd be fooled for a minute anyway. Not in this day and age. But heavens, all sorts of people are gay now. Can't he just come out of the wardrobe, or whatever you call it? Or is he a public figure?'

Harry tried a weak joke. 'Not quite public enough as far as I'm concerned. But, seriously, he's got a position he feels he'd have to resign if it came out. And a wife. And grown-up children who would be devastated. A whole lifestyle that can't just be torn apart to please me.' Privately Clara wondered why the wife came second to the job. Perhaps they always did. Harry patted her shoulder, and gave her a bright smile.

'Anyway, darling, enough of me. What are we going to do about little old you?'

They shifted about while the disco droned on. 'Who'd have thought that old Harry would fall for the oldest trap in the book? Romance.' The dance floor was beginning to fill out, and people kept crashing into them.

'Clara?'

'Yes?'

'Don't tell anyone, please. About me and . . . you know. Especially not Edward. It would just complicate matters.'

'OK.' Edward was now the last person she'd be chatting to over breakfast. She looked round, and spotted him across the other side of the room, dancing rather formally with Virginia.

'Lie,' murmured Edward to Virginia. At any other time it would have been bliss to be dancing like this, thought Virginia. She'd dreamt about this moment, imagining Edward's strong arms around her again, smelling the faint woody incense of his aftershave. Now she wondered how she could have endangered everything she loved for – well, a perfectly nice man. Suddenly Birmingham seemed no more than a warm glow – a pleasant, but distant memory, possibly one that belonged to someone else. She couldn't quite see why the thought of Edward had burned like a fever in her mind since. And Virginia did not tell lies, or at least only little white ones, and very occasionally stylish minimalist cream ones.

'Lie?' She had been really frightened by Simon's call, and had asked Edward what she should do about it.

'You should always lie to the person you're married to. *In extremis*, that is. If he accuses you of having an affair, just deny it. I've always lied to Clara. And we've been married for twenty-five years.'

'Then there'd be falsehood in my marriage. Rotting it to the core. Don't you think?' She was silent for a second, wondering who, except for Edward, could possibly regard Edward and Clara's marriage as a success. A thought struck her. 'You didn't tell Shirley about us, did you?'

He looked at her incredulously. 'Of course not.' Just for a moment, she had wondered. Shirley seemed so, well, knowing.

Suddenly Shirley appeared, swooping down in that manic way she'd taken on tonight. 'This is a ladies excuse-me. Colin's dying to dance with Virginia.' Edward handed her over, and Colin welcomed Virginia into his arms politely, although he could scarcely take his eyes off Shirley.

'Colin has asked me to marry him.' Shirley moved so that Edward could feel the hardness of her nipples through the thin fabric. That always turned him on.

'Congratulations.' His voice sounded dead, but he was singing softly along to the music.

'But *we*'re together now, aren't we? An item?' She ran one hand round the back of his neck and down his lapel. 'After all, it's time to leave Clara properly. Make it public. Announce everything tonight. Now that the children have finally gone.'

Edward drew back. 'I may have left Clara, but that doesn't mean I want to humiliate her in public.'

He always thought about Clara's feelings, never Shirley's. She thought about her own humiliation. Seen as the 'bit on the side' for all these years. She was not prepared to be second-best any longer. The time had come, she thought, to stake her claim in public. She slipped her hand under his jacket and moved closer. She knew his body so very well, and moved her lips to his. A kiss, a very thorough, lingering kiss. That would show Mrs Boring Wheeler.

And Edward had fallen for it. Responded the way he always did, his lips on hers, his hand stroking the golden curve of her back. The danger of it all, with everyone watching, was unbelievably exciting.

He suddenly broke free and walked out of the room. Shirley turned.

'Oh, hello, Clara.'

The people around them had stopped dancing to see what was happening, drawing back as Edward strode out of the room. Shirley was aware that she was standing in a ring, facing a white-faced Clara.

'Game, set and match, Clara, don't you think?' She smiled coldly, and slid through the crowd in search of Colin, who was sitting beside a distracted-looking Virginia. Neither of them had seen anything.

'I'm leaving now.' Virginia sounded controlled and pleasant but Shirley saw panic behind the elegant smile. Virginia, for the first time since she knew her, was desperately worried. 'I'm just going to find Clara to say goodbye.'

'Oh, don't bother, she says goodbyes are an awful nuisance . . .' Shirley didn't want Virginia mopping up Clara's tears. But Virginia hadn't heard, and was making her way through the crowd.

'Darling,' said Colin, 'you look ravishing.' Shirley could feel his hand fondling her breast as he tried to pull her on to his knee. Disgusting old lecher. Still, Edward needed to know that he didn't have an indefinite option on her. She treated him to a quick, but passionate, kiss. 'Wait here,' she commanded. 'I'm just going to the little girl's room.' He subsided, disappointed, but accepted her departure, and Shirley slipped off to find out whether Virginia was up to anything with Clara.

They were sitting together. Even under the flashing disco lights, Clara's face looked wooden. She was staring at the floor, and Shirley saw Virginia place a hand over hers.

'Are you all right?' Virginia kicked herself for not taking Shirley's advice and escaping while she could, but Clara looked so genuinely miserable she could hardly leave her.

Clara nodded, and Virginia saw a tear trickle down her cheek.

'Shirley?'

Another brief nod. 'Kissing,' she whispered. Virginia sighed. She knew that Shirley hated Clara, really hated her, but she'd hoped that once she gained confidence she'd be able to throw off the old Shirley, and move on. It seemed that she'd failed. Shirley needed a new life, and Virginia had offered it to her. For a moment, she felt as if it had been thrown in her face.

'I'm sorry,' she told Clara. 'I wish I could help.'

Clara shrugged. No one could help. 'Thanks.'

Virginia picked up her neat crocodile handbag, and rummaged around. 'Here.' She passed a key to Clara. 'You might need this.'

Clara gazed at it uncomprehendingly. Virginia scribbled on a piece of paper torn out of her notebook. 'Really,' she said. 'Our country cottage. It's yours. Nobody goes there. Except at weekends and we're not due . . . oh . . . for ages.' She stuffed it into Clara's bag.

Virginia squeezed her hand. 'I've got to get home now. But I mean it.'

Clara just sat there, glazed with unhappiness.

'If you do go down to the cottage,' said Virginia, in a last attempt to get through, 'I won't tell anyone. Unless you want me to.'

Clara nodded vaguely.

'A good party,' added Virginia, who could not leave her manners behind, even in a crisis. She pecked Clara on her cold cheek. 'Well done for organizing it.'

Neither of them noticed Shirley, standing on the

other side of the room, holding a glass of champagne and glittering dangerously.

She had seen Virginia give Clara a rustic pig key-ring. She remembered admiring how Virginia always had exactly the right accessories for every occasion – a silver Tiffany key ring for the London house, and the big pig for the 'cottage', 'so that we can't lose it in the Range Rover. Everything's so chaotic down there,' Virginia had explained, with the confident air of someone who called a missing Wellington boot 'chaos'.

You couldn't trust anybody, thought Shirley. You really couldn't.

She went to find Colin.

'Just one more little job, darling, and then perhaps we could go . . .' She ran her hand over him suggestively. Colin, for all his flirtatious ways, was a lump in bed, but Shirley was teaching him. The three wives had clearly had no idea, but then, wives obviously didn't. It was quite enjoyable, really. She too might just lie there and think of England once she'd got married. Because, one way or another, whether to Edward or Colin, she was getting married. Soon she would join that cosy little club that had blackballed her for so long.

'Harry's got a bit stuck with Clara Wheeler. She is the boss's wife, after all, but she and I have had a little disagreement. She's a bit menopausal really. Anyway, could you just take her a glass of her favourite tipple and rescue Harry? You only need to talk to her for a bit, but it would make her feel so much better.'

'You are sweet, worrying about her.' Colin took her chin in his hands. 'I just want to get you home and make love to you.'

Shirley disentangled herself, wondering how she was going to go home with two men without one of them noticing. 'Well, I feel very much to blame. But at least I can see she enjoys the rest of the party. Pink champagne with a big slug of vodka. A double – she gets very fed up if it's not strong enough.'

Seeing Edward kissing Shirley had been like a punch in the guts. Knowing about something, thinking about it, even imagining it – nothing was as piercingly painful as actually witnessing it. It had cut through the numb feeling that had partially protected her all day. She'd have expected to be immune, innoculated by the constant drip-drip-drip of Shirley's body language in the office, but she had seen Edward run his finger along Shirley's mouth in an unbearably intimate way. She'd only been aware of two people kissing at first, and she almost smiled, not recognizing them, thinking that the formality of the party hadn't taken long to break down into a typical Wiggins Frean binge. Then she saw the golden back pushing urgently against Edward, his big hands encircling it, and the warmth and gentleness of mouth on mouth. This kiss was in a completely different league from the clumsy encounter at their anniversary party.

The room felt loud and dark, and very, very cold. It was difficult to breathe. Clara sat down, wondering if she was going mad. Harry materialized out of nowhere, clutching two drinks. 'Bottoms up, darling.' He didn't ask anything, just sat down beside her with a quick hug.

'Life's a bitch and then you die, huh?'

Clara nodded, wishing the drink was stronger. She wanted a total anaesthetic. It didn't seem to be having any effect.

'I think the party's going well.' Harry was talking nonsense. It was a terrible party. He said a few more things but, cocooned in shock, she didn't hear them. She was vaguely aware of Virginia pressing something into her hand. 'For you. Do go,' she said, opening Clara's handbag for her and putting a piece of paper and a key inside. 'Don't forget.'

Colin appeared with another drink.

'Careful.' Harry put his hand out to take it from her. 'They're very strong.'

'Harry.' Her voice sounded tough and cold, even to her. 'Just let me go to hell in my own way, OK?' He almost flinched, as if she'd slapped his face, and she remembered to say 'sorry' in a vague sort of way, like a stranger who has trodden on a toe. She didn't notice him leave. There were cigarettes stubbed out in the remains of an avocado dip left on the table. She felt sick.

'Thanks for a great party, Clara.' A couple holding hands looked dishevelled and were dragging several others behind them. 'The bar's just closing and we're going down the clubs. Want to come?'

What a joke. Boring old Clara clubbing. She shook her head.

'Come with us instead.' Someone else grabbed her. 'Madam Jo-Jo's. Come on.'

She wriggled free. 'No, thank you. Have a lovely time.'

Max appeared. 'I'm seeing Judith home. Great party.'

'Life is full of surprises.' Judith was giggling away, hanging on to Max's arm. 'It just shows you,' she shouted over her shoulder. 'One man's meat is another man's poison.' One woman's kiss is another woman's poison, thought Clara,

They trickled past, all in a surprisingly good mood. Clara let most people kiss her cheek, leaning heavily against a table, feeling disembodied.

'Lovely time, great to meet everyone.'

'So glad.'

'Delicious food . . . quite a treat.'

'Thank you.'

'I was dreading taking my other half, but he's really enjoyed it.'

'How nice of you to say so.'

Then Harry came back again. 'It's all over. Time to go home.' He spoke gently, taking her arm.

She began to feel anger surge up in a wave with the last drink. She almost gagged on it. 'You're right, Harry. It's over. Quite over. I'm going.' She tried to walk in a straight line, and almost succeeded.

Edward appeared from nowhere and seized her arm. 'I'm taking you home. You're drunk.'

'It's over, Edward. Over, over, over. I'm going home alone, and I never want to see you again. Go to her. That's what you want.'

'I think you'd better leave, Edward.' Harry draped Clara's coat round her shoulders and took her from Edward. 'It's all right now. You're safe. I'm taking you back with me.' He very carefully steered her through the book-lined hall. Her elbow knocked a bowl of flowers to the ground, and later she remembered the startled, shocked face of someone trying to pick up the pieces, in isolation, like a photograph of the evening. She was just aware of people standing aside, looking worried, muttering to each other, and the sound of someone sobbing very loudly. Surely that wasn't her? Harry pushed her into a long black car.

'Very grand taxi, Harry.' She hiccuped through her sobs. 'Clever of you to find it so quickly.' There was another face there – one she'd met before, something familiar about him – who put a blanket quickly over her knees and got into the front seat.

'I know you, don't I? You don't look like a taxi driver.' Perhaps he looked like someone on the TV. Terence Stamp. She hoped she wasn't going to be sick all over the tartan rug.

'Shh. No, you don't.' Harry tucked the ends of the blanket in, and drew her head down to his lap. 'Time for sleep. Now lie down quietly. I'm taking you home.' Clara gave in, and the world began to spin. She was vaguely conscious of someone fussing around, doors slamming, some shouting and then darkness descending.

Shirley stirred in her bed, feeling the unaccustomed heat of another body beside hers at 7.30 a.m. God, it had been a good night. She stretched luxuriously. She'd managed to get rid of Colin after all, so that she could go home with Edward. There'd only been one worrying moment. She'd walked back into the party – just in time – to find Edward trying to take Clara home. The two-timing bastard. But before she could do anything Harry, bless him, had carried Clara off, and Clara had made a real fool of herself. At last. Shirley smiled to herself. Well, well, what a surprise. Mrs Perfect fallen off her pedestal.

Now Edward was asleep in her bed, for good.

She got up to make him a cup of coffee, thick and black, the way he liked it. She'd wake him with it, and they'd talk about where they went from here. Exit Clara. Enter Shirley. But not quite end of story. There'd be details to plan. Would they live in The Brambles? It would be typical of Edward to give it, lock, stock and barrel, to Clara out of sheer guilt. With details of registry offices and estate agents' particulars running pleasurably through her head, she started humming under her breath and snuggled up to Edward.

'What a relief to think we can go into the office together, without worrying about being seen.'

Edward opened his eyes sleepily. 'I think we'd better keep everything quiet for the time being.' He smiled and drew her to him briefly before jumping out of bed and stepping into the shower.

A silence shimmered between them as he emerged, towelling vigorously. 'What did you say?' Shirley asked, eventually.

He didn't notice the dangerous note in her voice

as he was pulling on his trousers and then reached out for his jacket. 'I mean, I don't think we should tell anyone until everything has been sorted out with Clara. It's for her to decide what to announce to the world.'

'Fine.' She almost choked on the word.

'I knew you'd understand. There's a good girl.' He straightened his tie, checked his briefcase and clicked it shut. 'I'll go in my car, shall I? So that people don't see us come in together?'

Virginia sat in her office in Wiggins Frean trying to pretend she was catching up on work. No one was in, except Naseem's cousin, who was Muslim and didn't drink. Lucky her. Squiggles of words drifted and floated in front of her eyes. She heard the crunch of Edward's footsteps.

'Hi.'

'Hello.' She waited for him to ask how the talk with Simon had gone. He went into his office and slammed the door. So much for friendship.

The telephone made her jump. 'It's Clara. I thought I'd take you up on your offer. If it still stands.' She sounded hoarse and tired, not like Clara at all.

'Oh. Yes. Of course. Let me tell you how to get there.' As Virginia talked, she regretted giving Clara the keys to the cottage. She felt like running away herself.

'Can you take Edward's calls, Judith?'

'Oh, yes, of course.' Judith seemed unaccountably cheerful. 'I don't blame Clara for not coming in.

Well, it would be above and beyond the call of duty. After last night.' She blushed, and scuttled away, as if she had said too much.

Derek walked past with a limp-looking bunch of carnations. 'Where's Clara?'

'Not in.'

He wobbled in the doorway, looking at the carnations as if they might explode any moment. 'Shauna and I wanted to thank Clara and we thought . . .'

Virginia sighed. 'There's a vase in my cupboard.' She waved a hand, and put her head down over the page proofs so she didn't have to hear what Shauna had thought.

'I can't find Clara.' It was one of the editorial assistants, blushing with nerves and holding a large white envelope.

'No one can. Leave a note.' Virginia got up and shut the door, hovering for a second as she saw a motorcycle messenger come down the corridor with a vast bunch of white flowers. Flowers round here usually came to Virginia. But he turned into Clara's office.

chapter 10

On her way into work, Shirley decided that she had better drive Edward down to The Brambles to collect his things. She didn't want to let him out of her sight. If Clara had any surprises up her sleeve – a fake suicide attempt, for example – she needed to be there to keep control of the situation. And if Clara was there, well, it would be an ideal opportunity to tell her about the divorce.

They set out at lunch-time. Clara wasn't there.

'Mrs Wheeler's off on holiday for a few weeks.' Dora Black, their cleaning lady, was vacuuming vigorously when they opened the door, and clearly knew exactly what had happened. Edward checked the hall table. Two brown envelopes, a circular urging him to join Neighbourhood Watch and leaflets for Pizza Deliveries, Carpet Cleaning and Instantly Unblock Your Drains. No goodbye note. Shirley's eyes raked the mantelpieces and the other tables in the drawing room. Nothing. The vacuum cleaner roared at her feet, and she had to move quickly to get out of Dora Black's way. Shirley wondered whether she could go upstairs with Edward, but somehow, with Dora here, she didn't like to. Although why she should care, she couldn't think. She ranged up and down the kitchen mantelpiece, picking up postcards and reading the backs of them. 'The Indian carvings are fabulous in the light of dawn. You must see for yourself. Love Caroline and Anthony.' Photographs of Eliza and Marcus as babies, drooling in a frame, snapshots of them as toddlers or children collaged together under plastic. Younger versions of Edward and Clara featured in these collages, wearing sunhats and sitting under beach umbrellas looking browner and younger, lifting elaborate cocktails to the camera. Some blustery cottage, probably in Kent, and the distinctive greyish-blue light of a British beach with the children standing on the edge of rockpools with nets, or making sandcastles. Well, Clara had her happy memories of her children and their holidays. Now it was time for Shirley to build some.

Edward came down with a suitcase.

'Is that all?'

'You've nowhere to put things. I can always come back.' He looked round the kitchen, picking off a fridge magnet. 'So she's taken that.'

'Taken what?' Shirley hoped it wasn't valuable.

He shook his head. 'Just a letter one of the children wrote her when they were small. It was sweet.'

Shirley decided to take him away before he got maudlin.

Dora was still vacuuming when they left, and didn't look up. Edward paused.

'Did Mrs Wheeler leave a contact number with you?' He'd hoped it could be made to sound casual, as if he wanted to check that Dora had everything she wanted. It was difficult to sound casual when you had to shout over the noise of a vacuum cleaner.

She didn't turn it off. 'I can't hear,' she yelled back.

'Mrs Wheeler,' he roared. 'Have you a number? For emergencies.'

'I'm not expecting any emergencies,' she shouted back. They were virtually vacuumed out of the house. Well, if they decided to keep The Brambles, Dora Black could definitely find another job, thought Shirley. Although, looking at its squat red-brick shape, punctuated with pillars, she thought something elegantly Georgian, like Virginia's house in Islington, would be nicer.

chapter 11

It was late afternoon by the time Clara found herself in Wiltshire, following the map to Virginia's cottage carefully, terrified that her pounding head was going to blot out her vision, or that the car would putter to a halt and leave her in a country lane. She'd spent the night at Harry's flat and Harry had accompanied her to The Brambles that morning to pick up her clothes, in case Edward was there. Unsurprisingly, their bed hadn't been slept in. It was like being slapped. Just for a few moments she had persuaded herself, as she put the key in the lock, that he might be there, furious, dismissive, or even – this a dwindling hope – repentant. He wasn't. He had gone to Shirley. It was really over. She walked through the cold rooms as if in a film about someone else's life, pulling open drawers and cupboards and pulling out items at random. Thick tights. Walking shoes. A little black dress. Her old pearls, that she had put away when she became 'fashionable'. An ancient letter from

Eliza, aged six, pinned up by fridge magnets and curling with age. 'You ar bewtiful, mummy. I luv you verry much.'

She didn't want Marcus and Eliza to worry about her. 'Oh, Harry,' she said, as they drove into the station forecourt. 'Tell the children I'm safe if they phone in from the States. I'll call you to get any messages. But please, don't tell anyone where I am.'

She dropped him at the station to take the train back to London, and the car seemed very empty. On her own now. The rain had started in earnest and she could scarcely make out the forms of the trucks thundering ahead. For a moment she was tempted just to drive into the back of one, but the thought of how pleased Shirley would be stopped that impulse. She turned on Radio 4 for company. A conversation was in progress about how female gerbils lost interest in their appearance when separated from their mate. 'Gerbils, like humans, mate for life,' explained the commentator. She puzzled for a while over how one could tell that a gerbil had lost interest in its appearance. Stopping at a Little Chef, she stared at herself in the mirror, panda-eyed with misery, hair wisping up in a frizz. Definitely up there with the gerbils.

'Turn right just after the Honey For Sale notice' – almost impossible to see in the dark – 'then left before the ford,' Virginia had told her. 'Up a rough track and Honey Tree House is on the right.' The rain had slowed to a drizzle, and the windscreen wipers slapped unsympathetically across her eyes. The wheels kept slipping in the mud. A tangle of black branches had almost turned the bumpy lane into a tunnel, and Clara felt like Prince Charming battling his way through the undergrowth to the Sleeping Beauty's Castle. If you ran fast enough, or far enough, she thought, you could, perhaps, run away from pain. But it followed her, persistent, dogged, determined not to be thrown off.

The house was in total darkness, with its front gate swinging off its post. A dog barked in the distance, and she tentatively opened the door of the car, putting her foot in an icy puddle. Stories of drug dealers using deserted country houses for meetings crawled down her spine from her brain, and lodged, cold and hard, somewhere in the pit of her stomach. It was very, very dark, and she wasn't even sure if she knew the way back. She felt tears begin to bubble up behind her eyes.

There was a loud creak, and the rasp of wood on stone. 'Hello?' An ancient voice, but a strong one, reassuringly female. Mrs Mudge did not sound like a drug dealer. 'Is that Mrs Wheeler?'

Clara staggered out of the car with such relief that she nearly fell into Mrs Mudge's arms. 'I've lit a fire, and got in a nice stew. Mrs Law said you'd be down about now and'd need looking after. I've made the bed in the spare room – third on the left as you go upstairs.'

She looked around her. The house smelt of beeswax, cedarwood, woodsmoke and home-dried lavender mingled with churchy aromas of balsam, mossy old stone and incense. Honey Tree House was old. It felt as if it was growing out of the landscape.

'There's whisky, gin or wine – Mrs Law'd want you to help yourself.'

'I'm feeling a bit hungover . . .'

'Best malt whisky, then.' She handed Clara an enormous glass.

Clara tried to see her future in the blazing fire, a game they had played as children, believing that they could see the silhouettes of the men they would marry in the glowing coals. If she'd looked long enough, back then, she wondered if she'd have seen the willowy outline of Shirley, burning vigorously away in the corner. There were no shapes in this fire. Logs weren't quite the same. Either that or she didn't have a future.

'I'll be off then.' Mrs Mudge reminded her of a hospital matron, doing her last rounds. Clara felt like an invalid and nodded, too weak to jump up and say thank you. After a bit of pottering, the door closed, and Clara realized that she was, at last, on her own. Down a muddy lane without a telephone. There really was nobody here.

She put her head down on her arm and howled.

'I can't talk to Clara about a divorce if I can't even find her, can I?' Edward was tetchy, the following day, just when things ought to be getting back to normal after the party. Guilt, thought Shirley. Guilt, guilt, guilt. 'And after what happened at the party, I don't think it's fair if we're the ones who break the news to the whole wide world before she knows exactly what the score is.'

She considered telling him exactly where Clara was, but decided not to. 'This whole business isn't fair,' she said. 'On me. On you. On Clara.' This was a lie. Frankly she thought Clara had been treated perfectly fairly. She didn't have to stay married to a man with a mistress, and if she chose to do so, then it was her lookout what she stumbled across at office parties. Why didn't she get a life? 'If you're really worried about fair, then we should get everything out into the open as soon as possible. So people can start the healing process.' She added the last bit to make herself sound a bit more caring.

'Healing, my foot,' said Edward. 'Being married for twenty-five years isn't something you can throw off in a day.'

'You aren't throwing it off in a day.' Shirley tried to be patient. 'You and I have been together for more than ten years.'

He kissed her, slightly absentmindedly. At least they'd come into the office together today.

Everyone was very subdued and hungover, and no one had quite met her eye. (For gawd's sake, it was the night before last, Shirley muttered to herself. However pink the drinks, they must have worn off by now.) Judith was gazing in despair at Clara's desk, which had four vases of flowers, and a pile of handwritten envelopes addressed to her, all threatening to topple over.

'Which hospital is Clara in?'

'Hospital?' Edward sounded startled.

'To send on all the flowers and cards from well-wishers. I assumed she must be ill.'

'Er . . .' Edward seemed at a loss for words.

'Just a little tired. These flowers are all "thank-yous" for the party. I must say, everyone has made a tremendous effort.' You could depend on Virginia, who had appeared as if by magic, to smooth things over.

A motorcycle messenger appeared in the door, almost obscured by another huge bunch of flowers. 'Where do you want these?'

'We don't.' Shirley didn't see why the place had to look like a florist's shop. No one had sent *her* flowers after organizing the office party. It was amazing what people would do when it came to the boss's wife. Well, this time next year, *she'd* be the boss's wife and they'd have to take a bit more notice of her. The messenger hovered uncertainly.

'Perhaps Edward could take them home?' Judith wasn't going to let go, was she?

'Edward isn't going home.' Shirley thought it was time things were made clear.

Everyone looked at Edward.

He flushed. 'Well, I certainly can't take this lot back to The Brambles.' So, he still wasn't going to admit anything. The fire inside raged even more vigorously. They were amongst friends, weren't they?

'I really don't think there's room for them here . . .' Virginia waved a hand to indicate the tiny office, piled high with paper.

'Flowers. How lovely.' Harry tried to get past the motorcycle messenger, eyeing his leathers apprecia- tively. 'Mmm. I like your outfit.' The messenger moved away hastily, thrusting the flowers at Shirley.

'Where's Clara?' Edward sounded just a bit too concerned for Shirley's peace of mind.

'I don't know.' Harry eyed the messenger's

retreating leather-clad bottom. 'She told me to tell everyone not to worry though. Although, frankly, I think a bit more worrying of that kind round here might be a good thing, but there you are.'

Great. It didn't take you long to change sides, did it? Shirley fumed silently. She looked at the flowers. She certainly wasn't going to have these testimonials to Clara's spurious popularity littering up her flat. She could just see the beginning of a message that read, 'With thanks and appreciation for . . .' She hastily passed them on to Virginia. Virginia, not used to standing round holding bouquets of flowers for other people, looked down at them as if they were unrecognizable objects sprung from Outer Space.

'Do you know where Clara is?' Shirley addressed Virginia, thinking about the rustic pig key ring.

'I wouldn't even hazard a guess.' That was interesting. Technically not a lie, but definitely along those lines. Shirley tried to think if Virginia had ever done any of this Jesuitical procrastination before. Not quite as white as she was so fashionably painted.

'Perhaps they could be sent to a local hospital. Or distributed round the building.' Judith was obviously trying to impress them with her sense of initiative.

'Oh, no.' Virginia made her first practical contribution to the conversation. 'I think Clara would want to see her flowers. If they're still alive when she gets back.'

'Yes. I'd say that's only fair.' Harry unfolded and re-folded his arms.

'As you seem to be so on top of the situation, Harry – ' Shirley smiled sweetly at him ' – perhaps you'd like to take them all and give them to Clara when you see her?'

'Anything to oblige.' Harry turned round and left the room, without taking any of them with him. Shirley took a deep breath, and followed Edward into his office, shutting the door behind her.

'Edward,' she said, determined not to be put off again. 'Edward, we do need to talk.'

'Do we?' He looked up briefly, and went back to skimming the file that Virginia had brought in. 'I think it would be better to wait until after this latest deal.' He looked up again and smiled at her. 'Really.'

If you spend your whole life looking at other houses when you open the curtains in the morning, thought Clara on her first morning at Honey Tree House, then there's something quite unnerving about just seeing trees, fields and sky. But she felt that she had space to breathe and think. There was no one else to think about except herself. In a way it was a relief.

She pottered around Honey Tree House. It was, of course, the perfect, unspoilt country home. She wondered why Virginia always spoke of it with a sigh in her voice, usually protesting about the constant shoring up it needed. Gutters cleared here, and leaves swept there. She could see, from the way everything glowed and gleamed, that the old furniture was lovingly polished. Honey Tree House was half-Jacobean and half-Queen Anne, with a tiny pretty sitting room and a hall that could obviously be turned into a dining room. All the floors were polished with beeswax, rising and falling unevenly as if following the line of the hill, and dark beams divided the creamy walls and ceilings into patchwork. Colours like moss and cranberry faded on horsehair arm-chairs and sofas, with velvet shawls, worn embroidery and needlepoint cushions piled up in comforting heaps. A series of Wellington boots in increasing sizes, starting with tiny ones, lined up beside the back door, as if their owners had just come in.

She walked for hours in the crisp autumn air, up the lane beside the house, scuffing her feet in the fallen leaves, playing Pooh-sticks on a little bridge, occasionally throwing stones at any stick that reminded her of Shirley. There was a sharp, cold tang to the brilliant sunshine, but she felt a sense of peace creeping through the pain. Perhaps her new life should be somewhere old-fashioned and safe. Towns and suburbs left you looking over your shoulder all the time.

In the evening, she climbed the stairs to her room, concentrating on the way the old copper runners clipped neatly against the hair-cord carpet and the polish of the dark wood glimmered on either side. She pulled back the heavy weight of eiderdowns and counterpane, slid between the crisp linen sheets and neatly turned blankets, and then, propped up on a thick feather pillow, fell into a terrible, restless sleep.

She dreamed of Shirley, a dreadful powerless dream where her feet dragged along in some kind of slime, her limbs were paralysed, and long, soundless screams struggled out of her leaden body. Shirley just watched, with that cruel, cat-like look Clara found so menacing in meetings. Clara struggled to wake up. She must wake up.

A sudden, heart-stopping twitch broke through the dream and she lay there, as still as she could, with her heart thumping in her ears, trying to see through the inky country blackness. Fear crawled in the pit of her stomach. If she even moved, or breathed a sound, she was sure that something was out there, ready to scrunch her up.

Gradually, as her eyes adjusted and her breath calmed, she could see shapes – the door standing ajar, the curtain blowing in the window, a tree creaking outside. All quite safe and peaceful. It was so quiet, just the rustling of the wind through the bushes, and the crackle of twigs under some animal.

She dropped off to sleep, then woke, far too early. The heaviness of the nightmare still hung over her, along with the ache and the emptiness. Better, on the whole, to get up, and look through Virginia's books and newspapers to see if there was anything to do in the area. Or give the place a clean. Anything was better than lying in bed, frightened, without the slightest reason to be.

Shirley was standing in the kitchen, looking immaculate and composed. 'You left the back door unlocked.' She didn't bother to say hello. 'I've been waiting for you.'

Clara wondered if she was supposed to apologize She moved towards the kettle, her heart thumping 'Really?'

'We're getting married. Edward and me. We thought you ought to know.'

Clara considered correcting her grammar, and decided against it. 'Edward is already married. He's said nothing about a divorce.' She wished she could think of something clever or witty to say. She couldn't bear to look at Shirley. Edward hadn't even come to tell her himself. Scared to face her, she supposed.

'He's been too busy. I said I'd tell you. He thought that was a good idea. After that scene you made at the party he decided that it would be better to do this woman to woman.' Clara could see that Shirley was watching her carefully. 'Anyway, we don't care about the piece of paper. If you make us wait five years for a decree absolute, we'll wait five years. We've waited long enough already.'

Clara thought about the waiting she'd done, night after night, for Edward to come home from Shirley. 'You know absolutely nothing about waiting. Anyway, how did you know I was here?'

It was her big mistake. She had offered Shirley triumph, and Shirley took it ruthlessly. 'Virginia told me.' It was a double betrayal. I have Edward, and I also have Virginia. You mean nothing to either of them. Shirley glittered in victory, and pushed a piece of paper towards Clara.

'Please communicate through solicitors at this address in future. That's what Edward wants. Have a good holiday.'

And she was gone, leaving Clara frightened, angry and terribly, terribly alone.

*

The car door slammed again.

What now? Forgotten something? Clara honestly didn't think she could stand another moment of Shirley's malice. She got up on trembling legs to lock the back door and found herself face to face with Virginia.

'Hello.' Close up, Virginia looked glassy, exhausted and older. 'You're up early. I hope I didn't wake you.'

'I can easily go.' Clara felt in the way. 'If you want to be alone.'

'Oh, no. Do stay.' Virginia smiled without her usual crisp sparkle. 'I'd like to talk.' She went out and came back with a suitcase. 'Don't answer this if you don't want to, but what was Shirley doing down here?'

'Filing my divorce papers.'

Virginia frowned. 'She's very young in many ways. Too impulsive.'

Clara was sick of people understanding Shirley. She was a bitch, an out-and-out bitch, and she wished she knew why Virginia had broken her promise and told her where Clara was.

'Let's have a drink,' Virginia suggested, rifling one of the cupboards and pulling out a selection of bottles that had clearly been abandoned for good reason.

Clara flashed a quick glance at the clock. It was ten to seven in the morning, and the first fingers of sunlight were beginning to warm the grey sky. Virginia plonked what looked like a bottle of sherry on the table. 'Simon's finest Madeira,' she said expertly extracting it from the village hall raffle offerings. 'Very appropriate for the time of day, I think.' She saw the expression on Clara's face. 'I've been driving around almost all night.'

'I'll have whatever you're having.' Clara was almost too surprised to speak.

'I expect you'd like to know what I'm doing here,' offered Virginia, pouring two huge glasses of Madeira.

Clara hoped she wasn't going to be sick.

'Well,' Virginia continued. 'I'd always wondered how you managed. Why you put up with it. The affair with Shirley. Everything. Whether you were just too frightened of being on your own to walk out. Or if you just loved him so much you couldn't bear to be without him. Or was it just the usual thing about the children? And what's made you leave now. So I've come to ask you. Because I need to make some decisions of my own.'

Clara felt utterly exhausted all of a sudden. Now she was being asked to explain herself.

'I'm sorry.' Virginia saw her expression. 'I'm so very sorry. I'm being thoughtless. You don't have to tell me, of course you don't. I was hoping you could help me, that's all.' She sounded desperate, Clara observed, feeling as if Virginia was at the other end of a long dark tunnel. Well, perhaps she should tell Virginia everything. Perhaps it would help her make sense of it all.

'Edward and I just never talked about it. Pretending everything is normal can get you through an awful lot. I never talk about Shirley, and he never talks about Tom. It's a deal, I think. Of sorts. I think I got the worst of it, though, and now it's over.'

Virginia drained the glass. 'Tom?'

'The baby.'

'The baby,' repeated Virginia, pausing as she selected another bottle. 'Do you mind telling me? Please.'

Clara tore a strip of flesh off her thumb, a bit too violently. It hurt, almost enough to make tears start in her eyes. 'Damn. Have you got a tissue?' Virginia had not run huge departments of 'girls' without keeping tissues around her at all times. She passed one to Clara with an expert flourish.

'Don't worry. I'm not going to cry. It was a long time ago.' Anyway, thought Clara, I didn't cry then. Only Edward had cried. She'd felt quite jealous of that really. It would have been a release somehow.

'What happened?' Virginia sounded kind.

'We always wanted three children. I don't know why, you must think we were mad. But we did. And the other two came so easily. It took ages before I got pregnant again – we'd almost thought of fertility clinics. But then it happened and we were thrilled. *Both* thrilled.' Clara emphasized this, because she could almost see Virginia thinking that women often wanted another baby when men didn't.

'He was a boy. Tom. One of those lovely, chunky babies with a big gummy smile, and chubby thighs. Really solid and cuddly.' Clara smiled at the memory. It was lovely to talk about Tom, because she never did. 'You're so much more relaxed when you've already had two, you can really enjoy a last baby.' She paused, thinking back. 'But in some ways, he was Baby Jekyll and Master Hyde. Gloriously cheerful during the day, grizzly and colicky at night. We hardly got any sleep. We were both going mad. Demented, and Edward had a big deal on. As usual.

'Anyway, one night he was particularly grizzly. We checked everything, tried Calpol, pacing up and down with him – I even drove off him around in the car for an hour, but nothing worked. Eventually Edward said he couldn't stand it any longer. "Put him in the top room, where we can't hear him. Just ignore him."'

She looked down at the sherry. 'We slept like logs. We were exhausted. So was Tom – we thought. At 8.30 a.m., we'd had a really good sleep-in and we went up to get him up. That was always my favourite time of day, because he'd always have such a big smile for whoever got him out of his cot.

'Not that day, though. He was dead. Not Tom at all, not even a feeling of him.'

Virginia paled. 'It wasn't anything Edward . . .?'

'Oh, no. The inquest couldn't find a reason. Perhaps a minor virus. Another Sudden Infant Death Syndrome victim. The coroner didn't even attach any blame to us. The room was the right temperature, new mattress, we didn't smoke, you know. But if we'd kept him in our room, I've always thought he'd be alive today. I should have gone upstairs with him. But I was so tired. He'd have been eleven next week.' She looked down at her hands. 'I've missed him so much.'

'I'm so sorry,' Virginia put a tentative hand on her shoulder. 'People do always blame themselves when someone dies. It's only natural.'

'It's only this year I've been able to start to say goodbye to Tom. You don't "get over" things like that, but I think you can come through them. The sad thing is that Edward and I didn't come through it together. I had to shut him out, to stay sane.'

'Did you?'

'I blamed him terribly. I didn't want to take Tom upstairs, leave him crying on his own. Edward persuaded me – even showed me a line in a baby book that said "if all else fails, and you're afraid of losing your temper, place the baby safely in his cot and shut the door". I just hate to think of Tom dying on his own, thinking we didn't care about him. But really, intellectually, I know it wasn't Edward's fault. I just don't *feel* that way. And I know that Edward feels he owes me. That he couldn't walk out on me on top of everything else. That's why, deep down, I always felt quite secure. Until now, of course.'

'No.' Virginia couldn't think of anything to say. Nothing seemed adequate.

'The awful thing is that I knew how isolated Edward became because of it. I used to hear people saying things like "How's Clara?" or "Is there anything Clara needs?" No one ever asked Edward how he felt, or if he needed anything. That's why I couldn't have left him. I wasn't much use to him, but I wouldn't have walked out. That would have been like accusing him to his face. And that's what everyone would have thought. It's as if men haven't got feelings. Once he snapped, "Tom was my son too, you know" and then went off and got very drunk. And never talked about him again.'

'Oh, dear.' Virginia felt her responses were wholly inadequate.

'I just couldn't reach out to him. There wasn't room in my heart. Once I found him crying in Tom's room, holding a little white bunny someone had given him when he was born, but I shut the door and never let him know I'd seen.' Neither of them had cried at the funeral, she remembered. They'd sat in the back of a black stretch limo, facing the most impossibly tiny white coffin screwed down in front of them, holding hands quite tightly in horror, but unable to find any words. 'We just stopped talking. Stopped making love. Stopped sharing anything much. Not because he didn't try. I just couldn't respond. It was my fault, too.'

'That's not what he thinks. He'd never have blamed you. I'm sure of that.'

'What really hurt is that he seems to have forgotten Tom completely. Just won't remember him. I suppose I can understand why, just like I've always understood why Shirley had to happen. Deep down, that is. It's just very hard not to be hurt by it. And I've only just got the courage to admit it all to myself. When it's too late.' She paused.

'I have to admit . . .' Virginia tried to suppress the memory of how quickly and easily she'd been unfaithful with far less justification ' . . . that in those circumstances, I'd have fallen to a Shirley myself.'

'So would I, if a male version had been around,' said Clara sadly, 'but understanding things doesn't give you the power to change them.'

Virginia sat for a moment in quiet agreement.

367

'Well, it certainly puts my problems with Simon into proportion.'

'Simon?' Clara's hand flew to her mouth. 'Not you, too? I thought your marriage was perfect?'

'It was. Until a little matter of someone called Hazel. Who was lonely . . .'

'And one thing led to another.'

'It did, I'm afraid.' Virginia sighed. 'I always told him that there'd be no second chances if he did that.'

'But?'

'But it wasn't really a perfect marriage after all. He wants something different. Someone who isn't me. Who, in his words, "is there for him".'

Clara was amazed. 'He adores you. I've seen his face when he looks at you.'

Virginia shrugged. 'Like you, we never talked about it. Until the night of the party.'

She had let herself into the house in Islington, giving the babysitter money for a taxi. She didn't like the fact that, after all the urgency in his voice, Simon hadn't even been there. Or the look on his face when he did come through the door eventually. Had it been it guilt, or simply a reflection of her own expression?

'I'm sorry,' he'd said; sitting down opposite her without taking his coat off. 'This just isn't working, is it?'

Virginia's mouth had gone dry, and she had had the sensation of the room closing in on her. She hadn't expected this. 'Not working' sounded terribly final. Irreparable, even.

'What isn't? In what way?' Too late, she'd realized she might start gabbling if she didn't get a grip.

He'd shaken his head. 'Our marriage. Don't come the top executive with me. This is our life we're talking about.' After fidgeting with a set of African bowls that Virginia had chosen to 'soften the hard lines of the coffee table' – as she had put it in *Heart & Soul* – he stood up and paced up and down, hands in his pockets. If only he'd take his coat off. He looked about to go out. For ever. 'We've always said that screwing around wrecks marriages.'

'But . . .' She'd wanted to say that it didn't have to wreck theirs. 'I haven't been screwing around,' was all she'd managed, in a very small voice. It wasn't a lie.

'No,' Simon had said. 'Neither have I. But I have been having an affair, and I think you should know about it.'

The words hadn't touched her at first. They'd been so absurd as to be meaningless. 'No, I shouldn't.' Virginia had jumped up, not wanting to hear. 'I don't want to know about it. Why can't you just keep it a secret?'

He'd gazed at her in amazement. 'Because we always promised to tell each other the truth, that's why.'

'We always promised we'd be faithful, but that doesn't seem to have stopped you.' Careful, Virginia, she'd thought. Don't get hysterical. Although she had felt a pulse thumping in her throat, had tasted the sick backwash of terror on her tongue. Or perhaps it had been a Pink Drink. She'd wondered what would happen if she mentioned her own night of passion. It seemed so trivial in the face of Simon's massive betrayal. Meaningless.

She'd shaken head. 'What are you going to do?'

'That's up to you, isn't it?'

Virginia had been puzzled. 'Me?' She had been bracing herself for the announcement of departure. A huge, empty hole – her life without Simon – had just opened up ahead.

'He told me I had two options,' she explained to Clara. 'He's been offered a posting in Singapore. Good money. Better prospects. I won't be able to work, and it'd be hopeless if I stayed here. If we can't hold a marriage together when we live in the same house, we certainly can't do it across three continents. And he says he doesn't want to try. If he goes alone, he won't be coming back.'

'And the other option?' Clara tried to imagine Virginia in Singapore, without the awards ceremonies and power lunches.

'I go with him. Forget my career.' She grimaced. 'When we come back people will be talking about restaurants I've never even heard of, let alone been to.' Clara wondered how much this really mattered to Virginia. It seemed an odd thing to worry about.

More importantly –' Virginia had obviously read her mind ' – people would think I was running away from failure. I wouldn't be such a hot property when I returned. I certainly couldn't just pick up my career where I left off. And sometimes, when you've been at the top, no one wants you further down the ladder either. I might never work again.'

'I'm sure you would.' Clara tried to be reassuring, but who was she to talk?

'I'd be nobody in Singapore. I tried to tell him.'

'What did he say?'

'He told me that I would be someone. I'd be his wife.' Clara could imagine how well that must have gone down.

'You know those statistics? One in three people who get divorced regret it? But what about the other two? Who change their lives and grow into new, more fulfilled people? Where do you think I fit in, statistically?'

'I shouldn't worry about statistics.' Clara could see that Virginia really wasn't thinking straight. 'I should concentrate on what you really want. Forget about what you think you ought to do. Forget about other people. Just think about the two of you.'

'I know,' murmured Virginia. 'I just love waking up beside him in the morning. He smells so sweet.' There was a silence. 'I need him,' she said. 'I love him.'

'In that case,' said Clara. 'I think you'd better take up his offer. Before Hazel does.'

'But I can't forgive him.'

'Join the club.' Clara decided that melon liqueur was not for her, and selected a vivid pink bottle which claimed to have something to do with cherries. She poured out another glass and tasted it. Funny sort of breakfast, but it might grow on you.

'By the way – ' Clara thought that Virginia still owed her an explanation ' – why did you tell Shirley I was here?'

Virginia looked appalled. 'I didn't.'

There was a silence.

Eventually Clara took a deep breath. 'So it was another case of Shirley's bullying. She must have followed me, or spied on us. She is, you know, quite seriously manipulative. Edward made me promise not to undermine her when I joined the company, but there comes a point when I have to say what I think. Even to you.'

'I can see that.' Virginia restored the corks to bottles, and gathered them back into the cupboard. 'Let's have some toast and a healthy walk. Then I'm driving back to London. And I'll sort Shirley out.' She smiled at Clara. 'Stay here as long as you like. I'll let you know what happens.'

For two weeks Clara ate, slept, walked, and cried. All the tears she'd never wanted to shed in front of Edward came pouring out. She hurled the Pooh-sticks into the river with increasing venom, then collapsed against the bridge sobbing. Underneath, however, she could feel something knitting together, something that told her she would survive.

Until she wandered into the tiny village shop for a pint of milk one morning, and looked at the magazine rack. It hardly carried any magazines at all. Just *Woman's Own*, *Prima* and *Viva*. Until now, she hadn't asked if there was any call for *Heart & Soul*.

The latest *Viva* was out, with a striking yellow strip across the side. 'Save £2 on our special offer. This issue just 50p. Our gift to you!'

'They're going ever so well,' said the shop

assistant. 'We've had to re-order twice, and they've only been in two days.' Clara asked for a copy of the *Guardian* and flicked to the media pages.

'Glossy price war breaks out' screamed the headline on page 7. 'Magazine giant Publishing Unlimited has started a glossy magazine price war that could push some smaller companies out of business. Just two days before the re-vamped *Heart & Soul* – edited by Publishing Unlimited's former star editor, Virginia Law – emerged with its own bargain 99p price, both *Viva* and its sister title *House & Home* hit the newstands with massively slashed cover prices, and major TV advertising campaigns. Media insiders estimate that *Viva*'s sales, already on the up-and-up, could double, and Publishing Unlimited confirms that an unprecedented 1 million print run has been ordered. "We've had a record year of profits at Publishing Unlimited," said the MD Paul Long, "and we decided it was time to give something back to our readers. The special 50p price tag rewards our current readership, and offers a unique opportunity to other women to try *Viva*'s best-selling package." Edward Wheeler, MD of Wiggins Frean, publishers of the rival *Heart & Soul*, was unavailable for comment.'

They had lost everything. Clara suppressed the familiar clutch of panic curdling somewhere around her bowels.

It was time to go back to real life. To find somewhere to live, a job, some friends. She folded the unused black dress and placed it neatly back in the suitcase. Heaved the suitcase into the boot of the

Volvo. It wasn't until she was on the motorway that she realized she didn't know where she was driving back to.

While Clara was buying a copy of *Viva* in the newsagent's shop, Edward was calling an emergency meeting. 'We've got a spy.' He thumped the 50p copy of *Viva* down on the boardroom table. 'Someone who wants to ruin us.' Virginia caught her breath. This made her look such a fool.

'It must be the printers.' Shirley tapped her notebook authoritatively, and leaned back in her chair, pushing her breasts forward. A button on her silk shirt strained for a minute and tantalizingly held until she relaxed her shoulders. Virginia saw Edward's eyes catch the brief moment when the fabric pulled and the shadows of her nipples darkened against the cream silk.

Virginia thought quickly and shook her head. 'No printer would stay in business for one second if they allowed any kind of industrial espionage. Anyway, there are only about ten days between the cover going to the printers and us hitting the streets – hardly time to set up an ad campaign and re-design the cover of two magazines, especially as they come out a few days before us.'

'How long would you need? Harry?'

Harry looked white with strain. 'Going like the clappers you could just do it in ten days. They'd still have had to know before the printers did, though, because they couldn't change their distribution slot in that time.'

'Perhaps it's a coincidence.' This was unusual. Shirley was usually the first one to suggest a conspiracy theory. Perhaps happiness with Edward had softened her. Virginia hoped so. After her strange breakfast with Clara, their close friendship seemed to have suddenly dissolved.

'Publishing Unlimited just never do these kinds of promotions. It's completely and absolutely out of character.' Virginia was anxious to justify her original position.

'Well, they're doing one now. What do you think, Harry?'

'I think you're right.' Harry spoke reluctantly. 'I think we have a spy in the camp.' Everyone looked at everyone else.

'I don't know if I should say this . . .' Shirley sounded unusually hesitant. 'I don't want to sound disloyal, or give anyone any wrong ideas . . .'

'Go on.' Edward moved papers restlessly round the table, just for something to do.

'But I saw Clara leaving the Publishing Unlimited building about three weeks ago. I heard some gossip that she was talking to them about a job.'

Edward picked up his papers and left the room. Virginia, Harry and Shirley looked at each other.

'You're wrong, Shirley.' Harry's voice was low.

'Well,' said Shirley with satisfaction. 'Perhaps you know more about it than I do.' She followed Edward out of the room.

Clara leant tiredly against the front door of the white stucco building that housed Harry's flat, peering through the bobbly glass panels and chicken wire that had been obviously been substituted for something more gracious. While she had been away, London had sprouted Christmas decorations, with twinkling lights strung across streets and advertisements proclaiming a sense of cheer that Clara could not envisage ever sharing again. It looked as if there was a Christmas tree in Harry's foyer.

She had rung three times, and there wasn't a sound, although she was sure she could see a chink of light under the curtains. It was the first floor, wasn't it? Perhaps she had been wrong. She turned back to the car. There must be somewhere else she could try.

'Darling.' The door opened behind her. Harry looked both ways down the street, as if he was being watched.

'Harry. I'm awfully sorry, but I couldn't think where else to go. I'll get a flat tomorrow, I promise.' Harry didn't look very welcoming. 'Perhaps I should go to a hotel.'

'No, no. Come in quickly.' What, she wondered, was all the rush about? 'You've heard the news? Edward's taking it very well for someone who's lost a packet.'

She climbed the ornately floral-carpeted staircase three steps behind him, to avoid tripping over her suitcase which he was dragging up the stairs. 'He's lost more than a packet, Harry. He's lost everything.'

Harry whistled. 'That means you have too. Pity you didn't leave him earlier really. Unless there's a hidden stash you can claim?'

Clara shook her head wearily. On the journey back from Wiltshire the worry about money had grown like a tumour. As if she'd been in remission for a few short years, and now faced more months and years of insecurity. She had given up pretending, even to herself, that the money didn't matter. She kept working out what kind of a mortgage a PA's salary would support – without any down payments to help it. A studio in Peckham if she was lucky. Where would Eliza and Marcus call home? Everyone deserved to go home some time, even if they were 'grown-up'. And would anyone want a middle-aged secretary with only one job behind her? In the light of Publishing Unlimited's strategy, she couldn't believe that that job was still on offer, although it would nice to think it was. Anger was beginning to warm up the cold pit in her stomach.

'I've got to call someone.' Harry waited, tapping his foot urgently. 'Damn! He's switched his mobile off.'

'I'd better go. I'm in your way.'

He pushed her back into her chair. 'Absolutely not. We've got to sit here and plan your escape from this nightmare. Now think logically. Are there any artworks that you could get out of The Brambles? Antiques? Shares in your name?'

She thought about the £100,000 spent on furniture, curtains and amusing little extras at The Brambles last year. She'd be lucky to get £20,000 back in the auction rooms.

'Well, it's a start.' Harry reminded her that £20,000 was hardly chicken feed. 'But you'll have to get it out before the gannets descend.' He watched her face pale at the thought of burgling her own home. 'For God's sake, Clara. If Edward's got any sense he'll want you to squirrel away as much as you can. And even if he doesn't want you to, he needs you to. Seize the day, darling! Or at least seize the goods and chattels.' He dialled again, feverishly. 'God, still not answering.'

A key rattled in the door. Harry froze.

Clara, used to people letting themselves in, hardly looked up. Until she saw who was standing uncertainly in the doorway.

'Sorry I'm late. I couldn't get away until now.' Framed against a backdrop of chintz wallpaper, a welcoming smile slipping off his face like snow sliding down a mountainside, was Sir Ralph Headcorn, chairman of Publishing Unlimited.

'Oops,' said Harry.

'This is my resignation.' Virginia slipped an envelope over the desk. 'With my regrets.' Edward didn't open it, but turned it over several times, as if it contained some kind of secret. 'I really am terribly sorry,' added Virginia helplessly. 'I feel dreadful.' They seemed such tiny words compared with the enormity of what she had done in suggesting this deadly strategy to Edward.

'Why?' He pushed his chair back, waving her to sit down and putting his feet on the desk, looking at her in a way that made her stomach flutter.

'I feel this is all my fault. This . . . disaster . . . was my suggestion.'

He grinned. 'Hardly. I've been taking horrendous gambles in business since I was nineteen. And I take it you didn't go running to Publishing Unlimited.'

Virginia nodded. 'Of course not.'

'I never thought you did, I must say. I have my theories on who it might have been. But then perhaps Shirley's right, it was some sort of leak from a disaffected junior or something.' He put the letter back on the desk without opening it. 'Not that it matters now. But I don't want you to go.'

'Doesn't matter?' Virginia was outraged. 'The whole magazine sabotaged and you say it doesn't matter? Well, it may not matter to you, but it does to me, very much. And you can bet your bottom dollar it matters to the staff, who don't have a nice little account in Switzerland to tide them over.'

'Neither, I can assure you, do I. I've never had anything sensible like that. Calm down. Of course it matters. But there's nothing we can do now, except control the situation. Possibly try to sell it off as a going concern. I think the receivers will be called in soon, and I'm afraid that means I'll be banned from the building. But I'd like you to stay and see us through. If you go, so does everyone's chance of a job.'

Virginia had been afraid of this. She and Simon had agreed to defer her resignation until after the figures from the new promotion had come in. She'd hoped she'd leave on a high, and, anyway, with so much riding on the new strategy, it wouldn't have been fair to pull out earlier.

'I was going to go anyway.'

He raised an eyebrow. 'Because of Simon?'

'How did you know?'

'I guessed. I've been meaning to ask you what happened, but I've been so worried about Clara . . .'

'Have you?' That was interesting. And unexpected. He really hadn't seemed either interested or worried. But then he seemed remarkably unconcerned about the collapse of his entire business. And he obviously wasn't going to talk about any of it. Virginia thought about the huge fissures that had so suddenly opened up between her and Simon, and how she had assumed they could simply be stepped over, fitted conveniently into her busy life like a hair appointment. She told Edward the story.

'We've sorted out our problems now. I think so, anyway. *All* our problems.' She thought that Edward would know what she meant. Bed. 'So I can stay for a bit, when he's first in Singapore, but I really don't think it's wise to let him off the leash for too long.'

Edward almost, but not quite, concealed a smile. 'I'm glad I've been an educational experience. I take it you didn't go in for any confessions of your own?'

'I thought I'd take your advice. For once. And Edward?'

'Yes?'

'I'm sorry about Tom.'

His face darkened. 'That was a long time ago. Goodbye.'

'My letter of resignation.' Harry made himself sound

unusually chirpy. 'I feel a bit *de trop* round here.'
Edward looked pretty grim, he thought. Still, not
surprising when you've lost a fortune.

'We're all a bit *de trop*. Especially me. I'm
expecting the receivers to come through the door any
minute.'

Harry shrugged, waiting for Edward to ask him
why he was going. He edged towards the door. With
any luck this wouldn't take too long. There were
rather a lot of things he didn't want to discuss.

But Edward waved him towards a seat. 'Park
yourself.'

Harry perched on the corner of a chair, determined
to give off the right body language. Not here for very
long, that was the message. He crossed his legs and
bounced one foot up and down to indicate an urgent
appointment elsewhere, trying his most practised
smile on Edward. A bunch of crimson and yellow
Gerbera wilted in a murky vase in the corner. Harry
wondered why you never saw a dead Gerbera.

Edward leaned forward. 'So. Do I take it that Sir
Ralph has offered you a better position, as it were?'

Harry felt himself go bright red. He forgot to go
on tapping his foot. 'How did you know about that?
Have you been talking to Clara?'

'I saw you together. Just talking in a restaurant.
Months ago. Although I didn't put two and two
together until recently, after something Shirley said.
And while we're on the subject, have *you* spoken to
my wife recently?'

This was not quite going the way Harry had hoped.
He stared at his hands. 'I'm not at liberty to divulge

that information.' How pompous that sounded, even if Edward did need a lesson.

Edward stood up, walked round the desk and grabbed Harry's jacket with both hands. He smelt of beer and anger. Harry maintained a surprisingly disciplined presence at the gym, but he could feel that weights and treadmills were quite simply no competition when up against the power of sheer rage. He felt like a rabbit in the grip of a terrier. And there was something slightly humiliating at having his heels just slightly lifted off the ground. A sort of social vertigo.

'Now I'm only going to ask this once, so listen very carefully. And if you don't answer I'm going to ram your face right into that vase of Gerbera. Where . . . is . . . my . . . wife?'

'Here,' came a voice from the doorway. Clara was standing there, surveying them both, arms folded. 'Now put him down.'

Harry had to grab a chair for support as Edward pushed him away roughly. 'And I haven't finished with you. I'm thinking of suing for industrial espionage.'

Harry and Clara exchanged glances. Harry adjusted the neck of his shirt and cleared his throat. It all seemed to be in working order. Bit sore just around the collarbone. 'That won't be necessary,' said Harry stiffly.

There was a silence. Edward was breathing heavily with the effort, and his bottom shirt button had burst.

Judith tripped in. 'Oh, Clara, you're back. How

nice to see you. Isn't it dreadful about *Viva* and Publishing Unlimited? Well, I always say it never rains but it p–' she petered out under Edward's thunderous gaze. 'I'll just pop this on your desk, shall I? It's the er . . . weekly sales figures.'

She escaped just before Shirley arrived, glittering dangerously in the doorway.

'Quite a party.' The tone in her voice made Harry wonder if she was on something. Whatever it was, she'd had too much.

'This is just like that scene at the end of Agatha Christie plays where everyone gathers to hear that the butler did it.' Shirley looked around. 'So tell me, do we know who the butler was? Clara?' The name sounded so out of place on Shirley's lips that Harry realized how rarely she voluntarily spoke to Clara. He had to hand it to her, not speaking to someone for nearly a year while appearing to be quite pleasant was a serious feat of achievement.

'You tell us.' Clara moved round the side of the desk to stand beside Edward. 'Hello. I'm so sorry the sales promotion didn't work out. Truly.' She kissed his cheek, and smiled blandly at Shirley, who was gazing at her with folded arms. 'He is still my husband,' said Clara softly but firmly.

Harry wondered whether she was justifying her behaviour or staking a claim, and moved his chair back nervously. If the latter, she was really throwing down the gauntlet with this 'my husband' business. Not for nothing did women's magazines caution you against taking sides, he thought.

Shirley appeared not to care, although Harry had

the sensation of watching a cat unsheath its claws. 'As you've become so friendly with the management of Publishing Unlimited, I would have thought they'd have confided in you,' she said in silky tones. 'I mean, I haven't got the wrong end of the stick, have I?'

'I have spoken to them, yes. But I'm hardly going to throw my own money away, am I?'

Harry wondered whether it was worth trying to sneak out and fetch Virginia, who was very good at keeping people under control. He didn't think he could get past Shirley without being noticed.

'Don't tell me – ' Shirley sounded as if she despised Clara ' – that you've never thought of vengeance.'

Clara smiled with deadly sweetness. 'You've got spinach on your teeth, Shirley. Or some sort of lunch, anyway. Would you like to borrow my mirror?'

Shirley hesitated for a second, and smiled back, admittedly not quite as widely as she might have done. 'Thank you, Clara. It's the latest fashion.' She looked her up and down. 'But you wouldn't know about that.'

There was a silence, and Harry certainly wasn't going to break it.

'I've come to talk about an offer,' said Shirley. She paused. 'I'd like to talk to Edward in private.' Harry gathered up his cigarettes, and pushed the chair back neatly against the wall, scooping up the stinking vase of Gerbera at the same time. He couldn't wait to get out of there.

Clara didn't move. 'As you know, as Edward's wife, I'm a joint owner of the company. In view of the circumstances, I'm sure you'll understand my staying.'

Shirley looked from Edward to Clara. 'Edward?'

Harry, halfway through the door, was aware of Shirley's scent, expensively choking him as he passed her. Underneath it he could smell something else. Desperation, perhaps. Or triumph. She was almost quivering with tension. He remembered the laughing girl of a year ago. He missed her quite a lot.

Edward looked down at his desk, and back up again. He took a deep breath. 'I think Clara's entitled to hear what you have to say, Shirley.'

Shirley paled, or perhaps it was the sun going behind a cloud. 'I suppose that's typical of the last ten years. Wifey comes first.' She turned to Clara. 'No matter how cold, or selfish, or slovenly you were, he just sticks by this Saint Clara image. I don't know how you've conned him into believing it. You ought to be ashamed of yourself.'

'Thank you, Shirley,' replied Clara. 'That's the nicest thing you've ever said to me.'

Shirley ignored her and placed an envelope on his desk. 'As they say, I've had an offer I can't refuse.' She walked out, turning round in the doorway. 'Two, in fact. In view of what Clara so quaintly calls "the circumstances", I don't expect you to hold me to my notice period.' She hunched her shoulders and clenched her fists inside the rich, velvety pockets of the trouser suit. 'Goodbye.'

'Shirley.' Clara was not going to let her get away with it. 'It was you, wasn't it? You're the butler.'

'Let's just say I decided to put myself first for a

change. As I could see that no one else was going to. But if you try to make it stick, I'll sue.'

'There won't be any need for that.' Edward looked very tired. 'I'll send a taxi round for my things.'

Shirley turned once more at the door, and looked at Edward.

'We could have been so good together,' she whispered. 'You just threw it all away.' Her voice rose. 'And now you'll be sorry for it. Because you've got nothing left.' She was gone, but her perfume lingered at the doorway, stifling Clara briefly, taking away her breath.

Edward looked at her. 'I'm sorry. I'm afraid that was all my fault. Once I knew it just wasn't going to work out between us, I told her that wherever you were, and whatever happened with our marriage, there'd be no Edward and Shirley. That it was over. Oddly enough, I thought she took it quite well at the time. I'd no idea that she'd try to hurt everyone.'

'It wasn't your fault, at all.' Clara was clear about that. 'It was Shirley's. Hers alone. She didn't have to destroy you to survive.'

Judith reappeared, holding two business cards. 'They say they haven't got an appointment. But they're . . .' she peered at the cards, before dropping them on the table and fleeing ' . . . some sort of accountancy firm.'

'The receivers,' said Edward. He handed a bunch of keys to Clara. 'They'll probably let you stay and help them sort things out. Or possibly Harry.' But Harry had already gone. They could hear the sound of him rattling the lid of the dustbin in the coffee area as he threw the Gerbera away.

Edward looked at Clara. 'I went to Tom's grave while you were away.'

Clara stood very still, watching him. 'I know. I stopped on the way back. I saw the flowers.' They had a card which read 'To a dear boy, always on my mind.' No signature.

'I went to say goodbye. To let him go.'

'So did I.' Clara felt her eyes fill with tears. 'I still wanted him back. Then suddenly he just went.' Taking her anger and guilt with him.

It's time to let Edward go too, she had thought. She still loved him enough to do that. She resolved that if Shirley made him happy – or even if she didn't – she no longer needed a marriage based on debt and guilt. It was time for everyone to start again. She would make a new life for herself, just like the women in Virginia's magazines. On her own terms. People did.

'I'm sorry. I've always known that Tom's death was my fault. I shouldn't have . . .' Edward moved closer to her. He cleared his throat. 'Tell me something.'

'What?' She felt very anxious, suddenly.

'This isn't a spur-of-the-moment thing. I've really thought about it.'

About what? thought Clara wearily.

'While you were away,' he added. 'Let's start again.'

Clara sat down on the desk and cried. For Tom. For Edward. And for herself. Eventually she blew her nose, and picked up the sales sheet. 'These figures,' she said to Edward, 'they're unbelievable. We might have something on our hands after all.'

'We?' asked Edward.

'We,' said Clara firmly. 'Without Shirley. Or Virginia, for that matter.'

'You *have* been chatting.'

'No.' Clara smiled weakly. 'I just knew. I know you, you see.'

'I do see,' he said. 'So, it's a deal. No Shirley, no Virginia, no anybody. The big one. At last.'

'The big one,' agreed Clara. 'Us.'

Epilogue

'I have to tell you, darling, that all this forgiveness isn't very Now. And neither, if you don't mind my saying so, are those loafers.' Harry and Clara were having what Harry called an Anniversary Lunch.

'What anniversary?' Clara had been bewildered on the phone.

Harry waved the practicalities away. 'Oh, the Battle of Hastings. The surrender of Sebastopol. The invention of the safety pin. Anything really.' He paused. 'Oh come off it, Clara. You know it's exactly one year since you took over Wiggins Frean.'

Clara smiled. The receivers, amazingly enough, had appointed her as temporary Managing Director after she'd sketched out a rescue plan that she and Edward had cooked up together. Just three months later, the banks, who had spent the first two months feverishly searching for a replacement for Edward, surprised themselves by confirming it as a permanent appointment. Clara had sold *Heart &*

Soul to *Viva* for much more than Paul Long had wanted to pay – the figures had been brilliant, after all. She was now doing surprisingly well with the technical journals. The Brambles had been sold, too – the renovations having added considerably to the value – and Edward had actually avoided bankruptcy, but had, rather to Clara's relief, been disqualified as a director. In theory this would slow him down a bit, but in practice it seemed to be giving him lots of free time to investigate other new ventures. 'We've only got my salary and we need that for the mortgage,' explained Clara. 'We don't own Wiggins Frean any more, you know. The banks do. We don't have any capital to start again.' That clearly wasn't going to stop him. They'd bought a flat in Hammersmith, and were renting Honey Tree House from Virginia and Simon for a peppercorn rent while they were away, provided that they looked after it.

'I can tell you – ' Harry was reverting to the theme of forgiveness ' – that Ralph's wife, who is very fashionable, darling, certainly wasn't into it. Mind you, she's getting married again herself awfully quickly, so she must have had a spare husband tucked up her sleeve anyway in case of emergencies. Honestly,' he sighed, 'I'll never understand heterosexuals, not if I live to be a hundred.'

'How did she find out?' After ten years of Shirley's vigorous clue-dropping, Clara was squeamish about people getting hurt.

'Detectives. Said she wanted out, and she knew she could get something on him if she tried.' He grinned. 'I don't think she'd quite expected to find this. Squealed like mad about AIDS, but we've both got certificates to prove otherwise. Shirley said . . .' He flushed, but Clara didn't want people whispering about Shirley behind her back.

'How is dear Shirley?'

Harry winced. He hated talking about Shirley to Clara or vice versa. It could only end in tears. His. 'Keeping Colin on a very tight rein, and now she's Consultant Sales Director at Dearest Cosmetics the sales are soaring.'

'And the staff are leaving in droves, I expect,' added Clara. 'Still,' she added, 'poor Shirley.'

Harry looked surprised, and switched topics hastily. 'Did I tell you Ralph saw Virginia in Singapore? She's making a stunning success of being a corporate wife. Everybody utterly adores her, especially Simon apparently.

'I knew she'd rise to the challenge.'

Virginia wrote often, and had had another baby in the last year, a boy. She'd rung up from Honey Tree House during a brief week in England, although there hadn't been time to meet.

'So are you really, really happy?' Clara had asked her.

'Not exactly.' But Virginia had sounded perfectly cheerful about it. 'Frankly, if this is downshifting, give me a nice quiet time in the fast lane any day. But it suits us. Now, anyway. I don't promise to do it for ever.'

Clara thought of those apparently endless days, marked out in park visits, nappy changes and an almost never-ending round of getting things collected or delivered, and the chance of completing a sentence uninterrupted just a distant memory. 'I know what you mean. This suits us, now. But I feel quite nostalgic about those days of waiting in for things to be delivered.'

Virginia had snorted. 'Don't mention waiting for deliveries. Yesterday we were supposed to have . . .' and she was off, on an interminable account of wailing children and non-existent delivery men, the frustrations of a fractious, bored baby, and the man who said he'd knocked at 11 a.m. but no one had been in. Drawing to a breathless close, she ended with 'Give me a board meeting, any day. At least, you feel you've achieved something.'

Clara had laughed. 'Maybe. Maybe not.'

'Oh, Clara,' said Virginia crossly. 'You still simply haven't a clue. You're probably still wearing last season's trouser suit.'

Clara grinned into the phone. 'Two years old actually. The one with the long-line jacket and boxy cut. You wrote that it was a flattering, easy-to-wear cut which disguises figure faults.'

'Never,' said Virginia. 'I couldn't have done. That shape makes a woman look like a tank.' She sighed. 'But I was talking lifestyle. Haven't you read the latest? Babies are out, boardrooms are in. I tell you,' she warmed to her theme, 'I must love Simon an awful lot to do this.'

'Good,' said Clara.